BelkA of
BABYLON

Book 1 of An Ancient Trilogy:
Light to the Nations

Joanne Kroeker Mahar

BelkA of BABYLON
Book one of an Ancient Trilogy: Light to the Nations
by Joanne Kroeker Mahar

Printed in the United States of America

ISBN 9781612156279

Unless otherwise indicated, Bible quotations are taken from The King James Version.

www.xulonpress.com

Dedication

To the glory of God, the inventor of
communication through words, and to my
husband Frank who has been my number one
critique person, as well as my encourager
throughout the entire writing process.

Chapter 1

The Summons

Babylon, Mid-May 589 B.C.

With a fluttering heartbeat BelkA Squash broke the seal on the scroll delivered by royal messenger. A summons to appear immediately before King Nebuchadnezzar? What could it mean? A new assignment? Surely not. He'd just returned from Egypt. Could he have incurred guilt for some wrong? If so he held in his hands the equivalent of a death notice. One thing he knew for sure was that tardiness always aggravated the mood of his majesty.

Turning onto Processional way he stretched his stride to the maximum, that the dignity of his position permitted, while the friction of the stiff papyrus attached to his belt rubbed sinister warnings into his flesh. Lions in blazing color, set in murals on the massive three hundred foot wall beside him, now appeared to chase after him with menacing fury.

With determined effort he rejected the thought and focused on the symbol they represented—Ishtar—goddess of love and war. Those lions were not roaring at him but declaring, "This is Babylon the golden city, glory of the kingdom, marvel of mankind, praise of the whole earth." The gods had favored him with a high position in the royal court and for the cause of such an empire, his own life held little significance. He slowed his pace slightly and raised his chin. He would prove himself worthy—by life or by death.

Nearing the palace he cast a whimsical glance at the hanging gardens that evoked in him a reverence surpassing even the temple of Marduk. Was there not a whisper of Deity in each tree, flower or shrub? Again he banished all frivolous thought. He must remain focused.

Babylon commanded awe. Straddling the Euphrates River, it stood secure with double walls reinforced by towers and a moat. Eight bronze gates allowed entrance to the city, the grandest of them all—the Ishtar Gate—now dazzled gold and blue above him. From among the three glazed-brick figures: the lion, the bull, and the dragon atop the fifty-foot arch, he focused upon the dragon, emblem of Marduk—Babylon's principle god.

Lifting his head he formed a plea, "Oh Marduk, urgency prevents me from offering a sacrifice at your temple, but according to your title, 'Great lord of heaven and earth,' I invoke your favor and a portion of your great wisdom."

Entering the palace grounds, with its five court-yards, BelkA chose the third that led to the principal throne room. There, upon presenting the summons to the guard, he had but a brief wait for his call to appear before the king. As he passed through the arched entrance into the throne room he reminded himself to stand straight and to breathe deeply. With deliberate steps—that he hoped revealed con-fidence—he approached the ivory-encrusted throne set in the niche of a massive forty-foot wall of gold and blue tile, and fell on his knees.

Impatiently brushing protocol aside Nebuchadnezzar spoke in his deep commanding voice that echoed throughout the hall, "On your feet BelkA. Your promptness pleases me."

BelkA fastened unblinking eyes on the king who appeared magnified in the strange light cast by clere-stories or narrow windows high on the wall above him.

"I'm sending you to Jerusalem BelkA. You are to deliver a message to King Zedekiah informing him that my patience has run out. I'm fed up with his games of pretension. His disloyalty amounts to treason. The city must submit and pay tribute or expect my battering ramps against its walls. It baf-fles me the way my lesser campaigns have been so easily forgotten, and repeated threats ignored. I am now preparing a major military deployment and will stop at nothing less than complete destruction. Undeserving as he is of a last reminder, out of con-sideration for my Prime Minister Belteshazzar, I'm sending you post haste."

BelkA bowed his head.

"I understand Bah-Ador will be leading a caravan to Egypt tomorrow at dusk. You will join it. I've decided not to give you an entourage, as I do not wish to draw attention to your person. If you remember, I sent an escort of twenty-four men with my last envoy and it was a disaster."

"I remember your majesty."

"You might consider posing as a merchant in search of jewels of which the markets of Aleppo have ample supply. Adept as you are with a dagger, and keen of mind besides, I'm confident you'll defend yourself adequately.

"Now BelkA," he said leaning forward in a way that bounced light off his black curled hair, "I don't want to lose you, so be on your guard. You are to discuss the mission with no one, not even your mother—especially not your mother. Do you understand?"

BelkA bowed once again, "I do your majesty. I am indeed honored and will let nothing prevent me from accomplishing this urgent mission."

A hint of a smile played on the king's firm jaw as he leaned back and sized up the tall young man standing before him, a replica of his stalwart father, the general who had fought valiantly at Nineveh only to lose his life at the peak of conquest. With difficulty he restrained any expression of cordiality. "Good," he said with deliberate harshness. "Now there's something else that you are to accomplish. Upon the request of Belteshazzar, whom the Hebrews call Daniel, I have agreed to his proposition that he will explain to you. Present yourself to him immediately

as he is expecting you. Upon entering the fifth courtyard you have only to mention your name. Is that
clear?"

"Of course, your majesty, I have but two
questions."

"Speak."

"Is my slave Parto permitted to accompany me
and share my confidence?"

"Agreed. The second question."

"Is my presence still required at your majesty's
garden party this evening?"

"Absolutely," the king chuckled. "You will be
well entertained. I would suggest, however, that
you go easy on the wine. But now, do not linger as
Belteshazzar is waiting."

Nebuchadnezzar turned his face indicating the
audience was over.

BelkA bowed and silently exited backward.
Turning south he entered the reception room off the
fifth courtyard where he was immediately ushered
into the prime minister's office.

"Get up BelkA," Daniel said motioning with both
hands from behind a desk piled high with scrolls.

Looking upon the man he had never before had
opportunity to meet, BelkA barely managed to conceal astonishment. In spite of dark, perfectly curled
hair, the official attire of a blue silk tunic bordered
with gold braid and the distinguishing gold necklace
of honor, a demeanor of kindness emanated from
deep-set grey-blue eyes that were now fixed upon
him.

"I want you to meet my assistant Ira," Daniel said indicating with his hand a small bald man sitting with quill in hand on a chair with a desk attachment.

BelkA bowed.

"The king has graciously permitted me to avail myself of your services. I've been informed that you're trustworthy, meticulous, and adventurous. Also, that besides your scribal training in the Babylonian dialect, you're fluent in Aramaic, Hebrew and have also knowledge of Egyptian and Arabic. Therefore, I dare to present you with a challenge of exceedingly great importance to me."

"I am your servant. Whatever you request I will perform even at the risk of my life. Tell me only your request."

Pointing to the scrolls Daniel said, "These are the sacred Writings of my God, BelkA. I treasure them above all my possessions. I was allowed to bring them with me when I was taken captive and brought to Babylon. They are but a few of what we Hebrews call *The Torah*. There are yet many other sacred Writings that remain in Jerusalem."

"I see, my lord."

Daniel once again engaged BelkA with penetrating eyes, "I'm troubled for my countrymen who face conquest and deportation. Conditions are about to become chaotic in Jerusalem. It has been revealed to me that the temple of my God is about to suffer destruction. My great concern is for the safety of these Writings. May I count on you to collect them and transport them safely to Babylon? They will be many, and they'll be heavy. For that reason I recommend that you travel by camel."

"You can count on me honorable Daniel," BelkA responded with earnestness.

A flash of relief crossed Daniel's face. "Thank you. I'm presently compiling a list of missing documents. I'll present it to you at this evening's banquet."

BelkA bowed his assent.

"Now before leaving on your mission, you must see the prophet Ezekiel who will doubtlessly have a message for you to take to Jerusalem. I believe you know where he lives?"

"I do sir. Five years ago I delivered a message from him to Judah. As I remember, the reaction of the populace was mixed."

Daniel sighed and shook his head. "Excuses BelkA," he said with a hint of exasperation. "Israel is a stiff-necked people determined to follow a self-destructive path. Agitators and activists in Jerusalem like to pick out little details to defend their agendas. Ezekiel prophesied that Zedekiah would be taken captive and brought to Babylon, while Jeremiah in Jerusalem claimed that the Jewish king would never see Babylon." Daniel pushed aside some scrolls, and leaned forward, "I'm confident that both of these prophecies will be proven perfectly accurate, though now they appear to conflict."

"But how?"

"If Zedekiah were blinded—the punishment he now faces for treason—could he not be brought to Babylon and yet see nothing?"

"Why! Of course my lord."

A far-away expression swept over Daniel's face. "As I see it, Judah uses any and every excuse to continue her lifestyle that is offensive to Yahweh. She's obstinate, arrogant and apostate."

"Apostate? Oh, excuse me honored one for my hasty reaction."

"You may not understand as, here in Babylon, many gods are revered."

"If you'll permit my saying so honored one, there are indeed numerous gods in the pantheon, but I find them confusing, so I usually address my petitions to Marduk, though at times I invoke Ea, god of wisdom, or as we say, 'Lord of the intelligent eye,' and for healing I appeal to Gula."

"I understand BelkA. In Jewish context it's quite different. You see Yahweh has entered into covenant with our nation. He is our one true God; we are instructed to have no other. Yet Judah has brazenly disobeyed and adopted the gods of surrounding nations. In so doing she has brought upon herself the wrath of Yahweh. Our God is merciful and patient, but now His reputation is at stake. The consequences stated in the covenant are therefore inevitable."

"I can see then how important it is to you that the scrolls be rescued."

"BelkA, you need to make preparations for your journey, but before you go I must request complete secrecy. Obviously you might need to trust certain people, but use discretion—for your own protection and that of the Writings. I'm sure you are aware that this could be a hazardous mission because there are many Jews who will resent your presence in

Jerusalem. I'm afraid they'll try to kill you. If you indeed survive—as I pray you will—it will mean a great deal to me if you could bring the scrolls to Babylon."

"My life belongs to the king. I will deliver his message to Zedekiah and do my best to serve you as well."

"The task you are assuming will have all the powers of evil against it."

"I know that your God is powerful. I have heard how He delivered the Hebrew slaves from Egypt."

Daniel smiled. "May the strong arm that rescued the Israelites from the mighty Pharaoh rest upon you, and give you a safe and successful journey."

BelkA bowed his head and quietly left the room.

Preoccupied as he was, he jumped upon reaching the outer court to hear a voice that struck terror upon his entire being.

The shrill call of his name came from Adda-Guppi, priestess of the moon god Sin, and the last person he wanted to see—ever—and especially not now. With resolute restraint he turned and responded with a polite nod and salutation.

"What brings you here?" the priestess bluntly asked.

"The usual," BelkA replied.

"My, my, we're rather curt today. Have we displeased the king?"

"Forgive me honorable priestess. I have a mission that requires haste. I must not allow myself to be detained."

"Go, you impertinent fellow," the spiteful woman shouted with a toss of her head that set the locks of her black wig swinging. Then twisting around she lifted her wrinkled brow and cast daggers from her kohl-lined eyes. "It may not appear to you that I possess information that you might find useful. Do you realize the prestige I enjoy in the king's court?"

"Yes, yes, Adda-Guppi. I recognize your prominence in the eyes of all. I do not wish to offend you."

"Just tell me where you're going."

BelkA hesitated momentarily then replied. "By the king's command I am sworn to secrecy."

"Is it not to Judah?" Adda-Guppi asked slyly.

BelkA — stone-faced — stared after her.

Chapter 2

The Garden Party

Babylon, 589 B.C.

To regain composure BelkA turned toward the royal garden where a section open to the public was also sheltered from the bustle of preparations for the royal banquet. Finding his favorite spot under a vine-covered arbor, he sank upon the stone bench and inhaled the air sweetened by jasmine that mingled with soothing sounds of gentle breezes playing in leaves. Here a mysterious tranquility infused mind and body.

Hearing footsteps he rose and looked around. Ah, it was the friendly chief gardener laden with a bulging basket. "Bazy-An," he called out, "How good to see you."

"Well, if it isn't BelkA. Greetings to you my good friend," he said putting down the basket.

"Are you all right, Bazy-An? You look weary."

"Indeed I am," the forty-year old gardener said wiping his brow with the ample apron that covered a faded tunic. "The watering system had me baffled for a time, but it's finally in place, thanks to my clever Hebrew assistant. The construction of the beds, that had to be perched at just the right angle to suit the sharp eye of Queen Amytis, is now complete."

"The queen is satisfied then?"

"We won't know till all the trees and plants are in place. I'm finishing that up now. But how goes it for you BelkA? Did you come to check on your plants, the ones that is, that you donated?"

"Not this time Bazy-An, I just needed to regain my composure."

"You didn't meet...?"

"I did," BelkA interrupted, "and at the most inopportune time. Just after receiving a new assignment— a secret assignment—and of course she pulled it out of me."

Bazy-An sniffed. "I never could stand the woman. I do all I can to mind my own business and let her mind hers."

"I don't know what it is about the old gal that grates against me like sandpaper on silk? I dislike everything about her from her wig, to her exaggerated eye makeup, to the gaudy jewelry she drapes all over her, to her pushy mannerisms and wiliness. How could an old woman nearing seventy exert such power over me?"

"You're telling me."

"Thankfully I managed to keep from telling her of another mission to which I have sworn secrecy, though she herself correctly suggested the destination."

Bazy-An anxiously scrutinized his friend. "A dangerous mission no doubt?"

BelkA shrugged. "It could be."

"And when do you leave?"

"Tomorrow."

Bazy-An's face dropped. With an air of resignation he said, "I'll miss you and be concerned."

"Please don't worry. All will go well. Perhaps I shall find a new plant or two for your collection," BelkA added with a wink.

"I just ask to have you back safely, my friend."

"I will do all in my power to satisfy that wish," BelkA said as he laid his head on the shoulder of his friend in the customary Mesopotamian fashion of friends.

●●●

"BelkA, let me straighten your toga pin," Ahktar said to her son who stood straight and tall before their full-length bronze mirror.

"And how about the fringes? They must not appear tangled up."

His mother ran her fingers through the gold cords on the sleeves and then knelt to perfect those on the hem. "All is impeccable my son. You may go in confidence."

"Ah, dear Mother, with all that has happened today, and all that must be prepared yet before tomorrow evening, I assure you, confidence fails me.

Look at my hair. Is my bald spot covered? I had no time to see the hair dresser."

"Have no concern my son, you're fortunate to have a natural wave that disguises all, and besides, it's your head band that commands the eye. The amber jewels reflect your eye-color in a most distinguished manner."

BelkA smiled. "Thank you Mother. You have always the words to encourage a son, and now I must go." He took from her hand the cane she held out that was once his father's, and descended the stairs of their second-floor living quarters. A few wide strides took him through the columned courtyard and past the entry where a chariot stood waiting.

Moments later he stood transfixed in a garden paradise more beautiful than any he'd seen or even imagined. While savoring the fragrant air his eyes feasted on a landscape where every tree, shrub, and flower stood in perfect arrangement. Here a waterfall surrounded by lush foliage, there a riverbed bordered with orchids and other exotic plants, and above, balconies draped in trees and trailing blooms.

Lost, as he was, a touch of a hand on his shoulder caused him to whirl around. A whisper close to his ear restrained him, "Don't be so obvious."

"Oh, it's you Ira," BelkA said recognizing Prime Minister Daniel's secretary.

"Daniel wants to see you. You'll find him in the alcove beyond the fountain of the seven palms." In a flash Ira disappeared behind a column.

BelkA wondered that Ira had succeeded in finding him, but he turned and cautiously headed in the designated direction where he found Daniel, his head hidden behind a vine.

Following a warm handclasp Daniel took from his leather girdle, that served both as a belt and a satchel, a scroll that he handed to BelkA. "Quickly tuck this away," he said. He waited until BelkA had concealed it safely then continued, "The message is for Jeremiah whom I'm confident will assist you. He's well known in Jerusalem. This is the promised list of scrolls missing here in Babylon. Also we need Jeremiah's latest Writings."

BelkA smiled and nodded. "I will do as you wish."

Daniel put a hand on BelkA's arm, "I will pray for you."

BelkA looked squarely into the prime minister's face where a pronounced twitch of anxiety pulled on the eye. It stirred within him an even deeper curiosity, and with it Daniel's burden fell more heavily upon himself. At a loss for words he simply bowed.

The garden was getting crowded now with the arrival of groupings of guests from whom he identified dignitaries such as satraps, governors, advisors, treasurers, judges and even captain Arioch, the distinguished chief executioner. As the sun was setting servants lit torches perched in various niches that highlighted palms, olive trees, and other foliage. By this time, however, BelkA's enthrallment with the garden had receded to the background of his mind.

He decided to find his reserved place, as others appeared to be doing, but he'd barely put a foot on the first step of the wide marble stairway leading to where the banquet tables were set in readiness, when he heard the voice that sent chills up his spine. Under the familiar conical hat of priestess was none other than Adda-Guppi. Thankfully her back was turned, and she appeared to be in deep conversation with people he knew to be magicians, astrologers, and sorcerers.

Quickly he turned in the opposite direction mingling with the crowd. While passing a fish sculpture spewing water in a pond, a waiter came by and conveniently put before him a tray of tantalizing delicacies. BelkA ran his eyes over the fancy presentation of deep-fried locusts, stuffed snails, preserved olives, dried fruit, and almonds while many other varieties passed his notice. With a smile of appreciation he collected a fistful of almonds—his favorite snack.

"Caught you."

BelkA looked up into the smiling face of Bazy-An, now appearing out of place in his fine tunic with details of braid, and a wide belt wrapped around his slender waist. Strange it was to see him without the usual apron, but his countenance still bore an unpretentious attitude that put him at ease. Beside him stood a Hebrew youth.

"Allow me to introduce Shai," Bazy-An said.

BelkA bowed.

"Shai, like his name, is truly a gift to me," Bazy-An explained. "Just an hour ago he found a leakage in the irrigation system and managed to fix it just in time, saving me enormous embarrassment."

BelkA chuckled at the thought of water leaking on the heads of guests, while also eying closely the young man, taking in his neat appearance, work-worn hands, and an aura of wholesome simplicity in his manner. The praises of Bazy-An had been acknowledged simply with a nod and a smile. Then, remembering that he was holding a fistful of almonds, he held out his palm. "Allow me the pleasure."

Gratefully the two gardeners accepted a sprinkling of almonds, and as they began munching BelkA glanced around. "This is not my night for wine, but I saw some goblets of pomegranate juice floating by on a tray. Ah, I see them, wait here and I'll find the waiter."

"Thank you gracious friend," Bazy-An said when he tasted the drink offered him, and rolled his eyes with satisfaction. "Just what a tired old gardener needs. The rest can have their wines. Nothing refreshes like the juice of the pomegranate."

The three made their way to the banqueting tables set with elegant copper plates. Though their places were not together they were all at the king's table. BelkA noticed Daniel and his friends, Shadrach, Meshach and Abednego sitting opposite him. A ways down on his right sat Adda-Guppi looking smug with her son, now the great general Nabonidus, seated beside her. It was common knowledge that his appointment had been achieved through her court machinations. Word had also leaked out that mother and son were intensely devoted to the moon god Sin, the patron of Ur and rival of Marduk. It was not sitting well with some.

A swish beside him caught his attention, and brought before him a vision of rapturous beauty in a young woman attired in a flowing pink gown. She glided gracefully into a chair beside him and turned on BelkA the most beguiling of smiles. A jeweled comb shimmered in her intricate hairdo piled high above her head, while long auburn curls trailed down her back, with a few falling forward on her chest. "My name is RimA and yours is BelkA," she said taking the initiative in the introduction.

Overpowered by her presence and intoxicating perfume, and while attempting to regain his composure, BelkA could only swallow and stutter, "Ah... Good evening. Should I know you?"

"Had you worshipped at the new temple Etemenanki you would indeed know me."

BelkA gulped at the audacity. "I have indeed worshipped there a time or two, Miss Rima, mostly out of curiosity, but my tastes are simple and I am accustomed to worshipping at the smaller temple Esagila. Besides, Marduk is the god of both."

"Ah, but you have to appreciate that Etemananki stands upon the remains of the ancient tower of Babylon, called the foundation of heaven and earth. It holds the power and prestige of the original ziggurat—our version of the pyramid."

BelkA took a deep breath and spoke with an unmistaken touch of combativeness in his voice, "I fully understand that the word Babylon comes from the Assyrian word Babel and that it goes way back to the period after the flood when a king named Nimrod wanted a tower to connect the netherworld to heaven. It took a long time to build and was destroyed before its completion by an earthquake."

"But our great King Nebuchadnezzar and his father went to so much expense to rebuild it, don't you think we should show our appreciation and loyalty by worshipping there?"

BelkA shrugged. "It's my opinion that we can show loyalty to our king primarily by being good citizens. But tell me, are you a priestess?"

RimA laughed. "No, but I help dress and feed the gods and make sure people are entertained. But please, promise me you'll come. It's a spiritual journey of great significance and beauty. At the top one reaches the very gate of god."

BelkA forced a smile. "I might just do that."

"Soon?" RimA insisted.

"Not soon I'm afraid for I have duties to perform that require my absence. Have you had opportunity to enjoy the gardens this evening?"

"Indeed. My favorite part was the zoo. I liked especially the baboons."

BelkA forced a smile. "Good for you." To his relief the conversation halted with the sound of a trumpet announcing the arrival of the King and Queen. People rushed to the balcony to catch a glimpse of Nebuchadnezzar, with Queen Amytis on his arm, standing regally between the statues of two winged bulls that framed the gate.

Nebuchadnezzar's powerful voice boomed out, "Ladies and Gentleman. The Queen takes great delight in your presence this evening. She hopes you will enjoy breathing with her the atmosphere of her homeland in faraway Media, while you partake of the banquet she has carefully planned. She and I wish you a most pleasant evening. And now, let the serving begin."

The guests clapped and cried, "Long live Queen Amytis, Long live King Nebuchadnezzar." Applause continued while the King and Queen mounted the blue-tiled stairs, their crowns and clothing shimmering with jewels. Following more applause and lifted goblets the royal couple took their places at the head table, and the meal commenced.

Speeches recognizing special services of citizens filled gaps between the shifting of platters. BelkA cheered and applauded with abandon when Queen Amytis showered Bazy-An and Shai with praise for their landscaping success.

As the evening progressed glasses were refilled again and again, and yet again. The banqueting hall grew louder. BelkA noticed a slur in RimA's words that were now pouring recklessly from her mouth as she leaned heavily toward him. Glancing across the table he noticed that Daniel had risen to his feet and was turning to leave. Gratefully he took the cue and did the same, though not before a sweep of the eye in the direction of Adda-Guppi where he noticed that her seat was suspiciously vacant.

Chapter 3

The Secret Council

Babylon, May 589 B.C.

Light from a few lamps flickered in the darkness of the late night and cast eerie shadows on
the wall behind Adda-Guppi. Attired in a black robe
and a pointed hat she stood with outstretched arms
while an assortment of priests, magicians, diviners,
incantation specialists, astrologers, readers of omens
and scribes filed into the clammy temple basement.
Most were a bit tipsy from the free-flowing wine of
the party. Even Adda-Guppi's own voice appeared
unstable, though she lost no time in coming to the
point.

"I have learned only today that our king is
sending envoy BelkA to Judah on a secret mission,
and I have reason to think that he is scheming with
Prime Minister Belteshazzar. Endowed as BelkA is
with intelligence, scribal skills and languages, I fear

he may convert to their God. There was a time when I was sure he was one of us, but now I have doubts."

"Wait a minute," RAdin priest of Marduk spoke up. "I saw BelkA only a few days ago and I can confirm that not only he, but also his mother, are faithfully devoted to Marduk."

"If you're concerned that he fails to share your passion for the moon god Sin, leave the poor man alone," added Nazir, assistant to RAdin.

Adda-Guppi's jaw muscles tightened. "NO," she shrieked stamping her fist on her podium, "I sense a pull at work in BelkA that is drawing him away from Marduk toward Belteshazzar's God. I mistrust this Daniel who has attained such a place of influence in the empire."

"Priestess Adda-Guppi is right," affirmed Shamil the diviner. "The Hebrew God has an undeniable power that our gods are unable to match,"

"It's true," ToulAn the magician said. "Let's not forget that He empowered Daniel to interpret a dream that King Nebuchadnezzar couldn't even remember! BelkA's association with that Hebrew is a danger to our religion."

"I fear both the Jews and their Writings," Adda-Guppi said now reaching the borders of hysteria. "They're invading our country with their religion. I want their Writings destroyed. You hear me?"

"B-a-a," exclaimed scribe Utabar rising to his feet. "If you remember, Adda-Guppi, the Jews are not here by their own choice. And I should think that we Babylonians are open-minded enough to allow their Writings a place in our literature collections. They can only enrich us. We don't have to swallow everything we read. There are many ways of seeing truth. A few more myths in our midst are a good thing."

"I disagree," hollered Eri-Aku as he turned around and glared at Utabar. "There's a mysterious strength in their Writings that could disturb our powers from the underworld. From what little I know, I say we don't need them. So let's wipe them out."

Arif the astrologer, already resentful toward Adda-Guppi for requiring his presence, now spoke up with irritation oozing from his voice. "I see no reason for a debate of this nature at this late hour. We're all overstuffed with wine and rich foods. Can't this wait? We need to clear our minds before engaging in such debates."

Adda-Guppi stamped her foot, "I want this settled now."

"Beware priestess," Arif shot back, "If my hearing is correct you want to get us involved in hindering a mission ordered by King Nebuchadnezzar himself. Does it occur to you that such activity could be interpreted as treason?"

"It's not treason. On the contrary it's about loyalty to our nation and our religion."

"My advice is to keep our hands out of it," Arif said shaking his head in disgust. "It sounds to me as though the mission is riddled with enough hazards as it is, without us barging in with more. I can assure you that in the present political atmosphere of Jerusalem, an envoy from Babylon won't be popular. My guess is that he won't even come out alive."

"Well said," Eri-Aku spoke up with a grin twitching his mouth. Speaking smoothly he quickly added, "The chances of survival for this envoy are minimal, so what hurt is there in planting a few more unsuspecting detours of our own. Let's say we're just having a little innocent fun. I'm thinking that a knock-out attraction for a woman might do the trick."

Adda-Guppi fixed a smug sneer on Eri-Aku. "It might not occur to you that you're not the first to come up with the idea. Surely you saw the beauty sitting beside him at the garden party this evening. I myself arranged that, yet BelkA, the snobbish fool that he is, sat as aloof to her charms as an old toad."

Laughter rang out.

"What did you expect Adda? The woman has the brains of a donkey," Eri-Aku said.

Muffled snickers stopped abruptly when Adda-Guppi, now beside herself with rage, clapped her hands, "He's a male isn't he? Like all the rest, he turns his head when a beauty saunters by. He has a reputation for drawing females like flies."

"BelkA would have married long before this were his father still alive," Arif said loudly. "Even so, BelkA is perfectly capable of choosing a suitable woman, and I still think he will. He's only about thirty."

"Thirty-two" corrected Adda-Guppi.

"If you allow me Adda-Guppi," Eri-Aku broke in again, " I would still like to complete my suggestion. The woman I have in mind is more than what meets the eye. She's intelligent, refined, and there's a special quality or charm about her. I guarantee that

BelkA will take notice. I also happen to know her father. I can assure you that he's one of ours. He trades in sculptures at the various markets in Aleppo, Damascus, Tyre and all the way to Egypt. I know that his daughter assists him and that they are on their way to Aleppo even as we speak. I recommend that one of us join BelkA's caravan party and then act as a spy and incognito matchmaker. I assure you, this is no ordinary woman. Her reputation has gotten around. Her father told me that someone has already spoken for her but he's holding out for better."

Adda-Guppi relaxed her frown and a smile escaped her crooked teeth. "I like the idea," she said. "The question is who?"

"I would be happy to make inquiry," said the diviner, "but it's rather late to bring out a sheep's liver. Some incantations perhaps?"

The mere suggestion caused Noushbar the incantation specialist sitting beside him to begin humming softly an otherworldly melody, her lips moving in a silent repetitive cadence at first, then bringing out a voice unlike her own. "The Scriptures speak. The Scriptures speak of Messiah who is to come. Messiah must not come. Time is advancing. The Writings must be destroyed."

The magician stood and raised his hands, "Is BelkA in danger?"

"BelkA is in grave danger," answered the voice.

"Is there someone in this room who should be sent along as a spy and go-between?"

"Arif the astrologer is the one I have chosen."

Arif gasped.

The voice went on, "Many will be killed. The ark will disappear. The Writings must surely be destroyed." The voice stopped.

A strange stillness hung in the air.

Adda-Guppi nodded gratitude in the direction of the magician. "Arif shall depart with the caravan party tomorrow evening."

"Wait," Arif shouted shaking with confusion. "I didn't offer myself. I'm no spy. I deal in the science of planets and stars, and I'm no matchmaker."

Utabar turned around and said, "You have wisdom and clarity of mind equal to BelkA, Arif. It seems to me that you would be a discrete spy and most convincing as a negotiator."

"But there has to be a reason for my joining the caravan."

"You'll think of something," Toul-An said.

"But what if it comes to a showdown? I'm not keen on fights."

"Hopefully, it won't, but I'd suggest carrying a dagger."

"But my career?"

"You'll be compensated," Adda-Guppi said smugly. "If you succeed you'll be well compensated."

Arif got up and walked toward the door. "Why should I endanger my life for Adda-Guppi's cause?" he mumbled to himself, "I've nothing against BelkA. Actually, I respect the fellow."

Utabar the scribe who'd caught up with him and heard the words nudged his fellow scribe, "Maybe it would be worth your while to go," he whispered. "It seems to me that a keen astrologer like yourself would find Judah an interesting case study. I'd be curious enough to find out about Judah's mysterious God, wouldn't you?" With a wink he added, "Besides, you might find a way to sabotage the old gal."

Arif stared at Utabar. "Perhaps I should connect with the stars. See if there's a message there."

"I think you've already gotten the message. Refusing to go would stir up Adda-Guppi's indignation." He leaned still closer, "You can count on me if you need advice. Remember, I've got pigeons that know well their way home. Once you're in an established place you can start using them."

Arif's frown smoothed as his eyes widened with inspiration. "Utabar, you're brilliant."

"You know, scribes and astrologers think much the same. Drop by my place after your noonday rest. Come on now, we're both tired, lets retire. Have a good night."

•••

Priestess Adda-Guppi was far from satisfied as she watched the group file out of the temple. In her way of thinking Arif was ill chosen. What she had in mind was a violent type.

Seeing Toul-An sauntering down the torch-lit hall she saw a ray of hope. "Toul-An, you are a man of wisdom. Allow me to consult with you an extra moment?"

Toul-An, flattered at Adda-Guppi's compliment, smiled, "You have my entire attention priestess. The night is yet young for such as myself. It must be that you retain negative thoughts regarding the conclusion of this session?"

"Is that perhaps your impression as well?"

"Exactly."

"Then allow me to confide in you," Adda-Guppi sighed with satisfaction as she leaned forward to scrutinize his every expression. "I can't help but feel that Arif and BelkA are... well... we might say too much alike."

"Ah, I would agree on that point." Toul-An affirmed with a wink of complicity. "Character-wise I would imagine they might have much in common. Were you considering me perhaps?"

"H-m-m perhaps," Adda-Guppi replied with a twist of her head. "It seems to me that we need an aggressive man, or even several with ruthless natures capable of instilling some fear in a wayward son or— if necessary—removing him!"

Toul-An stiffened for a brief moment, then grinned. "I see what you mean. A-h-h yes, I see exactly what you mean. But is this not taking it a bit too far?"

"Accidents happen all the time you know. You heard Arif mention the unstable conditions in Judea. Who'd know how or what?"

"Well, in that case I might be able to help you." Toul-An rubbed his chin. "Let's see now, yes, oddly enough I know some lads who might be keen on obliging you, but tomorrow is rather soon... A-h-h would you have the wherewithal to support them?"

Adda-Guppi laughed in a raw sort of way. "Of course."

"Well in that case I do know some fellows who would jump at the opportunity."

"So would you be able to bring them here by midmorning tomorrow?"

"That's indeed short notice priestess, but I'll do my best."

"I need a better answer than that."

"I will fulfill your wish exactly as you say, but... might I have some compensation for the effort."

"That will depend on who you bring."

•••

Toul-An followed by an oddly assorted group of six young men approached the temple and walked down the corridor toward Adda-Guppi's private apartments.

"Enter," Adda-Guppi said after opening the door. She lost no time eying each fellow from head to sandaled feet, focusing special attention on one large man in particular who stood bare-chested with serpent tattoos on both arms as well as his chest. "Well, what have we here?"

Toul-An began with the names but was cut short.

"We don't have time for names. What I want are qualifications. Are they the violent sort and ready to leave with the caravan this evening?"

"They are," Toul-An replied. "I've explained the mission carefully. They'll pretend to be merchants but will tag along discreetly—at least at first—following BelkA's movements and any show of the scrolls. They'll not hesitate to remove both BelkA and whatever scrolls they lay eyes on—hopefully at the same time. Isn't that what you had in mind?"

"Exactly?"

Adda-Guppi made another round of inspection checking especially for expressions of anger, cruelty, and daring. With a satisfied grin and a toss of her wig she addressed Toul-An. "A good gang you've rounded up I'd say. I think I'll send them all." She turned to her table and wrote on some pottery that she then handed to Toul-An. "If you present this to my accountant, he'll provide a bag of silver for each fellow—and you as well." Then addressing the group she added with a sinister stare, "Upon your successful return you'll be compensated tenfold in gold."

Eyes around the circle of men widened. Each in turn bowed to their benefactor before leaving.

•••

Adda-Guppi slowly closed the door behind her guests and waited for their footsteps to recede before erupting into a bawdy laugh that kept surging in chuckles of glee. Then she stopped and poured from her side table a goblet of rich wine, before sitting down on her divan facing a statue in the corner. Lifting her glass in triumph she toasted, "To you great god of the Moon, in praise of our first triumph. Two of them could easily do the job; the other four gullible fools will be sacrifices to our noble cause.

Let us congratulate ourselves, after all, we've got the vessels from Jerusalem's temple in our own temple and ancient Babylon is still mistress of the nations. That is how it must remain. We will allow no one to put her in jeopardy. Not BelkA, and especially not Daniel and his God."

Chapter 4

Ezekiel

Babylon, May 589 B.C.

E zekiel awoke in an agitated stupor that propelled him to his feet. Reaching blindly for his sandals and cloak, he crept out of his small home walking aimlessly, oblivious to the fog and chill of the early morning air. Stumbling on a tree stump he fell to the ground where he lay prostate and despondent.

From his facedown position on the damp earth he eventually tried to rise, but the mere effort overpowered him. "O Yahweh," he cried out, "It's too awful. I can't bear it."

Two hours passed as fragments of the last message he'd received played over and over in his anguished mind, though he wished only to erase them: "Woe to the bloody city; they dealt by oppression with the stranger; (they've) vexed the fatherless and the widow; greedily gained of neighbors by extortion;

despised holy things; committed abomination; forgotten me; (so) I have drawn forth my sword..."

The echoing words hammered his mind with their cruel reality.

Lying thus in his confused stupor he jumped when a hand touched his shoulder. "Honorable Ezekiel, it's BelkA here."

Ezekiel raised his head of tangled hair, disheveled beard, and bloodshot eyes. Though still in his thirties he looked old with lines that had already forged grooves on his forehead. In his present state he lay as if incapable of movement or speech.

BelkA reached out to help him up. "Your wife informed me that I might find you here. I've come upon the request of Daniel."

"Daniel!" Ezekiel managed to repeat.

"I am about to leave for Jerusalem, and Daniel has asked me to consult with you should there be a message to send along with me."

Ezekiel looked at BelkA with astonishment. "Ah, lord BelkA. Now I understand why the Word came with such urgency in the night."

"The Word?"

"I mean a prophecy from my God regarding Judah."

"Ah, I see. Is it ready?"

"It is. I presume you'll be seeing the prophet Jeremiah?"

"Indeed I will."

"Then I will need to prepare a letter."

The two walked toward Ezekiel's modest brick house. Once inside a smile of gratitude broke upon the prophet's face when he saw that his wife had set out a plate of food for the visitor. "Please be seated, lord BelkA while I attend to the letter." With an affectionate pat on his wife's shoulder he turned to his writing table, and prepared a reed pen before writing furiously in large letters. When the ink had dried he placed both documents together in a clay jar. From a pottery container on his table he pulled out a clump of softened wax that he used to secure the lid before stamping it with his seal.

BelkA took the jar and bowed.

"Let me assure you lord BelkA, that your mission has tremendous significance, more in fact than we presently realize." Then Ezekiel placed his hand on the envoy's shoulder. "Would you allow me to offer a prayer for your assignment?"

BelkA nodded affirmatively, and listened respectfully while Ezekiel requested favor for his mission and a safe return to Babylon. The prayer uttered in confident simplicity aroused a sense of awe within BelkA that he quickly dismissed by rationalizing within himself, that one more god no matter which one, was certainly to his advantage.

Ezekiel stood on his doorstep and waved till BelkA had disappeared from sight. He then turned and put his arms around his wife. "The end is near for Jerusalem, my darling. The vision of this past night confirms it all. Oh, how my heart breaks."

"I share your sorrow beloved husband, but let us not despair. Yahweh has a plan."

Ezekiel managed a wan smile.

Chapter 5

The Caravan

Babylon, May 589 B.C.

Sweat poured from BelkA's body as he struggled in the heat of the day with uncooperative camels. All the prodding, pushing and shoving met with indifference. The animals refused to budge.

He had his slave Parto to thank that they were among the first to arrive with loaded camels at the edge of the trading post—but here the animals had decided to remain. Parto had efficiently handled all the preparations of shopping, packing, securing the camels from the herder and even loading them up, while he had attended to business matters. Upon nearing the trading post in good time, BelkA had allowed his slave to take some time to attend to personal matters and to bid his friends good-bye. Had he remembered how unpredictable camels were he might not have been so generous.

He was reaching a point of exasperation when he heard his slave calling from a distance, "Coming Master." The two words eased his tension and the sight of his trusted slave, with his bouncing black hair, restored his sense of pride. Parto had been acquired by his father as a spoil of war and brought to the family as a young boy of six. The two of them had grown up together almost as equals—yet not quite.

"I don't know how you managed to load these stubborn beasts and get them this far," BelkA said with a sigh of relief. "Camels have no respect for me."

"You have only to pamper them with some sips of sour milk and call them by name."

"I tried that—calling them by their names that is. I didn't know where you put the sour milk."

Parto pulled a goatskin container from a basket on one of the camels and poured a little pool into a copper bowl that he gave each animal in turn, all the while talking to them soothingly, "There Hufer all is well. You're going to enjoy this journey Goli, once we get going."

With a little more coaxing the animals reluctantly pulled themselves up, first on their knees, and finally to full height. Parto put the reigns of Goli into BelkA's hands, and took the lead with Hufer as they began marching toward the collected party with all their squawking and bleating animals.

Now they had only to await the trumpet call from their caravan leader Bah-Ador who, at present it seemed, was in a screaming match with some camels and their owners. It was hard to tell from their vantage point what was causing the problem.

Their own two one-humped dromedaries had seated themselves once more square on the ground, and were taking in the scene around them from behind thick long eyelashes.

As they waited more travelers arrived, some in companies of ten or more camels each. All appeared loaded to excess with cages of chickens and crates of fruits and vegetables dangling on the very top. Others were clearly merchants with huge loads covered with colorful drapes. Among the late arrivals was a motley group claiming to be merchants, but lacking the professionalism of the other traders.

"What do you make of that bunch?" Parto asked.

"I don't like what I see. Whatever they are they're not merchants. I wonder?"

"Maybe they're toughened from bad experiences with brigands?"

"Perhaps."

"Look whose coming," Parto cautioned.

"Bah-Ador," BelkA said by way of greeting.

"BelkA Souash. Honored I am to have you join my caravan, and I promise I will do all in my power to protect you and make your journey enjoyable. I must admit that I've got problems with two parties of latecomers who failed to make advance reservations. That kind of thing annoys me because it forces me to make hasty decisions. Besides that, I don't like the looks of one group. The other party is a family with two children. Who wants the responsibility of children? Well, we shall see. Thankfully I now have the assistance of my eighteen-year-old son. His hand on the bow is fast and precise, and he's smooth with the javelin. Anyway I have a favor to ask of you. If I let the family join our caravan, would you allow me to place them behind you where I can keep a closer watch on them?"

"Of course," BelkA said.

Bah-Ador bowed. "We'll be leaving soon."

As he walked away, using his shoulder to wipe the sweat from his face, BelkA noticed with slight humor, that Parto's eye was fixed on the formidable dagger bulging from the man's belt.

"A nasty scar on his cheek," Parto commented.

BelkA grinned. "A good man. Experienced and congenial as well."

A first trumpet blast, calling for members of the caravan to begin mounting, halted conversations. Parto held the ropes of Goli and soothed the animal as his master climbed aboard. Then he too mounted. This time with little prompting the camels rose. Noises of shuffling, calling, crying, rose again, until the second piercing sound of the ram's horn announced that the journey had begun.

•••

Arif stood his ground while patiently bargaining with Bah-Ador for the privilege of joining the caravan party. His wife Tirza, meanwhile, was adjusting the load on the temperamental camels. "You are correct," Arif was saying, "I know the rules, but circumstances require my family to accompany me."

He refrained from telling the whole truth—that his wife had cajoled him into taking the family along. "Why not?" she'd argued, "SabA's, mature for his thirteen years and Sussan, at eleven, is as helpful as an adult. They'll learn a lot through the experience while also being a help to you. As for danger, the risk of not having their father home would equal any danger in traveling." She'd also argued that her own sewing business would benefit from the journey by allowing her to sell her handcrafts at markets along the way, and in finding exotic materials for new projects. Actually he needed little persuasion because he dreaded, most of all, the prospect of being separated from them.

"Please Bah-Ador," Arif now pleaded, "I promise we won't hold you responsible should a problem arise. Just let us accompany you and we shall comply with every other requirement you might impose."

Bah-Ador looked at each member of the family, taking in the upturned faces of the children, SabA with his eager expression and comical cowlick at the crown of his head and Sussan with a sprinkling of freckles around her nose. Finally he conceded, "They appear in good health, and you, unlike some others, have convinced me that you are worthy of your word. Just don't let me regret my decision." With that he moved on.

Arif breathed a sigh of relief and turned to help his wife balance the loads they'd hurriedly put together. As they themselves calmed down the ugly camels did the same. By then Bah-Ador had swung around and was motioning for them to follow, and soon they found themselves placed directly behind BelkA and Parto. Arif's heart now began to thud loudly in his chest, but he forced a smile.

BelkA turned around and nodded a greeting.

•••

As the caravan moved steadily along the dusty road, Babylon faded into a tiny dot before disappearing completely on the evening's horizon. They proceeded along the Euphrates, where the mist, that had begun to descend an hour earlier, was now thickening into a dense fog muffling the sound of the camels' gate into a surreal environment.

Chapter 6

Tamara

Anathoth and Jerusalem, May 589 B.C.

The first rays of sun pierced a purple sky as father and daughter, sitting side by side on their donkey-drawn cart, started down the road from their home in Anathoth. Birds chirped and sang merrily in the almond trees now in full bloom, filling the crisp morning air with fragrance. Tamara inhaled deeply and laughed outright, "My favorite time and favorite outing."

Her father Elzur shook his head in wonder, remembering the struggle of an hour before when he'd tried to rouse his teen-age daughter from slumber. What a transformation in the young woman beside him, now thrilling with the awakenings of nature.

"Hard to believe the desert is just below us, isn't it Father?"

"Yes, we breathe a different air up here, except when those hot easterly winds sweep through. Thankfully the orchards provide a reasonable shield."

"And also the almonds that keep us going to Jerusalem's market. I do hope we do well today."

"It would be nice if we could sell the rest of last year's crop so that we can have all our baskets empty and ready for this year's harvest."

"Well, what's most important of all is getting to see uncle Jeremiah again."

"You mean cousin, my cousin that is. He's your cousin once removed."

Tamara giggled. "He told me I could call him uncle last time we were together. I asked especially because his nieces and nephews treat him so mean. He deserves a niece who thinks highly of him."

"Call him what you like my dear, but don't let the relatives hear it. We can't afford to stir them up any more than they already are."

Tamara suddenly sobered. "What I can't understand is why his own family would try to kill him."

"Ah! Indeed. We must try to understand that what matters most to his family is their status with the powerful and influential folk in the city, especially the wealthy nobles. And these seem to be the very ones that Jeremiah manages most often to offend. So they all hate him."

"But really, all he does is announce the words Yahweh tells him to say. Every time he speaks out he begins with, 'Thus saith Yahweh.'"

"You're absolutely right daughter, and it would appear that our cousin stands between two fires— God and people. One can't always please both."

"Well, I hope he's at least feeling better. He looked so distraught last time we were together."

"Just seeing you will cheer him up. It always does."

Tamara smiled. "I'm glad for that."

"I wish you could have known cousin Jeremiah when he was young or when we were young."

Tamara smiled. "That's hard to imagine."

"Ah, but what fun times we had. The two of us along with Baruch and Shaphan were inseparable companions. We used to explore caves, or build little cities in the desert sands, or we'd send messages to each other through our pet goats."

"That does sound like fun," Tamara giggled.

"The scribal schools were no joke though, it seemed we were always getting punished for something. But it was good for us, and as a result we've remained intensely loyal to one another all these years."

"And now he's an old prophet with no children or grandchildren to care for him."

Elzur smiled, "But he has us."

"That's right, but we can't always be near to help, and it seems that the episodes of violence and cruelty keep getting worse. I get so fearful and angry about it all."

"I do too, but cousin Jeremiah doesn't. He loves and feels sorry for the people because they're hurting themselves by their own wrong choices and actions.

He even weeps over them, and when he receives messages that must be told he pours them out sorrowfully. Have you noticed?"

"Yes, I have indeed," Tamara, replied. "Yet, more often than not they fly into a rage and gang up against him."

Elzur sighed. "It's the truth that offends daughter. People don't want to hear it because they like their self-pleasing and sensual life-style. They don't want anyone to ruin their fun."

"You told me once that cousin Jeremiah didn't want to be a prophet, I think I can see why."

"Indeed, a prophet's life is not easy. At first Jeremiah resisted his calling with all kinds of excuses. He wanted to marry, have children and live a happy uncomplicated life. Besides that he was timid and didn't like to offend people. But Yahweh refused all his excuses, so finally he surrendered completely to God, and after that he stopped thinking about himself. He just goes where he's told to, and pours out God's messages not caring how people react. He knows that people need to hear from God, and that if they listen and take heed to what He says, it could save them a lot of trouble."

Tamara pondered a while. "Father, do you suppose I could be called by Yahweh to do something difficult?"

"Perhaps, and if He did would you obey?"

"I would," Tamara replied without a second's hesitation.

Startled at his daughter's strong and hasty declaration Elzur checked a chuckle while sobering.

"Your answer pleases me, and at the same time creates concern. You realize my child, that especially in the present confusion of our uncertain times, obedience could exact a heavy price?"

Tamara turned and looked at Elzur. "You think I do not understand Father?"

Seeing the determined set of his daughter's mouth Elzur replied, "I think you do daughter, it's just that of late I've been concerned about your future. Difficult days lie ahead and sometimes good people suffer with the wicked."

They were now rising over the hill toward Jerusalem and Tamara took in the massive walls and gates that towered before them. "You think an enemy could break through such walls as those father?"

"I do Daughter. If the LORD allows it, those walls could be as easy to break through as thin parchment. But let's not let fear darken this day. Yahweh knows and cares about each and every one who trusts in Him. You're like a sparrow in His hand."

"H-m-m. A sparrow in His hand, I like that."

Elzur smiled but kept focused on the road for fear his daughter would see the tears gathering in his eyes.

Chapter 7

Jeremiah

Anathoth and Jerusalem, May 589 B.C.

As Tamara and her father approached Jerusalem, other farmers from the surrounding countryside clustered around them. Elzur descended from the donkey just before their cart passed under the massive Potsherd Gate, flanked on both sides by towers.

Once inside the barely awakened city it became a game of push and shove as they slowly made their way down the narrow streets to the market square. Elzur stopped abruptly to allow a woman, heavily laden with produce, to thread her way through donkey carts so that she could catch up with her party. He cringed as he saw a farmer give an excessive rap on his donkey's neck with a stick. Poor animal. Its slim legs were already heavily taxed with an overload, and in any case, there wasn't room enough to walk faster. The moment's distraction resulted in a sharp bump in the ribs from a sack of meal carried by a donkey passing on his other side.

Tamara meanwhile took in the merchants at the shops lining the Street of David, who were opening their shutters and bringing their merchandise into the streets. One, she noticed in passing, had already arranged neat pyramids of lentils and grains. Beside the table a cat slept atop a sack of wheat unmindful of the commotion around her.

Father and daughter continued down David Street until they reached the market, completely arched over, with only here and there an opening that admitted shafts of light.

As they approached their designated site Tamara got off the donkey, and immediately began setting out baskets of almonds and a scale. The task took little time allowing her the opportunity to wave at familiar vendors before customers arrived. "Good morning Giddel," Tamara called out to the friendly old basket weaver who was stacking bundles of willow sticks and raffia around his workbench. His granddaughter Hodesh behind him was busy arranging baskets of every size and shape imaginable.

"How about coming over for a little chat," Giddel called back.

Tamara obliged. "How are things in Jerusalem?" she asked when she stood before him.

The nearsighted old man seated on his bench looked up, and took in Tamara's glowing face and expressive brown eyes, "I suppose what you're aiming at is news about your cousin Jeremiah?"

"Of course?" Tamara said with her usual giggle.

"Well, let's say that last week was not one of his best. You know Jeremiah. He's one of those few downright straightforward old prophets. This time he told about a vision he had of two baskets. One was filled with good figs, the other contained figs so bad they couldn't be eaten. He explained that the good figs represented the exiles in Babylon and the bad figs were the people still remaining here in Judah." Giddel scrutinized Tamara closely under his wiry grey eyebrows to see if she got the point.

Tamara caught her breath. "Oh dear! I'll wager that didn't go over well."

"Especially not since false prophets have been announcing that people still here in Jerusalem are better than their countrymen who were forced to go into exile. Puffed up, as these prophets were, they'd insist, 'those exiles got exactly what they deserved.'"

Tamara bit her lip and cupped her chin with her hand.

By then Hodesh, who had finished her task, came and joined the little group that now included Elzur.

"What do you think about all this Hodesh?" Tamara asked after embracing her friend.

"If you really want to know, I'm furious with those scoundrels. If I could get my hands on some, I'd twist their necks. All their sneaky questions are nothing more than plots to trap Jeremiah. As I see it, they're demonic. Jerusalem isn't worthy of Jeremiah."

Old Giddel stroked his beard. "My daughter speaks strongly," he said apologetically—but with a slight grin. "There is truth in what she says, however, because there is indeed an element here that will stop at nothing to make Jeremiah's life miserable, and it's because they can't face the truth. I fear for him — and the rest of us for that matter."

Someone shoved against Elzur causing him to glance at the stand. "Come Tamara," he said softly, "customers are waiting."

•••

Anxious as they were, it seemed to take forever to reach Jeremiah's house in the second district. The day had seemed long and sales unusually slow.

A surge of nostalgia welled up within Elzur as he halted the donkey and attached it to a post on the side of a small home. Next to it sat a larger one that had previously been occupied by his own aunt Huldah — the elderly prophetess — and his uncle Shallum.

Glancing at Tamara he noticed that she too was lost in memories, with her eyes fixed on the upper floor that hung over the courtyard, where she'd spent some of the happiest hours of her childhood.

Elzur thought upon the days when the modest little home had been lovingly built for Jeremiah, by his aunt and uncle, when he'd decided to leave Anathoth and move to the big city. His uncle and aunt had since died and now the larger home rang with the sounds of children at play. With a sigh he reminded himself that life's scenes shift with changing times. Deliberately he turned around and set himself to the task of unloading the packages from the donkey cart.

Then he knocked at the prophet's door. It opened almost immediately.

Tamara spontaneously made a dive for Jeremiah, throwing her arms around him just as she'd always done. His untidy graying hair hanging thin and limp around his round face, and his dismal tunic with frayed edges mattered little to her. She knew that her older cousin had weightier matters to be concerned about, and in fact, it was that unaffected aura about him that she found so endearing. She only wished she could make his burden lighter, and that people would be more kind and appreciative of him.

"Come in, come in," Jeremiah said pulling them inside, his face now aglow. "I was expecting you and have some soup, cheese and bread fresh from the Street of the Bakers."

"First let us give you some packages," Tamara said still clinging to his hand. "Mother has sent along some of your favorite foods and fruits, and I have just finished weaving a new tunic for you."

"Woven by your own hands, did you say? Why that's too precious to wear."

"Don't be silly uncle. Put it on so we can see you in it."

"Well then, seat yourselves and rest a moment. I'll be back shortly."

Jeremiah returned in his new bluish-grey tunic that matched his hair and brought out a hint of blue in his eyes. Tamara noticed that it took years from his face.

"Do you like it?" she asked.

"Of course my dear. Obviously I was needing one, and I must say, your weaving has much improved."

Tamara laughed. "I'm gaining experience uncle."

"Be sure to thank your mother for her thoughtful basket."

"I'll do that."

As they were eating Jeremiah asked for news of Anathoth.

"It's calm right now," Elzur replied cautiously. "The relatives are busy with their fields. A good thing."

Jeremiah sighed. "I miss country life but I'm not sorry to be away because, as you know, mistreatment from family and loved ones is harder to take than from strangers. But how are you getting along there?"

"Alas, we still keep aloof of the relatives, but at least they haven't hurt us as they did you. We speak in passing, but that's the extent of our mutual communication. The happy times of sharing the feast days are long forgotten."

"Are you lonely here Uncle?" Tamara asked.

"At times, I must admit, but my scribe Baruch comes daily and the work keeps me busy. How did the market go?"

"Slow, but tell us about Jerusalem Uncle. We've heard some snatches that arouse curiosity. Can you fill in the details?"

Jeremiah sighed once more. "O Jerusalem. Stubborn Jerusalem. She breaks my heart again and again. Sometimes I wish I were blind. What one sees on the streets is bad enough, but what goes on in the temple itself shatters all hope of reformation. We are the people who were to be the keepers of the covenant, but you wouldn't know it even exists. In fact, I've heard that the sacred scrolls have disappeared from the temple altogether, and an idol has been set up in the holy of holies!"

Jeremiah stopped abruptly upon seeing Tamara's expression of perplexity and sadness. "Forgive me niece, I got carried away. It's just that I'm troubled over all the consequences that are building up, and I fear are now reaching the exploding point. I continue to pour out the warnings I receive from Yahweh but the words die in the air."

"We wish we could be closer by so we could assist you but, for Tamara's sake, I'm glad we don't live in the city," Elzur said.

"Indeed," Jeremiah affirmed shifting his eyes upon Tamara. "I certainly wouldn't want *my* niece to see what goes on at nights in the town squares and on roof tops as soon as it's dark."

"We know about the worship of the *Queen of Heaven*," Tamara said, "but I can assure you Uncle that when I look up at the stars and moon I get a mysterious sense of awe for the Creator of it all."

"I'm with you there niece."

Tamara went over to Jeremiah and hugged him.

"We're still concerned about your safety," Elzur said bringing the focus back on his cousin.

"I'm sorry to be the cause of your anxiety dear ones," Jeremiah said still holding Tamara close, "perhaps it will encourage you to know that I've lost that fear of people I used to have. Elzur you remember how I used to struggle with it?"

"I sure do."

"It's strange but now when I stand before crowds, that are mostly hostile, I don't even see them. Words pour out of my mouth that amaze even me. And these days, I must say, they aren't of the pleasant variety. Actually I expect to receive fewer messages because Yahweh has told me that the cup of evil is now full. I might as well not even bother to pray for people because it's too late. Justice must be poured out." He turned to his cousins and asked, "Are you prepared?"

Elzur paled. "I suppose you mean we should prepare food in case of famine and plague. At least we'll have an ample supply of almonds by the looks of things. I'm not sure what to do about the danger of the sword."

"You must—or rather we must all—surrender to Babylon," Jeremiah said firmly.

"What do you mean? Babylon is a wicked city, more wicked even than Jerusalem."

"That was the message Yahweh gave me last week and as you can understand, it was most unpopular. We must understand that Yahweh has the right to choose the rod needed to bring His disobedient children in line. In Judah's case He will use a wicked empire to bring a wayward people back to Him, and He has indicated clearly that we must submit to that empire and trust Him for the outcome."

Elzur sighed. "We talked about this earlier today, but I hadn't realized it could happen so soon."

"I can't say exactly when it will happen, but this last prophecy is specific enough to cause me to feel we are standing at the threshold."

"How do we prepare spiritually?" Elzur asked.

"By trusting Yahweh and His Word and committing ourselves to Him. It's something I put to the test this past week as I narrowly escaped death once again."

"Oh no. What happened?" Tamara asked anxiously.

"The false prophets managed to get a mob stirred up against me and they were laying to kill me at the corner of my street."

"Oh! Uncle!" Tamara looked intently upon Jeremiah's face, her eyes wide with concern. "So what did you do?"

"Yahweh warned me to alter my routine."

"So what happened then?" Tamara asked.

"Nothing at all."

Tamara and Elzur broke into laughter. "As simple as that?" Tamara asked.

"Indeed. I was delivered—this time. But there's something you need to understand Tamara, Yahweh sometimes protects from danger or suffering—and sometimes He takes us through it. We can, however, count on Him to stay right beside us, and help us one way or another."

"It's like what we were saying when Father and I entered the city. We're—each one—like a sparrow in His hand."

"You've got the picture my dear niece."

It's getting dark." Elzur cautioned, "We must be on our way."

Chapter 8

Dust

Desert, June 589 B.C.

Riding side by side with Parto in the cool of the night BelkA slipped into light chatter to pass the time. "It's good to have you beside me Parto. Of late my expressions of gratitude have been few, but I assure you that your efforts have not gone unnoticed."

"My pleasure Master."

"Now this may surprise you, but I think it's time to leave off protocol when there's no official call for it. I'll give you clues when formality is required, but I've been feeling the need for friendship of late, and it came to me that you are the trustworthiest person I know. Thus friend, when in each other's company, lets disregard social standing. It would please me if we could interact as good friends and equals."

Parto stiffened, "Of course Master."

"You mean, 'Yes BelkA?'"

"Yes BelkA."

"That's better. Now tell me Parto, how is it that you have become so organized and efficient when you are illiterate?"

"Experience has taught me considerable lessons... BelkA. Each time I strive to correct the errors of the previous journey."

"Ah, that is good. Remember the time you forgot my almonds? I spared no words in expressing my discontent."

"Indeed, never again will your supply of almonds run out."

BelkA laughed, and then said, "But Parto, I've also noticed that you've become more skilled with the camels and especially in handling minute details."

Parto reflected a moment before answering. "I keep practicing, as with the camels, even though it's been a long time since we've needed them. For other matters I use pieces of brick or pottery to help me remember the various items, marking them with colors of dye or drawing pictures, then I make little piles of each indicating the quantities."

"Why Parto, that's a form of literacy."

"Please don't be angry if I tell you that I'm learning the Aramaic letters from a friend."

"So you have a friend who's literate. Might I know him?"

"You do BelkA. His name is Shai, the assistant of Bazy-An."

"H-m-m, Shai, the Hebrew."

"I hope you don't mind Master u-h-h BelkA."

"Not at all, in fact I'm pleased. It's to my benefit to have a literate servant. This Shai, I hear, has great intelligence and skill."

"Indeed he has, and wisdom too."

"Wisdom. Can he interpret visions like Daniel?"

Parto smiled. "No, he's never mentioned visions to me, but I might say that he discerns matters that are beyond knowledge."

"Such as."

"Important things of life like right and wrong."

"No doubt Shai's a worshipper of Yahweh."

"In honesty I must say that he is."

"Relax, Parto. At a previous time this might have been a concern, but since meeting up with Prime Minister Daniel I've become more... shall we say... tolerant and even open, especially since I am also under his command. Would you say that Shadrach, Meschach and Abednego also have this wisdom?"

"Indeed BelkA. They exemplify it in their uncompromising life-style."

"So it seems this wisdom has a basis of integrity?"

"Absolutely."

"King Zedekiah of Judah could use a little of that. His lack of integrity is going to cost him."

"Shai mentioned concern about the king's policies. He told me that King Zedekiah knows right from wrong, but he caters to his wealthy and influential nobles."

"He said that, did he? I'm beginning to like this Shai. He's got Judah's king sized up to perfection. It'll be interesting to see how Zedekiah's responds to Nebuchadnezzar's ultimatum."

Parto flinched and looked into the distance.

After shifting into a more comfortable position BelkA asked. "Tell me Parto, what do you think of Ezekiel?"

"Well, I haven't had opportunity to meet him. I only know that in Shai's mind he's a true prophet of Yahweh."

"Does Bazy-An know about your friendship with his assistant."

"He does BelkA."

"Has he expressed an opinion?"

"He has."

"Favorable, no doubt."

"True. He has great respect for Shai."

"Has he added Yahweh to the gods he worships then?"

"Oh no, BelkA, he has chosen to worship Yahweh exclusively."

BelkA's eyes widened but he controlled his voice. "And you Parto?"

There was a long silence before Parto answered softly but distinctly, "I have also BelkA."

BelkA again concealed shock. "So you two Babylonians have become Jewish proselytes. I hope Adda-Guppi doesn't get wind of this."

"I hope it won't cause trouble for you, BelkA."

BelkA shrugged. "We've left the priestess behind. I appreciate every mile that comes between us. But tell me, why would you choose Yahweh at the exclusion of all other gods?"

"Well, I feel no need for gods made by men from stone and metal. They cannot hear, nor can they speak. And... I doubt their supposed powers. The Hebrew God has eternal existence and power that is real."

"Now that's a weighty statement. I'll have to ponder on it."

The two men left off talking, each entering his own private world. Hours slipped by as the steady bounce of hoof-steps rocked them into fitful slumber. Travelers were beginning to shift and groan when a trumpet echoed over the plain just as the first rays of dawn lit the sky. Bah-Ador turned around and hollered, "Camp time." For their special benefit he explained that they'd reached a favorite spot with a spring. "You'll like it," he added.

Passengers descended wearily from their camels and began stretching and rubbing their stiff necks. Parto was one of the first to have his tent up, and then lost no time getting a fire going with a kettle atop.

BelkA meanwhile busied himself with papyrus and stylus making careful notations and observations of the journey. By the time he had finished Parto was ladling out bowls of warm broth made from dried meat and barley. "Do you mind if I offer a bowl to the family beside us master? There is more than we can eat here, and the mother is burdened with many tasks while the children are hungry."

BelkA glanced at the tent next to theirs and took in the disarray. "Good observation Parto. I can't see that it would hurt. Ladle it up and I will take it to them myself."

As he approached the neighbor's tent the children, who were arguing over a toy, abruptly stopped rousing the mother's curiosity. She jumped at the sight of BelkA, then caught herself and bowed.

"What is your name?" BelkA asked.

"Tirza," the woman replied, "and my husband's name is Arif." When the bowl was put in her hands she remained speechless. "For us?" was all she could say.

"For you," BelkA answered gently. "It will warm you."

By then Arif appeared and immediately bowed to the ground beside his wife. "Much gratitude to you honored one. But we are the ones who should be serving you. Permit us to give you some dried figs in return."

"Perhaps later," BelkA said. "Please partake while it is hot." Without waiting for further conversation he turned around and left.

•••

When they had consumed the broth Arif pulled his wife to the side of the tent and whispered in her ear so as not to be heard by the children, "Last night, while you were sleeping on the camel, I overheard a conversation between BelkA and his servant."

"About what?"

"About the Hebrew God Yahweh."

"Really," she shrugged. "I wouldn't be concerned. BelkA's an intelligent man. It was probably a philosophical discussion."

"I hope you're right."

Arif got up and called the children to help him feed the pigeons.

"What's that on their feet?" SabA asked.

"That's a canister for messages. We'll be sending one off to Babylon once we reach Jerusalem," Arif replied.

"Show us how it works," Sussan pleaded.

Arif carefully removed the little canister attached to the leg of one of the pigeons and a tiny roll of papyrus fell out.

Sussan picked it up and handed it to her father.

Arif unfolded the tiny scroll and read, "This is Zur, the male. Notice his purple-edged wings. He prefers lentils the best."

The young ones laughed.

"Now the other," Sussan said impatiently.

"I'll let you remove the message SabA."

Carefully SabA laid the frightened pigeon in Sussan's hands and while she kept a firm grip he carefully removed the canister and handed it to his father.

Arif read, "This is Ziza with a triangle of white on her throat. She's a female. She's most fond of let-tuce, but she'll eat anything if you gently stroke her head."

"We like lentils and lettuce best," Arif repeated in a mocking tone.

"I'm afraid that it's barley tonight for both of you." Tirza said, as she dropped kernels into the palms of her children's hands, that they in turn held out to the birds while Arif gently caressed both heads.

The family had gone back to organizing their belongings when a wind from the east started blowing. In minutes it became a gale hurling sand against the tent. As they scrambled to chase after their belongings the very air became gritty. "Get inside quick," the husband ordered as he began throwing all they'd left outside into the tent. "Now SabA, get the hammer in my tool box, and come help me tighten the ropes on the tent pegs."

"You must first protect your faces," Tirza called after them as she dived into a basket and pulled out heavy scarves. Then with adept hands she wrapped the faces of each family member in such a fashion as to create a protective visor over their eyes, nose, mouth and ears.

•••

The wind continued all morning and into the afternoon throwing up huge plumes of dust that the sun transmuted into gold and peach as they swirled skyward. Bah-Ador made his rounds checking the tents, screaming above the howling gales that they would have to delay their departure. "Too difficult to buck winds like these," he shouted, "and we risk getting lost. We'll see about tomorrow. Rest as best you can."

The following day passed and still the winds persisted, though somewhat abated. Sand was everywhere and all efforts to sweep it from the tent and shake it from belongings proved futile. Parto managed to keep busy refilling the camel-skinned water bags from the spring, and watering the camels while fighting even to stand up. He was lifting the flap to reenter when he saw Arif approaching.

"Greetings neighbor," Arif said.

"Greetings to you in return. Is all well at your tent?"

"All is as expected. Please permit me to invite you and your master to our tent to partake of a simple meal."

"You should not go to the trouble in such conditions," said Parto.

"It's no trouble, on the contrary, it's a good way to occupy the time for both ourselves and the children."

"Allow me then to inquire of my master."

BelkA had heard the request from within the tent where he had been busily working on various charts and plans. When Parto entered he said, "Tell Arif that we gladly accept."

Parto bowed and exited. "You heard my master," Parto said smiling.

"We are ready when you are," Arif said.

The family appeared overjoyed at the arrival of their guests, as though concealing a big surprise.

"Mutton?" BelkA exclaimed when he saw the dish set on a rug. "You sacrificed one of your sheep."

"No we purchased it from an Arab," Arif explained.

BelkA and Parto looked at each other and shook their heads.

"Clever of them," BelkA commented. "They know that once we get to Aleppo or Damascus they'll buy several to replace this one."

"Please sit down," Arif urged.

When he noticed that Tirza was keeping Sussan separate BelkA said, "Let us forget the formalities of the east and dine together, as we often do in the Babylon of today."

"If it is acceptable to you, then it is well with us," Arif said as he indicated with a nod of his head for his wife and daughter to approach. "My Tirza is a liberated Babylonian," he remarked. "As a dressmaker she often sews for people of the court who make their own rules, and what she sees done there, she brings to our home."

"It seems to me that the priestesses of our temples keep pace with the court," BelkA commented.

Arif laughed. "I haven't thought about it, but in fact they do. In any case the priestesses outnumber the priests, and they take full advantage of their power and prestige. Do you not agree?"

It was BelkA's turn to laugh. "Ishtar is almost as prominent as Marduk, in fact, sometimes I think she rivals him."

"Shall we drink to her?" Arif asked playfully.

BelkA was about to comment, but restrained himself with a glance at the children.

Arif sobered remembering the conversation he'd overheard two nights before. "We are open-minded about matters of religion."

BelkA raised his eyebrows and cast a quick knowing glance at Parto before detouring the conversation, "Pleasant it is to relax in the company of good people like you."

"The pleasure is ours," Arif responded.

In the course of the meal BelkA's curiosity regarding Arif kept growing. Finally he dared to ask, "Have we met before? There's something familiar about your face Arif?"

Arif had an answer all prepared, "Actually, I know you better than you know me. You are a man of importance while I mostly seclude myself in my work. It is possible that you remember seeing me in passing at the temple of Marduk—the ziggurat Etemenanki—where I am an astrologer of mathematics and recorder of astrological events, also of wind, rain and clouds. As I remember we had but one personal encounter."

"Why of course," BelkA responded. "I do indeed remember seeing you a time or two in passing. As I recall, you were fully engrossed in your scrolls, but there was an occasion when we discussed an eclipse I believe."

"You're right."

"Will this journey benefit your work in astrology then?"

"Hopefully. I plan to meet with some other astrologers in Egypt, and since my wife is a seamstress, she needed to find textiles and accessories to please her clients. On the side we do some merchandising of odds and ends as well. We brought our children along because we thought the experience would be good for them."

"You decided rather precipitously Bah-Ador told me."

"Yes", and then looking up Arif asked, "Might I ask the purpose of your journey lord BelkA?"

"It's the king's business and I'm not free to discuss it," BelkA responded rather abruptly, and then turned to the children asking them their age.

"I am thirteen," answered SabA, "and my sister is eleven."

"I am almost twelve," corrected Sussan.

"So, then you are no longer children?"

The two smiled their approval at the remark. Then SabA abruptly asked, "Have you seen our pigeons?"

"You have pigeons?" BelkA asked feigning surprise for he had earlier heard them cooing and suspected they were for communication purposes.

The parents exchanged anxious looks but the brother and sister innocently uncovered the blanket from the cage.

"This one is Ziza. She likes to have her head rubbed like this," said Sussan as she demonstrated the technique. "The other..."

"This is Zur, the male," her brother broke in. "See? He's the one with the purple-edged wings."

"Pleased to meet you," BelkA said as he ran his finger over Ziza's head. Then he looked at Sussan. "Do your pets like music?"

"I don't know," Sussan answered with a shrug and a giggle.

BelkA reached into his robe and pulled out a flute. "Let's find out." He began first to play some rapid scales with a quirky rhythm causing the birds to compete and everyone to laugh outright, and then gradually the notes flowed into soothing melodies while the volume gradually lowered, and eyelids became droopy.

Tirza, who had by then tidied up, excused herself and, taking the children, disappeared behind a blanket curtain while the men continued their conversation far into the night.

A trumpet blast abruptly terminated the visit. "Looks like we'll be traveling in daylight today," BelkA said.

Rejoined by Tirza, Arif bid his guests good-bye in response to a profusion of expressions of gratitude.

Once back in their own tent BelkA whispered, "Those are carrier pigeons Parto. There's something more to Arif's presence than he has thus far admitted."

"I'm afraid so," Parto agreed raising an anxious brow.

Chapter 9

Conspiracy

Desert, June 589 B.C.

"I've had about all I can take," Ghadir yelled as he walked toward the tent flap.

"Are you out of your mind. Where are you going?" Tahampton called after him. "You'll get blown away out there."

"I'm bored out of my skin. I'd like nothing more than to blow away."

"Come on we'll play a game," Tahampton said in as pleasant a voice as he could muster.

"Do as you like but leave me out," Ghadir shot back. "I'm sick of this miserable tent. I want action."

"Me too," KaVey said. "I'm fed up with this so-called adventure. All we do is trudge along one dreary day after another playing a charade. What we were paid is less than pigeon feed when considering the fact that we have no diversion, no women, no wine or beer, boring food and sand, sand, sand."

Ghadir jerked around and faced KaVey. Dropping his scowl for the first time in days he said, "Heh, you're a smart fellow. You want to talk?"

"About what?"

"About breaking the monotony with some action."

"Like what?" Tahampton broke in.

"Well, listen to this. I've overheard BelkA and Parto talking about the Hebrew God. It appears this Parto is a believer. Isn't this the very thing old Adda-Guppi feared? I think we need to sabotage BelkA's mission right now by killing Parto and stealing the gold in their tent. This will force BelkA to return to Babylon; it'll be the end of his mission including those Writings that seem so precious, and we'll be wealthy."

"You do remember that the agreement stipulated we were to kill BelkA and dispose of the Writings at the same time."

"B-a-a. Who cares? BelkA's carrying more gold than we'll ever get out of Adda-Guppi."

"Have you gone mad?" RAstin shouted above the roar of a blast of roaring wind. "We'll have the whole caravan against us and Bah-Ador will have us all executed."

"I agree," Tahampton said. "This is not the time to act. Let's cool down and wait it out."

"Let's first see what happens in Jerusalem," Abid suggested, "I've a feeling that a cold welcome awaits BelkA and that enemies are itching to get their hands on him. All we have to do is leave the dirty work to them?"

"Now we're getting somewhere," Tahampton added letting out a long sigh."Let's just cool our tempers. We'll soon be in Aleppo where we'll have some diversion. Think of it fellows, a full week to indulge ourselves day and night."

"I'm going to check on the camels outside," Ghadir said before ducking out of the tent with KaVey following after him.

"Have you noticed," KaVey said, "the winds are dying down."

Ghadir grinned.

The ram's horn sounded.

"We've got to get going, but while we're here alone let's decide on something. Would you be willing to cooperate with me in a plan?"

"That's what I'm here for. I like your idea."

"We'll discuss it as we travel, but I think the place to do it is at our next camp site."

"But what about the others?"

"They'll take the blame. What do we care? We'll be gone."

KaVey hesitated as a sense of fear fell upon him. "Could we not steal the gold without killing Parto?"

"I don't see how. Come on, where's your enthusiasm?"

Reluctantly KaVey nodded his head in agreement.

Chapter 10

Arif

Desert, June 589 B.C.

Arif, tired of sitting on his rather uncomfortable seat on the camel, often chose to walk, especially in the night when he could look up at the stars and make mental calculations and observations. It required a rather rapid step, however, to keep up with the camel's wide stride, but still, the exercise brought relief to sore muscles and other parts.

Thus far they'd managed to avoid bandits at least, but the delay over the dust storm had resulted in Bah-Ador's announcement that they would skip Aleppo. This perplexed him. In a way he was relieved, but it upset the main purpose of his involvement, and how would he explain it back in Babylon?

Well, there was no going back now. Might as well make the best of it. Since the dust storm the caravan had kept moving at a steady pace, sometimes covering thirty miles a day. The canvas of landscape had, for the most part, not been of great interest, especially since they traveled mostly at night. The first evening's distance had followed Babylon's flat agricultural lands, irrigated by canals from the Euphrates, but it had suddenly become arid and bleak about the time the dust storm struck. Now the air had an odor of sulfur from bitumen seepages nearby. "This is where Babylonians come to gather bitumen to make mortar for bricks," Arif explained to his wife and children behind him.

At Hit, a friendly herder of goats had happened by their campsite and let the children watch his milking of the animals, after which he served them fresh warm milk, encouraging them to drink to their full. Tirza had purchased a quantity to make a good supply of sour milk and curds that was a favorite family treat.

Above Hit the Euphrates narrowed, but continued muddy between high banks on both sides forcing the road out of the constricted valley onto a broad steppe like upland, rolling and rock-studded. Here in the poor country, too high to irrigate and too dry for rain-fed crops, the black tents of the nomads silhouetted the evening's sky. A few villages appeared with some semblance of civilization, but the miles between were monotonous and bleak.

Arif wondered how he and his family could have endured had it not been, ironic as it was, for BelkA and Parto's company. Many had been the conversations, better-termed discussions, between them that had melted the hours away. The subjects of those conversations were what occupied his mind in times like these as he walked by himself.

What he'd overheard thus far from the discussions between BelkA and Parto would have provided excellent information to relate to Adda-Guppi in Babylon, but without some form of permanent residence he couldn't have sent out the pigeons even if he'd wanted to—which he somehow didn't. He needed first to make sense of it all. At such times he might have welcomed direct conversation with Parto, not for the purpose of spying, but to ask some serious questions. Alas, he dared not even consider it.

Strange it was that thoughts of the Divine seemed appropriate at night as one looked up at a sky blinking with stars. In all his years in astronomy he'd failed to penetrate the mystery behind them. In past days he'd even attempted worshiping the stars and all the heavenly bodies, but somehow it didn't make sense. The myths and fables of cosmic creation also lacked the satisfying answers he longed for. Was life, after all, dependent upon fate?

The last time he'd overheard conversation between BelkA and Parto it had been—of all things—about love. Yahweh's love and care. Apparently the Hebrew Writings mention it. Parto had quoted some words that he said came from a collection of Hebrew hymns. "He who watches over Israel neither slumbers or sleeps." He remembered a piece of literature he'd read on some pottery in the library that he'd thought so clever that he'd memorized the whole poem:

"They have retired, the great ones.
The bolts are drawn, the locks in place.
The noisy crowds are still and quiet,
The open doors have now been closed.

"The gods and goddesses of the land—
The Sun, the Moon, the Storm, the Morning Star—
Have gone to where they sleep in heaven,
Leaving aside judgment and decree.

"Veiled in the night:
The thoroughfares are dark and calm,
The traveler invokes his god,
Claimants and plaintiffs are fast asleep.

"The one true judge, father of the fatherless,
The Sun, has gone into his chambers..."

Sleeping gods! Impotent, at a time when their assistance is most needed. Of what use could they be even as mediators between groping humans and an Absolute Power. A wonderful thing it would be to know a God who never slumbers or sleeps on a night like this.

How does one reconcile the Babylonian concept of fate—the natural sequence of nature that can be interpreted through incantations—with watchful love and tender care? Could it be possible that a totally different pattern existed where a God of love ordered man's ways?

He looked up at the stars. They were enough for his ancestors; perhaps they held the answers after all. They, at least, were concrete images. He tried to identify the various groupings, but tonight, they too, appeared absent. Where might "Mother Nature" be on a night like this? Of what use were incantations, offerings and prayers? Confused and desperate he found himself crying out, "Could there, in fact, be just one true God. *If only I could know?*"

He focused on a lone, distant star. The longer he looked the more he felt that the secret beyond that star would soon be revealed to him. For the moment, peace washed over his troubled being. The air was clear, the wind had stopped, and morning was dawning.

Chapter 11

Aleppo

June 589 B.C.

A t the first rays of morning light Bah-Ador, at the head of his caravan, reached a fork of the road and waited. When all the stragglers had caught up he called out, "Since we're making good time I wish to offer you the option of the detour to Aleppo which, after the dust storm, I cancelled. However, it would delay our arrival in Jerusalem. Would this inconvenience any of you?"

A low rumble followed until a merchant shouted, "Aleppo is good."

A wave of applause echoed above the camels.

"I thought you merchants would be pleased, and for all the rest of you I hope the stop will be enjoyable. The market's unbeatable and the city offers interests for all tastes. A word of caution, however: beware of brigands. The stretch of road ahead has a reputation for surprise attacks and the city swarms with crooks of all kinds. Take courage my companions. In two hours we'll be there."

As they traveled BelkA noticed that his slave was taking Bah'Ador's advice seriously. He sat straight and alert on his camel scrutinizing every rock and cave and watching all points of the horizon. He himself had just dozed off when Parto exclaimed, "Look Master, Aleppo's upon us." There in the distance the stone citadel, perched on a massive rock, glistened in the late morning sunshine.

BelkA rubbed his parched eyes and took in the verdant metropolis, a striking contrast to the arid landscape about them. He wondered that the several thousand-year-old city, lying halfway between the Euphrates and the Mediterranean, continued to survive and thrive while other great cities of that vintage had long since faded into dust. Seldom conquered, it had never been destroyed.

A haze like the drifting of centuries settled upon them as they tethered their camels at the campsite on the outskirts of the city. By then Bah-Ador's son Heydar was already making the rounds repeating the warning for bandits." Take every precaution and call for help at the slightest disturbance," he repeated from tent to tent.

"It would appear that the lad is thirsty for adventure," BelkA commented.

•••

The moon was rising by the time Arif had the tent set up, his weary family fed and safely tucked into their bedrolls. He now carefully unpacked valuables, placing them under his bedroll. With curved dagger in hand and his ears tuned he went outside and started circling his tent. For an instant a shadow fell upon BelkA's tent and a hint of a footfall caught his ear. Instantly he stopped all movement and stood watching and listening, while his heartbeat accelerated. Finally he picked up enough courage to inch his way around his neighbor's tent. He found and heard nothing. Was it his imagination? All seemed normal. With one last sweep of his eyes he inched toward his own tent where he silently entered, carefully fastened the hooks, and put a basket weighed down with food supplies in front of the opening. Lying down on his bed with his dagger under his pillow he tried to catch some sleep, but it was slow in coming.

Besides his wariness for the safety of his family — and now strangely for BelkA and Parto—his mind picked up other concerns. Snatches of conversations he'd overheard replayed their strange concepts before his mind. Why should they matter? He must get himself out of the strange mood. He was, after all, a learned astrologer, supposedly firm in Babylonian theology. Yet somehow it did matter. He had to admit, he was at least mildly intrigued.

Besides that, apprehension for the following day weighed heavily upon him. How ridiculous that he, a thirty-five-year old scholar, should be called upon to play go-between for a marriage proposition between two strangers. It was preposterous and so was the whole spy idea yet, oddly enough, unavoidable.

What if he should fail? What if BelkA and the woman would dislike each other, or that he should fail to even find this particular merchant and his supposedly gorgeous daughter? And what if, in spite of all these machinations, BelkA, instead of being diverted from a connection with Daniel's God, might actually embrace Him? The confidence he once felt about it all was definitely faltering and he hated the whole messy affair.

There was still, however, Utabar's comical suggestion of sabotaging Adda-Guppi that played curiously upon him and intrigued him enough to give it a try. That others shared his dislike for the old priestess had been reassuring, yet it provided no direct solution to his present dilemma. Oh well, he decided, might as well let the day run its course. He'd just have to deal with whatever consequences came of it later.

•••

The market place echoed life in full dimension. The yelp of full-throated haggling over prices rose above the bleat of dozens of sheep being driven through the main square. Competing with them were the numerous children of merchants who were taking advantage of their parents' preoccupations to engage in scuffling, kicking, and screaming matches.

Arif and Tirza had managed to set up their own stand that included a variety of items they'd brought along to sell: richly colored Babylonian yarns, embroidered garments of Tirza's own designs and handiwork, and some novelty jewelry she'd collected. When cleverly laid-out the assortment permitted an appealing and tempting array.

At another jewelry stand BelkA stopped to take a closer look at some gems when a hand fell upon his shoulder. "Are you not BelkA?" the stranger asked.

BelkA nodded with a questioning frown.

"Don't ask how I know, but I must tell you that your life is in danger. If I were you I would go back to Babylon immediately."

"Who are you and from where do you come?" BelkA asked harshly.

The stranger nervously answered, "My name is Helem. I've just come from Jerusalem and I can assure you that the atmosphere is alive with antagonism against Nebuchadnezzar. I have connections with a group of realists loyal to Babylon who are followers of the prophet Jeremiah, and who are aware that an envoy from Babylon is expected to arrive in Jerusalem. From fellow merchants I've learned that you must be that envoy. There are men in King Zedekiah's court who are even now planning to kill you."

BelkA stood back and stared at the young man before him, taking in his attractive though modest attire and obviously earnest demeanor. "My obligation is to obey the orders of my king, that's all I have to say." Noticing, however, the disappointed slump in the shoulders of the young man BelkA added in a more gentle tone, "but I thank you for your thoughtful concern."

Turning away BelkA pondered the strange and troubling words from the stranger. Perhaps he should have insisted on a royal escort after all, because obviously his merchant disguise had little effect. Rumors were spreading at lightning speed from somewhere. Could that tag-along crowd be up to something? And was Arif involved? He hoped not, yet caution was indispensable.

•••

Arif continued on his way eager to get the ordeal over with. He found the short bald merchant in a Syrian cape, of shocking orange, seated cross-legged on a carpet surrounded by sculptures. One sculpture that particularly arrested his attention was a depiction of Ishtar with a star on her head and a chaplet of beads in her hands. Obviously Babylonian, he mused. Approaching the merchant he said, "I am Arif, and you are perhaps Huram?"

The merchant immediately snapped his fingers at a passing beer vendor. "Two," he called out. "I'm expecting you Arif. Here, this will refresh you."

Arif accepted the beer and watched the merchant drain his cup with one gulp.

Huram pointed to a remarkably beautiful woman making a transaction with a customer, her raven black hair gleaming blue in the glaring sun.

"I've received a message from Babylon that a man of high esteem and potential is interested in a marriage arrangement with my daughter."

Arif gulped. "Well..." he began still taking in the glow of the woman and her attractive form. "She is indeed beautiful."

"Of course she is and I'm expecting a good dowry."

"But I think you've been misinformed. You see this Babylonian of whom you speak is still unaware of the plan that others have relayed to you."

Merchant Huram's mouth hung open. "What are you saying? Am I wasting my time? I was led to believe through a message from Eri-Aku that it was set to go."

"I regret the misunderstanding sir. I am, however, more than willing to introduce you and her to BelkA, but I cannot promise that something will come of it."

The merchant shook his head and scowled in frustration. For a while he held his chin disdainfully in the air, then suddenly changed his demeanor. "Well, at least that's something. Let's get going." He called to his daughter and beckoned her to come.

The woman finished with her customer and approached.

"Look Mahla. This is Arif who has been sent by my friend Eri-Aku in Babylon to acquaint you with one of the most prominent, wealthy, and intelligent men of that great city. His name is BelkA and you will go now with Arif so he can introduce you."

The daughter crossed her arms before her and said, "Helem has already spoken to you about me. The first step of courting has been taken. I don't just skip around as if playing games."

"Come daughter, Helem's just a poor Jewish merchant. One can't compare him with this man BelkA.
Let's go see him at least and take a good look."

"I won't go."

"You will go," Huram said now on his feet and
putting his fist in his daughter's face. Then noticing
the crowd congregating he changed his style. "Look
Mahla, just do me the favor of going with me. If you
don't like what you see I'll let you have your poor
little merchant."

Reluctantly the woman followed her father and
Arif without saying a word. They came upon BelkA
as he stood discussing items on a jeweler's table.
Noticing Arif he turned and smiled a greeting.

"BelkA, I have here a merchant by the name of
Huram and his daughter Mahla. They would like to
meet you."

BelkA turned around and looked at both,
approving the daughter's elegant carriage and confident manner.

The merchant bowed low and looked up at
BelkA, "My lord, do you not find my daughter to be
the most beautiful woman you have ever seen?"

Mahla in her turn bowed and asked in an icy tone,
"Do you like our city of Aleppo?"

BelkA looked at her with curiosity that he concealed with a casual tone, "Well, it's a nice place. I'm
fascinated in fact that it was once the capital of the
first great empire of history."

Mahla for the first time smiled. "You're interested in history?"

"Yes. You see there's a connecting link between my Babylon and your Aleppo. The ancient King, Sargon I of Akkad, conquered Aleppo and connected it to Babylon." Mahla was about to ask another question when she suddenly realized that she stood before a most interesting, intelligent, and charming man. When she opened her mouth to speak no sound came out. Never before had she seen such well-carved features or heard a more captivating voice.

At this point the father smiled showing a number of missing teeth. Turning to BelkA he said, "You would be interested in my daughter perhaps?"

"In what way? From our conversation I can tell that she's a woman of broad interests and conversing with her is truly a delight."

"So what would you say if I proposed a marriage alliance?"

BelkA jerked his head in astonishment. "For my part the season is not right for any such consideration. I have heavy responsibilities to carry out before thinking of personal matters."

Arif looked at BelkA with an embarrassed smile—and a sense of relief.

"Perhaps at a later time I would be interested in getting to know more about her."

"Come lord BelkA, I realize that I am but a humble merchant, and you are a man of high position and impeccable reputation. My daughter here may not have your social standing, but she is a woman of distinct beauty and character. Women of her quality are rare. The two of you are in many ways equal. It's a chance of a lifetime, don't you see, and if you delay too long another might get her."

BelkA looked at Arif with a perplexed frown. He then turned to Mahla. "Perhaps our destinies shall cross again some day," he said with finality and bowed his head.

Mahla smiled and responded, "Perhaps." But when BelkA had turned around she exclaimed under her breath, "He even knows how to handle my father!"

Merchant Huram looked at Arif in disbelief and murmured, "He seems interested and yet he's distant. How do you explain that?"

"I was afraid of this. It's evident that he is much concerned over his mission, but I think that you have at least planted a seed in BelkA's mind. Perhaps it will grow, and as we continue our journey, I shall water it."

"What more can I ask," Huram said with a shrug of resignation.

Mahla smiled and fastened inquiring eyes on BelkA one last time before turning around.

Chapter 12

Master and Slave

Aleppo, June 589 B.C.

S itting cross-legged on his mat, Parto pulled out a precious sheet of papyrus that BelkA had generously shared with him for the purpose of practicing his writing. While opening his scribal box he caught the sound of muffled footsteps in the sand. Instantly, but silently, he collected the writing materials along with BelkA's valuables, and laid them in a hole that had been dug as a precautionary measure. Then he covered it all up with heavy cookware.

He had taken an upright position near the entrance when he heard a hand on the tent. Immediately he reached for his weapon. His skill with the dagger was not as proficient as his left-handed master, but as a fighter he excelled at pinning a man down. Thus he refrained from action until the intruder offered the right position. When a knife started to slit the tent open he crouched in a corner.

A tall, muscled man entered. Without taking time to recognize the intruder he dived at the feet, knocking the fellow to the ground. He was about to grab for some ropes to secure the assailant when a second intruder appeared and jumped on him.

Parto twisted and lifted himself enough to shove his elbows into the second man's ribs, paralyzing him with pain. Taking advantage of this temporary disablement he flung the man aside. By then, however, the first had recovered enough to throw a dagger at point blank range. Parto ducked avoiding a direct chest impact, but the weapon implanted itself into his shoulder.

Paying no heed to the pain or bleeding, he dislodged the dagger and hurled it back at his adversary. To his amazement it hit a juggler vein with a lethal blow. The man collapsed.

By then the first who'd gotten a second wind had fallen upon him. A struggle ensued on the floor with bedding and various objects scattering in all directions. Parto now invested all his strength in giving the robber a flip before collapsing to the floor. His opponent managed to grab a convenient knife and was lifting his hand—when Parto fell unconscious.

Just as it appeared hopeless for Parto, a dagger flew through the air striking the back of his opponent, while the poised hand dropped its weapon to the floor.

Upon arriving BelkA had noticed activity in the tent and had sprinted into action. Now he knelt beside his servant and recklessly tore off his turban that he tied securely around the injured shoulder, and across the chest. Then he dashed outside and called for help, waiting only long enough to be sure he was heard.

Bah-Ador and his son Heydar appeared in prompt response. "What is it?" Bah-Ador shouted between gasps of breath as he rushed into the tent. Gazing with astonishment at the scene he exclaimed, "These are not bandits, they're members of our party. They're part of that suspicious band of six."

"Where are the other four?" BelkA asked.

"I don't know but I'll find out."

"I want them interrogated."

"I will indeed do that lord BelkA."

By this time Arif was returning from market, and upon seeing a curious crowd gathering around BelkA's tent, stopped and rushed toward the opening.

BelkA indicated that he should enter.

Arif took in the scene and went immediately to Parto feeling for a pulse.

BelkA meanwhile was pulling the dead bodies aside and ordering their removal.

Parto drifted in and out of consciousness as his master watched over him.

Arif disappeared but returned soon after with an assortment of medical supplies including liniment and herbs. Carefully he removed the turban and examined the shoulder still bleeding profusely. "The wound is long and looks bad but it seems relatively shallow with only one deep point where the dagger dug in." Quickly he bound the injury exerting full pressure. "The bruises on the body do not appear serious," he assured BelkA," but I'm worried about those on the head. I don't like the swelling."

When Parto opened his eyes BelkA whispered into his ear, "Can you hear me?"

There was a slight nod.

"Can you see me?"

The eyes closed.

BelkA rose and pondered. "Would you mind staying with him then while I take care of other matters?"

"I'd be honored my lord," Arif said.

BelkA found Bah-Ador returning from investigating all the caravan members. "Did you find the others?"

"I did lord BelkA. They seemed incredulous when we questioned them, but I think they're trying to save their own necks."

"They ought to be executed, but just get them out of the caravan because they are a threat to the king's business wherever they are."

"It shall be done lord BelkA, immediately."

Turning back to the tent BelkA sighed. "I may be sorry for letting them off too easy."

•••

About an hour later Bah Ador returned. "I have carried out your orders, honored one. We're rid of them."

"Good, I think never-the-less that we need to be wary."

"Of course lord BelkA." Bah-Ador bowed before turning around.

•••

Tirza was pleased. She'd had some good sales including several expensive Babylonian cloaks. Her trinkets had also lured a number of customers, the most popular being the hoop earrings for men, but the women's necklaces, anklets and nose rings had also sold at a better price than expected.

The children had been reasonably helpful, allowing her to purchase unusual fabrics and various novelties for future sewing projects, besides fresh fruits and vegetables to provide a change from the dried lentils, dates, and nuts that were the staple of desert travel. She'd even included a provision of lettuce for Zur and Ziza.

Upon her return to the stand she found the children tired and hungry, so she encouraged them to quickly help her pack everything up.

Nearing BelkA's tent she noticed a commotion and found Arif discussing something with the people around him. When they approached he explained also to his family what had happened.

BelkA permitted entrance but cautioned the children, "Let Parto rest."

Tirza knelt beside Parto and felt his head and hands and then gently inspected the bandages. "A fine job Arif. It would seem that the bleeding has stopped and I think we can wait till tomorrow morning to change the dressing. I'll bring over an herbal concoction that will ease the pain and serve as a sedative."

She got up and looked at the distressed circle around her including BelkA and her family. "Look," she said, "I bought food at the market that is simple to prepare. Please try to relax a while. The children will help me prepare a meal that we'll bring to you."

BelkA gratefully accepted and sat down once more beside his slave.

Within the hour Tirza and the children were back, and soon large bowls of broth and flat bread were passed around. BelkA attempted to get Parto to sip some broth, but managed to coax only a couple of swallows.

"You'll see what a difference some rest will make," Tirza said cheerily. "He'll be stiff and sore tomorrow, but he'll be back on his feet in a few days or less."

"What about his head?"

"We'll have to wait and see," Tirza said with a serious expression.

BelkA joined Tirza's and Arif's hands together and held them a moment before letting them go. His eyes expressed the gratitude that failed to come from his lips. The children were subdued in their embraces, but their obvious compassion left a warm glow.

A few hours later Parto opened his eyes.

BelkA leaned close. "Can you see me?"

"Sort of," came the reply.

BelkA sat back and sighed, "You're talking my brother."

"Thank you BelkA for…"

"Sh-h-h Parto. Rest."

A hint of a smile touched the swollen lips.

BelkA was in no hurry to settle down for the night. Sitting on the mat beside his friend he let his head collapse into his hands. Relieved as he was that his slave was still alive, he crumbled at the thought that he had almost lost the man, who was more a brother than a slave.

He remembered the day when his father, years before, had brought home this frightened orphan of about six years of age, hoping to give him the brother he would never have.

Parto was one person who understood him like no other, and their relationship had been one of open camaraderie. When his father had been killed the understanding between them had deepened into a mutual reading of each that required few words. His mother, however, had noticed the close-knit entente and had advised him to maintain authority over his slave. "You don't need to pity him," she'd insisted, "he's favored far more than most slaves." He did as he was told but not without an inner struggle.

BelkA wondered sometimes how Parto himself felt about his situation. Outwardly he displayed a meek and grateful attitude, but surely there had to be a yearning for acceptance on a higher plane. Alas, as long as his mother lived, she ruled the household. *"Someday,"* he vowed, *"It will be different."*

Chapter 13

Tirza

Aleppo, July 589 B.C.

B ack in their tent Arif and Tirza faced a torrent of questions. Both young ones were perplexed over the injury of Parto and the two deaths. "But why did they do that to Parto?" Saba asked. "He wasn't hurting them."

"It probably has to do with the gold that BelkA is carrying." Tirza said looking at Arif. "It's a reminder for us to be extra careful with our own box."

SabA's eyes widened. "Would you be able to fight off an attacker Father?"

Arif shrugged and tilted his head indecisively. "I think it might be wise to get some pointers from BelkA and Parto. I have weapons but I hope I don't have to use them. Perhaps…" He stopped short after a glance at his daughter's distressed expression. "Sussan, What's wrong?"

"What happens after we die?"

"Ah, that's a complicated matter daughter. According to our religion we believe one descends into the nether world."

"Where it's dark and demons are all around?"

"Where did you hear this?"

"In Babylon at my friend Anina's house. Her mother spoke of it. It's true isn't it?"

"Let's say it's a different world that we don't understand. We believe that people who have died need us to provide food and other necessities where they are. That's why we put gifts on your grandparents' tombs."

"But I don't want to die," Sussan said beginning to cry.

Tirza gathered her daughter in her arms. "Let's not worry about it now. It's a long way off for you and besides, we don't really know for sure," she said with a pleading look in the direction of her husband.

"There are some who have a different understanding of the afterlife," Arif said cautiously. "Parto, for instance, believes like the Hebrews that people who have faith in Yahweh continue to live with Him in a beautiful place."

"What do you think Mother?"

"It's something I don't understand myself."

"I'm going to ask Parto," Sussan said with a determined set of her chin.

"One thing both of you must understand," Arif said soberly, "is that Parto is BelkA's servant—actually his slave. You must be very careful always to request permission of BelkA before taking up Parto's time." Then he added as if to himself, "Strange irony that in some ways Parto appears to have more freedom than his master."

"Besides," SabA said with big brotherly airs, "Parto is wounded and can't talk."

"You're right son. What's good is that he survived. He's our hero."

"So is BelkA," SabA insisted. "He saved Parto."

"True. And now my young ones it's time to settle down on your mats. It's been an emotional day for us all."

When satisfied that the children were asleep, Tirza quietly crawled out of the tent with her basket of embroidery. Light was beginning to fade but even a few moments in the tranquil hush, she felt was what she needed. The rhythm of hand movement and the sound of the needle sliding silk threads through the fine linen soothed her tightened nerves. As she formed a rose in a bold satin stitch her mind traveled to Babylon where the palace gardens delighted the eyes of countless visitors. A wave of homesickness washed over her that she resisted and rebuked. After all she herself was the one who wanted the adventure. But it was different from what she'd imagined beforehand. Instead of snakes and scorpions—though there had been some—other matters had emerged that were more subtle. It troubled her that the belief system of Babylonian society, and of her own family that went back countless generations, was coming under scrutiny. Was this adventure a terrible mistake?

B-a-a she admonished herself, *there's nothing wrong with the Babylonian way.* It was comforting to know that when someone was sick they could call in a specialist to determine the cause by examining a sheep liver, or observing the formation of clouds, or flying birds. She liked the variety of gods, each with its area of expertise and, if solutions were not available from one's own family deities, there was yet the sun, moon, stars, and Venus.

It was alas, the questions of the children that had agitated her, as she realized that their innocence in such matters had shattered.

She stopped the delicate work in her lap, shook out her long auburn hair and massaged her sore neck. This was all part of the life cycle. One can't forever shield young ones from unpleasant realities. Folding her handwork and putting it in her basket gave her the feeling of packing up all the troubling thoughts, and putting them out of mind. After carefully closing up the tent she laid down beside her husband and children.

Drifting into slumber she fell into a dream where her dead ancestors' gods, amulets, charms, and jeweled figurines danced around her, but stopped at intervals to remind her of their powers to inflict harm should she desert them. The cutest figurine of them all—the one with roses on her dress—whispered in her ear, "You can have Parto's Yahweh, but just don't abandon us."

A week passed before BelkA felt confident that Parto could sustain travel by camel. During that time Tirza continued to struggle with her nightmares, and the children had more frequent spats than usual. She was restlessly tossing with another nightmare when she awoke to the sound of a trumpet. What a relief.

•••

As the caravan advanced through the rocky slopes of the mountains that composed the Anti-Lebanese and Lebanese range, Tirza sat on her camel behind her husband, and would have been grateful to entertain some conversation with him but alas, he seemed lost in his own thoughts and the children were dozing. It was now BelkA who imposed himself on her mind.

Subtle changes had occurred in him since the Aleppo stopover that she couldn't resolve. Though still polite he'd become distant. Why? Was it the break-in? Did the matchmaking attempt arouse suspicion? Or was he simply anxious about his mission? If only she knew.

She noticed that once again Arif had gently urged his camel forward to permit listening-in on conversation between BelkA and Parto. She determined to stay aloof, but curiosity nudged her ahead. With some straining she managed to catch a surprising drift.

"Why are some people monsters Parto?" BelkA was asking.

"Master BelkA, that is a matter upon which I have some convictions that I fear would offend you."

"I asked a question Parto. I didn't stipulate that it should not offend me."

103

Parto took a deep breath. "Sin is the cause, BelkA. It's within us and it also comes from outside forces in the way of temptation. Sin is acting contrary to the laws of Yahweh and thus it offends Him. Indeed, it causes people to act as monsters as you put it, and brings about suffering and death."

"Interesting concept. According to Babylonian thinking, sin is a breach in the harmony of the global order. It's the disruption of natural sequence, but go on with your view."

"There is much that I yet do not understand, but Shai explained that the ancient Hebrew King David confessed his sin and received relief that brought about in him a feeling of joy and peace. In my experience I find that it really does bring relief to that troubled inside feeling."

"Really? You also mentioned that sin causes death?"

"Sin is a curse, but apparently Isaiah wrote that someday an anointed One would come and swallow death in victory. I'm not sure what that means, but it comforts me."

"H-m-m... curious." In pondering a reply BelkA jerked his body causing an imbalance.

Arif noticed him pulling back on his camel and held his hand up warning Tirza to reign in—and just in time.

•••

Day after day the caravan moved on in tedious monotony. Gradually, however, the scenery changed.

The land, that had been riddled with rocks and hardly fit even for pasture, now snaked through uplands and green mountains, orchards and vineyards. They continued to rise in altitude till they reached Jabal Aqa, a farming area where they stopped for a rest, and purchased some apricots from a farmer on his way to market.

"Be careful, they are really juicy," Tirza cautioned her children.

"M-m-m. What flavor," BelkA exclaimed after biting into an especially large one. "They burst in sweetness on the mouth," he exclaimed while wiping his chin. Sitting cross-legged in the shade, he reveled in the soothing landscape around him and the company of his traveling companions.

The young ones meanwhile were looking at each other and then at BelkA, each signaling to the other to speak up. It was SabA who finally said timidly. "Lord BelkA, we've been meaning to ask you, could we sometime have permission to speak with Parto? We have some questions to ask of him."

"Go right ahead."

"Well, not now, I mean... we each want our time alone with him."

BelkA laughed. "I tell you what. I'll let each of you have a turn riding a ways with him on his camel for whatever distance you require. Just be careful of his shoulder."

The young ones glowed with bright smiles of gratitude and victorious glances toward their parents, who in turn, looked with mixed feelings at one another.

When the trumpet blew Sussan mounted, and sat proudly behind Parto on his camel, taking care to avoid touching the injured shoulder.

By the time SabA's turn was ending they were beginning to take in an expanse of the deepest blue imaginable with its edges lapping on rocky cliffs. "What's that?" Sussan exclaimed.

"The great Mediterranean," her father replied.

"Those cliffs are called the ladder of Tyre," BelkA added.

The children laughed with delight as if they were having the grandest vacation ever. It was a short reprieve from the harsher realities they'd been through, and others that still lay ahead.

Chapter 14

Tyre

August 589 B.C.

"This is one city I like," BelkA told the little group around him. "Actually it's two cities with two ports, alternately usable depending on the winds. One is way out there on that rocky island in the distance," he explained, pointing with his finger until the young ones' eyes caught the direction. "It's only two miles wide."

"And the Ladder of Tyre faces it," SabA said.

"Clever fellow, you remembered. Those jagged cliffs have kept out many invaders."

"I'll bargain that Nebuchadnezzar could defeat them," SabA added with a defiant grin.

"Time will tell."

The next day the young ones persuaded their father to take them exploring, which suited Tirza who wanted her own unencumbered tour of the market.

Parto decided he'd just as soon rest and work on his writing lesson.

"Are you sure you'll be all right if I tour the city?" BelkA asked.

"Of course Master BelkA. I'll be on duty as usual."

BelkA laughed. "It's obvious that I've got my valiant servant back."

Upon entering mainland Tyre BelkA's ears caught the melodies of tambourines and flutes, laughing, and whistling amid the usual noises of business. The city radiated celebration and success. As the principle seaport on the Phoenician coast it handled a bustling trade that dominated the whole Mediterranean and Aegean coasts.

He wandered through the market remembering Aleppo and his meeting with Mahla. What a woman. A vision of her graceful carriage, humor and intelligence danced in the back of his mind blanking out all previous experiences he'd had with women. He imagined her walking beside him as he took in the vast array of merchandise: wines from Aleppo, spices and gold from Arabia, brass and weapons from Georgia, elegant apparel out of woven fabrics from Media and on and on. Everywhere merchants were calling, bargaining, and jostling their heavy loads.

He stopped before a stand of specialties of Tyre: musical instruments, hand blown glassware, carved ivory, and then he spotted a mantle of hyacinth blue. Inching forward he managed to barely touch it when the tall lean merchant with a pointed beard stopped hollering the benefits of his wares and said, "You like it?" He approached and held up the sleeveless cloak. "What do you think?"

"I might be interested," BelkA replied nonchalantly. "But I also notice your musical instruments. I think I might purchase two of your flutes for my young friends."

"Ah, you must have an ear for music. Allow me," he said pulling a flute from his robe and demonstrating.

"I'm convinced," BelkA said laughing. "I'll have two if you give me a reasonable price."

"You buy the cloak, I'll give one instrument for free."

"And the other at twice the price no doubt."

The merchant laughed with abandon. "A clever one you are, but I play fair with men of distinction." Again he reached for the blue mantle twirling it around before the eager eyes of the admirer.

"Exquisite, you think not?"

"The color reminds me of the Mediterranean."

"Ah, it's the dye extracted from the murex snail that loves our beaches. Worth twice their weight in gold they've made Tyre wealthy." Then he leaned closer to BelkA and whispered, "If you would like a supply I have connections."

"For myself not, but I will inform a seamstress friend of mine. It's the cloak that interests me at present."

"Ah yes, here it is," the merchant said holding it up once more.

After a surprisingly short dickering episode, BelkA walked off with the cloak, two flutes and half an ounce of dye, careful not to show the satisfaction he felt.

Walking further he came upon a stand displaying parchments and papyrus where he abruptly stopped. Gently he ran his fingers over the samples laid out on display while a tall merchant with graying mustache and beard watched.

"Fine quality," BelkA said.

"You have the eye of an expert. You won't find better anywhere."

"Indeed, it is impressive. I only need a small supply at this time, but I'll keep you in mind should I need more."

The merchant bowed and prepared the package for his client.

BelkA sauntered on coming upon the animal section where a collection of riding horses drew his attention. He winced remembering his own horse back in Babylon.

Hurrying past he found himself facing a pen where men, women, and children bound in chains looked out from despairing eyes. The sight sent quivers of pity through his body, especially when he remembered that his own Parto had once been as they. Quickly he turned, leaving the market and heading toward the docks.

Before him pendants of brilliant color flapped in the breeze on ships built and equipped to show off Tyre's prominence as queen of sea traffic through her vast maritime empire. Ships entering the port joined a myriad of others already docked in the harbor where sweating backs of numerous shades glistened in the sun as they worked in frenzied haste. One elegant vessel kept him riveted in sheer admiration. Like an elegant lady making a grand entrance, it smoothly cut through the waves under the power of its team of rowers.

Continuing to walk he found himself passing a house with a porch where two merchants were ardently dickering over something, when apparently an agreement was reached for they rose exuberantly, each grinning and shaking hands. Looking up they noticed BelkA, and after a glance of agreement, walked toward him. Bowing before him one of the two asked, "You are perhaps a merchant from Babylon honored one. Would you be interested in some jewelry perhaps? We have just received a new supply that you must see."

"What kind of jewelry?" BelkA asked.

"Please sit down honored one and allow us to show you."

One of them poured goblets of wine while the other opened brass boxes.

BelkA randomly glanced over the selection noticing a bracelet with a large lapis lazuli gem attached. "How much?" he asked then winced at the price and pushed the bracelet away.

"It comes from Edom, my country. The price is negotiable of course."

"We have gems similar to this in Babylon."

"But you like it. Name your price."

BelkA made a reasonable offer and the jewel became his. Taking advantage of the sociable atmosphere the purchase had afforded he asked, "Would you by chance be acquainted with a ship captain making northern voyages in the direction of Syria?"

One of the two, a Phoenician, looked at BelkA with curiosity. "I do in fact, that very ship entering port as we speak, is headed in that direction. I can tell you the captain's name. It's Mar."

"And should I by chance encounter him, whom might I say informed me of his name?"

"Jagur is my name," the Phoenician said, "and my new Edomite associate here is Dassais. Might we also know yours?"

BelkA stated his name, thanked the merchants for their hospitality and turned toward the dock. When he was a few yards distant he heard the two discussing him. One was saying, "He's no merchant. A man of high station, perhaps an officer in Nebuchadnezzar's army, or possibly an envoy!"

BelkA strode toward the docking ship and stood amidst the crowd of merchants and workers waiting to perform their services. When a gangplank was lowered he attempted to cross, but was almost lifted from his feet by the jostling crewmen. Determined to brave the situation at all cost he kept searching for the captain. Upon reaching mid-deck he looked up to see a tall, well-built gentleman with outstretched arms shouting orders. A distinctive silk tunic with a cylinder seal attached at the shoulder, and a jewel-encrusted scabbard on his hip, left no doubt.

For a while BelkA stood and watched the scene, but it wasn't long before he himself was noticed and approached. "To what do I owe the pleasure?" the commander asked.

Though BelkA's request regarding the frequency of voyages northward appeared of little significance, his dress and manner conveyed the opposite.

The captain replied, "In maritime travel the weather plays a major role. But I would be interested in conversing with you when things are calmed down somewhat. Would you be available tomorrow evening? I would be pleased to entertain you at my home."

"That would indeed be agreeable," BelkA responded, and upon being assured that a servant would pick him up at the appointed hour, he bowed and made his way to the gangplank.

•••

Accompanied by Parto, BelkA sat in the distinctive chariot that was to take them to the home of Captain Mar.

They passed impressive buildings along the shoreline, almost the equal to those of Babylon, and boarded a ferry that took them to an island where they docked a short distance from a stately dwelling. Soon BelkA and Parto found themselves standing on the black marble floor of the entry hall where a whole wall composed a garden scene in Egyptian mosaics, with a set-in wall fountain that rained down waves of melodious water into a massive Egyptian urn.

BelkA had braced himself for an evening of starched manners but both the host, Mar and his wife Samantha, a slender woman almost as tall as her husband, attended them in a relaxed and amicable manner that put their guests completely at ease. The food, though elegantly served, seemed almost incidental.

In the course of the meal Mar complimented BelkA on his speech. "Your use of the Aramaic is masterful," he said.

"I would return the compliment," BelkA responded. "It would appear that Tyre is a city of scholars of which you are also one. I have noticed a number of tablets of ancient Sumerian in your home."

Mar laughed. "They're on display for their beauty and for what they represent. I limit myself to the Aramaic, though I dabble in Egyptian because of my business. Time does not allow me to learn the hundreds of signs involved in other languages." Then he looked at BelkA. "I have the impression that you, however, are fluent in many."

"I speak a few," BelkA said attempting to brush off further comment.

"Now let me guess," Mar said paying no heed to the attempt at modesty, "The languages no doubt include Aramaic, the Assyro-Babylonian dialect, Hebrew, with perhaps some knowledge of the Sumerians cuneiform script, Egyptian and perhaps Arabic,"

"I have the feeling that you read me like a scroll. Regarding the last three languages, you mention however, I have a writing vocabulary but lack fluency."

"What brings you to Tyre?" Mar winked.

"I'm a scholar and a merchant seeking to collect some Writings for interested parties in Jerusalem."

"I'm sure any Babylonian won't be popular in Jerusalem right now, but I wish you well. How might I help you BelkA?"

"Returning home I might require an alternate route."

"You think you might eventually be needing an escape?"

BelkA smiled at the candid remark. "Exactly. I understand that relations between Judah and Babylon are rapidly deteriorating."

"Are you not then taking a great risk in going to Jerusalem?"

"It may be my last chance to get these documents."

"Curious," Mar said. "These documents I mean. They must be some ancient scrolls of great value, something to do with the Hebrew Writings no doubt?" Then noticing BelkA's raised eyebrows he added, "But never mind an answer, you have your reasons for not including details."

BelkA sat tongue-tied while Mar nonchalantly continued, "Myself, I find Jerusalem fascinating. Presently she competes with us in luxuries and all manner of refined living. Young people are richer now than their parents ever were. Never have I seen more jewelry hanging from all parts of the body than there."

"Who are we to talk?" Samantha said with her large brown eyes on her husband.

Mar paid no heed. "Naturally we enjoy trade benefits with Jerusalem. Her products, especially wheat, are important to us since we're unable to grow it here, but what we don't like is the way Jerusalem detours merchants from the east scooping up the cream before it reaches us. Now, it seems, she has even adopted some of our gods as her own.'"

"Their Yahweh appears not enough for them?" BelkA asked while searching Parto's face.

Mar glanced a moment at his wife before continuing cautiously. "Samantha and I have tried many gods, but sometimes it seems that only demons are real."

BelkA shook his head and lowered his eyes. "I'm at a point too where I wonder about the gods. In all honesty I find myself somewhat drawn to the Hebrew Yahweh, but if the lines of separation are fading with the Hebrews adopting your gods, maybe He's not that exceptional after all."

There was silence for a while until Mar changed the subject. "How long will you be in Tyre might I ask?"

"Two more days."

"I'll tell you what BelkA, since you are unable to determine the time of your potential need of my services, this would not be the time for making any kind of firm arrangements. However, among my acquaintances there are a couple of pilots and several shore men who could assist you. Meet me at my ship at noon, and I'll introduce you so they'll at least recognize you if, and when the need arises."

"I would greatly appreciate that," BelkA said as he and Parto rose to their feet and bowed.

Mar also stood and smiled at them. "Let's just say that I've taken a liking to both of you."

Chapter 15

Damascus

July 589 B.C.

E very traveler on the ancient north-south caravan route knew Damascus. It's snow-fed, seven-branched Barada River gave it greener fields than any other town for hundreds of miles around. The city provided travelers a last oasis of scenery and culture before plunging into the desert.

As BelkA walked down the narrow streets merchants cried their wares or bargained, while water sellers clanged their cymbals and women patted their dough into flat cakes, slapping them one last time before placing them in stone ovens. The aromas of baking bread and other cooking mingling with spices and perfumes beckoned alluringly.

He stopped a moment before deciding what to do, and that was when his heart started pounding. There stood three, of the four suspicious characters expelled from the caravan, sitting in front of a tavern where they appeared to be laughing and gesturing with their jovial bar tender. Quickly BelkA turned into another aisle where he felt relatively sure he was concealed from their view.

Now how had they gotten there so soon? After thinking it over, however, he concluded that they'd probably taken the direct route to Damascus without the detour to Tyre. His first thought was of Parto, but he reassured himself with the fact that, three of them at least, were preoccupied with other matters. He only hoped that the fourth was not out looking for trouble. To insure his own safety he ducked into the confines of a booth shaded by palm branches. Before him on a display table was an array of bolts of the most exquisite silks he'd ever seen. Once again Mahla flashed back on his mind.

A balding middle-aged man in a blue-green robe urged him to approach and examine his wares more carefully. BelkA looked into the man's face, and realized that sightless eyes were staring into a private world where ears compensated far more than eyes could see. Silk cocoons dangled from the hands of a petite woman behind him, who flipped them with agile fingers. She smiled at BelkA, but spoke not a word. Beside her stood a foot-powered handloom, and at her feet a dog lay sound asleep.

"You like our silks," the merchant said.

"They are indeed exquisite."

The man gently ran his finger over a bolt. "How do you like this lavender color?" he asked.

Astonished BelkA responded, "How can you tell?"

"The texture of the thread varies ever so slightly with the color."

BelkA guided the hands to another bolt. "Tell me about this one."

"Ah, this buttercup yellow is of even better quality. You like this one don't you?" the blind man said placing his hand gently on BelkA's.

BelkA laughed outright. "You know that I do. Name your price."

"The price is of no significance," the man said. "What matters is the one for whom it is intended"

"Now that's a strange way of bargaining," BelkA said.

"Ah, young man. I sense great feeling within you for this piece of cloth. It must be that you see in its folds the form of a special woman."

"How did you know?"

It was the blind man's turn to laugh. "It appeared obvious to me that I had touched a tender chord. But if you really want to know, it's the tenderness and respect I feel in your fingers as they caress the silk." Having said that he removed his hand.

"Please tell me your price," BelkA asked again.

"The price," the blind man repeated as he scratched his forehead. "The price must be equal to the value of the woman, wouldn't you say?"

Startled, BelkA looked up from the silk cloth. "What do you mean, the woman is beyond price."

The blind man smiled. "In that case, young man, there is no price that I might dare to ask. All I can do, therefore, is to give it to you. Take it. It's yours."

"Come on," BelkA insisted. "Don't joke with me. Say your price."

"I told you it's yours."

"Then I must make you an offer."

"There is no price that you might offer that would suffice."

"Tell me what I must do?" BelkA asked with a hint of irritation in his voice.

"Accept it with gratitude and give it to the lovely woman. She's worthy of it."

"I don't understand."

"I find myself obliged to give it to you because it cannot be purchased with gold. My wife will wrap it carefully in linen and felt, and you will take it with my blessing."

BelkA, overwhelmed by the scene lost restraint. "Sightless one, the way you see is amazing."

"You have a story for me my friend?"

Caught unawares, BelkA lost his restraint and poured out the unusual meeting with Mahla at Aleppo. "The woman has stirred me like none other," he said. "I can't get her off my mind. She haunts me day and night. Though I try to erase the vision of her, I see her everywhere. My decision to purchase the material was an act of impulsive folly. Please excuse my intrusion."

Before BelkA could get away the blind man grabbed his arm. "Your name please?"

"The name is BelkA. And yours?"

"Mine doesn't matter, most just call me *Blind Man*, but would you be shocked if I mention the name of Yahweh?"

"At this point nothing shocks me, especially since you appear to be a Hebrew. Besides, the name has come up quite often of late."

"How is that?"

"Through my servant. He met an exile from Judah who has convinced him that Yahweh is the only true God. Is there something you wanted to mention concerning Yahweh?"

"It's this BelkA. When one gets as old as me, he begins to view life as a hieroglyph traced for a moment in the sand but vanishing with a puff of wind. Some, however, leave behind a standing evidence to benefit unborn generations, something more valuable than gold or silver or magnificent objects. I believe you are about to do something of lasting importance, but to accomplish it you'll need Yahweh. You need to become... shall we say divine."

Laughing, BelkA responded, "Are you saying that I must become a god?"

"Mercy no BelkA. There are more than enough already? I speak of the miracle that happens when the Spirit of Yahweh enters a person and abides in him."

"Please speak on," BelkA requested intrigued by the new angle.

"You see the body is like one of those old cocoons that my wife discards. The worm within becomes transformed into a butterfly and flies away leaving behind an empty shell. Thus it is with the soul."

"You are speaking of immortality?"

Blind Man nodded.

"H-m-m. Interesting concept. Quite different from Mesopotamian thought where the body and soul never separate."

"Is there not within every man a yearning for immortality?"

"Most certainly. It's the basis of some renowned epics where people seek immortality only to discover that it always eludes them."

"Rather disappointing isn't it?"

"Exceedingly so. But you claim it does exist. How is that?"

"Long ago the Hebrew King David, upon pondering this matter of death wrote, 'Yahweh shall redeem my soul from the netherworld for he shall receive me.'"

"He wrote that?"

"Absolutely."

"But how does one attain this... oh what shall I call it... understanding or confidence that it is true?"

"By faith in Yahweh BelkA. One reaches out and receives it like a gift."

BelkA looked astonished. "My servant has told me something similar."

"So you know."

"Well... it's an interesting concept."

"BelkA, you have heard perhaps of the prophet Habakkuk in Jerusalem?"

"No, but I do know of Jeremiah? I understand he's a prophet."

"Indeed he is and the prophet Habakkuk is an old friend of his. This is what he wrote, 'the righteous shall live by his faith.'"

"This is indeed interesting," BelkA said with a sigh.

"I think I perceive a struggle within you."

"You see too well," my friend.

"You have another story BelkA?"

"Since you know so much already, and since you speak so knowingly of Yahweh I dare to tell you something, though I must be assured first of confidentiality."

Blind Man took BelkA's hand and drew him into the stand away from any possible ear, and then he placed both his hands on his heart and said, "You have my word."

BelkA looked into the unseeing eyes. "I am going to Jerusalem to find and rescue the sacred Writings and bring them to Prime-Minister Belteshazzar or Daniel as you call him."

Blind Man took on an expression of wonder and amazement. "Then you must also be the King's envoy to Jerusalem. I have been made aware that you are in great danger. I will pray Yahweh to protect you."

"I'd be grateful," BelkA said squeezing Blind Man's hand again. "I've already encountered enemies following me from Babylon and have been warned of enemies awaiting me in Jerusalem. It seems that knowledge of my secret mission has traveled ahead of me. It causes considerable concern."

"I hear anxiety in your voice, my son. Would it encourage you to know that I represent a group that will try to help you in every way we can?"

BelkA's stared at the blind man.

"I in turn must ask confidentiality of you BelkA."

"You have it of course."

"I am the leader of a secret society that we call…" Blind Man leaned over and cupped BelkA's head in his hands before whispering in his ear, "*The lamp connection.*"

BelkA frowned. "A strange name that."

"The lamp suggests light. The prophet Isaiah wrote that the Writings would become a *light to the nations.* Do you see BelkA? The words of Yahweh are like a light to us humans who must grope in darkness as we try to find our way in life. It is the desire of Yahweh for this light to shine into the lives of people in all the nations."

"I find that puzzling," BelkA said. "It has seemed to me that this one God was for only one nation."

"Not so BelkA, and you are fulfilling a distinct role in His plan. It fills me with awe that Yahweh has brought us together today. Actually my colleagues are even now discreetly watching for you."

"This overwhelms me. Could we speak further on all this?"

"If you come back tomorrow I'll make arrangements to meet you secretly."

"How about tomorrow morning?"

"Excellent. And now Blind Man, the shadows are lengthening and my servant will be anxious on my account. I must be on my way. Please accept my deep gratitude."

"Wait," Blind Man said. "The silk."

BelkA looked perplexed. "I thought it was settled."

"It was, and while we've been talking my wife has wrapped it carefully for you."

As he spoke his wife brought the package to BelkA, and presented it with a bowed head and bended knee.

BelkA reached into his girdle or belt satchel and pulled out a heavy gold coin that he put into the woman's hand, and closed her fingers around it. "This is for the wrapping," he said. Then he turned and walked away. Before taking to the street, however, he looked around cautiously to make sure the three men were not lurking nearby.

•••

RAstin who had declined the invitation to join the other three of Adda-Guppi's henchmen in their expedition into the city for the purpose of finding BelkA now paced restlessly in circles within the tent. Things were not going at all the way he had hoped. Bah-Ador's threat to kill instantly any or all of them should he ever see them again, still rang in his ears and shook his confidence. The desperation within him kept mounting as the moments passed, and at its peak it seemed the only door of escape was to take his own life. He was at the point of reaching for his dagger when his three companions returned.

Noticing RAstin's disheveled hair and red cheeks Abid asked in a slurred speech. "What's wrong old boy?"

The appearance of the gang disgusted RAstin but he asked, "Did you see BelkA and Parto?"

"Not a trace," Tahampton replied throwing some food at RAstin. "Had a good time though."

"So I can surmise," RAstin grumbled.

"We did overhear a conversation, however, where a man spoke of another caravan that had arrived so we know they're in town," Shabazn said.

RAstin made no comment. Instead he bit into his bread and cheese.

Chapter 16

Gilead

August 589 B.C.

The endless unbroken plain south of Damascus stretched in dreary contrast to the life and color of the city of Damascus. The caravan had taken the trans-Jordan route following the ancient King's Highway that the Hebrews had long used. In the distance on the right stood the mountains—some still snowcapped—that separated the high Syrian plateau from the Mediterranean coastal plain. To the left lay the vast Arabian Desert. It would take yet a week to enter what, a century before, had been northern Israel. There the mountains would end and the Great Rift Valley would begin, and deepen as it ran southward to the Sea of Galilee, down the Jordan Valley, and all the way to the Dead Sea before continuing on into Africa.

The closer they got to Judah the more caravans they encountered, some composed of hundreds of donkeys, all heavily laden with merchandise, others entirely of camels—countless camels—all of which slowed their progress. Another element of change was the vegetation along the Jordan, through which their road now passed, that replaced the scenery from drab brown to lush green.

That evening they camped on the Jabbok River with Gilead on both sides. Parto decided to cook a special dinner, and Tirza had insisted upon helping him, while BelkA offered his services in giving flute lessons to the young ones.

They were conversing amiably after the meal when BelkA beckoned to Parto. "I must be ill. My body's on fire. Make me an infusion from the bark of the willow."

By the time Parto had brought the medicine BelkA had started to shiver and looked most uncomfortable. "I regret to say that my master is ill," Parto spoke up, "perhaps you would be kind enough to excuse him."

"We most certainly will," Arif said.

Tirza looked at BelkA with penetrating eyes. "Of late I have had the sense that demons are angry with you. If only we could get to an exorcist to reverse the curse or drive away the evil spirits."

"In the past I've always called upon Gula for healing, but presently I have no desire for even that. I'm sure a little rest is all I need."

•••

Later that evening when Parto was preparing another infusion for his master, BelkA suggested that Arif be sent to summon the caravan leader Bah-Ador.

When he arrived Bah-Ador showed grave concern. "We will delay the caravan a week if necessary, or until you are recovered," he announced.

"It might take longer than that, my friend. Please continue without me. I have traveled many miles alone, but this time I have my servant."

"You are the king's envoy, I must fulfill my duty."

"You have," BelkA insisted. "Judah is just across the Jordan. Your caravan has yet to go all the way to Egypt and back. You must not delay on my account. I urge you to take advantage of the season of travel, the rains will be coming soon enough."

Bah-Ador looked sad and disappointed.

"We'll surely meet with one another in Jerusalem. I'll search the caravan camp site for you," BelkA reassured him.

Bah-Ador fell silent.

"In any case our family will not leave you," Arif said firmly. "You have become like a brother to me, I wouldn't think of abandoning you. Are you in agreement Tirza?"

"Of course."

"You're our uncle now BelkA," SabA said anxiously. "We'll stay with you."

Sussan went to him and put her arms around him. "We'll help you get well."

Bah-Ador looked from one to the other. "Perhaps I do well to allow you to separate from my caravan." He fixed his eyes on Parto and said, "I'm counting on you to continue to protect your master as you have so valiantly already. But I must warn you that the four men I expelled will be coming through within two days with the caravan they joined at Aleppo. Hopefully they won't try to venture out themselves. Remember if anything happens to BelkA, I will be held responsible."

"I give you my word that I will protect him with my life," Parto said with as much reassurance as he could affirm from his own state of anxiety.

•••

Parto sat up most of the night. From time to time he would approach his sleeping master then return to his mat to pray. When BelkA called for him towards morning requesting the presence of Arif, he became even more alarmed, but he obeyed without saying a word.

Arif who had been sleeping poorly came immediately when he heard a sound near his tent. He knelt down and sat on his heels before BelkA and said, "I'm here BelkA. How may I please you?"

"I feel compelled to speak with you before the caravan departs." BelkA began. "You must know that I am an envoy of King Nebuchadnezzar to King Zedekiah. An informant has told me that there is a pro-Egyptian element in Jerusalem who is aware of my coming, and is seeking my life. Your association with me could endanger your whole family. I insist that you travel with the caravan party. The two men who tried to kill Parto, I am convinced, are connected with the remaining four who obviously are up to no good."

Arif put his head in his hands. After a moment of anguished silence he spoke. "BelkA I must confess something to you that distresses me exceedingly."

"Go on."

"I was commissioned to spy on you and to prevent you from being won over to Daniel's God."

BelkA opened his mouth feigning surprise, but then admitted, "I knew there was something more to your interest in me besides playing the matchmaker. Now I can understand that Adda-Guppi was behind it," he said with a little smile playing on his lip.

"Indeed," Arif said keeping his head down as he explained the details including the conclusion of the secret council and Utabar's offer of pigeons.

BelkA grinned especially at Utabar's thought of sabotaging Adda-Guppi, and also about the introduction to Mahla. "So your stated intentions of going all the way to Egypt were part of the ploy?"

"Of course," Arif admitted sheepishly.

"Don't be embarrassed Arif. But what about the six fellows?"

"I was never informed about them or their purpose, but I suspect Adda-Guppi was behind that too."

BelkA got up and began to pace.

"Master, should you do this?" Parto asked.

BelkA smiled. "I'm fine Parto. I feigned illness to separate from the caravan party because I'm convinced that my enemies in Jerusalem will be awaiting the arrival of Bah-Ador, and in addition, we have the four coming up behind us."

"Perhaps it would be best if we would go on ahead then," Arif said. "We could keep a watch and alert you if there is danger."

"That offer I gladly accept. Now you must realize that I'll be keeping a low profile from Jericho on. I suggest that we fix a meeting place somewhere in Jerusalem where we can leave messages for one another. Let me think... yes, there's a place on the southeast side that's removed from the most congested traffic of the city. We should be able to put messages there discretely. It's called the Pool of Siloam where water collects from the Gihon Springs. I'll use a cryptic word when passing you... how about *lamp*. If necessary I'll put it into a phrase like, 'Get the lamp,' or 'I need a lamp,' or 'Light the lamp.'

"There's a low wall where one can sit down and, behind a robe, deposit a message beneath the rim of that wall. BelkA then drew the form of a lamp in the sand. The symbol to put on the message is the outline of a lamp. Code it also in the first sentence so I'll doubly know that it's from you by inserting the cuneiform symbol for light. Would that be agreeable to you?"

Arif nodded pensively and smiled. "Yes, it sounds to me like an excellent idea. It'll be hard for the young ones to refrain themselves when they see you, but I'll explain it as clearly as I can, while also restraining them. I think they're old enough to understand."

"Assure your family that BelkA and Parto love them and will see them soon."

"I'll do that," Arif said, looking back one last time at his friends before ducking under the flap.

Chapter 17

Helem

Damascus, August 589 B.C.

H elem halted his mule on the overlook to con-
template the rectangular city of Damascus
lying on the opposite side of the Barada River, and
marveled that the ancient city had stood millennia
before his time. From a distance one could make out
the crooked streets that he now imagined as typifying
his own life with the seemingly inexplicable twists
and turns of recent months.

At Jerusalem he'd had the chance encounter with
Ebed-Melech, the Ethiopian court official who'd
confided overhearing a plot to fall upon the coming
envoy of Nebuchadnezzar. He'd managed to meet up
with this envoy in Aleppo, and took extra pains to
inform him of the danger only to have it ignored.

The final undoing had been Mahla's father.
Months before the man had approached him regarding

a marriage alliance with his daughter. At the time it had flattered him, but as he thought it through there had been some nagging differences. In appearance she dwarfed him. His short stature had always embarrassed him and in his dreams he saw himself connecting better with a petite Hebrew girl, whereas Mahla portrayed the typical Babylonian in character and style. He'd reminded himself that dreams do not always conform to realities and one must be prepared to adapt and accept. The fact that Mahla had become a follower of Yahweh had virtually convinced him to remain open to an agreement, but then, what a shock it had been, upon returning to Aleppo, to find the father cold and indifferent toward him.

He'd planned to continue on to Ecbatana when, still in Aleppo, he'd received a message through a passing caravan to come immediately to Damascus. It had something to do with *The Lamp Connection,* a secret group that he'd joined some time before that had become like a family to him.

He urged his mule on through the massive gate to the unique street called "Straight" and on to the market. To his dismay the stall of the Blind Man was not at the usual place. Where could it be? With a feeling of confusion he turned around trying to decide what to do when a hand fell upon his back. "You're looking for Blind Man no doubt," a sparsely bearded old man in a tan tunic, said.

"You can tell?"

"Of course, let me lead you to him."

Helem allowed himself to be accompanied to a stall, on the opposite side of the market, where his guide pointed straight ahead and disappeared. He then approached the stand, leaned close to the Blind Man and waited for seeing hands to touch his face.

"Ah Helem. I'm pleased that you came. Now come with me. I must speak with you in private." Almost instantly a replacement arrived at the stand and quietly took over.

Blind Man's wife led them through a labyrinth of narrow streets, often arched over and with frequent hangover balconies, till they reached a house of considerable size with no front windows.

Once inside Helem took in the freshly whitewashed walls and orderliness of draped sections allowing privacy for members to study or write, and larger carpeted areas for conversing or eating.

Once seated on a rug Helem gave a report of his activities in Jerusalem and Aleppo.

"I detect sadness in your voice," Blind Man said.

"Mahla's father perplexes me."

"Are you heartsick my son?"

"Perhaps not as you might expect. Mahla is a jewel of a woman. I'd begun to think that, like all arranged marriages, love often develops after marriage. Besides that her devotion to Yahweh is sincere."

"I understand Helem. "Would you allow me to give my opinion?"

"Of course, please do."

"From the start I have felt that Mahla was not the right woman for you, but I chose not to interfere."

"I wish I'd known."

Blind Man shrugged his shoulders.

Helem smiled. "Strange, but I find your words reassuring and ... freeing."

"I am pleased. Yahweh, I believe, has another fine woman for you."

"Now regarding the envoy you met in Babylon. You need not be overly concerned about his ignoring you. I can assure you that nothing would stop him from accomplishing his mission. He has the mentality of a soldier. When he commits to something he follows through at all cost. But there's something I must explain to you about him."

When Blind Man had finished his story of BelkA's appearance at his stand Helem sat in blank astonishment. "I can't believe what I'm hearing," he said.

"Now I must tell you that I have already arranged for you to meet up with him so that you can protect and guide him to the area of the Dead Sea, as I have been warned by one of our young fellows that some trouble-makers are heading that way. BelkA will be separating from his caravan and will then allow our group to collaborate with him from then on. Now you have to understand that Mahla will be helping you. Will this be a problem?"

Helem thought a while. "No, actually. It's strange how these assignments made us forget ourselves. It will be good to get back to just being good friends."

Blind Man relaxed. "I can see that you've matured. I'm proud of you my son."

"I'll admit that my heart dragged low when I entered Damascus, but I now see things in a different light. I'm eager to get going. Where do I start?"

"Ah here's the plan."

Helem laughed at the scheme. "This is going to be fun."

"Caution my friend. One must always be watchful for the unpredictable."

Chapter 18

Crossing Jordan

Jordan Valley, August 589 B.C.

A s soon as the caravan had passed a ridge and vanished from sight BelkA turned to Parto and said, "Come it's safe now to continue on our own." As they walked he added, "I must warn you about tomorrow. I know not all that will transpire but, whatever happens, try not to worry about the outcome. My advice is cooperate as best you can and do as you're told."

Parto asked no questions knowing that in good time BelkA would explain.

"I want you to know that I'm putting Nebuchadnezzar's scroll on your camel and in this bag," BelkA said patting the satchel. "Should we be separated, or if something should happen to me, you must take it to the king in my place."

"Of course Master," Parto said as he carefully observed the placement of the scroll and other documents.

They continued down the ridge toward the Jordan.

"A strange valley this," Parto remarked.

"You won't find anything like it anywhere else," affirmed BelkA. "It drops over a thousand feet below sea level; that's a three thousand foot drop from the high country. We'll be crossing the Jordan at the ford soon, and then we'll climb to the plateau of Jericho. But today I thought we might bypass that city for a night of quiet relaxation where thick vegetation will camouflage us."

The two men with their camels crossed the Jordan with waters up to their waist. Carefully they led the animals around the boulders to the opposite side and continued southwest, gradually climbing to the plateau.

Upon finding a brook with a modest trickle— enough to provide a source of water—they set up camp. The task completed they settled back and listened to the harp-like ripple of the brook that blended with the carefree singing of birds in the trees above.

"A paradise just for us," BelkA exclaimed.

"The only thing missing is the children?"

"I've been thinking that too," BelkA sighed though he was also thinking of Mahla and wondering how she felt about nature.

"Imagine this scene with spring flowers," Parto said. "Makes me think of Bazy-An and Shai back in Babylon. They'd so enjoy this."

"We'll enjoy it for them," BelkA said. "By the way, I promised to bring Bazy-An some plants."

"O dear, that's not an easy promise to keep."

"I know it was foolish of me."

"Wait a minute; there are roots or bulbs that retain life for years." Parto immediately set himself to the task of digging and managed to discover a few that he carefully laid out to dry. "I think these are anemones and I don't quite know what the others are. He sat down once more and inhaled the sweet clean air. "Might I suggest sleeping outside BelkA?"

"I'm afraid you'd share your bed with company you might not appreciate. Characters like gazelles, foxes, lions, coneys, hyenas, maybe even a wild boar!"

Parto laughed.

"Tonight we must soak up all the rest we can because surprises await us tomorrow."

Chapter 19

Jericho

September 589 B.C.

"Some oasis!" Parto exclaimed as they rode their camels under the shade of towering date palms bordering the entrance to the city of Jericho.

"Jericho is understandably called the city of palm trees," BelkA was saying when he noticed a team of mules pulling up beside them. "Don't be alarmed Parto," he shouted above the noise. "Remember what I told you."

"Descend from your camels immediately, both of you, and get in this cart," a man in soiled and smelly clothing shouted.

Parto froze at the suddenness.

BelkA had just enough time to remind him, "You're in charge of my bag," when an arm shoved him toward the cart.

BelkA's words shook Parto into action. Quickly he dismounted by jumping onto the box put out for him, and immediately dislodged the bag from the camel, and fastened it securely to his body with the rope he'd included with it. Seconds later he found himself being shoved roughly. Barely in the cart a blanket fell over him. "What is this?" He began to scream when a hand came over his mouth.

"If you utter one more sound we'll be obliged to gag you. Understand?" a gruff voice warned.

A younger voice spoke, "We can't take chances. Here, stuff these rags in his mouth and wrap this rope around his wrists." The blanket was lifted long enough for his captor to gag him and bind his hands. "Just be thankful I'm not blindfolding you," he said.

Parto opened his eyes wide to quickly take in the bushy haired old man with a full beard accompanied by a slender energetic lad in a soiled tunic and a sloppy turban barely holding together on his head, before the blanket once again shut out all light.

"There's a carpet underneath you and a crate behind you to lean on. If you sit still you'll handle the journey better."

"Why the concern?" Parto managed to say until a foul odor choked his breathing. A giggle sounded up front. "Never mind the smell. Just some baskets of nice fresh vegetables and a load of manure. It won't hurt you," the lad said.

When the cart began to move Parto attempted to determine the direction. The way the baskets and crates were sliding upon him he knew they were heading down hill in the direction of the Dead

Sea, and he found himself struggling to keep from sprawling into the manure. Why was there no sound or resistance from BelkA?

They'd traveled for a couple of hours when the mules stopped. The farmer lifted the blanket and freed the captors, allowing them to get out and walk around. Perplexed and disoriented BelkA and Parto breathed in large gulps of fresh air.

"Follow us," the farmer ordered.

BelkA, now wearing a sheepish grin, motioned with his head to follow. "By the way" he whispered, "welcome to the Dead Sea."

"You knew all the time," Parto exclaimed.

BelkA chuckled. "Not everything. I still don't know who these characters are. All I know is that Blind Man told me to be at Jericho on this day and he would send people to assist us and provide protection for our entering Jerusalem."

It was Parto's turn to laugh and he barely refrained jabbing BelkA in the side.

The party ascended a short distance from the sea and came upon a primitive hut that looked not much more than a pile of sticks propped up on posts, no doubt intended to avoid the flood level. They entered by a hole underneath just big enough for a human to crawl through that opened to a crude staircase. Upon reaching the top they were greeted by a tiny slip of a woman, and quite attractive, with a bronze complexion and angular features. BelkA judged her to be about his own age.

"Welcome to my home," the woman said with a big smile and bowing low.

Once inside the farmers removed their head-pieces and other disguises before staring eyes. It was Helem, the informer at Aleppo, and Mahla!

Mahla saved the moment by hugging the woman and introducing her. "This is Amineh. She lives here much of the time hiding escapees. She has kindly offered to feed us tonight."

BelkA, now recovering from shock, introduced Helem and Mahla to Parto. "These are people I met at the market of Aleppo," he offered. "They are courting, I believe?"

Helem and Mahla looked flushed and uncomfortable. "Well," Helem said in a subdued voice, "Things have changed. As members of the Blind Man's secret society we have agreed to lose ourselves in the duties assigned to us."

BelkA looked first at Helem, then at Mahla. "So you are both worshippers of Yahweh?"

"For sure," Mahla replied, with a wide smile.

Parto looked on as if in a dream. "I'm dumb-founded," he exclaimed brightening up more and more as the picture kept clearing.

"Please sit down," Amineh invited after they had all washed and refreshed themselves. She pointed to pillows on the rug where food and drink had been set out. Though just a simple meal of stew and some of the fruit they'd brought, stomachs were filled and satisfied.

After lingering a while over a sour milk drink BelkA asked about the camels and the belongings.

"Two of our collaborators have taken your camels to a stable in Jericho, " Helem said. "They will be well cared for until your return. One of our group had reported suspicious persons in town, so we had to take rather severe measures of caution."

"Suspicious people?" BelkA asked. "You don't know who they are or what they look like?"

"That we can't tell you. You see we rescue widows and orphans from Jerusalem and bring them to Amineh until we can safely take them on to Damascus and beyond. So you see, we have enemies who may not necessarily be your enemies, but given your position, we can't be too careful. Your belongings are even now being transported to a nearby cave in the area so no traces remain in Jericho. We men will sleep in the cave tonight while the women spend the night here."

Chapter 20

Friends and Enemies

Jordan Valley, September 589 B.C.

Amineh's house on stilts, that had at first sight appeared stark and primitive to BelkA, now took on a warm glow in the light of two oil-filled lamps. Windowless as it was, apart from a number of slits on the back wall, there were womanly touches: a colorful carpet, embroidered pillows and bedcovers, pieces of tasteful pottery, and hand woven tapestries that disguised the walls of unpeeled trees. One wall, however, had been plastered, whitewashed, and adorned with a strip of painted art. BelkA examined it carefully with approving eyes.

He watched the petite woman setting out bowls for the two other expected guests, and marveled at her apparent fearlessness in her remote dwelling. She spoke a perfect Hebrew, but her features betrayed an Arabic blend. She intrigued him.

By then two lanky boys with stubby beards were mounting the staircase, obviously disguised as shepherds. BelkA noticed concealed daggers in their belts, and in their faces the glow of adventure.

Amineh went toward them accepting warmly their three kisses and backslapping hugs. With obvious pride she introduced them as, "My adoptive sons, Azek and Ibzan of Bethlehem, and now that they're fifteen we've taken to calling them *the scouts*. They're identical twins—apart from the mole on Azek's forehead." She led them to a small back room where a basin was prepared to wash off the stinging salt that clung to their sandaled feet.

While eating the scouts told of conditions in Jerusalem and the territory they had traveled.

BelkA asked if they happened to notice the recent arrival of a caravan.

"We did in fact," Ibzan answered, "two days ago. It was the one of Bah-Ador. He's a regular. A second one is expected within a day or two."

BelkA appeared relieved. "But did you happen to notice something unusual happening?" he asked.

"We sure did," Ibzan blurted out. "There were some of Urijah's friends prowling around looking for trouble."

"Who's Urijah?"

"He's a guard at one or other of Jerusalem's gates depending on the rotation," Azek explained. "He's up to no good. When he's on duty I detour to another gate. His gang likes to make trouble for Jeremiah."

"It affirms the wisdom of Blind Man who advised me to separate from the caravan before it reached Jerusalem," BelkA said.

"Are there other enemies we should watch out for?" Parto asked of the young fellows.

"Be cautious with priests and prophets. Some are weird," Ibzan replied. "Are you planning on seeing King Zedekiah?"

"Indeed I am," BelkA replied.

"Oh-h-h no!" Azek groaned. "Of all places, be careful around the court. About the only ones to trust would be Ebed-Melech and Shaphan's son and grandson. We've heard that most of the king's advisors and court are cunningly deceitful."

At that point Ibzan nudged his brother, "We need to make a plan to get him safely into the palace." Consequently the two brothers immediately broke into a runaway discussion as they plotted a complicated strategy.

By then, however, Amineh abruptly broke in, "Let's not forget that we have in our midst an envoy of the King of Babylon. It seems to me that BelkA Souash should have complete command of his mission."

All eyes focused on BelkA who had remained silent and amused as the young fellows expressed themselves with the inventive enthusiasm of youth. Now he said gently, "I thank you for your offer of assistance, Azek and Ibzan. Perhaps at this time we should listen to some other suggestions. I notice, for instance, a pensive look in the face of Helem."

Taken by surprise Helem stuttered a moment, "Well, I may sound pessimistic but given the circumstances in Jerusalem, it is indeed possible that the fools will attempt to prevent your entering the palace."

BelkA looked around at each face and pondered.

Ibzan was about to speak once more when his brother nudged him in the ribs, but after some whispering between them he proceeded, though more carefully than before. "I was wondering if you had encountered the prophet Shemaiah in Babylon?"

BelkA focused on Ibzan with curiosity. "No. Tell us what you know about him."

"He's a false prophet who's been sending messages to Jerusalem contradicting Jeremiah's prophecies and urging authorities to shackle poor Jeremiah. What he's aiming at is to get Jeremiah killed."

BelkA raised an eyebrow.

Mahla spoke up. "Ibzan is absolutely correct. I hate to say this, but I fear that Shemaiah might have gotten word to activists in Jerusalem to prepare an attempt on your life BelkA. These are the types who presently have money, prestige and power, and they hang around the court bribing key officials to do what they want. And of course the officials are just like them anyway, so they get along superbly. Naturally they're anti-Babylonian and, in my view, dangerous."

Parto looked at his master. "Perhaps we should mention Adda-Guppi's gang."

BelkA smiled in acknowledgment of the suggestion and told about the schemes of the old priestess.

"She's originally from Haran where the moon god Sin rules as chief god, but since the destruction of the city by the Medes, she's been living in Babylon where she crusades for her god and her son. Presently she's popular in the court through sneaky twistings of truth, but there's a growing resentment toward her. She still happens to be in a position where she has sufficient power to achieve her goals, that are primarily to stamp out the spread of the Hebrew religion and their Writings." He then explained briefly about the thugs and the attack at Aleppo, paying a glowing tribute to his slave.

When he had finished Parto asked, "May I add some details?"

BelkA grinned, "Of course."

Parto explained about the spy turned friend and his family and then, for the benefit of the scouts, he told details of BelkA's arrival just in time to save his own life.

"Wow!" Azek and Ibzan exclaimed with exuberant applause.

"Can you tell us the name of the spy?" Mahla asked.

BelkA couldn't hold back a grin. "His name is Arif, Mahla."

Mahla's eyes widened and a reddish glow came over her face. "Uh-h-h oh no!"

But you have to understand that he really had no say in the matter. Cunningly selected, as he was, by an incantations specialist who is part of Adda-Guppi's entourage, as far as the group was concerned, the matter was settled, because no one stands up against the priestess without serious consequences. You must also understand that Arif dislikes Adda-Guppi as much as I do, and would like to see her evil plans fail. So please don't be offended Mahla."

"Where is this Arif now?" Helem asked.

"The family was part of Bah-Ador's caravan, so I expect he's now in Jerusalem."

"I look forward to meeting this family," Amineh said restraining a grin.

"By the way Amineh," BelkA asked. "Would you mind telling us your background?"

"I was born into a Moabite home, but as a child I was orphaned, and then adopted by a family in Jerusalem. They are the ones who told me of Yahweh. Alas they suffered wrongful death at the hands of some betrayers. If you don't mind I prefer not to tell the story."

"We understand," BelkA said, but even as he talked he noticed that Parto had his eyes riveted on Amineh, and his face had taken on a glow. "Has Blind Man told you about my secret mission?" he asked.

"He told us that it involved rescuing the Writings, but he said that the details would have to come from you," Helem offered.

BelkA told about Daniel's request.

"Daniel," Ibzan said with big eyes. "He's our hero!"

Azek energetically nodded agreement.

The rest of the group sat in awe. Finally Mahla spoke. "This is beyond my wildest imaginations. How can we help?"

"Give me this night to think upon it," BelkA replied. "I must admit that I too am amazed at the developments."

"You are welcome to return tomorrow," Amineh said. "Unless you think it safer to meet with you at the cave."

"The cave might indeed be safer," suggested Helem. Then turning to BelkA he added, "We must be careful not to draw attention on Amineh's home by unnecessary activity. I would suggest early dawn."

"Then we'd best be on our way," BelkA said, "but before we separate, allow me to express my appreciation for the atmosphere that has prevailed here this afternoon. I don't quite understand it."

"It's the Divine Presence," Amineh said softly.

"Strange things are happening that I've never experienced before. I feel as though another hand is hovering over me—and this mission. Perhaps it is your Yahweh. Whatever it is, discovering friends like you has been most delightful. I should also mention that Blind Man has insisted that he seeks no material benefits, though of course I will repay whatever expenditure this mission requires, and I hope you'll allow me to personally assist yours as well."

There were smiles, but no one dared speak.

Chapter 21

The Cave

Jordan Valley, September 589 B.C.

While Parto slept peacefully BelkA tossed and turned on his bedroll. Running into Mahla so soon had thrown him into a whirlwind. It was pleasant enough but he feared his own vulnerability. He must stay focused. At all cost, he must stay aloof.

He wondered what his mother would think of her. Somehow he felt sure she'd be pleased. In spite of their past differences in taste regarding women, there was something about Mahla that crossed over the divide.

He decided to prepare a letter that could be sent off with the first caravan leaving Jerusalem for Babylon—or perhaps with one of Arif's pigeons.

Sitting under a torch with his writing equipment on his knees he began:

"My Dear Mother,

Our journey is going well in spite of an incident that I'll explain in detail when I return. An amazing thing has happened. An extraordinary woman has burst upon my life.

I'm sure you'd like her instantly. It would take too many words to describe her on this scrap of papyrus, except to say that she's beautiful in every way. I long for the day when the two of you shall meet. Meanwhile my king's orders take precedence.

Your devoted son,
BelkA?"

He folded the papyrus carefully and put it back with his writing supplies.

Starting on a new sheet he set about outlining a plan for the following day's strategy. Hours passed as he worked and reworked the details. He finally gave up and dropped onto his mat.

It seemed he'd barely dozed off when he was shaken by his servant.

"Master, it's time," Parto called compassionately.

BelkA mechanically stood up, and upon hearing Helem shaking the young scouts awake, he hurried to beat them at the washbasin. As he dressed he watched the young lads with fascination. Somehow the blend of youthful spontaneity and ardent devotion to their God Yahweh, that radiated an uplifting aura about them, drew him to them. Should he ever have sons, he decided, he would wish them to be of the same mettle. Now concern for their safety struck him with a new force. He must not let them take reckless chances.

They'd no sooner finished their morning preparations, than the women arrived with a basket of food that included warm bread with honey and dried figs. In a few minutes all was consumed.

BelkA then began presenting his final plan while at the same time watching the reactions in the faces around him. To his amazement all eyes remained lowered. Finally he stopped and asked, "Is something amiss?"

There was a long silence that Amineh finally broke, "Well, I don't want to contradict your suggestions," she began cautiously, "but it would appear that, as yet, you don't know us very well. Take Mahla for example, she won't need a protector by her side at all times as you suggest. She has a keen ear and a sharp eye. Handy she is too with the knife."

"What do you mean?" BelkA asked resisting a chuckle.

"Show him."

In a flash Mahla pulled a knife from her felt-lined leather booties and with a straight throw pinned a spider on the opposite wall of the cave.

BelkA caught his breath. "Is your aim that precise every time?"

"Every time," Amineh answered for her, "unless someone gets in her way of course."

"I can't take credit for it," Mahla explained. "It just happens to be something I do easily."

"But who taught you?"

"Amineh," Mahla replied with a grin.

Again BelkA gasped, then laughed.

"But I'm not as sharp as I used to be," Amineh corrected. "Thankfully I recognized the odd trait in Mahla and was able to give her a few pointers. It has already proven useful a time or two. You might bear that in mind."

"Indeed, I wouldn't want her for an enemy."

By then Parto had wisely brought out the almond bag.

"Ah! Good thinking," BelkA said as he began cracking the nuts with a hook on his dagger, dropping the shelled almonds into Azek's lap, and motioning for him to pass them around. Tensions began to ease as light chatter continued.

Meanwhile BelkA took his time with the nuts, cracking each one with care and precision until he finally looked up. "Well then, the plans are extremely simple. We'll all proceed toward Jericho, and hopefully arrive without incident. There we'll pick up the camels, and then proceed toward the caravan staging camp in Jerusalem, where we'll spend the night. The next morning I'll present myself at the palace in a manner worthy of my mission with Parto at my side. It's a risk we cannot avoid."

"We'll all be careful," BelkA added. "I suggest that Helem, Azek and Ibzan appear as merchants in Jerusalem. Helem can operate his stand in the usual way, while the twins scout around the area, and stand ready to assist if something comes up." BelkA then explained the system that he'd previously arranged with Arif for dropping off messages at the Siloam

Springs. "Be aware, that after seeing the king, I may be offered quarters, but if not I will continue to lodge at the staging station."

Then to Mahla he said, "I suggest that you go to the area of the palace at the beginning of work hours to keep watch for any unusual activity. Does that sound reasonable?" he asked looking back and forth from Mahla to Amineh.

The two women smiled their assent.

"Is everyone satisfied?"

Heads nodded. Azek and Ibzan were in a hurry to get going and Helem followed them.

Mahla and Amineh picked up the empty basket and started toward the shack.

BelkA leaned back on the sturdy rock at the entrance to the cave and followed with his eyes the two most astounding women he'd ever seen.

Chapter 22

King of Judah

Jerusalem, September 589 B.C.

First thing the following morning BelkA gave an adjacent caravan leader the message for his mother and bid Bah-Ador good–bye. "Pleasant journey to you," he said, "perhaps when you return I will return to Babylon with you."

"It would be my pleasure," Bah-Ador assured him.

BelkA and Parto then mounted their camels and journeyed toward the palace. Upon arriving they noticed Arif in the distance with his family, but dared not wave for fear of drawing attention.

After attaching their mounts to a post opposite the royal grounds, they walked toward the gate of the walled citadel. A guard looked them over with narrowed eyes and asked the nature of their business, but when BelkA presented documents with Nebuchadnezzar's seal the gate opened immediately.

As they hurried down the palm-lined walkway leading to the palace Parto turned surprised eyes toward BelkA. "Not like Babylon," he said under his breath, "but impressive none-the-less." The lines of the palace and surrounding landscaped grounds clearly pronounced a regal environment. Upon reaching the entrance a massive door opened before them where a guard offered to escort them to a waiting room. As they waited, BelkA pointed out Judah's history depicted on massive carvings that hung on red walls.

When BelkA was called Parto accompanied him, but remained in the background while the envoy approached the King of Judah.

From his seat on a throne of carved ivory gilded with gold, the monarch extended his hand. "Good day to you lord BelkA," he said, "and welcome back to Judah. We had learned you were coming, but had no way of knowing the exact day. I'm anxious to know the nature of your business."

"Your majesty King Zedekiah," BelkA began, "I have a message from King Nebuchadnezzar. May I present it to you?"

"Of course," the king responded and took from BelkA the scroll. He read it over twice before lifting his head. "It's as I expected," he said at last. "I will send a reply immediately to King Nebuchadnezzar through my own envoy." With a touch of irony in his voice he added, "The message does not surprise me." He looked a long moment straight into BelkA eyes, and with a softened tone that obviously intended a show of graciousness, he said, "Please may we entertain you and make you comfortable? It's been a long journey with no doubt many hardships along the way. I desire to express our appreciation through hospitality. A banquet perhaps?"

"I am a man of simple taste," BelkA responded. "I do not ask for such. The message I know is not to your liking, and I prefer not to make much of my presence. However, I should like to request something of you privately."

The king responded by dismissing the officers, advisors, and attendants in the room—an order that was met with some disapproving glances and rolled eyes. Not surprising, in view of the fact, that the court advisors had not yet been informed of the contents of the scroll.

Once they were alone King Zedekiah asked, "What may I do for you?"

"If it would be convenient, your majesty, I should like to visit the temple."

"You realize, of course, that only the outer court is open to Gentiles."

"I do your majesty."

"I shall be happy to take you there myself and thus guarantee your safety." A hint of a smile played on his lips.

BelkA bowed.

"Also, I may need to call you back for further consultation, but in the meantime a house will be provided for your use. My own servants will be at your disposal for whatever needs you have."

After another low bow, BelkA joined Parto and the two exited the palace.

"Congratulations, mission accomplished," Parto said as they made their way down the path toward the gate.

"Well, not quite Parto. Now we face the real danger. Tell me everything you saw."

"I got a view of the officers and advisors up front. Quite a bunch I'd say. In some I caught a look of well, disdain, arrogance to say the least. In a couple of others I detected anxiety. One had his head slightly bent much of the time, I thought he might be praying."

"S-h-h, BelkA whispered as they neared the gate, there's a woman around the corner... an old woman," he added, "with a cane. One never knows."

The woman—apparently curious—looked around briefly before continuing down the walk. As distance increased between them BelkA gave in to the urge to get another view. This time his jaw fell open when he saw the old gal lift her skirts before breaking into a run. Quickly he put his hand over his mouth to hold back an explosion of laughter.

"What is it?" Parto asked.

"It's Mahla?"

"Where?"

"The old woman."

"No."

"I caught her running."

"You don't say and I missed it. I was looking around to make sure our camels were still well-tethered."

"A smart thing to do. You didn't by chance see Arif?"

"No."

They were about to mount their animals when a young man hurried toward them, calling out, "My lord BelkA, I've been assigned to show you your lodging. I've just to mount my horse down the row and then you can follow me."

•••

In spite of the coolness of the morning Helem sensed a sultry impact that weighed upon him as he began to set up his stand. The twins had fanned out and left him to the task of setting up his stand, an option he much preferred. By the time he'd laid out his carpets, and piled them with exotic trinkets, a southeasterly wind stirred. Weighing the potential damage to his precious silks, he decided not to display them. His supply, in any case, had dwindled considerably since Damascus where Blind Man had bought up a substantial quantity, and today he wanted to be able to dismantle quickly should an emergency arise. This left him with little to do but watch passersby and wonder about BelkA. He decided that it would be the ideal time for a break. A little walk about the market and a snack might perk him up.

He was about to alert the scouts when he heard a clatter from behind followed by yelling and screaming. Turning around he saw a collision of two donkeys and their carts. Produce was tumbling out and rolling over cobblestones, holding up the already jammed traffic.

"Impossible," one man yelled.

"Exaggeration" came from the other.

While the men argued, two women were busily picking up the scattered fruit, vegetables and myriads of almonds. One of the women, he noticed, was a young girl who appeared embarrassed. He decided they could use some help, so he put two fingers to his mouth and blew the call whistle.

The two scouts were by his side almost immediately. While Ibzan, with turban and silk cloak over a black tunic, watched the stand, Azek, in a similar disguise, helped Helem and the women, so within minutes order was restored.

Seeing that the damage was repaired the men settled their dispute with self-conscious grins, excusing themselves with conciliatory tones. "My donkey's got a mind of her own," one was saying, and the other responded with, "You'd think mine were blind the way she plows ahead regardless of what's in her way."

When they'd moved on Helem took note of the path and destination of the almond cart remembering that BelkA had an affinity for these nuts—especially the cracking of them. Later when assured that everything at his stand was as it should be he set out to find the almond seller. The girl recognized him, smiled and reiterated her gratitude for his help.

Helem now had time to look from close range at the dainty young girl before him. Long lashes shadowed expressive brown eyes set in an oval face. She lacked Mahla's striking beauty, but she had a gentle freshness about her, and when she weighed the nuts he'd requested he noticed delicate hands that spoke of craftiness. She wore but one gold bangle around her slender wrist instead of the usual six—a style he decided—all of her own.

"You must be an out-of-town visitor," she said as he held out his canvas bag for her to fill.

"Now how did you know that?" Helem asked.

"It was just a thought. I don't know everyone in Jerusalem, of course, but my father and I come regularly and we kind of recognize the locals. Also," she began with a hint of self-consciousness, "we come to the city to visit cousin Jeremiah."

"A cousin of yours is he?" Helem smiled. "A good man."

"Thank you for saying that and for your kindness this morning. It's rare for people to do that here in the city."

"I'm pleased I could help. My display was set up so I was just standing around. By the way, my name is Helem."

"Mine is Tamara. Quite a whistle you have."

"I learned that as a child."

"What do you sell?"

"Mostly textiles, especially silks."

"From afar?"

Helem nodded. "The silks yes. They come by way of the Silk Road from Central Asia."

"Oh, that sounds exotic. Where do you come from?"

"Ecbatana."

"That is indeed far."

"Well, you know how it is, all paths lead to Jerusalem."

The last word faded out on Helem's lips when he heard a clamor, and saw from the corner of his eye a stately camel, and another immediately behind. He hurled around and stared at an image of BelkA he'd never seen before. He sat stiff and erect in a blue robe edged with gold tassels, and a toga draped elegantly about him, fastened with a toggle pin on his left shoulder. His perfectly curled black hair and beard contrasted his rounded, slightly conical blue hat. Parto, perched as straight and tall as his master, wore a green tunic with black braid that provided the perfect contrast with his master. A turban now concealed his tumbling black curls. As they passed, BelkA dropped the slightest wink in his direction that disappeared in an instant, but was not lost on the girl.

"You know him don't you?"

Helem looked her in the eye and cautiously said almost in a whisper, "I learned of him through friends who live in Damascus."

"He's obviously an envoy from Babylon on a royal mission."

"He is," Helem replied, and then added hurriedly, "I must go now."

Chapter 23

The Temple

Jerusalem, September 589 B.C.

The small square two-story house of stone and mud plaster offered to BelkA and Parto as their place of residence in Jerusalem, sparkled under a fresh coat of whitewash outside and in. Like many Hebrew homes, a courtyard dominated the ground floor, flanked by a room for animals and another for storage, and behind it a communal room with minimal furnishings: a table, two tripod chairs or stools, and beyond a rug with bolsters and pillows lining the wall. A tiny room off the courtyard contained a tub, jars of water, and a stool. Sleeping quarters were upstairs where a room was provided for each of them. From a cursory inspection, it appeared free of vermin. The realization of this brought sighs of relief to both men.

"Not exactly all the comforts of home," BelkA remarked when he and Parto were alone, "but completely adequate. I would only wish such for Arif's family as well."

"Indeed Master."

They'd barely settled in, and were watering their camels from the reservoir in the courtyard, when the aroma of roasted goose awoke their appetites and sent Parto scurrying to the door.

Two servants brought in baskets of fragrantly spiced food, and served them in elegant style with silver cups and bronze plates, along with an intricately carved bowl containing salt.

"What have we here?" BelkA said as he picked up and examined the dainty little bowl. He dipped his finger into the salt and touched the tip of his tongue. "Ah, the genuine flavor of the Dead Sea."

The servers smiled but spoke not a word.

"The height of refinement," Parto commented.

"And much appreciated," BelkA added.

They ate the main poultry dish prepared with almonds and accompanied with leeks, chickpeas and olives, followed by fresh fruits and dainty fig cakes. When they were finished the servants collected the baskets and tableware, but left the remaining food.

"What are we going to do with the leftover food?" BelkA asked Parto when they were once more alone.

They hadn't long to find out. Responding to a knock on the door Parto ushered in Mahla, still attired in her old woman's costume. "There are others at the back door. Go quickly," she said.

One by one their surprise guests arrived including Arif, Tirza, SabA, Sussan, Helem and the two scouts, Azek and Ibzan. To the astonished BelkA and Parto, Arif explained their meeting up with one another at the Siloam Spring.

Parto lost no time seating them and placing food before them. The starving children ate till the last crumb had disappeared while BelkA sat back with a satisfied grin.

"The only one lacking now is Amineh," Parto commented thoughtfully.

Helem had a faraway look in his eye.

After dinner the children were anxious to explore the house so BelkA gave them a tour. When they returned to the communal room Mahla said, "We dare not stay long."

"Indeed not, you took quite a risk coming," BelkA said with a grin. "Arif's family, at least, must leave the city before the gates close."

"The children were begging to see you," Arif said. "They'd watched you at the palace from behind the bushes and it was all Tirza and I could do to keep them from making a dash for you."

"Is there any way you might rent a house such as this?" BelkA asked.

"After the staging stations, Bethlehem's Inn seems quite appealing at this time, and they have reasonable monthly rents," Arif said. "We think we'll try that for a while."

BelkA then explained his palace experience and his hope to be shown the temple. "It also appears that King Zedekiah wishes to have further contact with me. Maybe there's still hope. We'll let you know about it all by message at the Pool of Siloam. Also should any or all of you desire to return for a visit, I would suggest you ring a tiny bell that will be placed under a stone, that I'll indicate to you. Should it be missing or there be some other impediment, blow a few notes on a flute at the back door, or if you prefer, pretend to cough. If there's a hint of danger, and you are at all able to alert us, just cough. We'll respond immediately if we can do so safely. If you hear or see nothing you must disappear as quickly as possible."

"By the way Helem, I saw you speaking with a girl at the market. What was that about?"

"She's a young woman from Anathoth who sells almonds at the market with her father. I was in the process of purchasing some when you passed. By the way, here's a bag for you."

"Thank you," BelkA said with a wide smile.

"Also," Helem added, "she's related to Jeremiah. A second cousin I believe."

BelkA puckered his lips. "That is indeed interesting. I want to hear more from each of you, but I'm afraid you must all go now without delay."

The scouts left first, one at a time of course, and checked the situation before giving the all clear signal of coughing as the others exited in the same fashion.

•••

The following day BelkA received notification by royal messenger that the King regretted his inability to personally attend to BelkA in showing him the temple, but that a court official would arrive for that purpose the following morning.

So when Parto responded to the knock on the door he was pleased to see standing before him the sleek Ethiopian he had previously seen at the palace.

"Greetings," the tall young man said displaying shiny white teeth that contrasted strikingly with his ebony skin tone. "My name is Ebed-Melech. I am to be your tour guide today."

"Please come in," Parto said as he bowed. Then he ushered the official into the communal room where BelkA stood waiting.

When the two men had acknowledged each other, with the respectful greeting of a bowed head, Ebed-Melech said, "Please excuse the early hour. It's best to avoid the crowds expected soon for the celebrations of the feast of harvest."

"That was thoughtful of you" BelkA said brushing aside the excuse. "I have only to pick up my staff and then we'll follow you."

The three men, dressed formally in court attire, made their way toward the temple where the gate-keeper recognized Ebed-Melech, and permitted immediate entrance into the courtyard. Once inside they made their way to the back wall, opposite the entrance, where they stood and contemplated the gleaming limestone structure in the typical Phoenician style.

"It was built by King Solomon some four hundred years after the Hebrew escape from Egypt," Ebed-Melech explained.

"The two pillars in front are reminiscent of the Babylonian style of architecture," BelkA commented.

"Their names—Jakin and Boaz—symbolize a unique theocracy with king and priest accountable to Yahweh."

"Divine kingship then. In our minds that would make the king a god."

"Definitely not here," Ebed-Melech said, and then continued explaining about the inside rooms, the holy, and the holy of holies and all of the furnishings, each with its symbolism portraying Messiah— the Anointed One who is to come.

"The imagery is indeed magnificent," BelkA commented with a sigh. "Makes one wish for Hebrew ancestry."

Ebed-Melech looked at BelkA, "Yahweh extends His concern to all nations. I, a former slave, embraced the faith long ago."

"My servant Parto did the same back in Babylon."

Crowds were beginning to jostle them, and a group of women were pushing their way to a statue in a corner of the court. "You didn't mention the statue? It has much resemblance to the Babylonian goddess Ishtar."

Ebed-Melech frowned, but explained that she was the Canaanite goddess Ashtoreth whose origin was indeed Babylon. "Soon the air will be filled with incense that personally I find unappealing... Oh, please excuse my impertinence."

"That's quite all right," BelkA said appreciating the show of independent thinking.

As they were making their way to the gate another crowd seemed to be gathering around an older gentleman that BelkA judged to be in his later fifties. His lean body seemed to fade away in an austere-grey tunic, but there was something quaint in the round face and intense eyes.

"That's the prophet Jeremiah," Ebed-Melech said.

"Jeremiah! The very one I need to see," BelkA exclaimed.

"Would you like to hear him?" Ebed-Melech asked.

"I certainly would."

"Me too!" Parto said enthusiastically.

It wasn't long before the prophet began shouting, his voice ringing out above the din of the noisy crowd, "Here you are, come to observe a sacred feast to Yahweh but you loose no time in turning around and offering incense to another god. It's appalling."

"Yeah give it to them prophet of doom," a young fellow near Jeremiah shouted back at him. "All you ever say is negative stuff. Be modern. Loosen up. This is a new era old man. You'd be more successful if you preached positive."

Jeremiah appeared to take no heed. "Yahweh sees your outward observances as less than useless."

"Who cares," shouted a woman by the shrine.

"For you Yahweh's but the tutelary deity of the land," Jeremiah's voice rang louder still, "so you take on Canaan's Baal, Ammon's Moloch, Moab's Chemosh, and Babylon's Marduk. Why? Because you have to be like everyone else, and because you enjoy the pagan rituals that excite your depraved senses. You excuse yourselves because you call it all religious, while what it amounts to is acting like wild donkeys sniffing the wind in the heat of passion."

"Who's the jackass? You're the pitiful long face locked into a straight jacket," a young fellow shouted back.

"Sh-h-h," a woman said. "Don't you realize, he's speaking a message from Yahweh?"

BelkA noticed an unearthly look in Jeremiah's face as if he'd heard nothing at all.

"And you black-robed priests not only permit it but take the lead. You don't have to tell me what goes on in that filthy valley of Hinnon. Your garments stink with the smoke of those fires; the blood of little children is on your skirts. Those obscene and cruel rites are despicable.

"The trees of the groves are witnesses. They see what goes on under their shadows. The rocks on the hills are bursting with stories—hideous stories. And you say, 'we do no wrong. We follow the rituals of Yahweh, and we keep up with our times by adding some excitement to it all. Our young people want it.'

"And you too, you false prophets out there. You prophesy to please, and to get ahead. Money and power are all you care about.

"I've been preaching God's warnings ever since the reign of Josiah. Other prophets have also urged you to turn from your evil deeds, and stop provoking Yahweh to anger with all your dumb idols that you craft so skillfully.

173

"Here I am, a tired old man still preaching and warning you that time is fast running out. The joyful celebrations of bride and groom, the cheerful sounds of the millstones, and the sweet music of the harp and lyre are about to end because you have not listened or heeded the messages of Yahweh.

"The whole land will soon become a desolation and a horror. You and the surrounding wicked nations will serve the king of Babylon for seventy years. Yahweh will pour upon you the cup of His wrath. Jerusalem and the cities around Judah with their kings and princes will become ruins. Egypt, Tyre, Sidon, Moab, Elam, the land of the Philistines, Ashkelon, Gaza, and more will all drink from the cup because Yahweh is entering into judgment

"This is what the LORD says, 'A calamity is about to fall upon this city which is called by my name, wail you leaders, wallow in ashes you priests because Yahweh has left His hiding place like a lion. The days of your slaughter and dispersion have come just as I promised.'"

The prophet stopped preaching as suddenly as he started, and was beginning to make his way toward the gate when BelkA whispered in Parto's ears. "Detain him until I can speak with him."

Parto lost no time in reaching the prophet before whom he bowed and made his master's request.

Though obviously weary the prophet graciously agreed and waited until BelkA and Ebed-Melech had caught up.

When BelkA was introduced he bowed his head before the prophet.

Jeremiah offered his hand first to Ebed-Melech, giving him a warm smile and then took BelkA's hand.

"Revered one," BelkA began, "I have a message for you from Daniel, and another from Ezekiel."

Upon hearing the mention of the names Daniel and Ezekiel the prophet's eyes lit up and the creases in his forehead smoothed as if ironed out. "When may I receive them?" he asked.

"At your earliest convenience. The messages at this time are at the home assigned to us."

Ebed-Melech immediately spoke, "Perhaps BelkA and his servant could visit your home this afternoon, Jeremiah. Would that be convenient?"

"Perfect," the prophet answered. "I shall then await your visit with eager anticipation." A smile broke upon his face that appeared to ease the weight of sorrow.

Chapter 24

The Writings

Jerusalem, September 589 B.C.

Jeremiah carefully broke the seal on the pottery envelope that BelkA had put in his hand and removed the scroll. He took on a serious look as he read the letter from the prophet in Babylon, but in the end a smile touched his lips. Lifting his eyes toward BelkA he said, "It encourages me to hear from my friend. Thank you, lord BelkA for bringing the letter all the way from Babylon.

"Ezekiel and I share the common heartache of relaying warnings of doom—and it doesn't make things any easier knowing that our reward will be harassment, imprisonment, torture, and perhaps death. The task seems so unbearably painful that we succumb at times to bouts of depression."

BelkA shook his head indicating compassion.

Jeremiah turned to the scroll before him. After looking it over a moment, he laid it on his lap with obvious disappointment. "Unlike the letter, the print of the scroll is too small for my aging eyes," he sighed. "Ezekiel is more than twenty years younger than myself. I will have to wait for my faithful scribe Baruch."

"Perhaps I might read it for you?" BelkA offered.

Jeremiah looked up in surprise. "You read Hebrew?"

"Not perfectly, but I'd be happy to try."

Jeremiah handed him the scroll.

"Would you permit me to translate at the same time into our Babylonian dialect so my friend Parto can follow?"

"Of course," Jeremiah said enthusiastically turning an approving smile on Parto. "It pleases me to see him interested."

"It would appear," BelkA said, "that Ezekiel begins with a summary of a number of prophecies that you perhaps have already read. I will thus begin with that, but stop me if you wish to skip over them."

Jeremiah nodded and then sat back on his bed-divan.

BelkA began to read, at first falteringly, stopping to decipher or translate while keeping his place on the scroll, but with Parto's help in holding the papyrus at his eye level he began to pick up speed.

"This is what YAHWEH says to Jerusalem... in the early days of your nation, when you were born no eye pitied you. You were cast into an open field and left wallowing in your blood. I spoke life into you and made a covenant with you, and you became mine. I bathed and anointed you with oil and clothed you in silk and adorned you with ornaments: necklaces, bracelets, nose rings and a beautiful crown. You ate fine flour, honey and oil. You were beautiful and advanced to royalty and your renown spread throughout the nations for the splendor I bestowed upon you.

"Alas, you trusted yourself instead of me and lavished your beauty and splendor on passersby who took your jewelry to make their shrines and adorned them with the embroidered garments I gave you. My bread, my oil and incense you set before them as a pleasing fragrance and you delivered your children to be burnt on their altars. How could you have done that to me? Therefore, O prostitute, because of your lust and the blood of your children I will give you into the hands of your lovers who'll strip you and cut many of you to pieces with their swords. They'll burn your houses and scatter many of you in distant countries with only a remnant allowed to escape."

BelkA stopped. "What a sad story," he exclaimed. "It's like hearing the pouring out of both an adoptive father and a husband."

"Sounds a lot like the prophet Hosea," Jeremiah said. Then he looked up with hopeful anticipation. "Perhaps you might read one more?"

BelkA lifted the scroll, found his place and read. This time it was about Ezekiel's magnificent vision of the glory of Yahweh and ending with glory departing from the temple.

At this point Jeremiah put his face in his hands and wept. "It's over. It's all over for the once magnificent temple where His presence rested between the cherubim. He's gone. All that's left is an empty shell."

BelkA put the scroll down.

"Yahweh has brought you to Jerusalem just in time," Ebed-Melech said.

BelkA picked up Daniel's list of missing scrolls in Babylon, and read it to Jeremiah.

"I don't have all those scrolls," Jeremiah said.

BelkA's face paled and his brow wrinkled with concern, "You don't have these scrolls? Where might we acquire them then?"

"I need to send you to an old scribe. In fact, I'll have my own scribe Baruch accompany you to his house with a list of the scrolls I have, that you can add to the ones he has, and then compare it with Daniel's list."

"Is this man trustworthy?" BelkA asked.

"Unquestionably."

Jeremiah told of the old scribe Shaphan who'd once been the secretary of King Josiah. "You'll also find that he's pro-Babylonian so you need not fear."

"Good for him," BelkA said.

"He's now old, but keen of mind and spirit and I can assure you that he'll be intensely interested in your efforts."

Parto, always concerned about practical matters, now spoke up. "While we're together, perhaps we should discuss the transport of the scrolls. It seems to me that we should collect pottery jars or containers for that purpose."

"You do well to mention it young man," Jeremiah said. "That is a matter of utmost importance, because some of the scrolls will be old, and as you might know, extremely fragile." He thought a while then leaned forward, "Incidentally I have a potter friend who will surely be disposed to help us. His name is Nethaniah. He and his wife are devout followers of Yahweh, and ever concerned over me."

"Perfect." BelkA said.

Jeremiah grinned at the coincidence. "This Nethaniah is like a son to me. He's honest to the point of cheating himself. I'll take you to him myself in a couple of days. He has his shop down in the area of Siloam Springs. Let's say we meet day after tomorrow when the sun on the dial is past its high spot."

"Agreed," BelkA said after jotting down the information.

"We'll also need some kind of packing materials like woven cloth to secure the scrolls in the jars to prevent damage in transport," Parto said. "Perhaps some woolen or linen fabric strips?"

"Helem might be able to help us," BelkA responded, "though I think he deals in silks."

"I know who'll help us," Jeremiah said. "A young woman with fingers that are becoming quite adept on her weaver's loom. She recently made the tunic I'm wearing," he added proudly standing up to show off the weave. "She lives in Anathoth but she usually comes to market with her father on Wednesdays, and the two of them never fail to drop by to see me. I'll speak to her about this. By the way," he added, "I recommend that the cloth that is to envelop the sacred scrolls be woven with the purest white threads, like the tunics of the priests."

BelkA raised his eyebrows at the last suggestion but made no comment. "Do you have an idea of the number of scrolls there might be?" he asked.

"It's hard to say. Thirty or forty perhaps. Also, we must hide copies of the scrolls here in this area, and not let them all be taken away. Anything could happen to you or the scrolls in transport."

"A wise suggestion;" BelkA said. "And now we must leave you man of God. Your help has been most valuable to us."

"Speak not of it," Jeremiah said. "I'm thankful and relieved that you came."

Chapter 25

The Potter's House

Jerusalem, September 589 B.C.

BelkA and Parto arrived early at the Siloam Pool and easily found the Potter's shop but Jeremiah appeared nowhere. Trying not to make themselves obvious BelkA examined shoes, pouches and leather accessories for sale at the shop next to the potter's, while Parto sauntered toward the Siloam Springs, sitting down on the rim of the low wall where he looked carefully around before discretely depositing a message at the agreed-upon spot. In so doing he discovered two messages destined for BelkA that he carefully concealed in his tunic.

Returning to BelkA he found him wearing an anxious frown. "What is it Master?"

"I feel a little disappointed that there seems to be no trace of Arif, Helem, Mahla, or the twins. Where could they all be?"

"Well someone has been by because a message was dropped off."

BelkA's face brightened. "Ah, a good sign." He took the message from Parto, but feeling movement on his left, turned abruptly, and found his eyes locked into an individual sitting cross-legged in the shade munching on a barley loaf. In his simple brown tunic and ample black headpiece, he melted into the crowd milling about, but there was clearly no doubt in BelkA's mind as to his identity. The presence of Ibzan suggested that Azek could also be near. Sure enough, a young merchant walked by with a familiar gait. With difficulty BelkA restrained a smile of amusement and relief.

At the same time he noticed Jeremiah approaching with a crowd assembling about him. Some were jeering, making faces, and imitating his mannerisms. A few stood back as if dismayed or alarmed.

BelkA and Parto walked toward Jeremiah and greeted him.

"Go on in friends and speak with Nethaniah. I must first deliver an urgent message. I'll join you immediately after."

Reluctantly they turned around and entered the shop. The potter, a young man of medium height and build with a sensitive expression, got up from his wheel and came toward them.

"Please don't stop the wheel," BelkA said. "We understand that, when the clay is moist and in the process of being molded, the wheel must keep turning."

"No harm done," the potter said taking off the clay and dumping it in a large jar of raw material.

"My hands just don't have the touch today. With my wife feeling ill, and having to concern myself with her responsibilities in serving customers, I shouldn't even try." He washed his hands in a basin and was reaching for a towel when, through the open door, he noticed Jeremiah. An expression of alarm crossed his face.

"Jeremiah is the one who sent us to you," BelkA said to the distracted potter. "Your name, we are told, is Nethaniah. I am BelkA, and this is my friend Parto."

Nethaniah came back to full attention with obvious embarrassment. "Please excuse my impolite manner," he said. "You were saying that Jeremiah sent you?" His smile had now widened till it crinkled up his eyes into mere slits? "What might I do for you?"

BelkA, taking advantage of the fact that Nethaniah seemed preoccupied by Jeremiah's presence in the neighborhood said, "Perhaps we should listen to the prophet before discussing our business?"

Nethaniah gratefully nodded in agreement and the expression of anxiety returned.

"I feel compelled to repeat a message I gave you some time ago," Jeremiah was saying...

"Go right ahead old clown," said a young mocker, "you're entertaining us." Others danced around while one young fellow even lunged toward Jeremiah as if to push him over when he suddenly fell sprawling to the ground. The crowd laughed at the scene, especially since it appeared to be the cane of an old woman that had tripped him.

Heedless, the prophet continued with an astonishing tone of authority, "'Arise and go down to the potter's house, and there I will cause you to hear my words.' Then I went down to the potter's house, and there he was, making something at the wheel. And the vessel that he made of clay was marred in the hand of the potter; so he made it again into another vessel, as it seemed good to the potter to make. Then the word of the LORD came to me, saying: 'O house of Israel! Can I not do with you as this potter...'" Jeremiah stopped and wiped his perspiring brow.

"Let that be your last word," said a heavily bearded man BelkA presumed to be a religious leader, no doubt one of the false prophets Ebed-Melech had mentioned.

"You're a liar old man," a heckler screamed hurling himself as if to strike Jeremiah, only to find Azek and Ibzan in his way.

Jeremiah, dripping with perspiration and haggard, looked about him before adding, "I beg of you please return to Yahweh. Perhaps He will still show mercy."

He now turned from the turbulent, angry, jeering crowd and walked into the potter's house where he found BelkA and Parto standing in silence and awe.

Nethaniah was the first to move into action, "Come in honored servant of Yahweh. Please be seated here on this cushion." He left the room to return a few minutes later with a pitcher of water on a tray that also included bread and honey.

The weary prophet drank to the point of almost emptying the pitcher. The potter was about to replenish the jug when Jeremiah stayed him with his hand. Silence continued while Jeremiah ate, then leaned back against pillows and closed his eyes. Just a few minutes later, however, he sat upright. "Nethaniah, have you met my friends?"

"Only just."

"The business we thought to discuss can wait," BelkA said.

"No, speak BelkA," Jeremiah objected. "Time is short. I will sit back and listen."

So BelkA told of his mission and of his need for pottery jars. "The quantity will be considerable."

"About how many would you estimate?"

"Forty, perhaps."

"I won't have enough clay for that. Is it urgent?"

"Well..."

"Time is of essence," Jeremiah broke in upon BelkA's hesitation.

"Are you implying that there is no hope that Judah will repent and make things right with Yahweh?" Nethaniah asked.

"You heard the response. Actually I knew they would reject it as usual because Yahweh warned me, but since I was coming here anyway, I thought to give the people one last reminder because Yahweh is merciful. Alas, they truly have proved themselves without excuse. The cup of iniquity is filled to the brim. Judgment is the only cure and it will be coming soon."

"I will close my shop and spend my time on this project."

"Not so fast Nethaniah," Jeremiah cautioned. "You need the income. Also I would advise keeping a normal appearance about the place."

"That might not be so easy with the crowd you drew here today."

Jeremiah shrugged and smiled endearingly.

"I'm going to have to go to the mire by the Jordan where I get my preferred clay and bring back a supply. That alone will take me at least three days. Wet clay, as you know, is extremely heavy."

Parto, who was now collecting the vessels Jeremiah had used, suggested the scouts as helpers.

BelkA affirmed him by repeating it.

"I'd like to meet the fellows," Nethaniah said.

BelkA pulled out his writing equipment from his sash to take down some notes, but stopped with stylus in midair to explain about *The Lamp Connection*, and to ask if Nethaniah could be present at an upcoming meeting.

"By all means."

BelkA explained the location, which was also convenient for the potter as he could, at the same time, collect his clay from the nearby Jordan River.

Parto sat up straight and said, "I was thinking that we'll need baskets—strong baskets to protect and transport the scrolls."

"There's a man at the market who makes all kinds," Nethaniah suggested.

"Of course," Jeremiah burst forth. "Old Giddel, the grandfather of Hodesh, is indeed a skilled basket weaver."

"If you like I'll speak with him as we see each other regularly at the market," Nethaniah offered.

"Excellent," BelkA said. "And now Parto, we must return before our own food arrives. We dare not create suspicion."

Chapter 26

Gibeon

September 589 B.C.

O nce within the walls of their temporary home, BelkA sat down to read the two notes that Parto picked up at the Siloam Springs, and to ponder while his servant fulfilled his duty of making the rounds of the house, checking up and downstairs, the court-yard and attending rooms, and even the outside for evidence of prior or present intruders. He had just finished his rounds and had rejoined BelkA on the carpet when sounds at the door announced dinner. Quickly BelkA hid the messages under the carpet.

Again they were served in elegant style and gen-erous portions, but this time the servants presented a message to BelkA that requested permission to be excused early in order to be present themselves at another event. When BelkA had read the note one of the servers presented his apology silently by putting his hands together as if praying.

"Of course," BelkA responded with a smile. "Think nothing of it. No need to stay since you have attended with diligence to every detail already. You are excused."

When they were gone BelkA smiled at Parto. "Nice to be just the two of us tonight," he said. "Pity those who must dine in luxury every day."

Later when Parto began to clear the table BelkA stopped him. "You've already performed your dinner service for the day. Tonight you are my companion and friend. Together they put the leftovers in the baskets, covered them carefully and placed them at the back door under the branches of the cypress tree. Then they went in and sat on the carpet where BelkA read the messages left for them at the Siloam Springs. "Arif's family is staying at Bethlehem's inn and the twins are exploring the Gihon tunnel as a possible escape route."

"The scouts performed well today," Parto commented with a chuckle, "but I fail to see the interest in the Gihon tunnel?"

"The Gihon Spring is the city's main water supply. It's located just outside the wall, so there's a tunnel under the wall that connects the springs to what some call the pool of Siloam or what we've been calling the Siloam Springs. When the flow is low one can actually wade through it. I think the idea is good," BelkA said with a thoughtful expression.

"I would think that the location of the springs on the outside of the city's wall would make it vulnerable. Why the enemy could cut off the water supply."

"You're absolutely right Parto, except that it has been enclosed. The weakest point, however, is still vulnerable."

"I think our young spies have somehow learned that it has been used in times past as a secret tunnel."

"How about that?" Parto said with a grin. "And how about some almonds?" He asked setting out before getting a response, and returning with a bowl brimming full.

"Ah, there's another from the twins. They've been checking out Gibeon about eight miles away where there's the possibility of renting a stall for our camels, and a friendly home that could be used for hiding."

"What do you think of all this Master?"

"Well, I have to admit, we've got a pair of clever adventurers who get things done. We might have to rein them in from time to time, but I'm impressed with the way they project their thinking ahead. Definitely an asset."

Chapter 27

Shaphan

Jerusalem, September 589 B.C.

B elkA and Parto, accompanied by Jeremiah's scribe Baruch, stood before the stately home of the old scribe Shaphan. A servant assured them at the door that they were expected, and led them to an elderly gentleman sitting on a divan with a scroll spread out on his knees.

"Ah Baruch," Shaphan said putting the scroll carefully aside before rising to his feet.

"Good to see you honorable Shaphan, allow me to introduce two Babylonian friends."

"Welcome to the home of old Shaphan," the white-haired gentleman said offering both hands along with a bow of his head.

BelkA and Parto bowed in their turn.

Shaphan turned to his servant: "A tray of cakes perhaps Selig?"

When the guests were comfortably seated the host himself sat down once more beside his scrolls. "I was most pleased to hear about you from Jeremiah," he said, "and also relieved because, I must confess, I've had nightmares concerning the scrolls. You see, some thirty years ago we almost lost them, and now we face the same dilemma all over again."

"You mean it's happened before?" BelkA exclaimed.

"I'm afraid so. It all began during the reign King Manasseh when altars to Baal and Ashterah were set up in the court and even in the temple itself. To make room for the idols, certain furnishings were removed along with the scrolls. For a long time, those of us, who were loyal to Yahweh, feared they'd been destroyed and lost forever. But when Josiah, the grandson of Manasseh, came to the throne I was appointed secretary of state, and Hilkiah was named high priest. We were greatly relieved when King Josiah ordered a restoration of the temple putting Hilkiah in charge. As the workmen were cleaning out debris in some of the storerooms Hilkiah found the book of the law and brought it to me. I nearly fell over so great was my shock, but I managed to collect my wits, and to go directly to King Josiah who allowed me to read from it. When he realized how far we had departed from the teachings of the law, he became terrified and agreed to consult with the prophetess Huldah concerning Judah's critical position. To make the story short, the clean up continued and more scrolls were found and restored to their proper place in the temple. Alas, today we're back to where we were in the days of Manasseh."

The servant interrupted the conversation when he entered with a tray laden with tasty delicacies.

"Take it to my scriptorium please Selig," Shaphan ordered and invited his guests to follow him.

They entered a back room where a wall was lined with cubicles containing scrolls. "This serves as my library and scriptorium," he explained. "I had it built especially to accommodate the scrolls."

"They're all here then?" BelkA asked.

"No. I'm afraid not. I've searched throughout the temple in every room I could access, but a good number of scrolls seem to be missing and I don't know where they are. Someone or some persons may have disposed of them, or they could yet be in one of the storerooms to which I do not possess a key."

"Is there not some way of getting access to the key?" BelkA asked.

"I dare not inquire for fear that, if the scrolls were discovered by some idolatrous priests, they would be pounced upon and destroyed."

"Wait a minute. I have the list of Daniel's scrolls. Perhaps we won't need them." BelkA said as he gave Shaphan the list.

After carefully comparing Shaphan shook his head. "I have one scroll listed here but not the rest."

"Here's a list of Jeremiah's scrolls," Baruch offered.

Again Shaphan checked. "I have all these except the last Writings of Jeremiah and Ezekiel."

"So, quite a number are yet missing?"

"I'm afraid so."

"H-m-m." BelkA pondered. "The missing scrolls are locked in a room for which we have no key. What we need is a locksmith."

"Indeed, but who can we trust? Besides, in the hours of daylight there are too many people around. What would they think of people walking out with arms full of scrolls? The number, after all, is considerable."

"We've got another problem," Baruch said with tightened lips. "Jeremiah insists that at least one copy of all the scrolls must remain in this area just in case they get lost in transport."

BelkA frowned. "That would mean that if we do not find two copies of each,we might have a considerable amount of copying to do. Who could do that?"

"It's a problem because most of the scribes and faithful priests have been deported. Thankfully I'm near-sighted, but copying takes a long time."

"I too am a scribe," BelkA said, "but alas, the rule we adhere to in our land is to always copy in one's mother tongue. I'm sure you have the same."

"We do," Baruch affirmed, "it's the best way to avoid errors. They slip in all too easily, despite the best of intentions. There's the two elderly prophets, Habakkuk and Zephaniah, whom we could call upon but alas, their eyes have aged. If Jeremiah agrees— and I'm sure he will—I will gladly assist you."

"We'd best start with whomever we have available," BelkA said.

"There's still another problem," Baruch cautioned. "Right now there's no papyri available. I bought up most of the stock from a merchant who is leaving town."

BelkA scratched his head. "A shortage of papyi? That means we'll have to send someone to Tyre. I found a merchant there who has an excellent quality of papyri, and I believe a sufficient supply. I wonder if I could go myself?"

"Not so fast my friend," Shaphan cautioned. "From my experience at court, and with my son and grandson presently involved there, I can assure you that the prevailing atmosphere is, shall we say, troublesome. I worry enough as it is about my family who insist that their voice is needed there, but please don't add to my concern. I can assure you, BelkA, that your presence in town has sent out a sounding alert on the part of activists who have been pressuring the king for a long time to throw off the Babylonian yoke. Getting you out of here alive is going to be a big enough challenge as it is. Please be careful."

"Is my being here a risk to you Shaphan?" BelkA asked.

"I doubt it. I'm old enough to be considered harmless, and I don't meddle in court anymore."

Chapter 28

A Last Audience with the King

Jerusalem, October 589 B.C.

Dark clouds hung over the heads of BelkA and Parto as they descended from their camels in front of the palace. Today even the courtyard, that had previously offered such a strong first impression a few months earlier, lacked luster without that gleam of sunlight.

As they waited their audience they noticed servants occupied with moving furniture, dinnerware, and all manner of foods.

Upon their entrance into the throne room they were surprised to notice but few officials with the King. BelkA smiled with relief as he recognized Ebed-Melech standing soberly off to the side. The King himself seemed agitated, though he accepted them warmly. Following BelkA's bow King Zedekiah said, "You seem well, BelkA Souash. It is good to see you again."

"I am well your majesty," BelkA responded, "and I have enjoyed your hospitality for which I thank you."

King Zedekiah nodded acceptance. "The reason there are but few officials present with me today is that they are preparing to receive a royal delegation that has just arrived from Egypt. It is my regret to inform you that the sympathies of the majority of my advisors are with Egypt. I fear a palace conspiracy or anarchy if I oppose them. Thus I have permitted the alliance."

"Is Nebuchadnezzar aware of this?" BelkA asked.

"Shall we say that no envoy has been sent? Rather than send you back to Nebuchadnezzar with a negative message, and because I have concern for your safety, I have chosen to keep you here in Jerusalem."

"I see," BelkA said. "I am grateful for your concern about my safety."

A forced smile appeared on the king's face that quickly faded. "I must request that you remain within the city walls and in the house I have provided for you."

"In other words I am under house arrest."

"I regret the circumstances." The king looked around the room and his eyes rested for a moment on Ebed-Melech who stood straight and tall like a statue. "I have appointed Ebed-Melech in charge of your safety. Your dwelling will, of course, be under surveillance, and your needs will be provided daily. Did I make myself clear?"

"Very clear, your majesty. I was just wondering if there was a time frame with regard to my presence in Jerusalem?"

"Not presently. All further communication will come through my official, Ebed-Melech. I will thus dismiss you into his hands."

BelkA bowed, and followed Ebed-Melech to join Parto at the door. From there the three remained silent until they reached the courtyard. There Ebed-Melech invited BelkA and Parto to sit down on a stone bench in a secluded spot. With a grave voice he said, "The dye is cast. There is nothing I can do or say to change the king's mind. He fears his advisors more than he fears Yahweh. He's stalling and using you as a hostage."

"As a hostage?"

Ebed-Melech nodded.

"I'm sorry that you must bear the risk of our safety," BelkA said.

"Please don't feel that way. It's a relief for me to have charge over you myself. King Zedekiah has at least done one good thing. I would not want to think how dangerous your situation could be were some of the other characters at court given that responsibility. From the king's vantage point he wants you alive so he can use you later. The others—apart from Shaphan's son and grandson—don't care."

"Were it not for the prayers of the faithful we would be in grave trouble," Parto said.

Ebed-Melech nodded affirmation.

Hesitatingly BelkA said, "Hearing this, causes me great concern in making a daring request of you."

"Speak on."

"It's important that I meet together with those who are preparing to help me in fulfilling Daniel's assignment. Arrangements have been made to come together at a cave in the Jordan Valley as soon as possible."

Ebed-Melech wrinkled his brow and frowned, but refrained from speaking. Finally he asked, "How long would you be gone?"

"Four days," BelkA said looking squarely into the courtier's face. "It's the only way I can begin to carry out Daniel's request. I can promise you that you need not fear that I would try to escape."

"You are an honorable man I know, but you do realize that my life is on the line."

"I do." BelkA said.

Ebed-Melech was silent for a long moment. Finally he said, "It's a risk for all of us, but there's one thing in our favor. Presently the court is preoccupied with the Egyptian dignitaries, so you won't be of primary concern. Should the king hear of this I'll do all I can to convince him that he has no cause to fear your escape; I'll have the two servers keeping watch over you from a discrete distance, and I myself will personally escort you into the city upon your return."

"The servers are trustworthy to that point?" BelkA asked.

"Absolutely. Just remember that their safety also depends on yours."

"I do not take lightly the enormity of your generosity and trust."

Ebed-Melech got up and with downcast eyes said, "I shall await you outside the east gate before sundown on the evening of the fourth day." Then he turned back toward the palace with rapid steps.

Upon mounting their camels they'd gone but a short distance when a reckless rider on a horse caught up with them and passed at a rapid gallop, coming within inches of grazing their camels.

"Crazy young fellow," Parto exclaimed.

As the rider was about to round a turn and disappear out of sight, he suddenly slowed to a trot and signaled to them.

The two men burst into laughter upon recognizing their associate Mahla.

She in turn cautioned by putting her finger to her lips, "Arif and family are awaiting me at the crossroads of the Jericho road. I'll travel in their company. Helem will be waiting for you at Amineh's hideout."

"Fine" BelkA agreed explaining also that they would follow at a discrete distance as soon as the two servers required by Ebed-Melech arrived.

Chapter 29

RAstin's Dilemma

Jericho Valley, October 589 B.C.

With a scream of terror RAstin twisted and convulsed on his mat. In his nightmare he saw himself dangling from a pillar, in the eyes of all Jerusalem, while two children lay wounded and bleeding at his feet.

"What's going on," Tahampton called shaking him awake.

RAstin threw aside his blanket and sprang to his feet. Holding his head in his hands he shuddered, "A bad dream I guess. I'm going outside to calm myself,"

"You've been jittery since Aleppo. It's time to get hold of yourself man. You won't be of much use to us this way."

RAstin answered by throwing a cloak over his head and rushing out of the room.

When he reached the courtyard he stretched and let the memory of the evening's conversation run through his mind. The group had not only lost track of BelkA, but were now broke and driven by desperation. Here he was caught in the middle of a kidnapping plot aimed at innocent children. What could this lead to? How could he ever get himself out? If only he'd been satisfied with the modest income produced by his sculptures back in Babylon.

He stood under a tree and looked up into the heavenly bodies. "Oh Marduk-Bel, and all the gods of the starry host, help me now. I desperately need you, and I promise I'll do whatever you want if you just get me out of this fix? And if nothing else, just let me die."

Pacing back and forth and already shivering from strained nerves, an even more terrifying possibility struck him. What if Marduk were angry with him? Or, what if Marduk didn't exist? Or for that matter, any of the gods. Then what?

Laying face down in the dust his desperate mind suggested he might as well try the one-God that had come up in a recent discussion. It seemed preposterous, especially since most of what he'd heard about Him was mockery, but at this point, what did he have to loose. Pushing himself into a kneeling position he lifted his head and called out, "Yahweh, God of the Hebrews, if you exist, and if Arif's children are of any concern to you, and if you get me out of this situation, I'll believe in you."

But as his concern for the children kept weighing upon him he lowered his head to the ground.

"Yahweh, I don't know you, and you probably don't care about me, but I'll accept death if you'll only help me to save these children."

Chapter 30

Mahla

Jordan Valley, October 589 B.C.

As Mahla journeyed with Arif's family toward Amineh's hideout she noticed restlessness in the children as they kept complaining of thirst and discomfort. Finally she suggested to the parents, "How about taking a break? A little exercise and a short nap could make a big difference in the rest of the day that yet promises to be long for them. In fact, I could go on ahead to reassure the others on your account."

"You're sure it's safe for you Mahla?" Tirza asked.

"Have no care. If anything should come up, I'll know that you'll be following close behind."

After continuing a couple of miles she began to have some afterthoughts, realizing that she'd spoken carelessly. She knew all too well that danger lurked

everywhere. One could never be without fear of
bandits or wild animals in such places. So she kept
a slow but steady pace with eyes and ears alert to
every sound or hint of a shadow. At present the only
movement seemed to come from a frantic shepherd
chasing after some scattered sheep. When she came
to within sight of the dense foliage surrounding
Amineh's shack, she decided to stop and wait there
for Arif's family to catch up, so that they could join
up with Amineh and the others together.

Perching herself on a massive rock, and while
scanning the countryside that had already experienced the bite of winter, she satisfied her thirst with
sips from a sheepskin bag and munched on some
rations of dried fruit and nuts. The stillness eased
her mind into a reverie that brought BelkA onto the
scene.

The fact that her father had dared to suggest marriage with a man of his standing was absurd. But oh!
If only she could control those crazy feelings she felt
towards him. Now she realized that as far as Helem
was concerned, their relationship had been nothing
more than an open-ended arrangement. He had been
unwilling to show disrespect for her father, and she
had felt little more than an obligation toward a kindly
friend. Now, surprisingly, a sense of freedom and
relief enveloped her, and somehow she knew that
Helem felt the same.

Distracted as she was, she failed to see a man
creeping up behind the rock, and by the time she
noticed him he'd already fallen upon her. In a rush
of adrenaline she managed to free a hand and was

reaching for her knife when the attacker once again managed to pin both her hands against her body.

Paralyzed with fear Mahla stared into the face of her captor. "Who are you?" she finally managed to say.

"I'll tell you if you stop resisting. It's important that you listen. The safety of Arif's children depends upon it."

Her mouth fell open.

"My name is RAstin. I'm one of the group that Adda-Guppi sent to prevent BelkA from getting the sacred Writings."

"Thus you are my enemy."

"You have reason to see me as that, though I'm not in sympathy with my group that is indeed your enemy. I'm even now risking my life to try to get you to help me rescue the children who've already been seized."

"Arif's children? Why?"

"Because they mean a lot to BelkA, and because their father is a traitor in their eyes. Besides that they need money."

"What do you and your group know about Arif?"

"Maybe everything, maybe little. Time will tell."

"So what do you want me to do?"

"Follow me."

Chapter 31

The Second Cave

Jordan Valley, October 589 B.C.

U pon arriving at Amineh's dwelling, BelkA and Parto found only Helem and three mules with Jordan River mud on their hocks. "Ibzan and Azek want us to meet up with them at the new cave they've discovered," Helem explained. "The others, apart from Mahla and Arif's family, are already there. As soon as they arrive I'll lead all of you up."

"Wait a minute," BelkA said with a frown, "are you saying that Mahla and Arif's family have not yet arrived?"

Helem shook his head, "No."

"That's strange. They left ahead of us."

"I hope they're all right. But here's Ibzan and Azek coming now," He pointed in the direction of a water-course where a pair of mules were now approaching. "Perhaps they'll know something. Meanwhile I suggest we exchange your animals because camels just won't make it up the incline. If you'll follow me I'll lead you to a place where we may tether them."

Helem led BelkA and Parto down a path through a tangle of brush and thorny shrubs to a makeshift shed engulfed in vines where jugs of water had been thoughtfully placed in readiness for drinking.

When the brothers arrived BelkA greeted them warmly, but lost no time inquiring about Arif's family and Mahla.

The young fellows immediately jumped down from their mules and started looking around for footprints. "Look here," Ibzan exclaimed.

"Those are footprints of two others," BelkA said motioning for the two servers to come out from behind Amineh's house. He introduced them and explained the arrangement with Ebed-Melech. "These fellows will be watching out for me from here below. As for Mahla and Arif's family, we're going to have to go back and look for them."

"There's a lookout at the halfway point of the climb where one can view the entire plain below," Helem said. "I suggest we take a look."

"A good idea," BelkA said. "Azek and Ibzan would you mind staying below with the servers just in case they show up, and also to provide added surveillance?"

BelkA and Parto mounted the mules and followed Helem on a rough path that wound through a watercourse for a time, before climbing precipitously, till it reached a plateau.

"This is the halfway point," Helem said.

Each stood and searched the horizon in every direction for signs of movement.

Parto was the first to catch sight of flying dust down on the plain. "See those two clouds of dust. They're from two horses and they're heading back in the direction of Jericho. I have a feeling that one of them is Mahla's."

BelkA turned, held his hand over his eyes, and squinted through his fingers. "I'm not sure, but I think I see blue on the one rider. I know that Mahla was wearing blue so it has to be her. Something is definitely not right."

"We must go to them immediately," Helem said.

"I'm wondering," Parto said cautiously and while keeping his eyes in the distance, "if perhaps this is not a trap for you BelkA." Then he lifted his eyes to his master.

"You could be right. We must think carefully before we act. Let us return to Azek and Ibzan and find out if they've seen something. Then we'll decide what to do."

Climbing back down went slower than going up, but by following their guide in every step they made record time reaching the bottom, and from there they continued to Amineh's shack where the brothers assured them that they'd seen nothing.

"How would you two like to scout it out?" BelkA asked.

The two were only too eager, and were about to get their horses when BelkA called them back. "Wait fellows. Let's go over a plan. Since there's been little wind the last few hours the hoof prints should be easy enough to follow. That at least is in our favor. Now, what do you have in the way of weapons?"

"We have sling shots and bows and arrows?" Azek replied.

"Give each a small dagger Parto," BelkA ordered.

Parto pulled several from a bag and offered them a choice.

"Show them also a tactic for throwing off an attacking man."

Parto ducked and had Ibzan on the ground before he realized what was happening. Then he helped him up and demonstrated several holds and flips. "Success, of course, is dependant upon speed and surprise, but try it out on me."

"There's no time," BelkA said abruptly. "Get on your horses immediately."

Within minutes the boys were off.

"Now Helem, take us up to the cave," BelkA ordered. "We must inform the others."

Once again they climbed to the plateau where they stopped and watched for a time until the scouts came into view. No other movement appeared from any side.

Helem then led them to a fork where he took the right branch, which after a ways, became hardly more than a footpath. From then on it was very precipitous and in places almost a stairway. BelkA, not comfortable on heights, refrained from looking down and hardly dared to move while the mules slowly picked their way up the steep incline. Finally, after threading through a labyrinth of rocks, they arrived at a natural tunnel.

A series of torches lit the way into a small cave that eventually widened and became a cavern where animals were tied up. Here Helem stopped abruptly. "This is where we leave the mules." By continuing around the corner they entered the entrance to a huge chamber where they were greeted with shouts of welcome.

The Blind Man of Damascus was the first to come upon BelkA as he entered, grabbing him with one arm and Parto with the other. "We were beginning to worry about you," he said. "And where are the others?"

"Alas," BelkA replied, "we don't know!"

"You don't know?" Blind Man winced while anxious wrinkles collected around his eyes. He lifted his hand for silence. "Please listen everyone," he called. "BelkA has some important information to convey,"

"As of now we do not know the whereabouts of Arif, Tirza and the two children as well as Mahla," BelkA announced. "They failed to appear at the agreed-upon meeting place of Amineh's home. The two brothers, Ibzan and Azek, are even now attempting to find their whereabouts. Other than that we only know that we saw two riders galloping across the plateau. We think one of them was Mahla."

A heavy silence fell upon the group.

"It's my opinion that there's a plot to get at you," Blind Man said. "You are, after all, the key man in this matter of the Writings; thus it seems to me that you must be careful. Perhaps you should just stay here?"

"I can't do that."

"Well at least let the others take the lead while you keep a safe distance."

"I'll agree to that."

"Just give me time to quickly prepare some food," Amineh said in a soothing tone. "You'll be needing it."

As they sat down Blind Man introduced Elzur, his wife Arielle and daughter Tamara. "They've agreed to join us in our efforts."

BelkA acknowledged them with a nod and a smile of relief as Amineh came almost immediately with a basket heaped to the top. "Eat this when you have a chance." she said.

"Let's go," BelkA said to Parto and Helem.

Chapter 32

Kidnapped

Jordan Valley-Jericho, October 589 B.C.

Once more BelkA faced the one thing that bothered him most—the perilous precipice. The ascent was bad enough, how would he handle the descent? If only he had the same calm boldness others in the party seemed to have. His glance swept through the group lining up to descend. There wasn't a jittery fellow among them, not even older Elzur.

When his turn came to proceed Parto caught his eye and suggested going first. BelkA willingly made way for him. Then with whitened knuckles he held tightly onto the reigns of the mule while keeping his eyes solely on the path and the hoofs before him. The fact that Parto understood provided reassurance, and a hint of confidence.

Upon arriving at the midway plateau, they stopped briefly as before to view the horizon that now lay hazy but still. Then losing no further time they continued down to the lower plateau where hoof prints clearly led in the direction of Jericho.

"Let's trade the mules in for camels," BelkA suggested.

"The seven of us on two camels?" Helem objected.

"It won't be like riding in a chariot," BelkA admitted, "but we'll move faster than these fat mules. Time is of essence."

Helem conceded.

Parto took over the task of preparing the camels who were none too pleased to end their lazy comfort. With gentle coaxing and some tasty morsels of Amineh's food the animals finally complied, and once in movement, they picked up a racing speed as if sensing the urgency. Miles flew under the wide strides proving that the time lost in exchanging animals had been to their advantage.

Arriving on the outskirts of Jericho BelkA now signaled to Parto with his hand to slow down to a stop. "We need a plan of action. It's my opinion that one person should go on ahead to survey the city."

The group looked around at each other. "I'll volunteer," Elzur offered. "In my attire, and the hour being advanced, I'll appear as a farmer returning from the fields."

"Sounds reasonable," BelkA agreed. "Do you have a weapon?"

Elzur shook his head. "I wouldn't know how to use one."

"Give him a weapon Parto."

Parto immediately opened the bag and displayed its contents.

BelkA pulled out a dagger and handed it to Elzur. "I think you'll know how to use it if the need arises. We'll be in the orchard just behind that last vineyard ahead. Report back to us as soon as you can."

With a rapid pace Elzur walked toward the town and, just as he hoped, he joined some farmers who were returning from their fields and entering the gates. From there he made his way cautiously to the central square and looked around before choosing a side street. He'd walked only a short distance when he sighted a group of young fellows rounding a corner and was now approaching. Quickly he ducked under an arch leading to a stable and waited for them to pass. Coming out from hiding he bumped into two young men hurrying in the same direction. He was about to apologize when he realized they were the scouts, Azek and Ibzan.

"Sh-h-h," Azek said as he in turn recognized Elzur. Grabbing his arm he pulled him with them into an ally. "We just saw Mahla turn in here with a mystery man."

"Look, there she is," Ibzan cautioned. "She's approaching the inn that backs onto this ally. Let's be careful not to startle her."

After inching forward a ways Azek called softly, "Mahla."

Mahla whirled around, but in her movement managed both to acknowledge them and show relief. With one hand she beckoned for them to approach while with the other she cautioned silence.

"This young man is with us, I'll explain later," she whispered. "He has a key and in a moment or two he'll open the door, and I'll plunge in and throw my knife. Hopefully I'll do no more than frighten the men inside. You must back me up and attack in the best way you can. Do you have weapons?"

Ibzan nodded affirmatively.

"Try to incapacitate them. Look he's putting the key in the hole now. Stand back."

A few seconds later the door opened and Mahla flew in and hurled her knife with all her strength. It whirred through the air and struck the wall just above a man's head with a dizzying thud.

While the occupants inside were still dazed the three dashed in. Ibzan pulled out the carpet heavily laden with food and threw it over the head of one man, while Azek grabbed at a broom and shoved the kidnapper on the floor none to gently. A scuffle followed that ended with the thug becoming unconscious. By then Elzur had a third against the wall with a dagger poised before his face while RAstin flung himself on the first man who was trying to escape. Within a few moments the three adversaries were lying on the floor. Mahla noticing this yanked off her veil and wrapped it around the feet of one, and then took the scarf from around her waste and tied up the feet of the other. Following her example RAstin pulled out a rope from his own belt and took care of the last one.

"You little traitor," said Tahampton sneering up at him. "Just wait. This will cost you."

"Capturing children is not a game I play," shot back RAstin. "If you'd listened to me before, this wouldn't have happened. Do with me what you will; the children are going back to their parents. Now where are they?"

Elzur accommodated by approaching and placing the dagger inches from the man's eye.

"The next room," came the reply.

"Use your headpiece to gag the man, and find a way to do the same to the others," RAstin ordered of Elzur as he backed out.

Mahla then joined RAstin in the first room on the west side. There a stout woman sat trembling with the terrified children. Her head was heavily veiled and there were no less than twelve bangles on each of her bare arms. "You scream and you'll have a knife in your back," Mahla warned.

The woman fell on her knees. "Mercy, mercy! I have nothing to do with this."

"I know who you are. You'll do anything for money. Get out and go as far away as you can," RAstin said. "If we find you, you'll not live to tell about it."

The woman got up and scurried out the door.

Mahla made a dash for the children, and then took a brief moment to reassure them.

"Come with me" she whispered. "We've got to get out before the thugs manage to free themselves and follow us."

"By now the gates are locked," RAstin said when they reached the others, "but follow me, I know a place where we can squeeze through."

"I want Mother," Sussan began to cry.

"I know you do," Mahla whispered, "but first we have to get you out of here, so be brave and don't make any noise."

"I think I know where to find them," RAstin was saying. "I saw them checking into an inn on the south side of the city. It seems to me that they intended to use it as a base from which to search for the children. If you want to risk the time I'll take you to it?"

"Let's go," Elzur said.

RAstin led them through side streets and stopped in front of an inn. "Should we ask the owners or should we check around the back?"

"Check the back," Mahla shot back.

They rounded the side and crawled along listening at the windows. All of a sudden Suzann called, "Mother."

Mahla reached out and put her hand over the child's mouth just as a form came to the window. Relinquishing the children to the care of Ibzan and Azek, she edged up to the window and recognized Arif. Following a gentle knock on the windowsill she called softly, "Arif."

Arif put his head out, and at the sight of Mahla, he was about to exclaim when he caught himself. "Quick," Mahla whispered. "We have the children. Hand over your belongings and help Tirza to climb out. Hurry."

After passing over their bags Arif made a step with his hands and helped Tirza to climb out." Our horses are tied in front," he said. "Let's get them."

In little time the operation was over, and the relieved parents were allowed to embrace their frightened children a few brief and silent seconds before they were urged to follow toward the wall. "Tread softly with each step you take," RAstin cautioned.

They reached a section of the wall where some repairs were being made, and where RAstin, helped by the scouts, moved enough rocks and debris to permit the rest to find a stepping. Shoving and pulling on the horses followed until all came through the opposite side. Smiles and exclamations of relief began to break out, but RAstin silenced them once again.

Elzur pointed ahead, "They're waiting for us on the other side of the orchard," he whispered. "Since it's a dark night, you'll need to follow me very closely and not a word until we reach the others."

Arif and Tirza silently mounted the horses each behind a child, and followed the rest, headed up by Elzur as he led them on a fast trot till they reached BelkA and Parto. Then celebrating began.

BelkA grabbed Sussan pulling her off the horse, and Parto did the same for SabA, while Elzur, Nethaniah and Helem stood with grins from ear to ear.

Mahla then introduced RAstin who had led the operation. But before the group could applause she added, "He was one of Adda-Guppi's spies who has turned against the band."

The group sobered and looked silently upon him as if waiting an explanation.

With eyes down RAstin began, "I was bored in Babylon when I learned of Adda-Guppi's offer of adventure. At first it seemed like a gift from the gods, but I soon began to have misgivings. At the campsite of Aleppo one evening I was at the point of breaking. I went to Arif's tent hoping to talk it over with him when I noticed that I was being watched."

Looking suspiciously at RAstin BelkA asked "What was the purpose and what was your part in the attack on my servant Parto?"

RAstin stood trembling but determined. "The two fellows, Ghadir and KaVey, were truly treacherous men. The idea of sabotaging your mission was to their liking, but they didn't want to wait to complete the whole assignment. They wanted especially the gold, and knew that without it you'd be blocked anyway. The other three and myself tried to restrain them because we know full well that Adda-Guppi has a way of eliminating people who cross her, but they chose to go ahead with their own plans and believed that they could get away with it."

"So RAstin, it would appear that they wanted to sabotage my mission, steal my gold, and kill me and my slave as well?"

"It was the goal for which Adda-Guppi hired us."

"So she was acting as a traitor against King Nebuchadnezzar?"

"Add-Guppi has a many-sided agenda my lord."

"Does she? Explain."

"She pretends allegiance to Marduk, but she's passionately devoted to the moon god Sin. She makes frequent trips to Haran and it is whispered about that if she could, she would replace Marduk with Sin as Babylon's titular god. She also has a fierce hatred for Daniel and his God, and claims that you are influenced by Him. In her mind this is reason enough to eliminate you, or at the least, to sabotage your mission."

RAstin shivered but held pleading eyes on BelkA, then he lowered them as he continued with determination, "Some of us have heard or feel within us that she is trying to eradicate any and every competitor that might hinder her son from rising to power. She claims even that her only son has been called to succeed Nebuchadnezzar and to bring in *her* god." As if expecting a blow he lowered his whole head.

"Look up," BelkA ordered.

When RAstin obeyed BelkA said in a more gentle tone, "What you say confirms what Arif has already told me, and what I know about Adda-Guppi from my own sources. What I need to know is are you truly and sincerely with *us* now?"

"Yes my lord, I give you my word. When the gang leader came up with a plan to make away with the children, I knew I had to do something drastic to oppose them. Then when the group pounced on the children as they were taking a nap, I turned my horse around and raced after Mahla. And you know the rest. From now on, no matter what happens, I want nothing more to do with the group."

Arif put his hand on RAstin's shoulder. "By doing that you saved my children, please accept my sincere gratitude."

"I truly regret my involvement with Adda-Guppi."

"That makes two of us," Arif said.

"What do you plan to do now?" BelkA asked

"I don't know. I'm without friends and resources."

"For the moment come with us," BelkA said. "Later I'll give you some money to hide out in Jerusalem near us, because I'm sure that if the other three find you, they'll eliminate you."

RAstin bowed low. "I am most grateful my lord. I will do as you say."

Parto went to his camel and brought back the big bag of food. "This is from Amineh," he said pulling out large slices of bread and meat. "It would seem that she had faith that this rescue operation would be successful, and that we would all be very hungry."

Adults and children alike dived into the food like ravenous goats.

"What do you make of this incident?" Parto asked BelkA as they traveled back to the cave.

"I'm beginning to see light?" BelkA replied. "Your God seems to be watching out for us."

Parto smiled at the remark but continued intently, "What I don't understand is the matter of the gold. Did Adda-Guppi actually think she'd get her hands on your gold?"

BelkA chuckled. "Good thinking. My guess is that she expected all but one or two to survive, and even if they did run off with the gold, she'd have no further cost connected with them."

"So her scheme would have cost her little."

"Exactly."

At that point Arif motioned to BelkA and strolled a distance from the group to speak with him privately, "My pigeons have just come back from Babylon, my lord, with two messages. Here's one from your mother, the other read simply, 'Nebuchadnezzar's army is marching.'"

BelkA gasped.

"What do you make of this?"

"It would appear that time is running out, but let's try to remain calm and think clearly. Presently what we all need is to soak up some rest. Let's not say anything tonight."

•••

"What have we here?" It was the innkeeper's exclamation upon finding the men bound and gagged. "Can't one be absent for some personal matters without coming back to a disaster? You Babylonians are worse than the Egyptians. I want you out. I don't care what happened."

The three fellows, still confused and recovering from head pain derived from blows and the shuffle, decided in unison to get their animals and leave. But they hadn't gone far when thoughts of retaliation enflamed their passions.

Chapter 33

Impending War

JordanValley, October 589 B.C.

The first rays of light broke on the horizon as BelkA faced once more the dreadful trek up the mountain, though this time with a little more confidence in the sturdy old mule he'd recovered, but especially animated with a sense of triumphant wonderment toward Yahweh. Upon reaching the upper plateau the smell of smoke and slow-cooking soup heightened anticipation.

Barely on top of the ascent, and before he had a chance to dismount, Blind Man rushed to his side and grabbed him, "My son," he cried reaching for BelkA's hands. By then it was discovered that Arif and Tirza and their two young ones were with the group. This incited ever-increasing shouts of joy that echoed through the cavern.

In no time Mahla had also fallen into the arms of Blind Man. "My daughter, my brave one, you are safe," he exclaimed as his hands searched her face, and his head tilted upward in a prayer of gratitude and exclamation, "Oh merciful Yahweh I bless you, I thank you, I exalt you. My children are safe." Then he beckoned to BelkA, "Come now, you must tell us all about it."

Meanwhile Amineh had Sussan and SabA beside her on the ground where she was examining their white faces shadowed with the effect of trauma and fatigue. She then stood up and took the children by the hand while also addressing the parents, "Follow me," she said. The parents meekly obeyed as she led them to a quiet inner shelter of rock where bedding was laid out upon layers of dried reeds and straw, and where also a basin of water sat in readiness for washing. "I'll be back shortly with some soup," she said as she turned and disappeared.

Upon arriving in the central cave Amineh drew Mahla into her arms, and after a brief embrace said, "Come with me. I have a comfortable little alcove for you."

Mahla smiled. "Amineh dear. You have worked hard to make ready for us. Let me first help you finish up your chores. I'm too excited to rest just now anyway."

Amineh laughed. "You're impossible Mahla."

"I know, I'm a lot like you."

Amineh shook her head, "You can help Heleh...." But before she finished the sentence Mahla was already taking bowls of steaming hot leak soup to the group gathered around BelkA, who was reporting on the rescue.

When all was told and questions answered satisfactorily BelkA said. "Now noble friends I suggest rest. Tomorrow holds more challenges for us all. Does everyone know the sleeping arrangements?"

"I believe Amineh has everything organized," Mahla said, then seeing her friend approaching she added, "and here she is."

"There should be a sleep corner for everyone so please line up behind me and I'll lead you through the maze and drop you off along the way."

"Who is the young woman with the little girl?" BelkA asked in passing.

"With all the excitement I haven't had a chance to introduce you. Her name is Heleh, and her daughter's name is Biddel. Tomorrow I'll explain."

BelkA nodded and gratefully retired when Amineh pointed to a prepared niche.

•••

Rising early Blind Man and BelkA seated themselves on a blanket by the fire, where Amineh had busied herself in preparing her special flat bread for breakfast. For a moment BelkA's mind drifted to the next problem on the horizon, but jumped upon realizing that Blind Man was addressing him.

"I sense tension within you friend," Blind Man was saying. "Is there something you need to tell me?"

"There you are again Blind Man, seeing right inside of me. In fact, there is something I have just learned that I must announce to everyone. Would you mind if I refrain from speaking of it now?"

"Of course," Blind Man replied as he pulled out from his girdle a piece of papyrus with an outlined plan for the day that his wife had written, and that he now handed to BelkA. He'd barely finished explaining the main points when little by little the group came together around them, and gratefully devoured the stacks of flat bread and honey.

When Mahla and Amineh had collected all the plates Blind Man announced that a meeting was about to commence and that all should try to seat themselves as comfortably as possible.

After a brief shuffle Blind Man began, "Time is short and there's much to discuss, but first let's make sure we all know each other. I'll let you take charge BelkA."

BelkA's eyes rested upon Heleh who sat holding the hand of her daughter. Then he turned to Amineh sitting beside the two and said, "Tell us please about your friends."

"Heleh and her daughter Biddel are former residents of Jerusalem. Heleh's husband, and the father of Biddel, had been an elder and one of the judges that sat in the city gate, thus a rather prominent citizen. But unlike many of his associates, he refused to join clicks or accept bribes. Consequently he acquired enemies who tried to eliminate him by inventing tall tales about him that, thankfully, they were unable to prove. Unsuccessful in their more subtle schemes, they chose a more direct method of revenge. One evening after he'd stood up against his fellow townsmen by defending Jeremiah, he was walking home when he was attacked with clubs and left unconscious. When he failed to return to his home that evening Heleh and Biddel went out looking for him, and found him laying in a coma on the street. They managed to drag the poor man home, but he died the next day.

"Heleh succeeded in keeping her small olive oil business going for a time but creditors soon began harassing her, and making threats that escalated by the day. There was one among them—an evil man— who threatened to take Biddel as his slave and to have Heleh imprisoned. Mahla sneaked them both out of the city, and the twins brought them to me. We've had many conversations and I trust them completely. They are, of course, of the faithful remnant that worships Yahweh at the exclusion of all other gods, and they too await the coming Messiah. Since they're eager to help, I recommend that we consider them members of our group."

BelkA deferred to Blind Man who opened his hands as the group nodded. "Beyond a doubt we are unanimously in favor," he said.

Meanwhile Heleh and Biddel, who had kept their eyes down while Amineh spoke, fell on their knees and expressed gratitude.

BelkA, still affected by the story, cleared his throat and proceeded with the session by introducing other new members: RAstin whom Arif had already introduced to several, Giddel the basket weaver, his daughter Hodesh, and Nethaniah the potter.

"Thank you," Blind Man said taking over. "Alas, if only we could just relax and enjoy one another."

"I need to tell you that I'm turning over the leadership to BelkA. My wife, who was unable to accompany me, and myself regret that our activities in Damascus prevent us from being able to help you directly, but our prayers rise constantly for you. I urge you to assist BelkA in every way you can."

BelkA, feeling cramped and needing to exercise his legs, stood up and called for a short walk to take in some fresh air before continuing. When they returned he explained the arrangements made with Jeremiah and Shaphan for the copying of the Writings, including the possible delays it would entail. "This complicates my mission as I will have to wait for them to finish that task. There's something else that I've been turning over in my mind," he added hesitatingly. "While I'm unable to assist with the copying in Hebrew, I am proficient in Akkadian and Aramaic."

Blind Man gasped. "What is it? " BelkA asked concerned.

"It's just that I think I know what you're about to say, and I feel like a child unable to hide my excitement. But please go on."

"I was about to say that I've thought of translating the Writings into Aramaic."

"I knew it," Blind Man exploded with tears falling from his eyes. "I've been praying for this for a long time and can hardly believe what I'm hearing."

BelkA and Arif looked at each other.

"Thank you Blind Man for that affirmation. It touches me profoundly and increases my commitment to the task. Since presently I am under house arrest, I might as well use the time to do this."

"I hadn't heard you were under house arrest, BelkA," Blind Man said. "How is it that you were able to come?"

"There are two young fellows who have been appointed by Ebed-Melech to observe my movements. Even now as we speak they are at Amineh's dwelling watching for any intruder. Ebed-Melech is a believer in Yahweh and so are the two fellows. As a precaution, in case of betrayal, they've been forbidden to converse with us. They will be on duty until my safe return to Jerusalem."

"Good for them," Blind Man said.

BelkA continued assigning tasks to each one and then he cleared his throat once more and said, "I have been informed through messages that have arrived from Babylon by way of Arif's pigeons that something momentous is about to happen. I wish I could have prepared you, but I find no better way than to tell you simply that Nebuchadnezzar's army is marching."

The announcement sliced through the comfortable atmosphere like lightening. Stunned and frightened eyes focused upon BelkA.

"This means war," BelkA said. "I estimate that it'll take the army approximately three months to reach Jerusalem. Obviously my present mission for Nebuchadnezzar is over. My primary concern now is for the scrolls. Meanwhile we need to prepare for survival because siege means famine and plague. Food must be stockpiled and remedies prepared."

When BelkA paused a moment to catch his breath whispering broke out amongst the terrified group.

"Children, children," Blind Man called out, "We must look to Yahweh. This is part of His plan."

BelkA interjected, "I delayed making this announcement because I anticipated that we might all be paralyzed with fear and unable to think clearly."

Elzur suggested his daughter quote an appropriate passage she had recently learned.

BelkA said, "Please say it for us Tamara."

Tamara's spoke out in a melodious voice, "'I the LORD will bring the blind by a way they knew not; I will lead them in paths they have not known: I will make darkness light before them, and crooked things straight. These things will I do... and not forsake them.'"

The Blind Man stood transfixed and moved. "Thank you Tamara, a most appropriate passage for a group calling themselves, *The Lamp Connection*." Lifting his hand he quoted the blessing, "May Yahweh 'bless thee and keep thee ... make his face to shine upon thee ...lift up his countenance upon thee, ...and give thee peace.'"

Chapter 34

Ebed-Melech

Jerusalem, October 589 B.C.

E bed-Melech sat under the generous shade of the olive trees that seemed to thrive on the mound overlooking Jerusalem, causing some to refer to it as Mount Olivet. For several years now it had provided him a quiet, renewing shelter from the clamor of the town, and especially the frictions at court.

Though grateful for his position as courtier, the whole situation often drove him to despondency. Most of the court officials, driven by power and their own agendas, repeatedly drowned out any and every voice calling for reason and redress, and now the flattering politicians were finishing up the downslide with promises they'd never keep no matter what.

He'd learned, of course, the art of perfect control, as men in his position must, yet deep inside he groaned. If only King Zedekiah would be courageous enough to stand up for what was right and just. At times one could perceive in him a hint of conscience, even requesting counsel of Jeremiah, but when approached by his arrogant officials who knew exactly how to pull him their way, or who threatened by force of power and threats, he usually caved in. What could one yet hope for?

Here, on his favorite spot, he felt removed and at peace. Now as always he breathed in the luxurious air of tranquility that seemed to emanate from the generous trees. The gloomy clouds—normal for the time of the year—were allowing the sun a last piercing streak of glowing orange and mauve. It calmed his soul, and at the same time quickened his pulse as if announcing a violent outburst on the horizon.

He'd come early this afternoon to the spot that he also knew would permit a vantage point for the sighting of BelkA Souash who was scheduled to return from the area of the Dead Sea before the locking of the gates. Now the sun was waning, and his eye kept searching the road below that still appeared deserted of man and beast.

The ugly thought of what might happen should BelkA fail to keep his promise now crossed his mind, and with it a shudder raked his body. He had his own enemies, always waiting to catch him at some misdemeanor as a pretext to usurp his position. He'd risked his life by allowing BelkA these extra days of freedom, and the last hour before the closing of the gates was fast approaching.

As the sun lowered, almost to the horizon, he attempted to come up with a strategy. Should he inquire of the gatekeeper? No, Urijah was on duty. He would only welcome the opportunity to impose his authority, and even make trouble. He decided to mount his horse and make a little jog.

He'd barely settled into his saddle blanket when he saw a cloud of dust from a group of horses in the valley below. Prodding his animal forward in that direction he soon saw an odd assortment of strangers he could not identify. Reaching a fork of the road he turned around, and was about to make a dash back for the city, when he decided to pause and seek guidance from his God.

Slowing his horse to a trot he focused his thoughts upon urgent prayer. Meanwhile the men overtook him and as they passed he nodded a greeting. They had distanced themselves from him only slightly when he overheard them conversing in Aramaic and in a manner that aroused his curiosity.

"They must have gone around the west side," one of them was saying. "Let's angle round that way."

"Come on fellows," a second said. "I'm tired. Our last escapade was enough for me."

"For me too," said a third, "even if you do see them, what then do you plan to do? Let's turn here toward Bethlehem's inn and devise another plan for tomorrow."

"The two of you go on then. I'm going to discover his whereabouts."

Ebed-Melech turned around and noticed that one of them had taken the fork toward the west side of the city.

"Ah Yahweh," he breathed in gratitude, "Thank you for showing me what to do at this particular junction." Shoving his heals into his horse he made a dash toward the east gate, where he dared not shirk on the prescribed protocol for fear of arousing suspicion, but once inside the city he made a straight and hasty trot toward the west gate. To his utmost relief there came BelkA, Parto, the scouts, the two servers and yet another. As they approached the wall he began to circle round to avoid the east gate. Hurrying after them he called without formality, "Follow me."

BelkA looked up startled, but without a moment's hesitation rounded his camel and followed with the others close behind.

Refraining from even looking back until they had turned a corner and were completely out of the guard-view from the west gate, Ebed-Melech finally relaxed his commanding demeanor, turned around and smiled.

"Excuse my tardiness honored one," BelkA began...

"Think nothing of it BelkA. It's of no consequence. Please continue following me."

Upon reaching the wall enclosing the temple court they took side streets and alleys that twisted through modest neighborhoods until Ebed-Melech stopped under a sign that read, *Tovi's Inn*. Upon dismounting he said, "Allow me to offer you dinner. This is my favorite inn where the food is good and the owners are discrete."

"How thoughtful of you noble one," BelkA said, "but please allow me first to introduce you to our new friend RAstin. We'll explain more about him later."

After a nod of acknowledgment Ebed-Melech said, "It's been a stressful day for us all, so I thought a quiet dinner might help to calm us down." Once seated he added, "You might as well untie your sandals straight away because I've ordered that our feet be washed."

Parto's face took on a perplexed expression, while RAstin, Azek and Ibzan and the servers shifted their eyes downward. Ebed-Melech caught the expressions immediately, and added, "all of us."

BelkA gave the courtier a wink and a smile.

The others bowed to express their gratitude and amazement.

Having their dusty feet washed and massaged while they sat by the warmth of a crackling fire created a relaxed camaraderie, and also a boost to their moral.

"You had me worried there for a while," Ebed-Melech said explaining his nervousness.

"It troubles me not a little to know that we put you at risk," BelkA said.

"As for me, I'm embarrassed that you must be detained in Jerusalem. Things are so twisted these days."

"Has something happened since we're gone?"

"Not really, it's just that people are doing exactly the opposite of what Jeremiah advises." He was about to elaborate when the food arrived in abundance. Fish delicately prepared with trifles and garlic, followed by watercress greens and ending with honey cakes. The starving men ate with abandon. When the innkeeper came around to check on his guests Ebed-Melech introduced them.

BelkA, who was in the process of licking his sticky fingers, said, "Excuse my rudeness honorable Tovi."

The innkeeper ignored the comment. "What do you think of my cakes?"

"Delicious, the flavoring is rosemary I believe."

"Correct you are. It is not the usual date honey most have in these parts." He then leaned over as if to tell a secret, "I keep the bees also as a means of protection," and then he added in his formal voice, "I'm pleased you like my cakes."

"They're the best I've ever tasted," BelkA said.

When Tovi had left them BelkA asked, "What did he mean by the bees?"

"It's his way of keeping away the wrong kind; all he has to do is allow the bees to make the atmosphere unsettling."

"Now that's a novel idea," Parto said laughing, "but if it works, so much the better."

"Tovi's a good man," Ebed-Melech continued. "He and his family have deep faith, but now tell me of your meeting and about RAstin."

BelkA told of the kidnapping experience and RAstin's part in the rescue, causing the servers to gasp and sigh in relief. Then with a tremor in his voice he said, "I'm afraid I must give you also the alarming news that Nebuchadnezzar's army has set out from Babylon."

A look of horror and disbelief crossed the face of their guardian. "I wonder if the king knows," he gasped.

BelkA shrugged. "I couldn't say, but please know that we'll do everything we can to help you."

"I know you will," Ebed-Melech said taking on his usual stoic attitude. Smiling he added, "We must be quiet and confident in Yahweh. He won't forsake us. But now, I'm afraid I must see you to your house BelkA. But before we depart, might I assure you that if you need something, let the servers know by writing. They are, as you already know, forbidden to speak for your safety and theirs."

"Thus far we've managed quite well," BelkA said.

The servers grinned.

"They take it as a game," their boss explained. "Don't you love the sense of humor in these youth."

"We sure do," Parto agreed.

Ebed-Melech then turned to Azek and Ibzan, "By the way, where are you two staying?"

"At Bethlehem's inn," Azek replied.

"That's where the gang is staying," RAstin exclaimed.

Ebed-Melech frowned. "I'm not sure I like that. I suggest you transfer immediately to Tovi's inn."

"Then Arif's family should too," BelkA said with alarm in his voice.

"Allow me to take care of the arrangements," Ebed-Melech insisted and lost no time in signaling the innkeeper and asking about accommodations for the three fellows and also Arif's family.

"All I have left are two rooms on the roof," the innkeeper replied.

"With outside stairs leading to it?" BelkA asked.

"Exactly. What do you think?"

"We'll take them," Ebed-Melech stated. "You fellows might as well stay right here tonight and help Arif's family to move tomorrow."

"Agreed," the scouts said almost in unison.

"Well then, it appears that we must bid you good-night," he said reaching out his hands to the three. "You will be safe and well looked after."

"Thank you, thank you," the scouts said with RAstin joining and falling on his knees.

Ebed-Melech reached out his hands, "Thank you lads for all you're doing. I'm proud to know you. Have a good rest."

Chapter 35

The Break-In

Jerusalem, October 589 B.C.

Parto pushed back the shutters to discover sunshine streaming into the room. After a dreary week of rain, driving winds and menacing thunder, the warmth cheered him and provoked a sigh of relief, "Ah-h-h, a good wash day."

"While you do that I'm going to write a letter to Babylon," BelkA said with a tone of strong resolution.

"A pigeon delivery?"

"Of course. Is it not the most efficient and fastest we have?"

Parto nodded as he turned to the courtyard.

BelkA collected his writing materials and sat on a stool by the table. Picking up the triangular bottle of his favorite ink mix that had just the right balance of charcoal and lampblack, he shook it vigorously to make sure it was well blended. Then he began to write quickly and furiously as if needing to pour out his agitated feelings. When finished he sat back to read what he'd written and shook his head in dismay at the sharpness and exaggerated length. Never would it fit into a tiny pigeon canister. Abruptly he tore it to shreds and sat back to reflect, and also to seek guidance from the Almighty and true God. With a quietened heart he wrote.

"Honorable Mother,

I am concerned that you might be worrying about me. At present I am safe, though under house arrest. Since Nebuchadnezzar's army is fast approaching Jerusalem the future is unknown. We must prepare our hearts for any eventuality. I know this might sound strange to you, but I am finding in the Hebrew God Yahweh a sense of courage and comfort that I wish also for you. If I survive it will be thanks to Him.

Please greet chief gardener Bazy-An and his helper Shai for me.

Your devoted son,
BelkA"

By then a good portion of the day had passed but a burden had fallen from his shoulder. Though imperfectly stated, he'd conveyed the essential burden that had weighed heavily upon him for quite some time. After placing the message in Arif's pigeon box he sat and pondered, wondering if he should risk informing

King Nebuchadnezzar of his predicament. He finally decided that the risk of the message being discovered by the wrong person was too great. Besides, he'd probably already left Babylon.

Apart from food drop-offs there'd been no visitors for several days, no messengers and little diversion in the monotony of confinement, so he and Parto had begun wrestling to vent their pent-up energy. He was considering interrupting Parto's work with such recreation when he detected a flurry at the window.

Advancing cautiously to remain unseen from the outside he detected a figure in heavy dark clothes attempting to peer in. He hurried to the courtyard where Parto was stooped over the big tub of clothes and tapped his shoulder, "I think Mahla's out there, but stand watch, will you, while I look?"

Carefully he opened the door a crack and there in fact stood Mahla in her old woman's disguise. He grabbed her hand and pulled her in, yet keeping hold of her till they were past the courtyard and safely in the middle room. Then they looked at each other and burst into laughter.

"What is this?" BelkA teased. "Spying on us are you?"

"How about watching out for you?"

"The bell's out there."

"The house seemed somehow lifeless. I was curious."

"It was seeming that way to me as well. What's happening on the outside?"

"We're planning a break-in."

"You mean for the scrolls?"

"Of course."

"And when is this to happen?"

"Tonight."

"How?"

"I've come to discuss that," Mahla grinned as if conspiring a prank. "The challenging part will be to get past the guards and the people who come at night to do their secret rituals."

"And how do you intend to get into the suspected storeroom? Has someone found a key?"

"No, but I have a tool," she said as she dipped into her tunic and pulled out a tiny knife. "It works every time," she added with a smirk.

"Wait, I hear footsteps," Parto cautioned as he ran to the front door to call back almost immediately, "The food's here."

"Already? It's later in the day than I thought." BelkA grabbed Mahla once more by the hand and pulled her to the courtyard.

"What is this?" she protested. "It wouldn't hurt for them to know."

"Better play safe," he said.

Reluctantly she sat down and pulled some of the laundry over her head.

When BelkA returned to the central room he greeted the servers, and while they unpacked their baskets, he cut off a strip of papyrus and wrote a note with Ebed-Melech's name on the back and rolled it up. After sealing it he placed it on the corner of the table with the name visible.

Upon completing the task he noticed three place settings. He looked up at the servers and saw a smile on the face of the tallest. The two finished in silence, and like wooden soldiers, marched to the front door and let themselves out. BelkA was about to run after them with the note when he noticed that it had disappeared. "Parto did you see them pick up the scroll?"

"Actually I did not. The shorter of the two seemingly sucked it into the sleeve of his robe even as I watched. It was there, and then it was gone."

BelkA laughed. "Sounds like something Mahla would do."

"What was that you were saying?" Mahla asked from the door.

"Oh, Mahla, come on in. Your dinner has been laid out for you. Let's eat while it's hot and then we'll explain."

As they ate BelkA told about the note. "I have a feeling you know the trick Mahla."

"It's quite simple. A hint of distraction is all it takes to fool the most careful observer."

"We'll keep you in mind," BelkA said, "should such an act be required."

"How about trying it tonight?" Parto suggested.

BelkA looked at Parto with widening eyes. "You're onto something."

"First tell us what that note was about." Mahla said.

"I informed Ebed-Melech that we would be helping you with the break-in."

"Good. Shaphan and I were discussing this and we saw no other way than to involve you. It's going to be risky for both you and Ebed-Melech," she said soberly.

"It's risky for us all." Parto corrected. "But I suggest another disguise whereby you would distract the guards in such a way that would permit us to get in."

"My old woman costume's not good enough then? How about minstrel, shepherd, mourner?"

"No, I have it," BelkA said. "We'll turn you back into a beautiful woman."

"But I like my blackened teeth and wrinkles."

"So I've noticed," BelkA said, "but let me get something?"

He ran up the stairs to his chamber and descended like a plunging arrow holding in his hands a package carefully wrapped in felt. "I was enticed by the Blind Man in Damascus to purchase a length of silk the color of my favorite yellow lilies. Tirza pestered me till I showed it to her, and then she offered to sew it into a garment. I think it will suit you."

"You do have a clever way of blaming others for your actions," Mahla said as she opened the package. As soon as she untied the string the garment tumbled out in silky folds of gold with sprinklings of woodland flowers. With it was a veil of finest white silk with matching flowers embroidered along the front. Suddenly sober she held it up and looked from one man to the other.

"Try it on," BelkA said, "it might not fit."

"You know very well that it'll fit."

"Suit yourself."

"It's my opinion that this is too fine a garment for the errand," Mahla said.

"What do you think Parto?" BelkA asked.

"The idea's to distract," Parto replied trying to keep a straight face.

"Then how do you expect me to accomplish the acrobatics my little trick might require?"

"What acrobatics. All you have to do is force a lock?"

"And what about carrying out dusty old scrolls?"

"That won't be required of the lovely lady."

Mahla made a face before conceding. "Oh, all right. I'm outnumbered. So what am I to do besides appear at dusk like a phantom in a glowing robe?"

"You'll be looking for your lost earring," BelkA said.

"Start from the beginning. I've agreed to meet Shaphan at sundown. Then what?"

"We'll follow you at a distance. Should there be questionable characters about that you have failed to notice, one of us will clear our throat as a signal."

"That is when I look for my lost earring? Then what?"

"After you've distracted the guard and gotten in the gate, we'll hurry through. Now should we get separated, do you know the way to the specific storage chamber?"

"I do. Shaphan carefully explained it. He also gave me this little map."

"I'm going to need a copy of that Parto."

"I'll tend to that right now," Parto said, "also I suggest we collect many bags, blankets and baskets to carry the scrolls."

"Good thinking Parto. There may not be that many but its good to be prepared. I'll pick up the baskets in the courtyard if you can see to a lamp and the blankets."

Meanwhile Mahla disappeared to get into her disguise. When she returned BelkA shook his head as if to awaken from a stupor.

Parto noticing hinted, "Let's not forget anything."

BelkA quickly scooped into his arms what Parto had set aside for him. Moments later, and after carefully scrutinizing the landscape, they made their way toward the temple. When they reached the appointed corner they found Shaphan who was accompanied by the two servers, and also Azek and Ibzan. The eyes of all opened wide at the dazzling sight of Mahla who quickly explained about her costume, prompting Shaphan to explain the presence of the two servers who had been dispatched by Ebed-Melech to assist them. After reviewing the plans one last time they proceeded silently toward the temple gate with Mahla keeping a good distance in front of them.

At the gate Mahla put on her act of pretending she'd lost something. The guard noticing came to her. "What is it woman?" he asked holding up his lantern and taking in her appearance appreciatively.

"I lost one of my best earrings," Mahla groaned. "I know I had it when I was in the courtyard. Do you suppose I could go in and have a look?"

"It's dark. What do you expect to find?"

"Would you by any chance have a lantern?"

The guard let her in, and leaving the gate open, went to find another lantern. In those few moments her collaborators slipped inside unnoticed and kept in the shadows.

Returning with a brightly lit lantern he said, "Go woman, but don't get lost." He looked after her in wonder.

Mahla put a drape over the lantern and then joined the men as they continued to the side door where they needed to enter. Apart from a few stragglers whom they were able to avoid, they decided that the groups that came in the evenings for their exotic worship had reached their meeting places, so with a dash they cleared the open courtyard with Shaphan puffing and panting, though held up by a server on each side of him in order to keep pace. When they reached the side door Shaphan gave BelkA the key and stepped aside.

Upon entering they inched their way silently up the stairs and past several doors until Shaphan stopped and pointed. "This is the one."

Mahla handed the lantern over to BelkA, and then pulled out her precious little tool. With practiced movements she worked her knife into the keyhole until the lock clicked open. Silently they entered and shut the door behind them.

Even in the dim light Shaphan could tell that they'd found what they came for. "There's more than I thought," he whispered excitedly. "This could save us much time. Let's take them all."

The group immediately set to work packing up the scrolls. When the baskets were full Parto unfolded two blankets, carefully laid the scrolls upon them, brought the corners together, and with a rope attached them to the backs of the scouts.

After getting downstairs Mahla put out the lantern and left the others behind while she hurried out to deposit it near the gate where it would be easily recovered. She then returned to open the door for the men loaded up with their burdens. They'd barely gotten through the outer door when they heard voices.

"I tell you a woman came into the courtyard just before sundown claiming she'd lost her earring. I don't recall seeing her leave."

One of them kicked and knocked over something. "What's this?"

"Oh, it's the lantern I loaned her. She must have found her earring and left."

"Well, there you are. You'd better get back to the gate."

"What a break?" BelkA exclaimed.

"I'll distract the men further by showing myself." Mahla said.

"Go ahead," BelkA agreed.

Mahla edged toward the men pretending a slight limp.

"Why it's her," the guard exclaimed, "but she's limping. What happened?" he asked as she approached.

"I stumbled onto the earring and fell causing the lamp to go out. See here's my earring," she said as she pointed to one of the two earrings she was now wearing. "Thanks to you I can now face my husband. I am most grateful for your assistance. If you don't mind I'll massage my ankle a bit and then continue on home."

"Of course, but one of us will accompany you."

"Thank you for the offer, but it won't be necessary. My brother should be out looking for me even as we speak. I'll just slowly go on to our usual meeting place."

"You're sure?"

"Of course."

Mahla procrastinated as long as she dared by stooping over her ankle and rubbing it while keeping an eye on the gate, thankful that she was facing that direction. "I think I'm ready now," she said at length, then limped slowly in front of them as they walked before her toward the outer gate.

They were nearing it when two drunken men appeared outside and began pointing at Mahla while exclaiming loudly, "Somethin' inresting's happnin'n there. Let's go see."

The guard overhearing them shouted as he barred the gate, "You'll do nothing of the kind. The woman's injured, can't you see? Someone's coming for her."

Conveniently Ibzan approached, "Ah there you are," he said. "I've been looking all over for you. Are you all right?"

"I sprained my ankle."

"O dear, let me help you," he said putting his arm under hers. Mahla exited the gate and walked beside him along the wall until they had turned the corner where they quit pretending and made a dash for BelkA's temporary home, arriving just in time to help the men lay down their precious burdens.

For a moment they all stood in wonder until Ibzan slapped his brother's back. "We did it," he shouted. Shaphan collapsed onto a stool.

The others then let loose and began hugging and congratulating one another until Shaphan said, "Hold the noise. Let's rather thank Yahweh."

BelkA agreed.

When all was silent Shaphan prayed, "Accept our praise most holy Yahweh for watching over the Writings tonight. Forgive us where we have been devious in words and actions. We count on your help to preserve these precious scrolls."

When Shaphan had finished his prayer Mahla asked him, "Do you consider that we were devious with our acting?"

"Well, it's one of those fine areas. It was indeed acting as you put it, and for a good cause, but I have no doubt that Yahweh could have protected us and the Writings without it."

The group sobered a moment until BelkA asked, "Do you think these scrolls will be missed in the temple?"

"I can assure you they don't even know they're there, nor do they care. It was that way in the days of Josiah and it's that way today."

One of the servers was now nudging his companion and motioning with his head toward the door, and then pointed at Mahla.

Shaphan interpreted by saying, "Mahla we're going to accompany you to your lodging."

"I must first change my clothing," she said.

"That won't be necessary," BelkA said nonchalantly.

"But, I could damage these lovely garments."

"I don't think so. In any case, they're yours."

There was no time for Mahla to protest. Parto handed her the bag containing her disguise. By then one of the young fellows was already in the court-yard helping Shaphan onto his horse and the other stood ready to do the same for her.

Chapter 36

Living Words

Jerusalem, October 589 B.C.

BelkA and Parto stood looking in disbelief at the heap of scrolls. "Let's light some lamps and lay the Writings on the floor," BelkA suggested.

When all had been gently lined up against the wall in the central room BelkA grinned. "We could wait until tomorrow morning when the light is better, but I'm curious. How about you?"

"Enormously so."

"If you hold the lamp I'll have my hands free to open a scroll."

Eagerly Parto took the lamp from the table and held it as BelkA picked up the scroll nearest him.

"This one appears fragile and maybe they all are. I'll need to unroll it carefully on the table. Oh, looks like a smudge right over the title, but the text appears quite readable. Here goes," BelkA began translating as he went.

"In the beginning *Elohim* created the heavens and the earth..."

"It's the book of creation. It's called Genesis," Parto exclaimed.

"Well now. This should be interesting," BelkA said looking up at Parto eagerly. "Why *Elohim*? The noun is plural, yet the verb, I see, is singular? That's odd."

"He's three in one, remember? We speak of the *Messiyah* to come, of YAHWEH or Almighty LORD God, and the Spirit of God."

"Thus might we say that the Trinity agreed to create the cosmos" BelkA mused.

Both men looked stunned, hardly daring to breathe.

BelkA picked up the scroll once more. "The earth was without form and void, and darkness was upon the face of the deep. And the Spirit of *Elohim* was hovering over the face of the waters."

"There you have it," Parto exclaimed.

"And *Elohim* said, 'Let there be light... to separate the day from the night... for signs and seasons, and for days and years.'" On and on BelkA read of stars, living creatures to where Yahweh said, "'Let *us* make men (*humans*) in our image...and breathed into his nostrils the breath of life.'"

Reading on they were overwhelmed when BelkA pointed out that the name *YAHWEH came* from the Hebrew word *to live*.

"Yahweh has always existed. Life created life BelkA, and He created us to live forever."

"One can't help but compare this with our Mesopotamian epics where man is an afterthought or a whim. Even our Enuma-Elish story has a ring of depravity to it that makes one hesitate to believe it."

"You're thinking of Marduk creating heaven and earth from the King's blood after triumphing over him?"

"Exactly. Imagine Parto what meaning it might imply if you and I were created in the image of God Almighty. What value would that place upon us?"

"Enormous lord BelkA. Yahweh created us so that we could enjoy fellowship with him. He made us, loves us, and wants us to love Him back."

"This is getting too much for me Parto. Let's stop our reading for tonight and allow our minds a rest. Perhaps our subconscious mind will process this information and help us to understand it better tomorrow. It seems too good to be true."

Chapter 37

Eden Defiled

Jerusalem, October 589 B.C.

From the first rays of dawn BelkA and Parto hovered over the scrolls, sorting by author and antiquity—as best they could discern—with BelkA making index labels as they progressed. There were still a few to open and arrange when BelkA, from his seat at the table, looked down on Parto still lining up the scrolls on the floor. "I'm bursting with curiosity Parto. Come sit beside me while I read some more from the Scroll of Beginnings."

Parto needed no further prodding. He picked himself off the floor and slid onto a stool beside BelkA.

As BelkA read Parto interrupted from time to time with comments. He started with the account of man and woman being placed in the garden in Eden, and the story of the one forbidden fruit, but when he got to the part of the serpent's crafty deception,

BelkA put the scroll down with a puzzled look. "Do you know something about this Parto?"

"Do you mind if I tell it in the way my imagination sees it."

"Please proceed."

"I envision a beautiful woman meandering through the most exotic garden imaginable under a clear blue sky. Feeling secure and happy she hums a happy tune, skips across a gently flowing stream, pauses to caress a deer or picks some berries, and then drops on a carpet of moss where she enjoys her juicy treat knowing it is provided for her enjoyment. In such a state of bliss she sees movement in a tree and sits up straight. There before her is a most unusual creature radiating striking color and agility. The creature engages her now in an acrobatic performance that makes her giggle. Then slyly the serpent hints that Yahweh is unfair in withholding something good from her by forbidding her to eat the fruit of that one tree, and argues that it would help her become as wise as Yahweh."

"Yes, I can see the picture."

"The woman contemplates the fruit glowing with color and the fragrance is perhaps like that of a golden-ripe mango. She switches her gaze to the serpent that now swings around to face her, relaxed and confidant. He blinks in a beguiling way. The woman is faced with a choice. What is she going to do? Who is she going to believe?"

"Ah! You've got me hanging over a cliff. Go on."

"Well, here's a woman who has everything she could ever desire with only one thing withheld.

Feelings of resentment begin to enter her mind. What would it be like to have as much knowledge as Yahweh? Ambitions she'd never imagined burst into her mind."

BelkA turned to the scroll to pick up the story reading how Eve ate the fruit and gave it to her husband, and about the shame that came over them that caused them to hide from Yahweh.

"Their innocence is lost," Parto exclaimed. "They became knowledgeable about hunger and pain and death."

"So Eve was tricked."

BelkA read further about Yahweh making garments of animal skins to clothe them.

"That's the first animal sacrifice," Parto explained. "Substitution of guilt on an innocent creature. That's why they have the temple sacrifices. Isaiah wrote that we are all 'like sheep that have gone astray and the LORD has laid on him the iniquity of us all.' Some day Messiah will come and perform the ultimate sacrifice."

"Amazing!"

At that moment a bell was heard followed by a clearing of the throat. They looked at one another for a moment and then Parto ran to the courtyard and the back door. There stood Arif flat against the wall.

Parto beckoned him. "A good thing you came. We were so engrossed that I forgot Master's breakfast. Go on in while I prepare a tray."

Chapter 38

Buz, Land of Antiquity

Jerusalem, October 589 B.C.

A rif whistled when he saw scrolls scattered all over the floor.

"Don't say it," BelkA interrupted. "It appears a disaster but we're actually making order."

"Well eh-h-h. Might I offer a suggestion?"

"Go ahead."

"Why don't we leave a message for the scouts to find us bricks so that we can make cubicles for the scrolls. It would clear up some floor space."

BelkA stood up and scratched his head. "Suggestion accepted. If I can find my writing materials I will write out a message immediately. By the way, we were informed that our scouts brought the heavy clay through the Gihon passage last night."

"You don't say!" Arif exclaimed with a chuckle. Then he sobered. "BelkA, I've been thinking, would it not seem wise to consider escaping now that you have the Writings?"

BelkA put down his quill, and while stalling for time interjected. "Before I forget, here's a letter for my mother. Would you...?"

Arif took the messages.

"Now back to your suggestion regarding the Writings. I'm afraid that I must reject it because I believe we have already discussed all the requirements that have not yet been fulfilled. We still don't have enough clay to make jars; we need to find secure hiding places; we don't have sufficient copies; nor do we have the papyrus needed for copies."

Subdued, Arif said, "I'll send a pigeon off this evening."

BelkA thanked him and turned to the scrolls. "I want to show you an account of creation that challenges our myths and legends."

"You're serious?"

"Absolutely. If I can just find it."

Meanwhile Arif, who had a literary knowledge of Hebrew, had curiously opened another scroll. "This one is ancient, I mean really ancient. It has to go back almost as far as the flood. The setting is Buz, our own ancient land."

"What are you saying?"

Arif read for a while with some difficulty due to creases and cracks. "It's about a wealthy and apparently influential man named Job whom the LORD calls a righteous man because he shuns evil and helps others. It appears that Satan wants permission to test him to see if he will turn away from the LORD God and even curse Him."

Parto who'd let the others speak while he continued sorting, now sat and eased his sore knees by stretching his legs out, "Mysterious. I'm intrigued."

"Alas, it's a big scroll, in fact I think there are two scrolls here written or copied by the same hand."

BelkA looked up with a twinkle in his eye. "I have a proposition to make."

"Go ahead."

"Why not arrange to have a table set up here for you so that you can help us?"

"Are you serious?"

"Totally."

"Well, I have to confess that when you mentioned translating at the get-together and caused Blind Man to gasp, I got stabbed in the gut also. Something like this would be most fascinating... actually a dream."

"Are you saying that you would like to translate some scrolls into Aramaic?" Parto asked.

"That is my present thought. You have to understand that when I mentioned escaping earlier, I was searching out a plan for myself as well. Let's put it like this: We're in it together."

BelkA raised his fisted arms, but restrained a whoop. Then he let them flop upon the table. "This brings us back to our problem. The papyri, or lack of it. When we were in Tyre I purchased some of excellent quality from a merchant there. In fact I still have a sheet left." He got up and went to his satchel. "Here, what do you think of this?"

Arif held it up in the light and ran his fingers over the grain. "The smoothest I've ever felt." Then he laid it down. "Now let me guess, you're asking me to go to Tyre to get a supply of papyri."

"Correct," BelkA said nonchalantly.

"BelkA, like you I'm a scholar, but unlike you I am weak in the area of self-defense. I have no interest in weapons. I don't like to hold, touch or even see one used. Nor do I enjoy traveling, especially alone... But... well... perhaps I might endure it for the sake of these Writings."

BelkA again raised his fisted hands in a triumphant gesture. "Your fear happens to be weapons, mine is heights. We're both learning to face our weaknesses. But what about Tirza and the children?"

"I think they'll be sufficiently safe now that they're at Tovi's inn. It's time for me to face my enemy. I'll leave early tomorrow morning."

"Brave man, Arif. You have risen enormously in my esteem. I'm most proud to consider you as my friend, companion, and collaborator."

"Perhaps I can yet redeem myself from the guilt I feel over being on Adda-Guppi's side."

"Let's forget her," Parto said.

"Not so fast Parto," BelkA cautioned. "Her gang is still too near and too sly. Your idea to leave early tomorrow is wise. We must constantly be one step ahead of our foes. What we don't want is for them to follow you."

Arif stiffened at the thought and put his hand on his heart.

"I'm sorry if I alarmed you Arif. My intention is only to eliminate any possible danger by taking every precaution we can."

"I will pray for your protection," Parto said.

"Thank you friend."

"There's the gist of a pilgrimage song in the scroll of Psalms that Shai quoted when we were leaving Babylon that has been a source of encouragement to me. It goes like this: 'The LORD shall preserve thy going out and thy coming in.'"

Arif stood stunned. "Short and easy to remember. I'll remind myself of that all the way."

BelkA meanwhile had gone to his desk and when Arif turned around he handed him a map. "The merchant's name is Thomas. I've written his name and specifics about his stand here. Now, if you'll excuse me I'll collect the gold."

Arif studied the map while BelkA disappeared upstairs returning with a sturdy leather bag that he put into Arif's hand. The weighted hand plunged provoking a surprised grin. "BelkA, this is extremely generous."

"Think nothing of it my friend."

When the map and money were wrapped in an ordinary gunnysack Arif gripped BelkA's hand a last time before hurrying off.

Chapter 39

Zaccaria and Abigael

Gezer, October 589 B.C.

A rif flopped onto a bench in front of Gezer's main inn, his body limp. The last ten steps had taken every ounce of strength he had left. Unconscious of his disheveled condition, with his tunic caked with mud, he indulged his aching muscles in the luxury of rest. In spite of the damp weather, and unmindful of the hard bench under him, he drifted into sleep.

When jolted awake by a hand on his shoulder he sat up and tried to connect his mind to what this strange woman was saying. "Who are you?" he managed to ask.

"I'm the innkeeper's wife and I've brought you a cup of water and some bread, but won't you please come inside? You'll rest more comfortably."

"O, Thank you, for the water and food," Arif managed to say, "but I have an urgent errand to accomplish. Perhaps you would allow me to sit here awhile?"

His request was ignored. "I insist sir. You *must* come in. You are at the point of exhaustion. It would be dangerous for your health to ignore my request. I have a bed in a tiny room that will cost you little. Come now with me and I will show it to you."

Arif forced himself up, and reached for his bag, wincing at the weight.

The woman, whom he now noticed was dressed in Hebrew attire, took it from him. "Don't worry about your horse, he'll be taken care of."

Like an obedient child Arif followed the woman to a room the size of a closet, but with an inviting mat all made up and ready. "Rest now. I'll be bringing you water for washing in a little while," the woman said before disappearing.

Arif sunk to the mat, pulling his bag close to his body and wrapping an arm around it. Once he was sure that the dagger was still safely in its place he let himself drift into a fitful sleep during which he dreamt of water coming up to his armpits, of snakes swimming toward him, and of robbers mocking him.

From far off he jumped when a loud banging on the door roused him from sleep. Somewhat disoriented he sat up and realized that light was fading, and that someone was at the door. The rapping continued. "It's me, the innkeeper," the male voice was saying, "Are you all right?"

By then Arif had the door open and looked inquiringly at the middle-aged man standing before him.

"The wife's worried about you. She tried to bring you water but you failed to answer the door. Why don't you come on down to dinner."

"My appearance," Arif said apologetically.

"Never mind that, the food's hot and you'll find strength and courage to go on."

Reluctantly, Arif descended the stairs and sat at the table designated by the innkeeper. Gradually he began to filter through his mind from whence he'd come, and where he was.

He'd chosen the route through Gezer that connected to *The Way of the Sea* highway, but it had proven quite a challenge, winding as it did through forested heights infested with snakes and animals he cared not to think about, climbing, wading through slippery mud or gushing water while always keeping alert in case of brigands. Every traveler he'd encountered had been eyed warily with a hand on his dagger. At one point, when he'd slid down a wadi, a young man had reached to help him up, but he'd kicked him off. It had turned into a scuffle in the mud and ended with a good laugh for both himself and his jovial rescuer who, thankfully, knew and relished adventure. As he'd plodded mile after mile he'd rebuked himself for attempting the journey at all. But upon reaching the clearing and catching sight of the inn, he'd plunged forward with a last force of will. Now he vaguely remembered that his horse had been led to a stall. He trusted she was safe.

When he'd eaten the innkeeper came to him and asked. "Are you feeling a bit better now?"

"Indeed, I'm glad you woke me sir. I had only expected to sleep an hour, I must be on my way."

"Nonsense. One doesn't set out on a journey at dusk. You need all the rest you can get."

"I have to," Arif said curtly.

But a few minutes later the innkeeper's wife came and seated herself opposite him. "Ah, you're looking better. Still, I think it would be foolish to push yourself any further. A good night's rest will gain you time tomorrow."

Arif looked into the kindly face and read a look of genuine concern. "Very well. I will do as you say."

"What is your destination?"

Arif looked cautiously around the room. Business obviously was slowing with only a few lone stragglers and a young couple remaining. Still he hesitated. The woman didn't insist.

When he had finished eating, and was reaching his room, he heard footsteps behind him. He whirled around.

"It's only me," the woman said as she stood behind him with a basin and a towel. "You need not be fearful. We keep close watch on all our customers night and day."

"Thank you," Arif said, now realizing he'd been overreacting. "I must still be weary. Traveling alone is new to me."

"I understand." She put the basin on the floor, the towel on the mat, and then she left.

The following morning he awoke at dawn, this time feeling renewed. He jumped up, dashed water into his face and ran his ivory comb through his hair.

After grabbing his bag he hurried downstairs hoping to find the innkeeper to settle his account. Again it was the woman who was on duty. When business was taken care of she insisted he sit down, and set a barley loaf in front of him with a glass of ale. Standing above him she said, "I'm Martha. If you come back this way please stay with us. You'll be safe here."

"I'm Arif, I'll remember that."

Reclaiming his horse he mounted and road off keeping on the low coast route where miles sped under the horse's hoofs as he pushed her to near exhaustion, until he reached the plain of Dor. There, where the Mount Carmel range cast its promontory of high land almost to the sea, he stopped in the village to refill his water bags and to eat some dried fruit and bread. With renewed courage he continued to Acco.

The inn he found there was crowded and noisy. Having taken the precaution to unload his belongings and to secure them to his body, he feared lest his cumbersome burden be noticed. Staying close to the wall he inched forward until he reached a corner where a table still had one free seat. He decided to take his chance and sat down. "Do you mind?" he asked of the family seated there.

"Not at all," came the gentle response from a heavily bearded man who appeared to be about his own age. "I am Zaccaria, a cultivator by trade. This is my wife Abigael, and on your right my son Saadya."

"I am Arif. I left Gezer early this morning," Arif said trying to show some civility.

269

"And your destination?"

With a sense of new confidence Arif said, "Tyre."

"That is the same as ourselves. I am a merchant of wheat from Gibeon. When I go to the market of Tyre my wife and son like to come along. The journey is difficult but the city is interesting. Ah, here's a waiter at last. Since you're alone we'll allow you to order first."

"Thank you," Arif said and ordered a side of mutton with roasted grain and fruit.

In the course of the meal he began to unwind still more. Thus when asked about the purpose of his own visit to the city of Tyre he stated simply, "I'm seeking papyrus."

"Ah, I know a merchant you need to see. His name is Thomas. His merchandise is good and he deals honestly."

"Thomas, interesting that you mention his name. My friend met him some months ago in Tyre and suggested I find him."

"If you like I can lead you to his stand."

"I would be most grateful."

While they were eating Zaccaria glanced around the room as if watching for someone. About then a heavy set man lumbered through the door and sat down across the room from them and in full view of Abigael. She turned toward her husband with a look of alarm.

Zaccaria inched toward Arif to permit his wife to change the position of her chair. In doing so he whispered, "The man is a crook and not to be trusted around women. We had a bad experience at the market once when I left Abigael and Saadya in charge of our stand. We were hoping never to see him again, but we manage to run into him at times."

Arif had only a side view of the man, but he eyed him over, noticing harsh facial lines and a hefty dagger.

As if knowing what Arif was seeing Zaccaria asked. "Are you armed?"

"I carry a dagger, but I'm hoping never to have to use it."

"It's a bit late to try to find another inn, but it might be to the benefit of all of us here if we shared a room together."

Arif looked with questioning eyes at Abigael and Saadya.

Abigael spoke. "From past experiences we've found that when an inn is as crowded as this one is tonight, one must expect to sleep with strangers. Though we've only just met, we feel trustful of you."

Arif looked once again at the character who was downing a pitcher of ale, and then at the family sitting around him. He suddenly found himself saying, "There's something providential about our meeting. The gods have brought us together."

Zaccaria took the hand of his wife. "We believe that Yahweh directs destinies."

Arif smiled broadly. "You understand, I'm a Babylonian, but I've heard much about your God in recent days and am impressed with many things about him."

Zaccaria smiled while Arif turned to Saadya in an attempt to draw him into the conversation, and told the youth about the pigeons.

"Did you bring them with you?" the lad asked.

"No, they're with my wife and children. They've been very useful in sending messages back and forth to Babylon."

"By the way," Zaccaria asked. "How are things in Babylon?"

"The last message from the pigeons, in fact, was that Nebuchadnezzar's army is marching on Judah."

The news produced gasps of surprise.

"Perhaps we should continue this conversation in our room," Zaccaria said with a hush.

Silently, and as inconspicuously as they could manage, they went to find the innkeeper to be shown their room. There they sat down and conversed for several more hours with Arif telling of the reason for his journey to Tyre and the copying of the scrolls.

Upon hearing this his new friend Zaccaria asked, "Would you mind if we prayed for the success of your efforts?"

"Not at all."

Thus Zaccaria poured out his intercession asking also that Yahweh would protect Arif and his family.

They rose before dawn the next morning and silently went to the stalls to reclaim their animals. It was then that Arif noticed that his horse was missing. He was making a more thorough search when he heard the sound of hoof beats, and rushed to the front of the inn just in time to see his horse disappearing in the first rays of dawn. "What am I going to do?" he wailed.

"Nothing friend. I saw who it was. It's best with such as him that you have no contact. The worst thing about him is that he's a man of high standing and wealth. When caught he just buys himself off."

"If he has money why would he take my horse?"

"He probably doesn't care for his own horse properly, or it could have just been easier to take yours."

"Oh dear. Now what am I going to do?"

Zaccaria turned to his wife. "We could perhaps ride together and let him borrow my horse."

Before Arif could answer Saadya said. "He can have my horse father."

Arif looked in shock at Saadya.

Zaccaria smiled. "Thank you son for that generous offer."

Arif put his hand on Saadya's shoulder and said, "I'll be very careful with your horse and return him when we get to Tyre where I'll buy another."

"I'm giving you my horse Amal. His name means *Hope*."

"That is a most generous gesture," Arif said gently, "but I assure you that I couldn't take your horse. I can tell that he's a good friend of yours."

"It's because I want to help you in your important task, and I'll be proud to let Amal do the same."

"You can be sure it's a serious offer," Zaccaria said.

Arif tried to speak but his voice choked up. "What can I say...?"

The lad put the reigns into Arif's hands, looked up at him and smiled.

Arif ran his hand over the horse's mane. "Amal is a gorgeous animal."

"We purchased him last year at the fair of Tyre," Saadya explained. "He was still young then, but he has grown big and strong."

"I will never forget such a gesture Saadya. I hope you and my young ones will be friends some day."

Arif and the happy family mounted and set the three horses on *The Way of the Sea* towards Tyre.

Chapter 40

Gadua

Tyre, October 589 B.C.

"Looks like a big ship," Saadya commented as he looked upon the island city of Tyre.

"It does in fact?" Arif smiled at the observation of the young fellow. "It's surrounded by water, yet its water supply must come in by boats. Of course, with gold all things are possible."

"No," Saadya objected. "Our priest Amit says that it can't buy lots of things like love, peace, or contentment. Those things are gifts."

Zaccaria put a hand on his son's shoulder. "We need to explain to Arif that Priest Amit is a good friend of ours. He's one priest we highly respect because he's different from most of the others. Since we live in the country he comes to visit us whenever he feels the need to get away from the atmosphere of Jerusalem. When he comes he brings his scrolls and we read together. After that we discuss the passage. Of late he's been talking a lot about the pursuit of gold. He says gold is a god to many people."

"Gold a god?"

"He says that these days a lot of people, including priests, are bowing at the shrine of money."

"Interesting concept. In Babylon priests and priestesses live quite well and in fact, I myself receive a living from the temple. I must also admit that I like gold and all it buys. But tell me about this priest of yours. He sounds interesting."

"I think you'd like him Arif. He's a small man getting on in age, but his knowledge of the sacred Writings is astounding. He can recite large portions from memory and he's constantly encouraging us to do the same. Saadya is really picking up on it now too. Incidentally, would you like to hear the passage from the Isaiah scroll that prompted Saadya's remark?"

"Most certainly."

Saadya closed his eyes and recited, "'Ho, every one that thirsteth, come ye to the waters, and he that hath no money; come ye, buy, and eat: yea, come, buy wine and milk without money and without price.' Would you like to hear Amit's explanation of it?"

"Of course." Arif grinned.

"The kind of thirst meant is the thirst of the soul or the need for God. One cannot buy satisfaction for the soul with money."

"So how does one quench that kind of thirst?"

Saadya eagerly answered, "You go to the spring of pure water and drink the water of God's Word. It's another gift that money can't buy."

Arif laughed. "That priest of yours must indeed be a sage," he said squinting his eyes. "I would love to speak with him sometime... By the way, does this priest friend of yours copy scrolls?"

Zaccaria answered, "He does indeed, why do you ask?"

"There's something I would like to explain to you, but it might take some time. Perhaps we should first check into an inn."

They stopped before a small tidy building where they secured rooms, and made sure the horses were tethered in such a way that a thief would have difficulty making off with them. Then they went to the dining hall and relaxed.

Over dinner Zaccaria told Arif that, since learning about the peril that lay before Judah, and sensing keenly the importance and urgency of his mission, they wanted to share the burden. "Upon our return we will speak immediately with Priest Amit, but is there some way that we might be of assistance beyond that?"

"Would you be willing to speak with BelkA about this?"

"We sure would," Zaccaria said, "but let's retire to our room where we can talk privately."

•••

The following day Zaccaria introduced Arif to merchant Thomas. After exchanging greetings Arif asked if he remembered a Babylonian who had bought papyrus from him quite recently.

The man thought a moment and then exclaimed, "Of course, a tall man of distinction with the voice of a commander, but the attitude of a scholar. I remember him well, and indeed he did mention something about needing more papyrus."

"That surely is him, and he has, in fact, sent me to purchase papyrus."

"Marvelous. I will show you the exact kind he likes." Reaching for a stack behind him, he laid it before Arif. "What do you think?"

Arif stroked the grain of the papyrus with experienced fingers and smiled. "This is it all right."

"What quantity might you need, honored one?"

"About twenty packets."

Thomas raised his eyebrows. "Allow me to check on my supply." The merchant returned a few moments later shaking his head. "I'm sorry to disappoint you. I have only the equivalent of about half."

Arif winced. "We're needing it urgently," he said as he continued to stroke the papyrus.

Zaccaria, noticing the tension in Arif spoke up. "Thomas my friend, I dare to share with you a matter that is confidential and that is the reason why this papyri is urgently needed."

"Of course. I am indeed curious."

When Zaccaria had finished explaining, Thomas rubbed his forehead and sighed. "I have also just heard through caravan reports that Nebuchadnezzar is marching, but I could not have even imagined the other problem. I want to help as best I can, but technically speaking, the earliest possibility is a ship due to arrive tomorrow, weather and other factors permitting. Most of the shipment is destined for our home base in Byblos, but I will send an agent there to explain that we will need it here. Would that work for you?"

Arif shrugged. "It would appear that I have no other choice."

•••

While Zaccaria rejoined his wife and son, Arif took a stroll through the market by himself hoping to work off the stress that lay upon him. Surely the extra time of waiting would alarm BelkA, and could jeopardize his own safe return as well as that of the papyrus. What could he do? His mind was a blank.

Walking, however, soothed some of the tension and a flash back of Zaccara's prayer the night before broke into the forefront of his mind. It had seemed to him a bit quaint—even childlike—but it had the ring of sincerity and frankness that appealed to him. It was as if they'd been simply conversing with a friend. He wondered how it might feel to offer prayers without pretense and fear of being rejected over some deviation in ritual, or some minute detail of fate. He began to realize that this was the reason why he had rejected most of the family gods. Now, to his own astonishment, he felt drawn to this approachable God. Why not at least try a connection.

His footsteps meanwhile had brought him into the horse-traders section of the market and before him stood a magnificent stallion.

"Would you like to try him out?" came a voice behind him.

"I'll be back." He replied turning away.

An hour later he stood at the same spot with a perplexed Saadya at his side.

"What do you mean another horse?" Saadya argued. "Don't you like the one you have?"

"Most certainly. But I know a fine young fellow who needs a horse because he gave his away. What do you think of this one? Would you at least try him out?"

Saadya took the reins, guiding the animal to a trial arena where he urged the stallion into a trot, then a full gallop before returning.

"Well, what do you think?"

"He's a powerful horse and I would imagine that he needs a stronger master."

"Do you want to know what I think?"

Saadya shrugged.

"I think Amal misses you."

"Are you saying that I should take Amal back. I'd be too embarrassed and ashamed to do that."

"How about looking at it like this. You gave me a gift and now I give you a gift."

Saadya's pulled back and thought over the suggestion, until a wide grin lifted his face. "Well, if you put it that way. I was kind of missing Amal, but why don't you first give the stallion a try?"

Arif took the animal on a restrained tour, and upon returning he winked before approaching the merchant, "Let's make an agreement."

"What are you going to name him?" Saadya asked when the transaction was completed.

"His name is Gadua which means gift of course. Your gift to me."

That night Arif awoke with his mouth dry. Reaching for his water skin he remembered Saadya's remarks about soul thirst. Now, he decided, was the time to put the whole matter to the test. Imitating Zaccharia's style, he prayed for the quenching of his soul's thirst and for a safe return to Jerusalem.

Chapter 41

Four Phoenicians

Tyre, October 589 B.C.

Arif's frustration grew upon learning that the ship had been delayed an extra two days, but when Zaccaria told him that those two days had brought him some exceptional customers who had bought out his entire wheat supply, he cheered up, at least outwardly.

Now, as the sun was getting low in the sky he approached the stand with a sense of foreboding. To his relief Thomas greeted him with a broad smile. "It has come in," he shouted above the heads of some customers. Coming closer he added, "I talked with the captain himself upon his arrival and you, your friends, my wife and myself are all invited to his home tomorrow evening. You will accept I hope."

Arif looked astounded. "Of course," he replied, "but it surprises me since he's never even met us."

"It appears that your Babylonian friend made quite an impression on him."

"I'll send off a message immediately, a chariot will be arriving at my home tomorrow at this time to pick us all up."

•••

When the four arrived at Thomas' home they were introduced to his wife Idra. "You'll find my wife timid and retiring at first, but I assure you that she's full of energy."

Arif smiled and took the hand of the woman who stood taller than her husband, but whose graceful gestures overshadowed the difference. Her lavender silk gown highlighted her black hair that was pulled straight back and mounted on her head, giving her the typical Mediterranean statue-like appearance. She contrasted sharply with Abigael who wore a delicate cream wool tunic with a yoke of colorful embroidery. Both, however, reflected unique and fascinating personalities.

As soon as introductions were made the six crowded together in the chariot, but since none were heavy they managed each to have a reasonable standing space. The main problem was for Saadya to restrain his movements, eager, as he was to see everything.

Upon entering the same elegant home that had mesmerized BelkA, they were greeted by Mar who approached them with outstretched arms, his purple tunic shimmering and his long hair flowing from a jeweled headband. "I am Mar and this is my wife Samantha," he said while allowing her to approach and reach out her hand. Dressed in a red gown in the Egyptian style with a red hibiscus attached to her shoulder, Samantha cast a spell of happiness upon her guests that banished all feelings of stiffness.

"It's an honor to receive friends of BelkA-Souash," Mar said enthusiastically.

When they were seated comfortably two young women servants entered, one with trays of drinks, the other with finger food composed of all manner of sea creatures, prepared and displayed elegantly on glass dishes of varying shapes. When they had left Mar interrogated Arif. "And how is my friend BelkA?"

"He is well..." Arif said hesitatingly, "Though the circumstances are not exactly to his liking. You see... He's under house arrest. His mission of delivering a message from Nebuchadnezzar to King Zedekiah was not well-received."

"I'm sorry to hear that. Is he safe?"

"Presently he is," Arif replied soberly.

"Is there a possibility that he might escape?"

"Not yet," Arif said, and then prompted by Zaccaria and Abigael, he told the story of the scrolls, with even Saadya adding the details of the Aleppo attack.

"At this time he doesn't want to escape as he's gathering the Hebrew Writings and wants to make as many copies as possible to insure their preservation."

"And for this he's risking his life. It shows how deep this Hebrew God has influenced him. I thought as much when he was here."

"I can't speak for BelkA, but I find myself involved with him and taking the same risks."

"So you are a scholar as well?"

"I'm an astrologer but languages are a hobby of mine."

Mar smiled. "Obviously you form a good team. But what about your own safety, and that of your wife and children."

"It does concern me, and I hope to have a plan soon."

"Well, I have to say you both have my highest esteem."

They were interrupted when the servers returned with the main course of delicate racks of lamb with pomegranate sauce. As they ate Samantha looked at the Hebrew family sitting opposite her and asked about Zaccariah's profession and the changes in Jerusalem.

Zaccaria responded by telling about his farming, then added, "We're very concerned that our people have forgotten their history. They fail to remember that in the past, when they relied entirely on Yahweh, He delivered them."

"You know," Samantha said with a far-away look, "sometime ago we were in Jerusalem, and while walking through the market, we stopped to buy some almonds. I remember hearing a peculiar little man nearby shouting, 'Thus saith Yahweh.' We learned that his name was Jeremiah."

Zaccaria felt compelled to come to the defense of the prophet. "Jeremiah gets criticism from people who don't understand him. He's sensitive and caring but when it comes to messages he steps on toes."

"He sure does," Mar said, "I felt him pointing his finger right at me when he spoke out against oppressing the helpless. You see I trade in slaves so his words sliced right into my very core. It bothered me so much that upon returning to Tyre, I broke my contracts with traders, so I'll be buying no more. The ones we now have live with us in our home as if they were our own children. But enough on this, it's getting late and Thomas, you and I need to talk about the papyrus transaction."

Thomas rose and sat beside Mar where a whispered conversation lasted but a few minutes when an agreement was made. Thomas then addressed Arif, "We want to share in your expenses so we have agreed that you should pay only what they cost Mar."

Arif immediately argued that BelkA had made provision, but neither gentleman appeared to hear what he was saying. So finally Arif bowed his head. "I'm grateful beyond words, he said as he thanked his friends. The two couples beamed with delight as if they were the ones receiving the gift.

"Tomorrow we'll deliver the papyrus at your inn," Mar said.

Chapter 42

Tovi and Eliana

Jerusalem, October 589 B.C.

As the last customers left the dining room, Tovi plunked himself down on a chair by the window overlooking the front garden with a mug of soured milk. He smiled as he watched his eight-year-old son Elasah playing with their dog, coaxing it to retrieve a stick.

How proud and thankful he was for this child who was Yahweh's answer to years of his own, and his wife Eliana's prayers. Now, however, they shared deep concerns for their child's social life. If only they could find a suitable playmate for him. All the children they knew were already wise in pagan ways, and one had already invited him to a ritual of star worship on their family's rooftop. Tovi knew that, as their son got older, the temptations would only increase. What should they do?

With his last sip he noticed that after the night's rains a new crop of weeds had sprung up and were spoiling his little garden bed in front of the inn. Reluctantly he rose and went to the storeroom to collect his tools, and when walking out the front door, he noticed a man in foreign attire talking with his son. What could this be about?

As he approached the fellow bowed his head politely in his direction and walked away.

"Who was that?" Tovi asked.

"I don't know."

"What did he want?"

"He asked if a Babylonian man called Arif was here."

"What did you tell him?"

"I told him he'd gone to Tyre."

"What else did you say?"

"Well, he wanted to know who he went with, so I told him nobody because the children and their mother are here."

"Then what did he say."

"Nothing. He just left."

"You're sure he didn't say anything else?"

"Yes, I'm sure."

"I don't like the sound of this Elasah," Tovi said. He scratched his beard, and then dropped his tools. "I want you to come with me. We need to talk with Arif's wife." Tovi took hold of his son's hand forcing him to follow his rapid steps toward the chamber occupied by Arif's family.

"Excuse our interruption," Tovi said noticing the children seated cross-legged on the floor with papyrus in their laps and a bottle of ink between them.

"It's quite all right," Tirza said. "The children are due for a break from their exercises. Perhaps Elasah would like to join them sometime?"

"Why that's a most kind offer dear woman. Perhaps we might discuss it when your husband returns. What we came for is to tell you that a Chaldean stopped to talk with Elasah in front of the inn, and asked if Arif was here. Elasah, repeat once more exactly what the man said."

Elasah relayed the same story he'd told his father.

"I'm very sorry for this compromise in your family's security, dear woman. Ebed-Melech has made it very clear that you needed protection, and I promised your husband as well. My son didn't realize what he was doing. I should have made things more clear to him, but since the damage is done, should I contact Ebed-Melech?"

"No," Tirza replied, her eyes wide and her voice shaking, "It's imperative that I notify my friends."

"I believe RAstin is still here," Tovi said, "I'll speak with him immediately. Is there some way I might contact others?"

"I'll write a note that can be deposited at a secret place."

Tirza turned around, grabbed the papyrus from Suzann's lap and began to write. When she'd finished, and while still holding the message she asked, "Did Ebed-Melech tell you about the attempt to kidnap my children?"

"Yes, and about the Writings also."

"Ah," Tirza said with a sigh of relief, "so you know. Then I believe there's no harm in your knowing the place where we exchange messages. My son knows where it is but I'm afraid to let him go alone. Perhaps you would accompany him?"

"We'll be glad to do that?"

When Tovi had taken the message from Tirza's hand he was about to take leave of her when Elasah tilted his face upward and asked, "Can I go along?"

All eyes focused upon the child who in turn became self-conscious.

Tovi bent over to look into his son's face. "Listen to me Elasah. This is a situation where you must be very careful with whom you talk. If you have never spoken to someone before, say nothing. Come directly to me and let me talk with that person. You may go with us only if you promise not to say a word to anyone else about it except your mother, is that clear?"

Elasah soberly nodded his head.

Tovi couldn't refrain himself from giving yet another emphatic warning to his son insisting, "You have put this family at great risk son. You're eight years old now, Elasah, old enough to understand that there is danger involved here because the one you talked with earlier is not a good man. From now on you must keep secret all you see and hear about Arif's family or any of our guests at the inn. I will allow you to go with us, but what we're going to do is a secret. Do you understand?"

Elasah nodded now fully aware of the gravity of the situation.

"What are you to do if you see or hear something?"

"Come get you or Mother."

Tovi tousled Elasah's hair. "You did right in telling us everything. I know I can trust you."

SabA led the party to the rock at Siloam Springs. As previously instructed he first looked around to see who might be watching, and then he took the message in its clay envelope and laid it into the hole.

They were beginning to return when an old woman approached and gently put a hand on SabA. Elasah immediately pulled back and grabbed his father's hand. SabA smiled at Elasah, and then whispered. "It's another secret. She's not an old woman but our friend Mahla in a disguise."

Elasah looked totally confused, but when Mahla stood up straight and lifted the heavy black veil he wanted to laugh. Mahla put her finger on her lips and quickly rearranged the veil before saying, "And who are you young man?"

Elasah looked at his father.

"His name is Elasah and mine is Tovi."

"Ah yes, the inn where you are now staying SabA."

SabA nodded.

"What's going on?" Mahla asked. "I saw you leave a message."

"It's about father. I think someone wants to harm him and perhaps us!"

Mahla looked at Tovi who explained the story.

"Tell your mother that I know where the scouts are. I'll get hold of them immediately, and also the potter Nethaniah. I'm expecting Helem here anytime so I'll watch for him."

"Is there anything I can do to help?" Tovi broke in.

"If you could see to the protection of Arif's family and perhaps accumulate provisions for a rescue operation?"

"Gladly," Tovi agreed. "RAstin is now protecting Tirza and the children during my absence, but he would probably be of great assistance in the rescue operation as he has a cool head about him, and he knows what these fellows are capable of doing. I give you my word that my family and friends will protect Tirza and the young ones with our lives."

"Good. Then if you would notify RAstin to prepare, we'll plan to leave immediately."

Mahla hugged SabA and then Elasah before saying, "May Yahweh help us all."

Chapter 43

Manua and Martha

Gezer, October 589 B.C.

The curtain of night had fallen when the weary travelers arrived bone-weary at the Red Bird Inn that Arif had suggested. Thankfully a small lamp in the window guided their groping footsteps to the door where a dark figure enshrouded in an ample cloak received them.

"Ah, it's you Arif I believe." Martha, the inn-keeper's wife said in relief.

"You remembered me. This time I bring with me some new friends, a family: Zaccaria, Abigael, and their son Saadya."

"Well what do you know?" the woman exclaimed pushing back her cloak and throwing her arms around Abigael.

"Martha? What are you doing here?"

"It's a long story but do come in. Welcome to you too Zaccaria and Saadya. What a surprise."

Martha took one look at the travelers and said, "I'm anxious to talk with you, but that must wait. You must first rest. Follow me. My two best rooms are still available."

"The small room I occupied before will do nicely," Arif said.

"There's no need this time," Martha broke in. "Perhaps you'll sleep better with more air."

The next morning Arif descended to the dining room before his fellow travelers. The innkeeper came to him and introduced himself as Manua and took him to a table with ten place settings. "My wife and children are now busy, but they'll be coming soon. With fewer customers, we should be able to enjoy a meal together."

A short while later Martha came to him with her four children. "This is my oldest, Joel; his name means *Yahweh is God*; my second Aliza our *joyful* girl; Eitan who I hope will always be as *solid and enduring* as his name; and my youngest Hannah blessing us with *grace* indeed." After bowing each in turn, the youth passed out fresh-baked bread and soured milk before seating themselves.

Arif looked happily at the wholesome young people and told about his own children who were in the same age range of the youngest two, then he curiously prodded them with questions on their life and points of view.

Answering at first stiffly, they gradually became quite candid until Joel reversed the focus back on Arif, asking him, "How did you, from far-away Babylon, become friends with Zaccaria and Abigael?"

At this point the latter entered the dining room and the atmosphere exploded in a grand reunion.

When all were settled and eating their flat bread Joel rephrased his question, "How did all of you get together?"

Arif wisely deferred to Zaccaria who explained their meeting and all he'd learned about BelkA, Parto and Arif, as well as the business transactions in Tyre.

Joel looked at Arif and asked, "How do you see it?"

"A series of providences," Arif said simply.

"I knew there was something about you," Martha exclaimed. "I see a priest in you."

"A priest?" Startled Arif sat back. "How?"

Manua laughed. "Don't be alarmed Arif. Martha has her own way of classifying people."

Martha quickly elaborated. "I connected you with a good priest and friend we knew in Jerusalem who had the same sincerity as you, and always had a scroll in hand. The way you came up with the simple explanation of providence sounded so like him."

Saadya's eyes sparkled, "She's speaking of Amit."

"Of course. By the way how is he?"

"Fine. And we're going to introduce Arif to him."

"Well of all things," Martha said with her family as enchanted as she.

Zaccaria still sensing some puzzlement in Arif said gently, "I'm just an ordinary cultivator while you're a scholar of distinction, but in the traditional

Hebrew view a priest is one who sees the hand of God in all that happens."

"Ah-h," Arif said as his shoulders relaxed and a smile widened his face, "Thank you Zaccaria. Your explanation helps. I find it all profoundly interesting. You see, in my mind, a priest performs or overseas certain religious rites and intervenes with gods on behalf of individuals, but essentially he's an administrator or politician with many secular duties. He rules from a temple or ziggurat where he controls matters of economy dealing with agriculture, rents of land, construction, literature, astronomy, technology, and of course war. For instance, we have them to thank for the wheeled chariots and bronze weapons that serve us all."

The young people laughed at the astounding comparison, but quickly hushed as their parents turned stern faces in their direction.

Martha now hastened to speak. "Arif, please forgive me for my careless remark. It was enlightening for me to hear your view."

"Thank you dear woman, but no apology is necessary. On the contrary I find your classification of me most flattering, and I am most pleased to learn of your evaluation of a true priest. Indeed I look forward to meeting Amit."

By then customers were needing attention. Manua leaned over and whispered in his wife's ear, "I'll take over my dear. Don't get up."

"Fancy our meeting in this way," Abigael mused. "If only we could have more time together to fill in all the gaps since last we were together. But perhaps, before we part, you might tell us what caused you to leave Jerusalem so suddenly and why you came here?"

"We just had to get out of Jerusalem. It's not a place to raise children these days. Night after night we saw things that upset us. Situated in a prominent place as we were, we found our inn becoming a house of prostitution with religious leaders approving and even participating. So we decided to move away from the city. We're not sorry. We have fewer customers here so we must pinch a bit all around, but we are content. With the children helping as they do we don't have to hire outside help, at least at present. We miss the temple, of course, and here we have no priest to teach us, but we celebrate the feasts as a family, recite the precepts by memory and write them on plaques to keep them constantly before us. But now tell us about you."

"Not much has changed for us in Gibeon," Abigael replied. "We were happy to sell all of our wheat, but we need to attempt a crop of barley so that we can harvest it in early spring. These are uncertain times. The big news of Nebuchadnezzar's army marching is already all over Tyre."

The family sat up straight. Manua noticing came to them.

Abigael suddenly caught herself. "Oh, I'm sorry, I didn't realize you did not yet know."

Martha repeated to Manua what Abigael had just said.

"So Jeremiah's predictions are about to happen!"

"Let us not be alarmed," Zaccaria said. "Yahweh will never abandon us."

"Do you suppose we could pray before parting?" Martha suggested, her eyes pleading reassurance.

Zaccaria looked at Arif. "Would you mind?"

"Of course not. In fact I think it's a wonderful idea."

Martha suggested that the young people pray on their behalf.

Simply but enthusiastically the youth spoke their requests with ease just as Zaccaria's family had the night before.

Arif sighed wishing that his own children might experience such an atmosphere of trust and openness.

When they'd finished Manua spoke seriously, "We don't know what lies ahead of us or if the army will come through Gezer as the Assyrians once did, but I have the sense that they will focus primarily on Jerusalem and the surrounding areas. Perhaps we could provide a safe-haven for all of you. When do you think Nebuchadnezzar will reach Jerusalem?"

"About two months hence," Arif said solemnly.

"A thought comes to mind," Zaccaria said. "A siege means famine. There's not much use in planting a crop in my field as soldiers will probably plunder it, but would there be land available for that purpose here in this area?"

"Actually there is. I'll check it out—today."

"We really need to start on our return journey," Arif said with a squint of anxiety in his eyes, "so perhaps we should settle our accounts with you and be on our way."

"The account is settled," Manua said. "I never charge my friends."

"That's not good business," Zaccaria insisted.

"Please allow us the joy."

Goodbyes completed the travelers walked toward the door. As Arif passed the innkeeper's children he dropped a gold coin in the apron of each and extended a last heart-felt thank you to the parents.

Chapter 44

The Thugs Plan

Bethlehem, October 589 B.C.

It was high noon when Abid shoved his horse into the stall of Bethlehem's inn. He darted through the central courtyard, up the rickety steps taking three at a time, and ran down the long balcony to burst through the door of the room his gang occupied.

"I've got exciting news," between gasps he shouted at his two companions taking their afternoon nap.

"Can't it wait," one of them protested, his eyes filled with sleep.

"No ShabAzn there's no time to lose. Wake up Tahampton. We've got our break. Arif is traveling to Tyre all by himself and carrying a bag of gold. Do you hear me? This time we've got him in our hands. All we need to do is lay for him in the rugged pass between Jerusalem and Gezer."

"Where did you hear this?" curly haired ShabAzn asked.

"Never mind that now, I have my connections."

"How well we know," Tahampton said sitting up and yawning. "And once again you've worked out the perfect plan." He flopped back on his mat and shut his eyes.

"Come on fellows. So my past schemes haven't all worked. If only this one works we'll have it made. Do you hear fellows? Arif has been sent to Tyre on some errand, and is expected to be absent five days. Chances are he's returning today. There's no time to loose."

"I think we deserve to know where this information comes from," Tahampton insisted.

"All right. I heard of it at Tovi's inn. That is, outside the inn."

"From who?"

"The son of the owner. I was asking him if a Babylonian was staying there. He told me yes, but that he was on a journey to Tyre. He assured me that he went alone about five days ago, and that his wife and children were still at the inn."

"How do you know it wasn't some other Babylonian including RAstin? He's the one I really want. Besides, there are plenty of foreigners in Jerusalem, and how old was the boy?"

"The name Arif came up, I forget if it was he or me who said it, and the lad might have been seven or eight. How do I know?"

"Are you expecting us to act upon the word of a seven year old?" ShabAzn said to affirm his derision.

"Look ShabAzn, time is of essence. If we don't move now we'll miss what could be our great opportunity. It's our chance to settle the score once for all with Arif for switching loyalties. After he's out of the way we can more easily go after RAstin."

"For all we know Arif hasn't even started on his return journey or he could be just outside Jerusalem. Why don't we rather get the wife and children?" Tahampton loudly asserted sitting up and fastening his sandals, "or even better wait for the big fish—BelkA."

"There are too many people around Tovi's inn and there's all kinds of surveillance around BelkA. We may never get the chance but this is worth the effort, so let's get moving. You Tahampton, get the weapons together and prepare the horses, you ShabAzn the food, and I'll put together the blankets, heavy rainwear, and the tents. We could be facing a cold wet night."

"Now wait a minute, who gives the orders here?" Tahampton asked, standing to his feet and facing Abid.

At that moment a loud knock fell on the door.

Abid moved aside to let Tahampton answer.

"What's all the noise about during rest hour? We're getting complaints from all around."

"Pardon us, we were about to leave on a journey."

"Then get out," came the angry response, "and don't bother to return." Having said that the innkeeper walked out leaving the door ajar.

"Now look what you've done," Tahampton said as he quietly shut the door.

"What have I done? It is *we*—all of us—who just had a little discussion."

"Sh-h-h" ShabAzn cautioned. "We're in enough trouble as it is."

The thugs packed up and quietly stole out of the inn.

Chapter 45

Thugs Revenge

Between Jerusalem and Tyre,
October 589 B.C.

The air was heavy and muggy matching the glum moods of the three young Babylonians, each on his own horse, as they left Jerusalem through the Ephraim Gate. Once on the open road, ShabAzn, who'd managed to keep out of the most heated arguing apparently, determined that it was up to him to drum up some light conversation. "I predict showers by nightfall," he said nonchalantly. "Could be even to our advantage."

"Or disadvantage," Tahampton said with a look of disdain in the direction of ShabAzn.

"We'll make sure it *is* to our advantage," ShabAzn said as a means of justifying himself. "Once we're past Gibeon we'll need to keep our eyes and ears open for clues."

ShabAzn, still in a grumbling mood, now vented another complaint, "If we had a guide with some savvy he'd advise us to circle around and come in from behind Arif without leaving tracks, but I still think this whole thing is stupid."

"Hold your tongue curly head," Tahampton gruffly admonished, then suddenly changed his tone. "Actually, you've got an idea there. When we see a way of climbing a cliff or a rock we'll send you up to check the road below so we could perhaps circle around behind Arif. Surprisingly there appears to be some brains under that tangle of curls."

ShabAzn was about to shoot back a retort like, "At least I have hair," when Abid, riding in front of him turned around and gave him a warning frown. "You won't accomplish anything with a crack like that," he said in a low tone with his hand muffling the direction of his voice.

"He always makes remarks that belittle me."

"And me too, but if you're smart you'll avoid disputing. He's at least giving you credit for a good idea. Besides, since we've decided to do this, we need to quit bickering and concentrate on striking."

•••

Upon reaching Gibeon they stopped at an inn to eat and replenish their water skins. Tahampton took the opportunity to ask the innkeeper if he, by chance, had seen a traveler with Arif's description.

"There are travelers all the time but I don't recall seeing a Babylonian, at least not one obviously so.

No, today there have been only Jews and mostly in groups."

Again they started up the winding road that could barely be called that, rutted at places, or virtually washed away at others. When they reached a spot with a high rocky embankment on the side, Tahamtpon turned around and said, "Here's your opportunity ShabAzn. We'll wait on the side of the road while you survey the territory from up there."

ShabAzn climbed the steep slope, inching his way by digging his feet into the dirt, and pulling himself up by hanging onto brush and branches until he reached a rocky ledge. Turning slowly in all directions he surveyed the landscape. The tangle of trees prevented a clear view of the road but as far as he could see in the fading light, there was not a person in view nor could he see an alternate route.

"There's too much vegetation to see clearly and it's getting dark," he said upon his return to the others.

"I was afraid of that," Tahampton said. "I think that the smartest thing for us to do now is to set up camp while we can still see. If Arif should happen by, which I think given the hour he won't, we'll at least be in place."

"Good idea," Abid said. "Now fellows, it's not a bad site."

While ShabAzn prepared the food the other two set about sharpening their weapons. In so doing Tahampton began to feel a sense of confidence heightened by a rush of adrenalin. "Just think fellows. We're three against one this time. We'll be returning home with a fat bag of gold."

"Home. Are you dreaming?" ShabAzn retorted.

•••

Helem, Mahla, Ibzan, Azek, Nethaniah and RAstin had managed to come together within the hour and Tovi had hurriedly accumulated victuals, rainwear, blankets, and tents.

With their knowledge of the terrain Azek and Ibzan advised taking an alternate route by going straight up to Ramah before veering west, as a precaution in the event that the gang had set out too and were already laying for Arif. "It's a bit longer, but the area surrounding Ramah is a plateau so we'll cover more distance and even be ahead time-wise," Azek explained.

"There's also a short cut we know, but we'd need to reach it before dark," Ibzan added.

"That's right," his brother affirmed. "When the water's high it's impassable. We'd risk getting lost or drowned."

"Already it could be muddy but let's give it a try," Azek insisted.

The sun was low, nearing the skyline when they reached Ramah and so they dared not take time even to eat. Once back on the road to Gezer, they'd traveled but a short distance, when the scouts led off down a valley, through a rocky waterbed, and then climbed once more to a summit.

Mahla sniffed the air. "I think I smell smoke," she cautioned.

307

Azek and Ibzan looked at each other. "Let's check it out," Azek said, and then turning to the rest he added, "It won't take long."

There were nods of approval as the group got off their animals and sat down on logs and rocks.

As they waited Mahla thought out loud, "What do we do if they spring on us?"

"A good question," Nethaniah said thinking the same thing.

Before they could come up with a solution the scouts were back puffing and panting. "It's Adda's gang all right," Azek said. "They've set up camp and there's three of them. We've come in above them. It appears Arif hasn't yet come this far."

"Should we begin with an attack or try to alert Arif first?" Ibzan asked.

"I suggest we alert Arif," RAstin said. "He should be in on the planning."

The others nodded agreement.

"From now on we'll have to go on foot leading our horses, so let's get our lanterns lit and then all of us, by all means, keep together no matter what," Ibzan said. "We need to warn you that there are wild animals in this area including bears, so keep your weapons handy and keep quiet."

They made their way slowly winding through ravines, around clusters of trees, sometimes even cutting through thickets with the help of a sword, other times tripping over stones or stumps. A snake slithered over a rock near Mahla, but she had her knife ready, and with lightening speed, plunged the sharp blade into the serpent's head. Further on they met up with a jackal that Azek took care of with his sling-shot. Finally upon rounding a bend the boys stopped. "The road's just below us," Azek said. "Let's just hope Arif isn't between us and the gang, as we're a good distance ahead of them now."

"It's a chance we'll just have to take," Helem said, "unless you boys want to risk going back to make sure."

"It's safer," Azek said. "We'll be quick."

The scouts had barely set out when Mahla noticed tiny flickering lights moving. "Look ahead," she whispered. "There's more than one person coming."

"Let's move off the road and wait till they get closer," Helem whispered back.

By the time the twins rejoined the group they could make out the forms more clearly. "Arif's one of them," Mahla said quietly. "I'm sure of it."

"Does he appear to be bound?" Helem asked.

"No, but it's him for sure," RAstin confirmed.

"Do the others look like enemies?"

"Not a chance," Mahla said. "There's camara-derie among them and one's a woman."

"I'll call out his name," Helem said, "no rather you Mahla."

"Arif, have no fear, it's us your friends," Mahla called softly.

The group fell silent for a time, and then Arif jumped from his horse and ran to them. "What is this, a welcoming committee?"

"Sh-h-h," RAstin replied signaling caution. "The thugs who kidnapped your children are waiting for you down the road."

"But who is the family?" Mahla asked.

"New and wonderful friends that I want you to meet. I'll tell you all about them later."

Following quick introductions Arif asked, "How far ahead is the gang?"

"We know exactly where they are, they're barely out of earshot," Ibzan said, "I suggest immediate attack while they're off guard. Besides there are only three of them."

Arif stood still thinking it over. "We've got to avoid unnecessary bloodshed," he said reflecting. "I think it best that we stay in this area till light of day, then while all of you stay in the background, I'll proceed slowly toward them alone. Let me be the bait."

"I wouldn't trust them," RAstin said. "I know this bunch. They're not especially brave but they are desperate. I'm more than willing to accompany you."

"You have a point, RAstin, but if they see two of us they might lose their heads or maybe turn and run. Then we'd have to deal with them again later."

Nethaniah who'd been listening carefully now spoke up, "I'd agree to that, but Arif we'll be fully prepared to back you up."

A concerned frown crossed Mahla's forehead but she refrained from a comment.

"In any case," Arif said, "If I'm injured, the rest of you could perhaps get the papyrus to BelkA. I want Abigael and Saadya completely removed from the scene, and you too Mahla."

"Yes, well," Mahla said non-comittedly.

"Thank you Arif," Zaccaria said to the precaution. "The women can take charge if there are wounded."

After setting up camp—though without making a fire—and partaking of the food Tovi had sent along with them, they gathered together in a circle and earnestly petitioned protection and courage for the confrontation ahead. Not all slept that night. Arif reviewed his life and caught himself addressing a plea to Yahweh, though he made sure no one heard.

By dawn rain started falling. While they silently ate breakfast Azek and Ibzan, who'd already been out surveying, returned and announced excitedly. "They're coming this way. At the speed they're going they'll be here in ten or fifteen minutes," Azek said gasping for breath.

Helem looked at the scouts and asked, "Where's the best place for the rest of us to hide?"

"We've already chosen the spot," Ibzan replied. "We'll need to get in our places right away."

"Arif, you should probably continue on horseback so they'll not suspect anything," Helem suggested, "and I'll be in charge of the animals. And if you like, I'll give the call of alert should something unforeseen come up."

"Thanks Helem," Arif said. With a whispered prayer, and remembering the quotation from the Writings: "the LORD shall preserve thy going out and coming in," that Parto had spoken back in Jerusalem, he mounted his horse. When poised to go he said in a shaky voice, "If anything happens to me, friends, please take care of my wife and children." Then he turned to Mahla. "In a moment now would you give me you the go-signal?"

From her position behind some trees with Abigael and Saadya, Mahla softly said, "GO."

Arif proceeded on his horse, hesitatingly at first, then confidently toward his enemies. When he had come within their view he dismounted and walked toward them.

Laughter broke out among the thugs and then teasing, "Well, well, nice to see you again pal. This calls for celebrating, don't you think?"

Then a dagger came out of it's sheathe, a sword flashed, and arrows were removed from a shaft.

"Let's talk," Arif said. "I'll cut a deal with you. Wouldn't you rather just take the gold?"

"Are you saying you're giving yourself up without a fight?"

"I'm saying that I want an agreement that you'll stop making trouble for my family and BelkA, and return quietly to Babylon."

Raucous laughter was the answer, then an arrow whipped through the air and struck Arif's right shoulder and a dagger hit his arm. He staggered for a while and began to fall. In seconds a man was on the ground beating him with a club.

Meanwhile Helem's signal had rung out in the distance that resulted in an instant pelting of arrows coming as if from nowhere. The man beating Arif fell forward and then the second with the sword fell, the third was also wounded, but managed to turn around, mount his horse, and begin to flee only to slump over and fall to the ground.

Abigael and Mahla rushed toward Arif helping him to a comfortable position and then gently washing and applying dressings. Mahla held up his head enabling Abigael to put a mug of wine to his lips.

"I was afraid of this," Mahla groaned.

"If you'll help me I'll try to get up."

Abigael cautioned, "You've lost a lot of blood Arif, but we'll give it a try."

By then RAstin had rushed over. Arif looked up at his friend and attempted a smile. "This is the second time you've come to my rescue."

"Don't talk Arif. We'll get you to Jerusalem."

Arif whispered, "Oh Yahweh," and then fell to the ground.

"Is he dead?" the others asked.

RAstin touching his pulse affirmed, "He's alive."

"What do we do about the bodies?" Azek asked.

"We can't afford any delay. Push them over the cliff. It's the living we care about most right now," Nethaniah said.

While RAstin, Helem and Nethaniah helped Arif onto his horse, Zaccaria solemnly performed the unpleasant task of disposing of the bodies. Then RAstin mounted behind Arif and the others led the extra horses.

•••

The sun was low but had not dropped from the horizon when the weary group reached Tovi's inn.

Chapter 46

Papyrus

Jerusalem, October 589 B.C.

Tirza was attempting to keep her rambunctious adolescents quiet in the tiny room at Tovi's Inn while her husband slept. As hours passed her anxious eyes kept hovering over him. How long would it yet be? Again she sighed.

Fnally Arif jerked, groaned and screwed up his face as if wrestling with a nightmare. Then he opened wide his eyes and attempted sitting up. "The papyri, I must check on it," he shouted, but fell back helpless. Every muscle in his body felt yanked apart and his back, arm and shoulder burned with pain. Once more he tried, and again fitfully gave up.

Tirza tried to soothe and speak gently to him, but Arif ignored her. The only success she had was to put a light shawl over his shoulders and even that caused him to groan. After an hour it seemed that her husband was calming down once more when suddenly he was up, and even stumbling into the hall.

"I must get to Zaccaria's room," he whispered.

All Tirza could do was help to steady him as he walked. "We're getting to it now," she said. "I know it by the humorous graffiti on the door. Here we are." She gave two raps on the door, which opened almost immediately.

"Arif, what are you doing up?" Zaccaria asked.

"How's the papyrus?"

"All is well, take a look."

Even Arif's hazy mind registered stacks of papyrus spread out neatly all across the room.

"No need to worry Arif. Mar's a professional importer of papyrus. It was all carefully wrapped and it's in perfect condition. As a precaution I spread it out and checked each package carefully to make sure there was no leakage, and all is intact."

"You're sure."

"Absolutely. But its you I'm concerned about."

"I'll be fine," Arif said turning around. "You coming down for breakfast?"

Zaccaria stood with open mouth. "Well, sure."

As they ate Tirza whispered to Abigael that Arif refused to let her see his back. "I didn't want to put him through the nuisance of taking his tunic off last night, but I know there are wounds. He still won't let me touch him."

"I'll see what I can do." She turned to Arif and gently said, "When you get back to your room I'll be coming by to check on your wounds."

"The first thing that has to be done is to get the papyrus delivered to BelkA. After that the whole world can worry about me if it wants."

The women shrugged their shoulders.

Arif asked Mahla to give instructions for moving the papyrus to BelkA's residence, which she easily and efficiently performed. "We'll each take turns, those of us knowing the way intermingling with those who don't. Let's walk at a normal gait and as nonchalantly as possible."

"Agreed," Saadya said. Being the oldest he naturally took on the role of leader.

"I'll lead the way," Arif insisted. "I suggest you follow me Abigael while the scouts bring up the end."

"Of course," they all agreed.

The young people, led by Zaccaria, set about bringing the papyrus down the stairs. When it was all stacked near the door, Arif slowly got up and reached for a stack, but this time Abigael stood in his way. Reluctantly Arif obeyed and set out walking slowly over the uneven paving stones. He'd almost reached BelkA's gate, however, when he realized that he'd overestimated his endurance. Dizzy and faint he collapsed.

Abigael put down her load and stooped over Arif, while the scouts quickly moved forward and scooped up her load. After depositing it within the gate, they returned to help Arif.

Arif groaned as Azek and Ibzan picked him up and took him to BelkA's central room where they gently laid him on the rug.

"What's wrong?" BelkA asked in shock and dismay.

"An incident yesterday," Azek said. "We'll explain later."

BelkA looked on with mingled joy, anxiety and guilt. The papyrus was stacked up and ready, but his friend's condition looked serious.

Abigael administered herbal remedies and continued bathing his face. Eventually Arif opened his eyes and looked around. Then he drew in his breath and tried to sit up.

Abigael tried to restrain him but it was no use.

"Our scriptorium!" he exclaimed, taking in the second table with writing equipment neatly set out and ready. Parto pulled back a curtain to reveal shelves of carefully classified scrolls. Arif smiled and attempted to edge forward only to collapse once more.

Tirza and Abigael arranged pillows around him and Tirza stroked his hands trying to keep him calm.

"I need to check his wounds," Abigael said. "Do you think we can manage that?"

"Allow us," Azek said as Ibzan squatted down to help. Gently they propped him in a sitting position.

BelkA looked on anxiously as Abigael gently probed and uncovered the injuries. By then Parto had already prepared water and liniments that he brought to Abigael.

When she had finished the dressings Arif was laid on his uninjured side in a position where he could look at the group.

BelkA fell on his knees before his friend and took his hand. "Arif, forgive me. I should never have made you go. It was foolish of me."

Arif opened his eyes and whispered. "Have no concern BelkA, I'll be all right. If only you knew. Ask Zaccaria to explain."

Though not yet introduced to Zaccaria BelkA looked up and smiled.

"I'm Zaccaria and allow me to introduce my wife and son."

BelkA requested that the group sit in a circle around Arif and Zaccaria, and when everyone was settled the account was told in detail.

Even then a shower of questions fell upon poor Zaccaria who let his wife answer some, allowing Saadya some of his own interpretations as well.

Finally a prolonged silence fell as tears were wiped away and eyes filled with wonder.

Now once again Arif attempted to sit, but this time he urged Zaccaria to explain his plan.

"Promise you'll rest?" Zaccaria bargained.

Arif laid back with a more contented smile.

"The friends in Gezer are making arrangements to secure a plot of land for the purpose of cultivating wheat and other crops in view of creating a stock pile for future emergencies. Since I'm a farmer I've offered to do that. It would seem that Gezer is far enough away from Jerusalem to miss Nebuchadnezzar's invasion, so we've also been offered a place of refuge should any of us need that."

Once again a hush fell upon the group.

After some time Mahla asked to speak. "There's a detail that Zaccaria might not have noticed, that I think you should know. It was RAstin's arrow that struck the one who was clubbing Arif."

Arif jerked up and looked at the young man sitting quietly. "You helped me yet again my friend," he exclaimed.

BelkA with his jaw set to prevent an emotional outburst now turned toward the young fellow and put his hand on his shoulder. "I commend you for a task accomplished with skill and devotion."

"I cannot take the credit," RAstin said with a shaky voice. "It was Yahweh who helped me."

"We can all say that," Arif said in little more than a whisper.

Looking at Parto who sat smiling through his emotion, BelkA said. "I must also confess that I have my devoted slave to thank for patiently opening my stubborn mind to discover a God beyond my wildest conception. Yahweh is no longer a stranger and this week I've seen how He really does hear our petitions. You, my friends, have each one demonstrated the difference He makes in a life, and I thank you for showing me the love and acceptance I've always longed for."

Enthusiastic clapping broke out until Helem waved his hands. "I think I hear knocking."

Parto went to the door and there stood the two servers with unusually heavy baskets brimming with food that they brought in, and set down in the middle of the group. Then noticing Arif on the floor they showed sympathy while BelkA explained. "We nearly lost him and the others as well."

The servers looked at each other and put their hands together indicating that they too had been praying.

"Be sure to tell Ebed-Melech as well," BelkA added. "He'll be glad to know that the three remaining thugs are no longer a threat."

The young fellows nodded and collected the empty plates, and when they'd left Arif asked once more while breathing heavily, "What's the status of the scrolls?"

"We now have the entire collection, but the copying is going slow."

"And the translating?"

"As you well know, I've been out of papyrus."

"No more," Arif said with a grin, and then pointed to himself as he formed the silent words, "and I'm helping."

"Of course," BelkA said gently, "when you feel better of course."

Zaccaria looked at Abigael and asked, "Might we suggest two priests who could, perhaps, help with the copying?"

BelkA grinned, "What are their names?"

"I've already mentioned Amit to Arif, but now I'm thinking also of another one named Uzziel. If you like we could speak with them."

"Please do."

"By the way," Zaccaria said. "Should you need a place to hide scrolls I have a cistern on my property that is dry. It could easily be concealed with vegetation."

"My gratitude to you, new friend," BelkA said. "We already have some scrolls in duplicate that we could hide immediately. We will discuss this with Azek and Ibzan. But now I must insist that Arif be allowed to rest, and I know most of you have need of the same." He then turned to Tirza, "Would you allow Arif to stay here tonight, and for that matter, your whole family could stay as well."

"I think it best if the children would stay with me at Tovi's inn. But I'll leave the herbs in case he needs them."

"I'll see to that," Parto affirmed.

When BelkA saw the disappointment in the faces of the young ones at not being permitted to stay over-night he said, "I'll tell you what, I really should get permission from Ebed-Melech first, but let's plan on your staying here one last night when your father is feeling better. How's that?"

Faces brightened immediately and soon the only sounds being heard in the small house were the deep breathing of Arif and the shuffling of scrolls.

Chapter 47

Siege

Jerusalem, July 587 B.C.

I t had been more than a year since the siege had
begun. Like an enraged lion the Babylonian army
had descended upon Jerusalem in clouds of blinding,
suffocating dust. The earth and the very walls shook
with the pounding of a myriad of hoofs, screeching
chariots and shrieks of soldiers. As intended, it had
struck terror into the hearts of the inhabitants.

Next came the hammering, sawing, and chopping
of timbers, and the dumping of earth for the building
of ramparts.

Prior to the siege, King Zedekiah's court had
returned to the old palace within the city walls, and
the magnificent new palace was dismantled to permit
using the bricks to fortify the walls. Now the Judean
archers stood perched from dawn to sunset on the
walls where they kept up a constant battering of

flying arrows. Presently they were resisting against the pounding catapults from the siege weapons, but could they hold out?

While some officials paraded the streets attempting to raise the moral by affirming that all was going as planned, and that the Chaldeans were sustaining the heaviest casualties, others with insight knew that it was just a matter of time.

As the city swelled with locals and their cattle from the surrounding areas crowding into the city, it wasn't long before the atmosphere became disruptive and sober. Prophets meanwhile droned on that Egypt would soon deliver. People watched and hoped day after day as things got worse, and food supplies ran lower and lower.

Even BelkA and Parto noticed reductions in their own rations from day to day. Reassuring it was that their own courtyard still had a stockpile of lentils, seeds, and nuts through the tireless efforts of Elzur, Zaccaria and Manua who had managed to harvest a crop just before the siege had started.

A considerable number of the scrolls had already been hidden in Zaccaria's cistern, prior to the siege, with a map of their placement carefully filed in BelkA's satchel, while others were deposited on the property of Manua in Gezer. That, at least, was reassuring, but the rest of the copying continued slowly with Shaphan insisting on accuracy at all cost.

Meanwhile, within the walls of their confinement, BelkA and Arif had continued at the tedious task of translation. Parto, now quite literate in Hebrew, had the responsibility of choosing which portions of the various authors to translate, placing markers as he went. The selection included passages from Moses, Job, Psalms, the earlier prophets and a few of the contemporary ones as well.

Having toiled late into the night under a flickering light BelkA now raised himself from his tense position to stretch his arms and rub his aching neck. "Time for a break," he called to Parto who was busily washing clothes in the courtyard, though using water sparingly as the supply was running low, and every drop had to be paid for in advance.

Parto came in with a handful of almonds and a smile of relief.

"Come, Arif," BelkA said gently prodding his friend to break away from his tedious work. "Your body needs stretching and relaxing too." He'd recovered from his injuries but needed still to temper over-exertion. Gratefully he got up and joined his friends.

Sitting on the carpet with their feet spread out before them, and their arms crossed behind their necks, the three men breathed deeply as each dipped into their own thoughts. Finally BelkA broke the silence. "It seems quieter today. I wonder what's happening, and about our situation. Sometimes I wonder if we made a mistake by not escaping sooner with what Writings we had, but then I remind myself that it probably would have been a death sentence for Ebed-Melech to have us disappear."

"And let us not forget how indebted we still are to him and his companions." Parto added, "who are still taking risks on our account, and still attempting to feed us."

"You're right," Arif said. "The only choice we have is to plod on."

BelkA sighed.

"Yahweh is working out a plan," Parto said. "We don't see it now but some day we will."

A key in the lock of the door announced the arrival of Ebed-Melech. After warm greetings the three invited him to join them in the central room.

"I'm on the run as usual," Ebed-Melech began, "but I wanted to update you on some events."

"Good," BelkA said. "We've been wondering."

"Day before yesterday King Zedekiah received word that Egypt's auxiliary was advancing. The Babylonians must also have received the message because they have withdrawn."

"So that's why it's been quiet today," BelkA exclaimed.

"Exactly. And of course the prophets are out there gleefully proclaiming that the Babylonians won't be back."

"Thus the siege has stopped?" Arif asked.

"Yes, but Jeremiah is cautioning that the reprieve is only temporary."

"And how is he?" BelkA asked.

"That's really what I came to tell you. He's been arrested."

"No," all three men said at once with a gasp.

"He was trying to leave the city to go to his own territory of Benjamin, and had reached the Benjamin Gate, when Urijah—now captain of the guard—accused him of deserting to the Babylonians. Jeremiah tried to defend himself, but Urijah brought him to other officials who have been waiting for a chance to pounce on him. They in turn took it as an excuse to beat him most cruelly, and now he's in the dungeon under the house of Jonathan the secretary. It's an awful place. Dark, moldy, rat infested, filthy and smelly."

"This Urijah," BelkA said trying to remember, "seems like we were warned of him before."

"He's the grandson of the late false prophet Hananiah. A few years ago Jeremiah was instructed by Yahweh to make a yoke—the kind we use to team two animals together for plowing—and to go to the palace and tell the King of Judah and his court that Yahweh's advice was to put themselves under the yoke of Babylon. It so happened that the false prophet Hananiah was present, as he'd just prophesied that within two years all would be well, and that the exiles already in Babylon would return safely to Jerusalem. Jeremiah confronted Hananiah, accusing him of lying, to which Hananiah responded by taking hold of the yoke and breaking it off of Jeremiah's shoulders, while at the same time injuring him quite severely. Later Yahweh gave Jeremiah another prophecy specifically for Hananiah in which he was told that the yoke of wood would be replaced by a yoke of iron—the kind used by kings to yoke prisoners of war together before being marched off into exile."

"Ah, yes, he's the one who died a year or so later fulfilling a subsequent prophesy of Jeremiah."

"Exactly. So that's the reason Urijah has carried a grudge against Jeremiah—and his friends—

ever since. I've got to hurry on, but let me tell you about a new prophecy by our dear prophet that I hope will encourage you as it has me. He affirmed that a remnant of exiles from both Israel and Judah will eventually come back to Jerusalem, and that the city will be rebuilt. He also proclaimed that a new covenant totally different from the old one made with the fathers would come into effect. Unlike the previous covenant written on stone—implying the intellect—this one will be written on the hearts of people who will accept it joyfully and obey it, not because of obligation but out of love. I hope I can get Baruch to give us a copy soon so you can read it in private. Jeremiah claims it's as sure as the moon and stars, sea and waves. I'll leave you with that."

Ebed-Melech was walking toward the door when he turned around once more, "Oh, by the way Amineh's back in town."

"Oh really," Parto exclaimed.

"The task of rescuing people is hindered by unsafe transportation in the area. Amineh feels she's most needed within the city walls so she took a room at Tovi's inn, and will help with the herbs they're preparing there."

"If the siege resumes she too will be at risk," Parto said sadly, "but she'll not stop her activities for anything no matter what. That's how she is."

"Given the break in the siege, is there a chance to get out soon?" BelkA asked.

"No, the king claims that you're now a more useful hostage than ever before. I think he senses that the end is near." With those last words Ebed-Melech disappeared.

The three men reviewed what had been said.

Arif spoke for them when he said, "Jeremiah's message is indeed a glimmer of light in the darkness."

"I'm going to record what he said right now before I forget," BelkA said. "It's the kind of message we need to ponder carefully."

"I think I'll send the pigeons off with a message," Arif said. "By the way, I received one from Babylon telling that the very day the siege began Ezekiel had been made aware of it by Yahweh. It also mentioned that he'd lost his beloved wife, yet on the evening of her death he was out prophesying as usual at the command of Yahweh."

"Brave soul. The life of a true prophet must be riddled with sorrows," Parto said.

"Perhaps I should write another letter to my mother."

"By the way, I forgot to ask you about her last message. Was it more congenial?"

"Not really. She wrote about meeting up with RimA and couldn't imagine that I'd resisted a woman so beautiful... and there were warnings of being true to our Babylonian religion... But yes, there was one good thing, she has talked with Bazy-An and was even impressed with him. Tonight I'm going to have to tell her that, with or without her approval, I've made my choice."

Arif gently said. "I'll send off the messages tomorrow."

•••

Jerusalem, January 586

Days, weeks, and months passed, and the pile of unused papyrus became smaller and smaller.

"What will we do when we run out?" Arif asked.

"I have a strange feeling," Parto said. "It came to me the moment I awoke this morning."

BelkA looked at him with inquiring eyes.

"I think everything's about to explode."

About midday, as Parto was preparing a tray of food, footsteps were heard at the door. Immediately he went to see.

It was Ebed-Melech, and he seemed out of breath and agitated. "I've come to inform you of important matters."

Parto stood aside to allow his guest entrance, and then followed him to the central room where BelkA and Arif rose from their worktable to great him.

"Please be seated honored one," BelkA said.

"Thank you, but since I'm short of time I'd best not. May I first ask how the copying and translating are going?"

"Very well," BelkA replied, "in fact our supply of papyrus is running low."

"I see," Ebed-Melech said straitening his shoulder, "I've come to inform you of what's happening at court. The king has just received word that the Babylonian army forced the Egyptians army to retreat, and are now returning to Jerusalem to resume the siege."

"So much for the alliance," Arif commented.

"Also, Jeremiah has gotten himself in trouble again. His enemies who've long tried to eliminate him have been lobbying at court with accusations of treason against him."

The three men shook their heads and sighed. "Accusing Jeremiah of what they themselves are guilty of," BelkA exclaimed.

"You are sadly right," Ebed-Melech agreed, "and this time they demanded that Jeremiah be silenced, and our spineless king meekly responded with, 'Do with him whatever you please. He's in your hands.'"

"No!" Parto exclaimed.

"So they took Jeremiah and dropped him into a cistern in the dungeon of prince Malchiah and have left him to sink in the mud. Fortunately there was no water in it or it would have meant immediate death, but if nothing is done for him soon he'll get buried alive. Thankfully I was in the palace at the time and heard it all, so when they left the palace I ran to the King, who was leaving for Benjamin's Gate for a court session, and implored his majesty to let me rescue Jeremiah before he died."

"You took your life in your hands," BelkA said almost in a whisper.

The anguish in Ebed-Melech's face told it all. "Thankfully, Zedekiah was already feeling remorse and even had the courage to agree to my plan. He has given me permission to collect thirty men willing to rescue Jeremiah. I've already managed to inform some of the loyal ones at court as well as the men of our group: the servers, the scouts, Helem, Nethaniah, and Zaccaria who are all, hopefully, coming together as we speak. Time is of essence, but since you're the leader of the secret society, BelkA, I've taken time to inform you. I must now run back to the palace storehouse to gather up some old clothing to save Jeremiah's armpits from the hefty ropes we're going to have to use to pull him up. I've also alerted Mahla. She, Abigael and Amineh will be coming to treat Jeremiah's wounds and tend his present needs. Now friends, I must be off. Pray for us."

"Indeed," the men called after him.

At the thud of the closing door BelkA stalked down the hall and into the courtyard with Arif and Parto hastening after him. "This makes me extremely angry. If I could get my hands on those traitors I'd squeeze the life out of them."

"Nebuchadnezzar's army will do that in due time," Parto said gently.

"You two go on in and do some praying. I have to deal with this alone. I'm going up to my room." BelkA said.

•••

For long moments BelkA struggled on his knees. At first he'd just wanted to pound the mat, but with determined discipline he focused on his newfound God. *Yahweh, I do believe that you are the one true God, a righteous God, a just God, but presently I fail to see your justice? Why must Jeremiah take the punishment that these criminals deserve?*

The struggle went on for some hours until Parto entered the room with a warm piece of bread and some broth.

By then BelkA had gotten hold of himself and gratefully accepted the bowl with a smile. "I have peace now Parto. As you were saying, Nebuchadnezzar will soon be squaring the account. I think it would be beneficial for us to spend some time reading in the scrolls for our own encouragement. Perhaps some of the hymns that we could combine with prayers for our friends."

As the three men worshipped in their confined quarters, their friends succeeded in rescuing Jeremiah from his distress with everything going as planned.

•••

Several weeks later Ebed-Melech visited once again. This time he accepted the invitation to sit down. "The siege has resumed," he said, "the battering rams are positioned and ready. I expect we'll be hearing blasting tomorrow."

"And how's Jeremiah?" BelkA asked.

"He's been transferred to the court of the guard in front of the palace. We'd hoped they'd allow him to go home, but in a way it's for the best as his enemies can't get to him where he is."

"How did this come about?" Parto asked.

"King Zedekiah called him to his chamber, as he often does when his conscience acts up, or when he gets the jitters."

"Go on," BelkA urged.

"Well, you know Jeremiah. He has no regard for status. A peasant or a king is all the same to him, and his resounding authenticity is always even. Interesting it is that in the past, every time King Zedekiah asked him to come and prophecy his future, Jeremiah seemed to have a message from Yahweh. This time when the king asked him to prophecy concerning himself, Jeremiah answered, 'I have no message for you. You've never had regard for what I've told you in the past, why should I have a word for you now? Go rather to those prophets who prophesied that Nebuchadnezzar's army would never come back?'"

"What irony," BelkA commented with awe.

"The king, never-the-less kept insisting. Jeremiah then went right close to him—at face-to-face range—and pleaded with him to surrender. 'If you do,' he insisted, 'you'll save yourself, your family and the city.'"

"But apparently he hasn't," Arif said.

"No, but Jeremiah did take advantage of the opportunity of being alone with the king to plead for his life. So the king ordered his transfer to the palace, and that a ration of bread from the street of the Bakers be supplied to him daily as long as the city holds out."

The men sighed with relief.

"You can imagine that Jeremiah, undaunted, continues to prophesy even though incarcerated. He's also purchased a field through his right of redemption, as an act of faith regarding the prophecy he received, that the day would come when exiles would return to their land."

"Is that not presumption on his part?" BelkA asked.

"No, that's faith."

"Thank you friend for your kindness and consideration of Jeremiah and of us," BelkA said.

"I'm grateful to God for the privilege." Ebed-Melech said graciously. Then he stopped and took a deep breath. "Alas my friends, I fear I have yet another message to convey to you from the king, a secret message in fact. The king is now afraid of harsh repercussions upon himself on the part of Nebuchadnezzar should you still be in custody or worse dead, as some are intent upon. He wants me, and a few others, to see to it that you escape the city. I must tell you to prepare immediately. Do whatever your duties require for the movement of the scrolls and be prepared to leave by midnight. We dare not wait a day longer."

"But I'll need to get the camels!"

"I'll be sending over race horses. You'll have to leave the camels behind. They're dromedaries chosen for their ability to carry heavy loads, not for agility."

"But what about my promise to Daniel? I need to take all the scrolls."

"Take what you can, and write out specific orders. You'll have to trust the rest of us to protect, and perhaps even to get them to Babylon. Today it's a matter of saving your life."

"Bah!" BelkA exclaimed. "How did power get in the hands of children anyway?" Then noticing

Ebed-Melech's concern he got hold of himself and a spirit of compassion replaced the anger. Gently he said, "I'll probably be seeing Nebuchadnezzar and that will give me an opportunity to intervene on your behalf, friend. I owe much to you and some day I hope I will be able to compensate you more fully. I would be grateful if you could write a list including the names of other deserving persons as well."

"You might also plead mercy for King Zedekiah," Ebed-Melech said sorrowfully. "He knows to do right but his companions have been his downfall. I must say that, in spite of all, he has treated me well."

"I'll remember that, and please forgive my anger."

Ebed-Melech bowed and said, "On behalf of those you will remember and for myself, I thank you." He then stood up and looked BelkA straight in the eyes a last brief moment before turning around and hurrying out.

Chapter 48

Escape

Jerusalem, March 586 B.C.

When the door closed behind Ebed-Melech, BelkA, Parto and Arif stood speechless. For a long moment they remained in a stunned shock, looking at one another as if hoping to be convinced that it was just a crazy dream. Then they quietly entered the central room where they sat down at the table.

After some moments of silence BelkA began to speak. "At times like these the old habits, like appealing to the gods or finding a specialist, tend to resurface."

Arif nodded agreement.

"Parto, you're the most experienced one. Give us some advice."

"There's no secret formula or magic words. Yahweh sees right into our hearts and knows what we can't even put into words. Many of the prayers we've read in the scrolls are not especially eloquent."

"I've noticed," Arif agreed. "But they come from down deep in the heart. That's what I experienced when I faced Adda-Guppi's last three thugs that day on the pass. I didn't know what to say so I just repeated that passage you once mentioned Parto: 'The LORD shall preserve thy going out and thy coming in.'"

"Thank you for reminding us of that hymn Arif," BelkA said, "and I must say Parto, that when you pray I sense the Divine Presence. I think it would help Arif and myself to hear you pray on our behalf."

"I'll be happy to do so."

The three men knelt down and Parto led the prayer.

•••

"Mighty God of Abraham, and all who come to you in faith, show us mortals who seek your face the guidance we need at this time.

"We implore your protection over our dear friends here in Jerusalem, also in Gezer, Aleppo, Damascus, Tyre, and Babylon, and also for these precious scrolls.

"Thank you for allowing us to have the sacred Writings in our own hands, and for all we've learnt from them. We also thank you for the friends who have helped us find and copy them. Please grant us protection tonight as we attempt to escape the city, and help us to trust you to protect those we love who might have to fight on our behalf. Thank you for the promises that encourage us, for your faithfulness and for your enduring love."

•••

The three men rose from their knees with more tranquil spirits, and sat down once more at the table.

"We all need to think with clarity," BelkA said as he put papyrus before each of them.

Lists were made, and a plan drawn up that included alternative options for the unpredictable.

It was agreed between them that Arif's family should escape the city with BelkA and Parto, but that they should make their way to Gezer. The obvious factor was that, apart from a few scrolls, they would have to leave the rest behind. With saddened hearts they selected two copies and two translated scrolls.

"As Ebed-Melech said, we'll just have to trust our friends and Yahweh," Arif reminded his collaborators.

BelkA looked grave. "I have failed."

"The end is not yet," Parto said trying to reassure his master.

"You're right my friend. I'm going to prepare clear instructions for Ebed-Melech and our group. Blind Man will have to resume charge of *The Lamp Connection*. That is all I can do."

•••

Late that afternoon when the servers arrived with food, they brought with them four horses and a cart with Mahla, Amineh, RAstin and the scouts as passengers. The last rations provided for a meal together with the servers also participating.

As they ate Mahla explained that famine in the city was becoming critical and that plague was already sweeping away the elderly and children. "Bodies are accumulating and there's nowhere to bury them. The streets are filthy and reeking with foul odors. People are hungry and selling their treasures for food, so naturally profiteering has escalated."

BelkA looked at Mahla. "And what are your plans?"

"My place is in the city."

"You're sure?"

"I'm sure BelkA. People are sick. The only medicines are at black market prices. Amineh and I feel compelled."

"How's the supply of food and medicines holding out?"

"It's dwindling but we're managing. The reserves that you'll leave us will provide some relief over at Tovi's. However, we're going to have to be discreet about getting them there. We can be grateful that all the supplies collected in advance are now saving many lives."

BelkA nodded and took her hand. "It grieves me to leave you in this situation. If only..." he dared not trust his voice.

Mahla forced a smile.

Meanwhile Parto had been talking with Amineh as she explained how the city had swelled during the break in the siege when more and more people from the surrounding areas had sought refuge within the walls of the city. "It's getting catastrophic," she said. "Babies are screaming with hunger and thirst, their tongues sticking to the roofs of their mouths. There are parents who've been so hungry that they've eaten their own children. It's become inhuman. I've had to assist at some births where one wonders what's the use. They're going to die anyway. The best one can do is recite those parts of the Writings that speak of Yahweh as the shepherd being with us in the dark valley of death."

"You are a brave and courageous woman Amineh," Parto said with a shaky voice. "I fear for your safety and health."

"Thank you for your concern Parto," Amineh said with her usual brave spirit, though a nervous shaking of the hand, and a flutter around her mouth told of turmoil within.

Parto had to restrain himself from taking her in his arms. He'd always known Amineh to be a strong and self-sufficient woman, tending to the needs of many before her own. Now even she, he knew, was reaching a breaking point and there was nothing he could do for her. What words were there? Their own time had run out. He could only hope that the members of *The Lamp Connection* remaining in the city would hold each other up till their rescue.

•••

The stars were out by the time Ebed-Melech came accompanied by Helem, Nethaniah, Tovi, and other trusted assistants who had volunteered as reinforcement to insure BelkA's safe escape. Lines of anxiety now played on their faces.

"We must go now," Ebed-Melech said soberly. "We'll leave by way of the garden gate. I know the guard and have notified him, so hopefully it will go well. However, should there be treachery, this is the strategy we'll use. All of us must stay together and be prepared to fight at close quarters. Mahla and Amineh can stay in the background with Tirza and the children, while also remaining alert and prepared to use their knives if necessary. You scouts, get your bows and arrows ready. The rest of us are well armed with daggers and short swords. Should you lose those, there's always your fists and stones." He turned then to BelkA and said, "I know you are an excellent fighter and that you're amply capable of defending yourself and others, but please, let us do this for you. Your getting out alive today is more important to us than anything. Don't pay attention to us. When I give the word *go,* don't look back."

When they arrived at the gate a group of men swept in out of the darkness and moved in upon them. "What's this," Ebed-Melech called out when he saw the guard looking on without doing a thing to stop it. "We've been betrayed," he cried out as his little army grouped to fend off the attackers.

From all directions men advanced with daggers toward them. Parto jumped from his horse and threw himself in front of BelkA who had his head down and his body as if glued to the horse. Mahla's knife flew through the air and downed an assailant who was poised to cut the children down. The rest had pulled together, ducking arrows as they ran toward the attackers with an outright thrust. Screams rose above the sounds of zooming arrows, the clamor of swords, and flying stones.

The surprised assailants, soon realizing that they were outnumbered, scattered and fled in all directions. BelkA, who had sustained the edge of a javelin that grazed his face and arms, caught from the view of one eye a knife flying from Amineh's hand into a man's back. By then he realized that it was the gatekeeper himself who had stopped in his flight to make a last attempt to eliminate him.

Within minutes several bodies lay on the ground with some sort of incapacitating injury, and by then it was discovered that Mahla had sustained the worst blows. Her robe was ripped and blood gushed from her nose, forehead and lower body. Amineh made a dash for her while Ebed-Melech shouted, "BelkA, Parto, Arif, get going NOW!" He ran forward and slapped BelkA's horse. In an instant they were dashing forward through the open gate.

•••

The moon lit up the landscape on the opposite side of the gate as the six refugees on their horses moved forward with increasing caution toward a cluster of soldiers sitting around a fire. Hearing their approach one of them shouted, "Halt!"

Within seconds they were encircled. "State you names and intentions," the sentinels shouted.

"I am BelkA-Souash, envoy of King Nebuchadnezzar with my companions. I desire to see your commander."

"BelkA," one of the soldiers shouted. "You're supposed to be dead!"

A torch was put into BelkA's face. "It's him all right," another shouted. "Risen from the dead."

Laughter broke out, then whistling. Heads began to appear at nearby tents. "Come on fellows there's cause for celebrating," they shouted. "We've got Babylonians here."

"Please announce me to your commander," BelkA shouted above the racket.

"Yes sir, with pleasure," a fellow said. "Follow me."

But when they reached the commander's tent a sentry standing guard gruffly pushed them back. "The general's sleeping, can't this wait till morning?"

By this time Commander Nebuzaradan himself appeared, and demanded to be informed on what the ruckus was about.

"It's BelkA-Souash," one of them called out.

"Wait, I'll be with you shortly."

A few moments later the general appeared holding up a lamp.

"You're wounded," he exclaimed and ordered treatment.

"Minor wounds sir. There was a skirmish getting out. The important thing is that I've been released from confinement by order of King Zedekiah."

"Well, well. We thought they'd done away with you."

"It was attempted," BelkA said nonchalantly.

"Like father, like son," the commander said with a grin.

"Actually, it was the courtier and some sympathizers who saved our lives," BelkA corrected.

"I hear a wise prophet in there is advising surrender."

"His name is Jeremiah, Commander."

"That's right."

"There are others as well."

"Their names?"

"If you'll allow me, I'll present you with a list."

"In any case, they've been told to surrender, why are they not doing it?"

"You see, what happened to me. The Jews are still laying wait for people who try. Jeremiah's incarcerated in the court of the guard in the front of the palace, and the others are trying to help the weak and sick."

"And who is this family with you?"

"My assistants from Babylon, Arif, his wife and children."

"I see."

To BelkA's relief he asked no further questions, but turned around and ordered that two tents be put up immediately. "See that all their needs are met. In the morning I require that a meal be prepared—an ample meal."

"We'll speak with one another then," he said to BelkA. "Follow my men."

"Thank you for your kind attentions Commander," BelkA said bowing his head.

The general waved his hands, "Get some rest."

•••

The following morning BelkA and Parto were escorted to a large tent where a meal resembling a banquet was laid out for them.

BelkA and Parto looked with wonder, and a strange queasiness at the food displayed that included a variety of meats, fresh and dried fruits, and even baked goods. Thinking of the distress of their friends still in the city robbed them of appetite.

"Please be seated," the commander said when he entered and caught their roving eyes. "I have a feeling you've not eaten well for some time. Your bodies are leaner than they used to be."

"We have fared better than most," BelkA said. "Alas, the city has little food left."

"We'll have them starved out soon enough now," the commander said appearing not to notice their restrained eating. "Let us speak of your plans."

"My first obligation is to report to King Nebuchadnezzar. I need to know where he is."

"A courier has arrived telling us that he will be setting up court at Riblah."

BelkA looked at Arif and his eyes widened. "We could get to Riblah by way of Tyre. From there a ship could take us to nearby Byblos. The rest we'd manage on horseback."

"Nebuchadnezzar wants to extend his control over Phoenicia and the coastal regions on down to Egypt, so a siege is being prepared for Tyre, but people can still come and go somewhat freely."

"Is the harbor still functioning?" BelkA asked.

"Of course. Tyre is a complicated and strongly fortified city. I have a feeling it will take a long time, probably years to cut it off. Commerce continues as usual."

"In view of the dangers of overland travel, I think we should take that route."

"In that case I'll provide an escort, perhaps not all the way to Tyre, but at least through the most dangerous terrain."

"As far as Gezer perhaps?" BelkA asked.

"That can be arranged."

Chapter 49

Translation

Gezer to Tyre, April 586

The escort to Gezer had greatly facilitated the journey. Upon their arrival and following a cordial reception at the inn, the escort left them to return to Jerusalem.

Arif's excitement while introducing his wife and children to Manua and Martha's family was so intense he could hardly contain himself. "My prayers are answered," he exclaimed with tears coursing down his cheeks. "The circumstances are not as I had hoped, but we are thankful none-the-less."

BelkA received special attention for his wounds but his hosts wisely refrained from pounding him with questions. Manua and Martha declared the inn closed to permit giving full attention to their favorite guests that now also included Zaccaria, Abigael and Saadya, who were staying there. As they sat on cushions by lamplight BelkA noticed the weariness on all the faces. Manua told of the efforts to grow special survival crops including herbs for medicines, while the women dried and prepared them for transport to Tovi's inn with directions for the use of each, all carefully written on potsherds.

It was Saadya who served as spokesman telling of the adventures and frustrations in getting the supplies over the pass, through the wall, and into the hands of Nethaniah and Tovi.

"Alas," Arif sighed, "there was never enough, and now with the siege once again in rigor, it's still more challenging."

"The plague was becoming severe as we left the city," BelkA added. "Thus your efforts were, and still are most useful. Obviously Amineh and Mahla insisted on staying there to help."

"Those women are astounding," Abigael said, "but I fear for them."

BelkA and Parto looked at each other. Both felt a tightening of the knots that had planted themselves within their stomach before, but especially after the escape. BelkA, knowing that his guests deserved hearing the details of the escape, cleared his throat and told about their last days in the city causing their hosts to weep with them.

After a time of prayer for Jerusalem and especially their friends still trapped in the city, Zaccaria asked about the Writings.

Once again BelkA and Parto felt their stomachs twist. BelkA insisted that Parto tell about it while he struggled with some twitching of the eye and control of his emotions.

"The present status is not to my liking," BelkA added when Parto stopped speaking.

"So most are still within the walls?" Zaccaria asked.

"As far as I know. All, that is, but the ones that you buried on your property Zaccaria, and also here, and the few I have along."

"We've got to do something," Saadya spoke up in alarm.

"No, we must wait upon Yahweh," his father said. "He will make a way."

BelkA told of Jeremiah's messages of hope, and about his purchase of a field as an act of faith in the midst of hopelessness, and of his amazing statement: "Is anything too hard for the LORD?"

"If we ever needed to hear such words, it's now," Zaccaria said softly.

"This is the promise I'm clinging to" BelkA said.

"My, how good it sounds to hear you say that," Zaccaria said with the others smiling in agreement.

●●●

Early the next morning as they sat around the table Arif reflected out loud, "I was thinking this past night, and it came to me that my family would do well to remain here for some time yet."

The young ones clapped their hands in joyful assent.

BelkA looked up thoughtfully and said, "That's an excellent idea Arif. I fully agree."

"Wonderful," Martha said beaming. "Our children were telling us last night that they hoped you'd bring them and stay with us as long as possible, but I dared not speak of it."

"Then the matter is decided" BelkA said.

The parting of BelkA and Parto with Arif's family was not without an added ache in the core of their beings, but seeing the children enjoying one another eased somewhat the strain of the final good-byes.

"Keep up your writing and your music," BelkA urged as the children embraced him.

"We will," SabA promised. "Perhaps we'll translate the Writings some day ourselves."

BelkA smiled, "Perhaps."

•••

The cramped quarters BelkA and Parto shared on the ship were luxurious compared to the conditions of other passengers sailing up the northern seaboard, most of whom were fleeing, but not sure to where. All shared that feeling of disorientation and being far from home.

The previous day they'd reached the docks with little difficulty, and with only a few Babylonian soldiers scattered about. Obviously the siege had not yet commenced. Parto, who had spotted Mar's ship, urged BelkA to hurry on ahead.

BelkA's appearance contrasted with all the fugitives boarding the ship and his request to see the captain immediately got the attention of the crewmen who, soon after, brought Mar to him.

"Excuse our late arrival..." BelkA started to say when Mar came to them.

Mar brushed aside the comment and ordered his men to find a place for the horses. "I insist that you join me for dinner in my own quarters tonight," he said and ordered his crew to find a room for his honored guests.

Later that evening as they sat in the captain's cabin BelkA said, "We were extremely relieved to see that you were in port. We feared you'd be on a voyage somewhere."

Mar smiled. "Please eat friends," he urged.

"Allow me first to show you something." BelkA got up and took from his bag a scroll and presented it to Mar.

"Is this what I think it might be?"

BelkA smiled.

"Dare I?"

"Of course," Parto couldn't resist saying.

Mar broke the seal and opened the scroll, then tried to speak but his voice refused to cooperate. "You... you did this for me?" he finally managed to say as he held the scroll to his heart.

"Just a sampling, alas," BelkA said.

"I cannot tell you what this means to me to have in my hands these sacred words that I believe to be the authentic Word of Yahweh. I am confident that some day all the scrolls will exist in my language. But how can I thank you for these first fruits of your labor."

"You have many times over," BelkA said.

"What I gave was material. This is priceless. I have a feeling that the scroll will change our lives."

"It might very well do that," BelkA said with a wink in Parto's direction.

"Now please eat," Mar urged.

BelkA and Parto obliged as best they could.

Chapter 50

New Assignment

Byblos to Riblah, May 1, 586

"We must now reorient our thinking toward Babylon," BelkA said as he and Parto rode their horses from Byblos to Riblah.

"Difficult it is to predict the reaction of Nebuchadnezzar upon seeing you," Parto reflected.

"That is of great concern to me as well, but what I fear most is facing Daniel."

"It's very possible that all the scrolls are now outside the city," Parto said trying to be reassuring.

"But I have so few with us."

There was nothing Parto could say to reassure his master.

•••

As they neared the outskirts of Riblah the road became increasingly congested with all manner of war machinery: chariots, mounted and foot soldiers, and an endless train of wagons heaped up with supplies. "This is probably going to go on for quite a while," BelkA said. "We might as well avail ourselves of an inn and wait it out."

"Sounds like an excellent idea," Parto agreed.

Upon inquiring, the innkeeper had but one room to offer. "There aren't many left in all of Riblah, honored one. This is the best I can do."

"Is it as congested in the city itself as it is here?" BelkA asked.

"Worse, far worse. That's where you'll find people sleeping under the stars."

"We'll take it then," BelkA said with a tone of resignation. "By the way, would you happen to know when King Nebuchadnezzar is expected?"

"Not exactly. A week or two I presume."

BelkA winced. "Then it would appear that we'll be your guests for awhile."

They settled into the room as best they could with Parto finding cleaning equipment to scrub down the grime and to reduce the crawling population.

"Not everyone has a practical servant such as mine," BelkA said as he saw debris collected and hauled out, and everything in the room clean and smelling fresh. "With a turn of the hand my servant has made us a lodging that will be quite acceptable. I commend you friend."

"Thank you Master."

"Come Parto, I'm sure you're hungry working so hard. Let's wander about and see what we can find." They walked up and down the narrow crowded streets only to discover that food was as scarce as lodgings, and not very appealing either. Thankfully the innkeeper had informed them of a vendor on a side street who had reasonably good fare to offer, but even his appeared to be in meager portions. The shopkeeper cut two thin slices of lamb roasting over a spit and added to it some tired looking leeks.

"We still have more than many," Parto said when they had eaten. "I'll never look at food in the same way again."

"I know what you mean," BelkA said with a sigh.

Upon returning to their room they leaned back against the wall and let their weary muscles unwind for a time, and then Parto suggested they read.

"Your turn Parto," BelkA said with the hint of a smile.

Parto timidly picked up a scroll and read until their eyes became droopy.

The same pattern of life continued for almost two weeks when a trumpet sounded announcing the arrival of King Nebuchadnezzar. They waited yet three days. Then BelkA got out his regal attire with Parto finding his slightly more modest, but equally formal clothing. After bathing, dressing, and helping each other with all the small details, BelkA picked up his jewel-encrusted sword, and the two set out among the bystanders who stepped aside to let them pass. Picking up the horses that Parto had carefully manicured and dressed, they made their way to the entrance of the barracks where rows of chariots were lined up under fluttering banners.

When BelkA announced himself as envoy of the king, he was immediately admitted into a waiting room of an enormous tent, heavily carpeted with elegant hangings, and furnished in the Babylonian style.

Upon his entrance into the temporary throne room a single glance at his king revealed in him an ill-concealed humor.

"Is this a phantom before me?" Nebuchadnezzar said when BelkA had risen to his feet. "I did not expect to see my favorite envoy alive. Are you well BelkA?"

"I am, your majesty."

"Reports were circulating that you were dead."

"My enemies have wished me thus," BelkA replied.

Nebuchadnezzar winked mischievously. "And Zedekiah?"

"Actually he treated me well, my lord. I had food when others had not, also..."

"Yet he incarcerated you did he not?"

"He did."

"And judging by your obvious weight loss your rations were on the meager side."

"But I must say on behalf of King Zedekiah that I owe my life to him. He gave orders to his officials to release me from custody, and to get me out of the city. The attempts upon my life failed. The last was a narrow escape."

"Is that the explanation for those recent scars on your arms and face?"

"It is, my lord."

"So, BelkA my son, you have bravely and courageously fulfilled your mission. I commend you."

"Thank you your majesty" BelkA said with a low bow. "I will perform whatever further duty you ask of me, but may I also request of you... a favor?" The last two words were said with BelkA lowering his head to almost touching the carpet.

"Speak."

"You see, I have learned much about Judah since my arrival there. I have met arrogant enemies of my king, and others of noble character who have backed the prophet Jeremiah in his advice to submit to Babylon. I have a list of names of those for whom I would plead mercy and leniency before you."

"They have only to surrender as the prophet has advised."

"There are enemies of my king who lay in wait for those attempting to surrender. It is in this way that Jeremiah himself was accused and arrested."

"I see." He ordered a guard to bring the list to him.

Nebuchadnezzar glanced over it. "A considerable number, and you know each one?"

"I do your majesty."

"With the prophet's name on the top."

"An honorable man, your majesty."

"What I've heard of him would agree with your evaluation." He looked straight at BelkA, carefully scrutinizing his face and body from every angle and from top to bottom.

BelkA stood looking straight ahead without a single flutter of a muscle.

"I should send you home for your health's sake, yet I see that same old spark still lives in you, and you are the perfect one for a new assignment."

"Yes, your majesty?"

"With your knowledge of certain citizens undeserving of the fate of the rest, I have determined to assign you to assist General Nebuzaradan in the transportation of exiles. You will review the people being taken into exile, and be in charge of those most deserving of mercy. Does such an assignment arouse questions within you?"

"Your majesty, I am most agreeable to the assignment, the only concern I have is that my incarceration prohibited me from completing satisfactorily the assignment of Prime minister Belteshazzar."

"Explain yourself."

BelkA told of the problem of locating the existing scrolls, the tedious copying, and even of the temple break-in.

The king sat back and laughed with abandon at the irony of it. Then he looked seriously at BelkA. "I'll make mention of it in my orders to Nebuzaradan under whom I now place you."

BelkA bowed low. "I will do my utmost to carry out your orders, your majesty."

Nebuchadnezzar called for a scribe to appear before him. Then he began his dictation.

"I, King Nebuchadnezzar, order BelkA Souash to remain in Riblah for a briefing under General

Nebuzaradan, commander of the imperial guard. He is to review the exiles, both those who have surrendered and those being captured, and is to be in charge of the conditions of the exiles deserving mercy at my hand. If, and when possible, he is to be released to complete a previous assignment that the political situation has prevented. I also require his presence here at Riblah for the passing of judgment."

When the dictating stopped the scribe handed the sheet of papyrus to the guard who presented it to the king.

The king read it through, applied his signet ring, and handed it back to the messenger.

Upon receiving it BelkA fell at his feet. "I am undeserving of such an honor in your service, your majesty."

"Go my son. You have found favor in my sight. I will now turn you over to my chamberlain who will lead you to an officer in charge of my personal servants. He will direct you to a suitable lodging."

Once more BelkA bowed. "I thank you, your majesty."

Chapter 51

Zedekiah's doom

Jerusalem, July 18, 586 B.C.

BelkA stood beside General Nebuzaradan who was proudly pointing out intricacies of the siege and attack upon the walls of Jerusalem. All around the city ditches had been dug and huge banks of earth piled up, topped with towers equal to the height of the city walls. From these the Babylonian soldiers were pitching missiles at the walls where the Judean archers had given up their defense.

The general pointed out the cracks. "We should break through by tomorrow. It's a tough target. The city's a fortress and the Jews have siege engines that are quite sophisticated, but now weakened by famine and plague, it's over for Jerusalem."

The words stung sharper than any scorpion. Stoically BelkA kept his dignity as he responded with, "That is clearly evident." Worries crowded his mind causing him to miss all but Nebuzaradan's last sentence.

"...in fact it wouldn't surprise me if we broke through the walls tonight!"

"Tonight?"

"That's right."

BelkA winced in spite of himself.

"You show concern BelkA. A woman perhaps?"

"Forgive me General Nebuzaradan. I have been in the city now almost three years and during that time have formed friendships with some."

"Which explains your present assignment of course. But you did not answer my question. What about the woman?"

BelkA flushed, much to Nebuzaradan's delight.

"To be honest, there is indeed a woman, though I've not expressed anything to her, nor am I assured of her feeling toward me. She was wounded while assisting in my defense as I escaped the city."

"Surely you didn't allow a woman to defend you?"

BelkA then explained Mahla's unique talents. "Now I wonder if she's alive or dead."

Nebuzaradan shook his head in dismay. "My advice at this point BelkA is to brace yourself. There's going to be a lot of ugliness played out before your eyes. You can at least console yourself that your position permits some intervening, but you can't be everywhere in a situation of massive confusion. Take it from me; the only way I survive is with the help of strong drink to deaden the senses. "

"I prefer not to take that route."

"Suit yourself. In any case, no matter what you see, remember that the city deserves all she's going to get, for nothing else than for abandoning Yahweh and failing to honor her agreement with Babylon. Whoever heard of abandoning one's own national god? From what I've heard of this God, if I had a God like Him I'd cling to Him and forget all the others."

"Yes, this Hebrew God is indeed unique, and above all other gods."

"I suppose you have learned much about Him."

"Indeed," BelkA replied.

"I'd like to hear more, but I can't afford any softening up today. I must go now. Stand by, we might be needing you tonight."

BelkA bowed and lingered when the general left. If only he knew what was happening on the other side of those walls.

•••

BelkA and Parto had determined to stay dressed and ready in case of a trumpet call, but had dozed into a restless sleep. Sounds of pounding, crashing, grating, clashing, smashing, screaming emphasized the urgency that prompted BelkA to run in the direction of the middle court overlooking the lower city, the place he had been advised would be the meeting ground of the officers and their assistants should the wall give way. Upon arriving he noticed that the generals Nergal-sarezer, Rab-saris, Sarsekim, Rag-mag, and Samgar-nebu were already occupying their designated seats. BelkA entered and stood beside General Nebuzaradan.

"BelkA, I won't need you here at present. I want you rather to go to the camp of the deserters to check out conditions there. Take the records from the box in my room and make annotations according to the knowledge you have acquired. You need to be aware of who is there and you'll no doubt find some you'll want to reassure."

BelkA's bowed his head and silently left. He was walking away when suddenly there came the sound of shuffling and running. The officers who were facing the lower city began shouting, "The soldiers are fleeing, chase them," then one of them screamed even louder, "There's Zedekiah himself. Grab him!"

For the space of an eye blink BelkA identified King Zedekiah's dark form among those of his officers as they disappeared into the night, and knew that the dreadful day had come. There was no doubt in his mind but that Zedekiah's destiny would include the system of punishment for which the Babylonians were famous and the thought caused him to shudder. If only he'd listened to Jeremiah, none of this would be playing out. Now it was too late. There was no way to turn back the tide.

But as fast as the image of Zedekiah crossed his vision, the memory of Mahla came to the front of his mind. Her injured body lying on the cobblestones provoked a searing pain within him followed by intense anxiety. With determination he got hold of himself and hastened to the task assigned to him.

After picking up the documents under the surveillance of a guard, he continued to the deserter's camp. From a quick glance around there were but a few he personally recognized, though most knew of him. Among all the faces it was that of Tamara that caught his eye first, then he recognized her father and also her mother, all of them lean and gaunt.

When they saw BelkA they cried out his name and he came immediately to them. Tamara threw herself into BelkA arms and clung to him, while her father embraced Parto who reached a hand out to his wife Arielle. BelkA took her other hand and in so doing he noticed she was with child. The realization made him cringe. "So good to see you got here safely. I'll do all I can to make the journey comfortable," he said gently.

"It was cousin Jeremiah who insisted that we come," Tamara said sadly. "He was afraid that we would come to harm, but leaving him behind breaks us up. Thankfully Baruch has promised to stay with him."

"Are there others of the group here?" BelkA asked.

"Nethaniah and Naahma were finishing up and planning to surrender. It's difficult also to leave with a toddler. I hope they get here soon."

"Does that mean that the Writings got out of the city?"

"We hope so," Elzur said with anxiety. "If they come we'll know for sure."

"But BelkA, you haven't told us how it happens that you are here?"

"I've been assigned to the exiles by Nebuchadnezzar."

"That's encouraging at least," Tamara said lifting her distraught eyes toward him.

"I'm concerned about the others of the group," BelkA said, making every effort to restrain his emotions. "I see no sign of them. I'm going to have to leave you now, but please let me reassure you that things will go better for you than the captured exiles. So take courage. I'll do everything I can to protect you."

"Thank you," they said, reluctantly letting him go.

As BelkA continued down the aisles where families were grouped, or where individuals huddled alone, he wondered at the stories behind each one. Then it was that he found himself looking into some faces that called out to him.

"We are from Gibeon the father said bowing before him. Your camels are still in our stables. We left them with all the water and food we had."

"Thank you for informing me," BelkA said. "I will have my servant remove the animals as he will be happy to be reunited with them. Allow me to reassure you that I will repay you for your expenses and care. But how are you?"

"We're in turmoil," the wife said burying her head in her hands.

"I understand," BelkA said with compassion. "The departure will be difficult, but I'll be watching to see that your needs are met as well as I am able."

"Thank you, thank you," the husband said standing back to make room for BelkA to move on.

Leaving them he made his way to the center of the area and called out, "May I have your attention. The king wishes to acknowledge your surrender and has placed me in charge of your transportation needs during the journey to Babylon. Because you have voluntarily surrendered, those of you who desire to remain in Jerusalem will have the opportunity to do so once the conquest is over, but I warn you that life here will be extremely difficult. Should you choose exile in Babylon, unlike those being captured in days to come, all of you will be unfettered once the journey has begun.

"Accommodations in the tents will not be comfortable, but traveling through arid lands is never pleasant. Be courageous. Once you arrive in Babylon you will have assigned dwellings in an area being prepared for you by Prime Minister Belteshazzar whom most of you know as Daniel.

"Your patience and cooperation will be required in all details along the way. The more you assist me, the more favor you will be shown by my superior Nebuzaradan. Tomorrow my servant will be with me as it is possible that our number will be greatly increased. For tonight I advise you to rest as best you can."

BelkA left the tent and returned to his own small one where Parto was anxiously waiting with their food rations. They ate and retired immediately after, but were awakened by the sound of tramping feet and loud talking. Quickly they got up and scrambled out of the flap of the tent to find a group of soldiers holding King Zedekiah and his family.

"Ah there you are BelkA," Nebuzaradan said. "I want you immediately to accompany King Zedekiah and his family to Riblah, and to return as soon as Nebuchadnezzar releases you. Tell the king that it is urgent for him to come. The city is falling."

BelkA bowed acknowledging the order. He took but one brief moment to scan the scene where all the important men of the city were being herded into wagons. Then he hurried to collect the belongings that Parto was rapidly putting aside.

•••

BelkA stood on the right hand of King Nebuchadnezzar under the elaborate canopy protecting them from the harsh rays of the sun. Before them stood King Zedekiah, the queen, and their sons. Behind them knelt Seraiah the chief priest, Zephaniah the priest next in rank, the three doorkeepers, further behind stood the secretary, the chief officer in charge of the fighting men, the seven royal advisors, the sixty fighting men along with many conspirators.

"Well *King* Zedekiah," Nebuchadnezzar's authoritative voice rang out. "Here you stand before your advisors and bodyguards who left you stranded as you escaped the city. You were a fool to listen to them all those years. They are deserving of punishment for betraying their king. Thus I sentence them to be executed on the spot."

Scuffling and piercing shrieks filled the air as the men were cut down.

BelkA meanwhile stood like a statue looking straight ahead.

When the ordeal was completed the King looked at Zedekiah once more. "Take a good look at your proud sons for this is the last time you will see them alive, I order for them the same sentence. Kill them all without mercy."

Again BelkA stood hardly daring to breath as Zedekiah screamed at the sight, and as swords cut them all down to the ground.

"And now Zedekiah it is just you and I. You betrayed me. You are a traitor. I do not like traitors. Had you been loyal, your city would not have been destroyed. I therefore sentence you to be blinded and exiled to Babylon."

BelkA kept standing, but this time praying for mercy on behalf of Zedekiah in Babylon. From the corner of his eye he saw blood dripping from his head as bronze shackles were snapped on his wrist before he was led away.

Chapter 52

O Jerusalem!

August 586 B.C.

J eremiah sat in the court of the guard in a state of paralyzed terror and sorrow. His heart thumped so loudly it seemed to compete with the shrieks of terror and pain, and the crashing of swords as soldiers ran through the streets randomly beating, slashing, and piercing everything and everyone in sight. Houses were crumbling all around under blows of hatchets, mallets, clubs and fire. Most involved were Babylonian soldiers but mingling with them were Jerusalem's own allies, neighbors from Moab, Ammon, Tyre and Sidon, as heartless and cruel as the rest, acting as if possessed. Clouds of dust darkened visibility, and polluted the air making his breathing labored. Cries of anguish, desperation, and beating of breasts filled the air with some even screaming,

"Where's Yahweh?" Others blasphemed, as unrepentant as ever.

Jeremiah tried to concentrate on doing something, but his distraught mind, usually so clear and collected, now felt the pain of the whole city as if falling upon his own shoulders. Suddenly he felt strong hands on his wrists but, as one in a morbid nightmare, he froze.

"Come Jeremiah," a familiar voice was saying. "We've got to get you out of here."

"Ah, it's you Ebed-Melech." With gritted teeth he forced himself up and was led out into an alley and down a side-street where they had to step over bodies and slide through blood and vomit as they went. Beautiful bodies along the way lay silent at the feet of the idols they worshipped. The image of the prophecy of the wine press entered his mind and he groaned.

"Are you all right?" Ebed-Melech asked as he stopped and drew Jeremiah into a doorway. Pressed as he was against Ebed-Melech's chest he could hear loud heartbeats that matched his own, yet now they had a calming effect upon him.

"We need to surrender," Jeremiah said.

"Not just to anyone we don't. We have to wait for the right ones to come by, someone who will listen before he acts." For a few hours they sat and waited amid the sounds of violence, screaming and crackling fire, this time seemingly closing in on them.

"They're starting on the temple," Ebed-Melech said.

"O Jerusalem!" Jeremiah wailed.

"We're too close we've got to move away from here," Ebed-Melech said. "Flames are spreading. Follow me closely."

They moved along slowly, trying to scoot from doorway to doorway.

"Prepare to make a dash," Ebed-Melech said pulling him forward, and then suddenly back again as he saw a woman with a child in her arms being clubbed and forced forward while soldiers chased other fleeing people out of their view.

"Now's the time." Jeremiah felt his rescuer almost lifting him off his feet. "I see one ahead. We must get to him."

It was all Jeremiah could do to keep up, but they had barely stopped when already Ebed-Melech, speaking in Aramaic, was saying his name.

"Follow me," the soldier said holding his sword in hand and leading them past the broken down wall. He brought them to an area where exiles were being herded, and left them only with the words, "I regret that I cannot stay to help you," before hurrying away.

Ebed-Melech found himself looking into the eyes of a soldier of about his own age. He bowed his head and spoke his name, and a few words in Aramaic. "Along with me is the prophet Jeremiah. We hereby surrender."

The soldier looked from Ebed-Melech to Jeremiah. "Jeremiah the prophet you say? Have no fear. I will do what I can to defend you. Alas I am required to put shackles on the wrists of every prisoner that passes me."

Jeremiah lifted his slender wrists for the shackles and Ebed-Melech did the same. A strange calm fell over both men as they were led away and connected to a rope with other exiles, and from there they followed the countless pairs of feet walking ahead of them.

•••

BelkA stood and watched the tragic scene before him. From his vantage point on a hill he could see the soldiers carrying away pots, shovels, wick trimmers, and dishes along with many articles of bronze, silver and gold including the bronze sea. He almost screamed when the twenty-seven foot pillars were hacked down, their bronze four-foot capitals with their beautiful carvings of pomegranates severed and loaded on carts. The memorable symbols of kingship and priesthood destroyed. What did this mean? Then came the flames, crackling slowly at first before exploding into an inferno even while some continued to feed them with broken up furnishings. The fire rose like a massive wall of flames as the temple crumbled.

It was over. O Jerusalem. If only she'd listened. The word *Messiah* came to His desperate mind and he lifted his arms and prayed, "Messiah, Light of the Nations, King of Kings, come quickly and take possession of your kingdom."

Chapter 53

Shattered Dreams

Jerusalem, July 584 B.C.

Perched on a rock on the Mount of Olives BelkA looked down on Jerusalem. His eyes lingered on the temple mount area sitting forlorn like a charred stump and remembered how it had been.

For two years now he'd been traveling the arid waistbands, most of that time with departing exiles. He'd hoped that by now the scenes of savage butchery, fire, destruction, and death might have faded, but the memories still haunted his subconscious, like glowing embers in his bones that refused to be quenched.

His servant Parto had stood loyally beside him all the way with hardly a complaint. On the blackest days his silent presence had provided stability in the chaos, but it was the Writings themselves that had carried him through.

Among the exiles there had also been some stalwart figures like Elzur whose faith defied the obstacles of the journey. He recalled how the beloved priest had kept telling the pitiful prisoners inching along the dismal road into exile, "Set up sign posts that will enable us to find our way home because we shall return. Yahweh has promised." Thus, at regular intervals, and especially at crossroads, markings were written on rocks and trees, or they'd set up heaps of stones pointing the way to Jerusalem.

BelkA wondered how Elzur and Tamara were getting along in captivity. Arielle, Elzur's gentle wife, had died in childbirth just as he feared she would, and there had been hardly enough time allotted to them to bury her and their baby son. Even while mourning Elzur had gathered the people together at camping spots to read to them from short portions copied on tiny papyrus scrolls that he'd managed to bring along in the one small bag allowed each prisoner of war. Other times he'd have BelkA read from his Aramaic scroll. Together they'd memorize favorite passages like, "Be strong and of good courage... fear not, nor be dismayed: for the LORD God... will be with thee; he will not fail thee, nor forsake thee."

As the procession of prisoners neared the gates of Babylon they'd encountered Bah-Ador leading a caravan south who had informed BelkA that his mother had died six months prior. Since there was now no compelling reason to enter the city, General Nabonidus had allowed him to join up with the departing caravan heading back to Jerusalem.

So here he now sat looking down upon a city so different from the one he remembered from years gone by. The sun was shining and the air was clear, yet it seemed to him that the smell of smoke still lingered. To one side a grouping of makeshift, or still unrepaired homes showed a hint of life, but the bustling proud city was no more.

He told Parto that he wanted to be alone for a time, so he'd come to this tranquil spot to ponder and put together the shattered pieces of his life. Doubts now flooded his mind. Had he irresponsibly overemphasized the scrolls and thus put everyone and everything else at risk. Where were they now anyway, scattered in the Judean hills or lost forever? He wondered about Mahla. There'd been no communication between them since that fateful day when he'd caught only a glimpse of her wounded and bleeding body lying on filthy streets. He'd put his career first and lost her forever. All, in fact, was lost.

Overcome with the anguish and grief he forgot his professional stoicism, and let the pent up emotions surface and spill out into loud sobbing. *Why? Why? Why? O Jerusalem, my life is like yours, a history of shattered dreams.*

In his abandonment he failed to hear footsteps climbing the hill behind him till a hand touched his shoulder. "BelkA, it is I, Zaccaria."

He jerked straight up alarmed and embarrassed. "O Zaccaria."

"I came to welcome you back to Jerusalem, friend."

"How foolish I feel to have you find me this way. Please forgive."

"Never mind BelkA. I come here quite often to pour out my own grief," Zaccaria said as they embraced. "Would you mind if I sat beside you?"

"On the contrary, I'd be pleased."

For a few minutes they sat each with their own thoughts. Then Zaccaria broke the silence. "You know BelkA, the scene below speaks of horror, but in a way I find it meaningful and reassuring."

"You do?"

"It's proof that Yahweh keeps His Word."

"You're right about that, Zaccaria. Jeremiah's prophecies have been fulfilled."

"I also see in those ashes the purity and love of Yahweh?"

"Love?"

"Love that cares enough to discipline, to cleanse, and to renew. You'll notice that the altars honoring foreign gods are gone."

"But the temple!"

"The temple was only a building. Yahweh still lives. He is the *I Am*. The Eternal. He'll always be. You are His earthly temple because the Spirit is in you, as He is in me."

"I am a temple!"

"A temple not made with stones of course, but the temple of your body that now houses the Spirit of God."

"Amazing."

"We here in Jerusalem are broken. Remorse over the past and anxiety about the future weigh heavily upon us. We still mourn over the loss of good people taken from our midst and harsh conditions still persist. Yet promises of renewal stand as sure as ever. We just have to keep on believing."

BelkA sighed. "I'm afraid I don't see it like that. My life is in shambles. I've ruined it all somehow, and now I even doubt the goodness of Yahweh. I embraced Him as my God, but He has either betrayed me or else I've displeased Him, and thus caused Him to abandon me."

"Ah, BelkA. God understands that we are mere humans confined to our limited viewpoint. We so often attempt to bring Him down to our level because we fail to grasp how much higher He is than ourselves, and we fail to realize that His timetable is often different from ours. We make our own plans that sometimes conflict with His."

"Are you implying that preserving His words was not His plan?"

"No, not at all, but He may have chosen to accomplish that in a different way from all our careful calculations. Are you prepared to let Him have His way?"

BelkA shook his head. "I don't know."

"There may also be more to His plan that just the scrolls. Have you considered, for instance, that His purpose included that of testing you to prove how much you really loved and trusted Him?"

"You mean like Job."

"Exactly."

BelkA stood to his feet and began pacing. Finally he dropped himself on the bench "You mean there could have been two plans, His and mine and I have not only failed to grasp His plan, but have insisted stubbornly on my own."

Zaccaria nodded in the affirmative. "Why don't you open your hand and let go?"

"I guess I'm independent, headstrong, and proud. I planned and counted on achieving my goals through my own self-discipline and determination. Besides that I expected Yahweh to compensate my devotion by giving me success. So in essence, I've been demanding my own way."

"Afraid so."

"Ah, but how does one accustomed to doing the directing let go?"

"BelkA, do you still believe He created the cosmos?"

"That I do."

"And that He created you?"

"Naturally."

"Would that God not be capable of directing your life and all you do, especially when it's a service for Him?"

"Ah," BelkA laughed. "How foolish I am. By faith I believe He created me, and by faith I trust Him with my life. "

"It's like a child trusting his much wiser father."

BelkA's turned and looked into Zaccaria's face, "Of course. So now what do I do?"

"Talk to Him about it."

BelkA fell to his knees and prayed, "Here I am LORD God Almighty. I confess my selfish will and

I here and now hand over my life to you. I'm your servant; you're my Master from now on."

Zaccaria continued to wait until BelkA looked up with a smile. "I feel lighter. The contest is over. I'm ready now to see His plan."

"Delighted I am to hear it dear friend. Might I suggest you come to my home? Abigael has prepared a meal to welcome you."

"But how did you know?"

"Is that not Bah-Ador's caravan down there in the valley?"

BelkA laughed.

"It seems that you've also doubted your friends BelkA. Did you think that we had forgotten or forsaken you?"

BelkA stood aghast. Looking into Zaccaria's eyes he exclaimed. "Indeed, I've been accusing you as well. Please forgive me."

"You are forgiven friend. Come the food is waiting."

BelkA was more than ready. Hustling onto his camel he prodded it forward and followed Zaccaria.

Meanwhile, Helem had caught up with Parto at the caravan site, and had told him to be prepared for a surprise. "Just follow me." It was thus that Parto and BelkA arrived at the home of Zaccaria and Abigael that had sustained damages, but was patched up and still reasonably comfortable.

Abigael opened the door with a flourish and before a greeting was exchanged voices all around exploded with shouts of, "Welcome, BelkA and Parto!"

With their eyes still adjusting to the inside the two men had difficulty distinguishing all the forms around them, but one by one faces took shape. SabA and Sussan were already hanging onto them, and there stood Arif and Tirza grinning. "How did you know?" BelkA asked.

"The pigeons of course. We were informed at the time that the exiles were approaching Babylon, and that you were not among them when they arrived. Then we learned that you were on your way back. We had thus only to calculate the approximate time of your arrival."

"I'd forgotten about the pigeons but thank you dear friends."

Continuing on around from Helem to Nethaniah, Naahma and baby Axella, Manua, Martha and all their children, and on he went to Giddel, Hodesh, Tovi, Eliana and Elasah, and then he saw a form that had changed somewhat, but still retained the vision he'd carried close to his heart for five years now. A rush of adrenaline surged through his body, weakening him with anticipation and excitement.

As he came close he noticed that she had aged. Her thin body now leaned upon a cane. An urge to rush to her and hold her to his heart almost won over his determined restraint, but the reminder that he first needed to be sure of her own feelings toward him held him in check. Thus he bent his head and whispered in her ear, "I need to talk to you Mahla. Would that be possible?"

"Tomorrow morning if that suits you?" she replied.

"Of course."

He followed Parto in holding Amineh's hands, noticing the weary lines and circles shadowing her eyes. A sense of deep admiration welled up within him that could find no adequate words. All he could say was, "Amineh."

He embraced with tears Mar and Samantha along with Thomas and Idra and their children who had come all the way from Tyre. "I hear the siege has not yet commenced." BelkA said.

"You're right," Mar responded. "However we live continually with apprehension. Soldiers are ever present."

BelkA sighed. "I understand," he said before turning to the man next to them. "No!" he exclaimed and fell into the arms of Blind Man, unable to say a word.

Having made the rounds BelkA and Parto turned and faced the crowd. "What can we say," BelkA said for the two of them, "We are shocked. Is it a dream? Please tell us it is true."

"It is true," came a loud shout in return.

BelkA turned to Parto, "Say something friend. I'm overcome. Never have I imagined that such joy could be mine."

"That joy is equally mine," Parto said in a shaky voice. "Thank you dear friends. We are overwhelmed by your kindness and self-sacrifice."

"Our meal is waiting outside," Zaccaria announced.

The makeshift tables that BelkA had failed to notice upon arriving now rapidly filled up with a vast array of food.

"What we have before us is compliments of our friends who brought it all the way from Tyre," Zaccaria announced. "We have not seen this much food for years it seems, so we will now offer thanksgiving for them and the feast laid out before us."

As they ate BelkA looked around, and suddenly asked in desperation, "Where's Jeremiah? And Baruch? Shaphan? Ebed-Melech and the servers?"

Everyone looked at each other wondering who should reply. Zaccaria was singled out.

"Jeremiah was forced to go to Egypt. Baruch, Ebed-Melech and the servers offered to accompany him."

"I'm utterly confused. Explain this to me."

Zaccaria told of the horrors of the assassination of Gedaliah whom Nebuchadnezzar had set upon the throne at Mizpah when Jerusalem was destroyed.

"But Gedaliah was Shaphan's grandson and a good man?"

"Indeed," Zaccaria affirmed. "But there was an evil conspirator, a jealous man who claimed to be the rightful heir. He managed to stir up followers who pretended to be in sympathy with Gedaliah, but then acted treacherously. It got ugly. Bloody. A lot of people, encouraged by a certain Johanan were fearful of Nebuchadnezzar's reactions following the assassination of his appointee, so they determined to flee to Egypt. Jeremiah counseled against going, but they wouldn't listen, and they forced him to go with them.

"Then you have undergone still more trials my friends."

"It has indeed been extremely harsh," Zaccaria said, "and many uncertainties remain still."

"And Shaphan?"

"He died the night the copying work was finished and just before the walls caved in. His last words were, 'Get ready for Messiah.'"

"Shaphan!" BelkA exclaimed. "Never will I forget the man."

After looking around once more BelkA asked with rising anxiety, "Azek and Ibzan. Where are they?"

It was Blind Man who answered his question. "Look down the road."

BelkA turned in the direction being pointed out and saw three young fellows unloading a cart. Then his eyes widened. "Azek and Ibzan, and who is that? RAstin!"

"Those three fellows have become some of our staunchest helpers. After Tovi's inn was ransacked they endured untold conditions hiding in burial chambers, cold and clammy underground cisterns, caves, forests, enduring extreme heat and cold, but Yahweh kept them, and what you are about to see."

"The scrolls, but how?" he exclaimed as basket after basket was placed at his feet.

"Actually, it was RAstin who drew plans for tunneling under the wall near the Bethlehem Gate. Yet it was risky with soldiers all about."

BelkA looked at RAstin with astonishment.

Timidly the young fellow explained. "You see my father is an architect. I learned from him."

"Check the scrolls off the list you left us," Azek said putting a wrinkled papyrus into BelkA's hand.

BelkA opened each one and compared. "They're all here!" he exclaimed. "What can I say? I'm stunned."

"I think you should know," Blind Man began, "that after the terrible confrontation when Arif was injured, priest Amit spent a lot of time with RAstin and the scouts, Azek and Ibzan, teaching and encouraging them. As a result they've matured and become stronger in their faith than ever. They are the ones who helped Mahla, Amineh, Helem, Tovi and the priests to escape."

BelkA fell at the feet of the three men. "I am not worthy of you my friends," he cried with a total forgetfulness of himself. Then he got up and embraced each young man mingling his tears with theirs. Finally he said, "I commend you for your sacrifice my brothers, or should I say *my sons,* for that is how I feel toward you. Never shall I forget this night as long as I live. Thank you, each and every one for your link in the chain that has made this possible."

Blind Man then explained about the two priests who had given themselves so completely to the copying. "They have been very ill since their rescue from the city by our boys and are yet recovering. They send you their greeting."

BelkA shook his head with a mix of concern and amazement.

Blind Man cleared his throat. "I have just one more clarification to make with you BelkA and Parto. The rest have known since the fall of Jerusalem that my real name is Uri which means light."

"Light!" BelkA exclaimed laughing. "That explains *The Lamp Connection* of course."

"*A Light to the nations.* The idea struck me when reading from the Writings of Isaiah where he wrote that the law of Yahweh and his judgments are a light to the nations. Jeremiah himself, through his life and prophecies, has lived it out before us. It's our desire that these scrolls will be multiplied, translated, and scattered throughout all the nations."

Chapter 54

Betrothals

Jerusalem, July 584 B.C.

BelkA supported Mahla's body with his arm as they walked toward a shady spot on Zaccaria's property. Once she was seated upon a stump he knelt opposite her and said, "Mahla, I've waited a long time to tell you this. Now, at last, the moment has come. I love you dear Mahla. You've been in my mind day and night ever since we met back in Aleppo. I have regretted setting you aside for my assignment, and now for two years I've struggled daily with anxious thoughts over you. That last scene of you lying wounded by the gate has tortured my mind every day since. I'd given up hope of ever seeing you again. Then yesterday, when I saw you, I thought I was dreaming. Now my heart begs for just one thing: to keep you always at my side. What I'm saying Mahla is, would you marry me?"

"O BelkA," Mahla said in a shaky voice, "look at me. I've aged; my body is wasted away and I'm a cripple."

"But Mahla, in my eyes you're more beautiful than ever before. Your limp reminds me how brave you've been and how you sacrificed yourself for me and for others. I'll never forgot how you looked the day we met, but this lovely lady before me glows from a radiance within that heightens her natural beauty. You're a feast for my eyes and thrilling to my soul."

"Lord BelkA, you are a dignitary at the royal court, I'm just a little peasant way beneath you. You deserve a woman of class, a woman whose status is equal to yours."

"Nonsense, Mahla. I desire only you." He lifted her face and looked into her eyes. Then he moved closer to her and his lips gently touched hers, at first hesitatingly, then with increasing intensity. To his great delight and relief he felt her beginning to respond to him, then abandoning herself to him.

"I love you BelkA," she said between gasps for breath. "I've loved you from the day we met, and secretly, I've been hoping..." her words were cut off as his lips sealed hers. Time ceased.

During a brief pause BelkA asked, "When should we announce our betrothal?"

Mahla giggled. "How about tonight?"

"Tonight it will be then, but wait a moment, I haven't spoken to your father."

"Father died five months ago, " Mahla said. "It was his heart."

BelkA held Mahla close. "I didn't know precious one. I must also tell you that I lost my mother six months ago."

Mahla jerked upright. "BelkA! My darling. So we're both orphans."

"Thankfully we now have each other."

"And Yahweh."

"Forever."

•••

"I need to speak with you Master," Parto said when the group was gathering for dinner.

BelkA, noticing concern reflected on Parto's face, left Mahla's side to walk a ways down the path with his servant. "What is it friend Parto?" he asked.

"I don't quite know how to tell you this. It's just that, well... from the start I've held Amineh in admiration. Then somehow it became blinding love. I've been frantic with anxiety over her these past months to the point where I thought I was losing my mind. When I saw her draw her knife that day in Jerusalem I knew she was putting herself in the midst of the battle, and I felt sure that I'd lost her for good. When we were sent to Babylon with the exiles I was sure of it.

"Yesterday when you were gone I finally surrendered her and asked Yahweh only that I might love Him more than any earthly creature. Shortly after Helem came to the camping spot and found me. He was warm and kind so I told him everything. Then you arrived with Zaccaria and you know the rest."

"No I don't know the rest. Tell me," BelkA said slyly.

"Well imagine my shock when I saw Amineh yesterday, and this afternoon I told her of my love for her."

"Congratulations to you Parto," BelkA said embracing him.

"But are you not displeased?"

"Of course not."

"Actually I have a similar story to tell you."

Parto grinned. "I think I know. It must have happened about the same time."

"You guessed right, but come Parto, they're waiting for us. We'll speak more later."

"Please Master. Would you announce it for me?"

"No, you'll do your own announcing. And don't master me anymore. As of now I give you your liberty. You are no longer my slave. I have an official scroll already made out to that effect. We are true brothers at last."

"But I don't want to leave you, and Amineh is comfortable with that as well."

"How does the word 'brother' sound to you, or 'collaborator'"

Parto 's face exploded in smiles of disbelief and wonder.

•••

As the dinner was ending BelkA got up and said, "It's my turn to surprise you. In the absence of parents it's for me to announce that Mahla has agreed to become my wife."

"What do you mean surprise?" Ibzan said with Azek punching him in the ribs. "We've been waiting for this a long time."

BelkA and Mahla looked at each other, pretending innocence, while clapping broke out. Eyes then turned expectantly toward Parto who blushed as he rose to his feet.

"Amineh has conquered my heart and I'm proud to announce that we have promised ourselves to each other."

The friends got up and, while some clapped, the younger ones chased each other around the tables.

Uri rose and put his hands out to silence everyone. "Wait. There's one more."

It was now Helem who stood. "Yahweh brought Tamara into my life through *The Lamp Connection* and also with the help of innocent pigeons who carried love messages across the miles separating us. From a distance she joins me in sharing our betrothals with you."

Clapping and backslapping echoed once more through the hills, while showers of congratulations fell on happy recipients.

When they had once more settled down Mar stood up. "Helem is looking forward to celebrating his wedding in Babylon with Elzur officiating and with Tamara at his side. But since Samantha and I have no children of our own, we offer ourselves as surrogate parents to the two other couples. We propose a wedding celebration in our home town at our expense."

More cheers burst forth.

"Thank you Mar," BelkA said upon recovering from shock. "We're overwhelmed by your kindness."

Uri the Blind Man raised his hand to speak. "There's a physician in Damascus, a shepherd actually, who has straightened the limbs of many an animal, and he has done the same for a number of our wounded ones. As a believer in Yahweh he never meddles with incantations, spells, and omens. I also know that his services are sometimes called for in Aleppo. I'm sure arrangements could be made for him to see Mahla, thus I suggest that they stop there on their way to Babylon."

Mar and Samantha whispered to each other a moment and then Mar spoke for them both, "We suggest that all of the wedding party accompany them as they travel on our ship to the nearest port. This will make for more comfortable travel for Mahla and for some special days of recuperation for all of our valiant soldiers."

The young ones stood and Ibzan shouted, "Cheers for Mar and Samantha," as laughing, whispering, planning, and celebrating electrified the air.

Chapter 55

Nuptials

Tyre, August 584 B.C.

Mahla and Amineh sat with wonder in a flower-
bedecked litter, born on the shoulders of
four muscled men, who gently carried them through
cobblestone streets in the neighborhood of Mar's
home. Young women walking before them carried
steaming pots of fragrant herbs while others trailing
behind sprinkled scented water on passers by. Mahla
had insisted that she would gladly endure some discomfort in walking on foot this last promenade with
her maidens of honor, but BelkA had already ordered
the litter and his thoughtfulness allowed her to enjoy
every step.

Meanwhile back at Mar's home musicians tuned
their instruments as male friends of the groom prepared to leave on a circuitous procession for they
must be absent when the brides arrived. Arif, as the

official *friend of the groom,* was standing proudly beside BelkA as they greeted guests entering the door when he exclaimed, "Utabar, what a surprise."

"This is one event I just couldn't miss," the richly clad scribe said with a broad grin.

"Meet Utabar," Arif said introducing him to BelkA as the owner of the pigeons.

BelkA grinned. "Welcome friend. Honored we are to have you."

"The honors are mine, and please accept my congratulations and wishes for a happy life ahead."

"I am indebted to you for those clever pigeons of yours that provided a most excellent form of communications on my last assignment. It was an ingenious idea."

"He also played a part in your meeting up with Mahla," Arif said. "Were it not for his affirmation and suggesting that I might sabotage Adda-Guppi, I would never have joined that notorious caravan, or been at Aleppo to introduce you to Mahla."

"That's right, I remember, so I am doubly indebted to you. Please be assured of my profound gratitude, and should you need something, do not hesitate to let me know."

As Utabar bowed with a smile, Mar gave the signal to depart.

•••

Upon their return to Mar's home the brides-to-be were led to separate chambers to ready themselves for the celebrations. Upon entering they found five complete outfits along with gold jewelry and a garland of lilies laid out on a divan. Mahla noticed a papyrus note tucked into the garland and read, "A token of love for my beloved Mahla. The crown is for the Queen who is for me like the loveliest of flowers—the pure and glorious lily. The gold is to remind my bride that she is more precious than rubies. From this day on I pledge you my all."

With trembling fingers Mahla chose the creamy gown ornamented with delicate cutwork design encircling clusters of pearls, with the accompanying veil of the same opaque silk fabric. She was about to pick up her veil when a professional beautician entered and announced that she had been hired by Samantha to prepare the bride. With experienced hands the woman applied potions on hollow areas and shadows under her eyes that succeeded in bringing back the face of pre-war days. When a brass mirror was placed in Mahla's hands she exclaimed incredulously, "How did you do it?"

"I had only to hide some temporary infirmities," the old woman explained, and after placing and adjusting the veil she offered wishes and disappeared. It was time now for the brides—along with their maidens—to await the midnight *hallel* or call of praise that would announce the approach of the men's party. Standing near the door the maidens nervously adjusted their lamps in readiness for a hurried exit when they would rush out to light the path to the door.

Tensions mounted as they listened and then suddenly, seemingly without warning, the door burst open with the announcement, "Hallel, the groom is coming." The maidens rushed out with their lamps burning brightly, and Mahla and Amineh sat down once more to listen and wait.

Time seemed to drag endlessly as they looked at each other with ears cocked, then suddenly the sound of singing reached their ears followed by faint foot-falls that gradually became louder and louder. With hearts racing they listened, until a hand on the latch began to turn ever so slowly, and then the door swung wide open.

Mahla and Amineh had time only for a quick straightening of each other's gowns and veils before the grooms—crowned with garlands of red roses— stood before their brides. Hands linked while the attending maidens gathered in front of the party to light their way down a long dark hall toward the great room. Singing as they went the maidens entered the banquet hall. There all came together as trumpets blasted a triumphant crescendo.

All the while BelkA had sustained Mahla's weight with his arm, and now he led her gently under an arch, where a banner with bold gold letters read, *His banner over me is love.*

Somehow the blurry form of priest Amit appeared before the two couples, and a steady voice spoke of the design of the Creator to unite man and woman in the holy union that typified His love for them. From the Isaiah scroll Amit read, "I will greatly rejoice in the LORD, my soul shall be joyful in my God; for he hath clothed me with the garments of salvation, he hath covered me with the robe of righteousness, as a bridegroom decketh himself with ornaments, and as a bride adorneth herself with jewels...For as the earth bringeth forth her bud, and as the garden causeth the things that are sown in it to spring forth; so the Lord GOD will cause righteousness and praise to spring forth before all the nations..." The prayers that followed, on the part of volunteers, added to the impression that the very ground under their feet was holy.

All too soon the mystery had happened. With veils removed spouses looked into faces wrapped in wonder. BelkA couldn't help whispering into Mahla's ear, "I've never seen you so beautiful, my darling."

"I am yours my beloved and you are mine."

Priest Amit pronounced the blessing, "The LORD bless thee, and keep thee: the LORD make his face to shine upon thee, and be gracious unto thee: The LORD lift up his countenance upon thee, and give thee peace. Amen."

Chapter 56

Babylon

October 584 B.C.

Across the plains the almost square city of Babylon shimmered like a mirage in the setting sun with its high white terraces nestled in luxuriant greenery, massive crenellated walls and towers, columns and ziggurats. BelkA's heart lifted with joy and thanksgiving. What a contrast to his previous return with the exiles when all seemed dark and foreboding.

Babylon still retained its sinister aura of idolatry, and its political and economic control, but now he had a new outlook. The thrill of a mission accomplished contrasted and gave meaning to the rescue operation. The Holy Writings now secure in their pottery jars and baskets, and firmly attached to the camels' backs proved the reality. What a change these precious Writings had already made in his life, and what impact they might have in the world, he could not even imagine.

The unexpected bonus had been the gift of a precious wife, and friends who now composed the family he never had. Their return journey to Babylon had not been without challenges, especially the time in Aleppo when Mahla had endured a painful surgery performed jointly by the shepherd from Damascus and an Egyptian of Mar's acquaintance, She was recuperating nicely, and already her face had gained some color and her cheeks had lost some hollowness.

How many times he and Mahla had reviewed the extraordinary happenings of the nuptials. Obviously another wedding would soon happen, for Helem had already asked him to be the acting friend of the groom. What a joy that day would be. If only the rest of the group from Jerusalem, Gezer, Tyre, Damascus and Egypt could be there for the occasion as well. How he missed them already.

Arif and his family, along with Utabar, had decided to establish themselves temporarily in Aleppo, where some scholarly opportunities had been proposed. With Tyre standing at the edge of a siege Mar had told BelkA that they were preparing to walk away from their home there. They and their servants would reestablish their business on the northern tip of Africa, though commercial ventures on the Euphrates were also under consideration. Memories of their separation after the seven days of feasting aboard Mar's vessel brought a tightness to BelkA's heart, and the vision of their scarves waving in the wind as a last good-bye still caused a churning in his stomach. Now he must force himself to look forward.

He glanced around at his five traveling companions. How thankful he was for each one. Helem's face glowed with the anticipation of seeing his sweetheart Tamara at last. Azek and Ibzan, he could tell, looked upon their new homeland with mixed feelings, while he and Mahla, looked upon them as adopted sons and had already decided that they'd do their best to guide them and provide whatever training they'd require to fulfill their callings with Parto and Amineh helping as well. How thankful he was that they had all become one family that also linked with the little flock they'd become so attached to that included Elzur, Nethaniah and Naahma, Bazy-An, Shai, Ezekiel, Daniel, and the others hinted of the potential that still lay ahead. He looked forward to getting more firmly grounded himself in his faith through interaction with them all.

He feasted his eyes upon Mahla as she dozed with her legs in splints spread out before her. How precious it was to that she was actually his—at last. Gently he took her hand.

She opened her eyes and smiled up at him. He leaned over and folded her in his arms as together they watched the last rays of the sun fade upon the outlines of the vast city of Babylon.

"It somehow fits to make our approach at sunset," Mahla said. "A curtain has fallen on our difficult past, and a new life awaits us."

"I'm looking forward to it," BelkA said, "though I know it won't be all rosy. The next few weeks, I fear, will be hard for you my darling as duties will require my immediate involvement."

"Don't worry my husband, there'll be other legs to run for me and other arms to replace mine. Our dear ones continually remind us of that."

"Thankful indeed we are for them,"

•••

The day after reaching Babylon BelkA had notified King Nebuchadnezzar and Daniel of his arrival. Now three days later he had his summons, that included also his wife and helpers.

The potential opportunity of seeing Bazy-An and Shai in the Queen's garden had prompted him to set out early. Hurrying down Processional Way in a chariot loaded with scrolls and passengers squeezed together, he looked as if in a dream at the old landmarks. The lion, the serpent, and the dragon on the walls of Ishtar gate, with the ziggurat in the background, had all lost their hold on him because Yahweh had conquered his heart.

As requested, the charioteer stopped in front of the royal gardens to allow BelkA a short stop. With a spring in his feet he walked down a familiar path where, to his great joy, he found both his friends hovered over a leaky fountain pipe. As BelkA approached they looked up in wild astonishment.

"BelkA!" the two men cried out together and ran toward him.

"My good friends," BelkA said. After hearty embraces and backslapping they sat down and listened with emotion as he told briefly about his return with the scrolls.

In turn Bazy-An explained that all was well with them, and that Adda-Guppi had fallen from favor in the land because of her impertinence in trying to impose the moon god upon the city. "People are tired of her and some are openly speaking their minds. It's the opinion of some—mine included—that she is preparing the way for Babylon's fall. There's also something unwholesome about her son. Indeed he is now married to the king's daughter, but he lacks the honorable traits of a kingly bearing, like discretion, wisdom or discernment. He's nothing more than a spoilt child." Bazy-An stopped abruptly. "Forgive me BelkA. I've got to watch what I say," he added sheepishly.

"Not with me," BelkA said slapping his friend once more on the back. "My how I've missed you, and yet, I've felt somehow connected to you."

"As I, or we have also," Bazy-An said with Shai nodding his head in agreement.

"I can't stay," BelkA said. "I'm scheduled—along with my wife and helpers—to appear before Daniel and then before King Nebuchadnezzar. But wait, I almost forgot," He put his hand into his bag and pulled out a tiny basket that he handed to Bazy-An. "I promised you this."

Bazy-An looked perplexed as he opened the lid. Then a wide smile parted his lips. "Bulbs!" he exclaimed.

"From the Jericho area," BelkA said. "It was Parto who remembered the promise I made, and since plants are hard to preserve, he carefully dug up these bulbs and kept them safe for this day."

"Well, Shai, what do you think of this?"

"Amazingly wonderful," Shai exclaimed in his turn, especially considering all you've been through. Please relate to Parto our profound gratitude."

"We'll plant these with great care," Bazy-An affirmed.

•••

Adda-Guppi stopped short as her eyes took in a familiar form from a distance. Why it was BelkA Souash walking with his usual confident gate. She'd heard that he was back, and that he'd married. She chuckled to herself in the thought that indeed she'd at least partially succeeded one aspect of her scheme, as meeting up with this woman at Aleppo had heen part of it. She'd had no news of the fellows she'd sent out after him, but then, what did it matter anyway? She hadn't lost much in the venture.

When the couple, walking arm-in-arm, came into full view she blinked several times. Was she not seeing right or was the wife limping? Could she be a cripple? Surely not. But indeed she was. What a strange irony. BelkA married to a poor little waif? And even BelkA himself looked wasted. Why they both had the appearance of returning war heroes. What a pair. Well anyway, what did it matter? She had far more important things to occupy her thoughts and her life.

When they neared she noticed servants with them carrying... scrolls! Lots of them. How she wished now that she'd chosen a different route. Those infernal Writings now here on her territory. How dare they? Instantly she decided she'd have nothing to say to them. As they passed she kept her head in the air and pretended to be deep in conversation with her escort to whom she now made reference about the Judean refugees.

"Indeed, Madame," her escort said, "the city is flooded with them."

"Well I despise every one of them."

"Actually it's not such a bad thing, Madame. They'll do a lot of our hard labor, and without any place of worship they'll soon be converting to our gods, don't you think?"

"Why of course," Adda-Guppi agreed. "I hadn't thought of that." Things were definitely looking up now. The cause was not lost after all.

•••

Walking through the five courtyards of the palace BelkA wondered about the way Adda-Guppi had ignored him. He'd planned to be congenial to her should he encounter her, but there was now no need to invent small talk. Oh well. He shrugged his shoulders and straightened his and Mahla's cloak as he awaited the summons of Prime-Minister Daniel.

Upon entering, BelkA, his wife and helpers noticed two men standing together in the room, but without looking up they all fell to their knees.

"Rise all of you," Daniel ordered and please take seats around me.

It was only when they all stood up that BelkA realized that the second man was the prophet Ezekiel.

"Welcome to Babylon," Daniel said, and turning to BelkA he asked for introductions.

"A great joy it is indeed to be back," BelkA exclaimed after which he introduced everyone with him.

"We've been following the reports concerning you BelkA," Daniel began, "and are overjoyed and much relieved to see you alive and well. Congratulations also on your recent marriage."

BelkA bowed. "Allow me also to inform you that I have chosen Yahweh as my God—my only God."

"We were praying you would," Daniel said with a broad smile and a wink in the direction of Ezekiel. "It is indeed a joy to hear such a statement from your own mouth. We're impatiently waiting to hear a full account of your adventures in bringing these scrolls to us. For this purpose, and following your interview with King Nebuchadnezzar, I have arranged a luncheon for the eight of us and I've also scheduled a banquet to take place a month from today that will include others who have assisted you, along with acquaintances of Ezekiel and myself who are particularly interested in the scrolls."

"You have seen much," Ezekiel said looking at BelkA with piercing eyes.

BelkA nodded remembering the tragedy of Jerusalem and the events of Riblah, and as he did his face twitched nervously.

Ezekiel reached out his hand and touched his shoulder. "And how is Jeremiah?"

BelkA explained the events as concisely as he could. "He suffered most at the hands of his countrymen, but there is a remnant, of Jews and Gentiles alike, who have stood with him."

Ezekiel exchanged a nod of sorrow with Daniel. With disciplined restraint he continued, "We have some gifted scribes here in Babylon who will be introduced to you at the banquet, BelkA. They're prepared to translate the scrolls into Aramaic, which is fast becoming the language of the exiles and the world at large. Would you be prepared to share some thoughts on this?"

"I'd be delighted," BelkA said with a bow.

"First you must recuperate," Daniel said. "But now, might you have some questions?"

"I am concerned about the exiles. How are they getting along?"

"They are still in shock and mourning, of course, but they're now all housed and settling down. Are there some in particular that you might be concerned about?"

"A father and daughter, honored one, a man by the name of Elzur and his daughter Tamara who is betrothed to Helem here. As you probably know Elzur's dear wife died in childbirth on the journey."

Daniel looked at Ezekiel. "Would the names be familiar to you?"

"Indeed. Elzur is an outstanding priest among the exiles. He and his daughter have provided stability in their midst." He then turned to Helem and bowed,

"My congratulations to you dear man on the fine wife you have chosen."

"And mine as well," Daniel added.

It was now Helem's turn to bow, and he did so slowly to conceal the emotions that had welled up within him.

BelkA also beamed and said, "Thank you Ezekiel for your kind words to us all."

"Now are there any other questions that you might need answered," Daniel asked.

"There is, honored one. My recent experiences have led me to have enormous respect for the true prophets of which you and Ezekiel are also included. Thus my question is, what is going to happen next?"

"Ah BelkA! There is within all of us a natural desire to know the future, especially in critical periods. Prophecies differ from the oracles that are around us here in Babylon. They do not rest on human wisdom, or on theories of probability. They are not intended to satisfy curiosity, but rather to edify and magnify the God who spoke them.

"Messages have come to me that surpass my ability to comprehend. At first they troubled me deeply, but Yahweh told me to 'seal them up' until a time when they would be understood. It is enough to know that He is sovereign over His creation, governing with infinite wisdom all the affairs of the world."

Ezekiel then added, "They and all the Writings teach us how to live in the evil world around us, while at the same time they comfort and restore us daily. As the hymnwriter wrote, "Thy Word is a lamp unto my feet." Presently we're entering an era when the words of Yahweh will go beyond the confines of the Hebrew community, It's fascinating to watch this happen. The prophet Isaiah would have rejoiced to see what is unfolding before our eyes as this light spreads throughout the nations."

"Perhaps we might conclude our conversation with some words of a hymn," Daniel said taking BelkA's hand, and encouraging each in the group do the same, "'The mercy of the LORD is from everlasting to everlasting upon them that fear him… the grass withereth, the flower fadeth, but the word of our God shall stand forever.'"

Epilogue

Mid-May 539 B.C.

Having served throughout the reigns of Nebuchadnezzar, his son Evil Merodach—until his assassination—and briefly under Nabonidus, we might imagine BelkA, now a great-grandfather and in his late seventies, enjoying an evening in the company of his older friend Daniel. Both are still engaged in diplomatic service, now adding up to some sixty-six years.

The rise of Adda-Guppi's son Nabonidus to the throne had been a trial for BelkA, Daniel, the exiles and the kingdom as a whole. Tensions provoked by the continual propaganda on the part of the King and his mother for the moon god had finally led to the monarch's withdrawal to the Arabian oasis of Tayma, leaving the rule of Babylon in the hands of his son Belshazzar.

We might now imagine BelkA and Daniel reminiscing side-by side as they watch the last glimmers of the fading sun. "Remember Daniel," BelkA might have suggested "how the exiles in those days grieved over their homeland?"

And Daniel replying with a poem he still remembered so clearly:

> *"'By the rivers of Babylon we sat and wept*
> *when we remembered Zion.*
> *There on the poplars we hung our harps,*
> *For there our captors asked us for songs...*
> *How can we sing the songs of Yahweh*
> *while in a foreign land?*
> *If I forget you, O Jerusalem...*
> *May my tongue cling to the roof of my mouth...*
> *If I do not consider Jerusalem my highest joy.'*

"Alas," Daniel might have added, "I fear that many of the exiles, if given the opportunity, would not return to Jerusalem. They're comfortable here. Babylon, with her luxurious and materialistic lifestyle, her freedom from the boundaries of morality, and her arrogant defiance of Yahweh, has become their god. They are once more wayward."

Perhaps BelkA might have brought up the name of the priestess Adda-Guppi, the old votaress of the moon god Sin whose biography had been written upon a paving stone in Haran. "Who would have imagined the woman would live to the age of one hundred and two years, and actually see the reign of her son."

"Ah BelkA," Daniel might have said, "I once thought that you would fill that high position. Nabonidus on his own had no claim to the throne apart from his marriage to the princess, and who knows, if Adda-Guppi hadn't maneuvered in the court, you might have won the hand of that princess instead of him—and also the throne."

BelkA in turn might have smiled with a far-off expression on his face. "Indeed I did win the hand of a princess—without the heavy crown. My life has been far richer and happier than his."

"And oh the compromises you would have faced BelkA. Like him you would have been hassled over many issues, perhaps blamed for the present two hundred percent inflation, and now worrying about being invaded by Cyrus."

"Indeed."

"It's winding up. The New Year's Banquet is going on tonight for the first time in nine years. It gives me an eerie feeling," Daniel says, "Something ominous is about to happen, and what is that I hear? A messenger at the door! What could this mean?"

Even as the two are together, Daniel receives a summons to appear at the banquet. Upon their arrival they gaze with disbelieving eyes at the thousand guests, including the king's wives, concubines, and nobles, who revel in a drunken stupor as they mock the God of the Hebrews while drinking from the gold and silver goblets from Jerusalem's temple. Yet, while some are still singing loudly, oblivious of all but their drink, a strange hush is gradually falling over the guests, as before their distorted eyes, fingers are writing on the wall words that are foreign to their minds. Belshazzar trembles in fear and promises advancement and gifts to any who might have the wisdom to interpret the message.

Daniel is hastily ushered in and presented to the king who points with a trembling finger at the hand and asks in a shaking voice, "Can you... ah... understand what is being written?"

Daniel stands up straight and with a clear voice translates the mysterious words, " *God has numbered the days of your reign and brought it to an end."*

Even as those words were being spoken the young prince Cyrus—grandson of Persian Camrbryses through his father, and of the Median King Astyages through his mother—was already leading his armies into the city through the diverted Euphrates. The glorious empire of Babylon was over.

In the course of the next three years Daniel would become the victim of a vicious plot upon his life that resulted in his being thrown into a lion's den. Yet he survived miraculously and lived to see the first contingent of exiles returning to their homeland, under the leadership of the Babylonian born Ezra, and taking with them the carefully preserved scrolls. The light of the eternal Word of Yahweh had survived war, famine, plague, fire, and dispersion and was now ready to wing its flight throughout all the nations and kingdoms of the world.

Cast of Characters

Historical Characters:

Nebuchadnezzar	Babylonian Emperor
Daniel	Jewish exile, Prime-minister and prophet
Ezekiel	Jewish exile and prophet
Adda-Guppi	Babylonian priestess of the Moon god Sin
Jeremiah	Prophet in Jerusalem
Baruch	Jeremiah's scribe
Shaphan	Elderly scribe once secretary of King Josiah
Zedekiah	Last King of Judah
Urijah	Jerusalem guard, despiser of Jeremiah
Ebed-Melech	Dignitary in King Zedekiah's Court Jerusalem

Primary Characters:

Babylon:

BelkA Souash	Babylonian envoy and scholar
Parto	BelkA's slave
Mahla	Babylonian woman BelkA meets in Aleppo

Arif and family	Babylonian scribe: wife Tirza, children SabA and Sussan
Bazy-An	Gardener
Shai	Jewish exile, gardener, and assistant of Bazy-An
Utabar	Babylonian scribe, owner of carrier pigeons
Bah-Ador	Caravan leader
Thuds:	Ghadir, KaVey, Tahampton, RAstin, Abid, ShabAzn
Helem	Jewish exile and traveling merchant

Tyre:

Mar	Ship captain and wife Samantha
Thomas	Papyrus seller and wife Idra

Damascus:

Blind Man	Real name Uri, leader of the "Lamp Connection"

Jericho area:

Amineh	Rescuer of widows and orphans
Azek and Ibzan	Teenage twin orphans, helpers of Amineh

Anathoth:

Elzur   Farmer and wife Arielle
Tamara   Daughter of Elzur and
                                Arielle

Gibeon:

Zaccaria and family   farmer and wife Abigael,
                                son Saadya

Gezer:

Manua and family   Innkeeper, wife Martha, and
                                children

Jerusalem:

Nethaniah   Potter and wife Naama
Tovi and family   Innkeeper, wife Eliana, son
                                Elasah
Amit   Faithful priest
Servers   Unnamed for security
                                purposes

9 781612 156279